Dear Reader,

My name is Holly Denham. I wanted to write and say, first of all, a huge thank you for buying this book. I also thought I should explain how my personal e-mails came to be published! It all started with the website www.hollysinbox.com. Before that, I was your ordinary, boring 9—5 receptionist, working in London, seeing my friends Jason and Aisha, having various disastrous relationships, and generally getting on with my life. After my inbox was posted on the web, I was told that thousands of people from 120 countries (!!!) were logging on every day to read my e-mails — how spooky is that! To be honest, it's been amazing and I've received loads of messages from the loveliest people, saying how much they've enjoyed reading the site. And it was this overwhelming response from fans that led to a publishing deal!

Anyway, I really hope you enjoy reading this book, and that you'll visit the site www.hollysinbox.com.

Thank you again for all your support!!!

Lots of love,

Holly x x x

Acknowledgements

Mum for being so loving, kind, hardworking and generally wonderful.
Dad for being the funniest person I've ever known.
Sister for being a hero and inspiration to anyone and everyone.
Brother for always being amusing no matter what!
The fab In-Laws — for always being so helpful.
Broo, my agent — for returning my email when no one else did!!! Then being so lovely, like a female Jerry Maguire, but more fun.
Sherise, my editor (I still can't get over saying I have an agent and editor, it's just like being in a film) — for removing the bits I should have removed (but was too scared to do so) and for working ridiculously hard on this (in such a tiny space of time).
Everyone at Headline who are so much fun and have made this a dream come true!
Dr Ash Alom from Fluent2 for building Holly's Inbox website and for putting his heart and soul into it.
Neil, Julie and George.
Tom for general advice.
Granny for giving me so many memories xxxx

Big kisses and hugs to . . .
Katy Stardust, Joyby, Tim O, Janey, Juleigh, Tigger, Dobby21, Manisha, Seliji, OnixLou, Karin, Vicki, Lexiloucs, Rina, Media Chick, Azure, Agatha, Sallyb, Nicole, Sammi, Pickle, Leannev84, Wishingangel, Dearbarbie, Daxz, Sophicoast, Dryadwombat, Fifitrixi, Laney, Emilyp, Jazzij, Mg1983, Queen of Chaos, Princess Smiley, Jenny20, City Angel, Flounder78, Samie, Dignity, Innocent, Sofie, Sylar, Mummy2CandL, RooRoo, Bristolmary, Shiny, Hkdkat, Mike Manic, Harvey, Emma, Atenea, Lavinia, Lulubellxxx, Rhiannon, Michelle, Deadgirl, Louisebw, Ciara22, Kate007, XKaighbeex, Mrs Weasley, Shany, Jade, Vicychopra, Lauricha, Daniella, Jeditinkerbell007, Trish, Ekatgirl, Ann Marie, Romeo, Voyeur, Geeklady, Jack, Emerald Skies, Aaron, Inges, Cinders284, Chrissywissy, Kaymoo, Elliejc, QueenofCool, Pinkycat, BadHairDay and Chandleo.

The English teacher near Brighton who really inspired me, and started me off on this road.
Monkey and Grettal — for helping me sleep, relieving stress and for being cuddly and furry (cats).

Lastly to you know who, for being the love of my life, being my lobster, and for sending the 'Ara' to my heart xxxxx

Holly's inbox

Holly Denham

R

<u>headline</u>
review

Copyright © 2007 Hollysinbox Ltd

The right of Holly Denham to be identified as the Author of
the Work has been asserted by her in accordance with the
Copyright, Designs and Patents Act 1988.

First published in 2007 by HEADLINE REVIEW
An imprint of HEADLINE PUBLISHING GROUP

1

Cataloguing in Publication Data is available from the British Library

ISBN 978 0 7553 4374 4

Typeset in Trebuchet by Avon DataSet Ltd,
Bidford-on-Avon, Warwickshire

Printed and bound in Great Britain by
Clays Ltd, St Ives plc

Headline's policy is to use papers that are natural, renewable and
recyclable products and made from wood grown in sustainable forests.
The logging and manufacturing processes are expected to conform to
the environmental regulations of the country of origin.

HEADLINE PUBLISHING GROUP
An Hachette Livre UK Company
338 Euston Road
London NW1 3BH

www.reviewbooks.co.uk
www.headline.co.uk

HOLLY'S
INBOX

MONTH 1

WEEK 1

MONDAY

Subject: To Holly — New Job

FROM Mum and Dad
TO Holly

Holly
   Exciting news about the job, are you enjoying it?
   Your sister has a parcel (books or something) that needs bringing out with you, when you come to see us. Alice says it's very important and 'Ferret', a friend of hers, is passing by Maida Vale next week to drop it off.
   Love Mum
   PS Send us your flight details!

FROM Holly
TO Mum and Dad

Job — I don't know yet, only been here an hour, very busy.
   Ferret — what? How does anyone get to make a friend called Ferret? Parcel — no problem, as long as it's not too heavy.
   xxxx

Subject: Welcome

FROM Roger Lipton
TO Holly

Dear Holly
   Glad to have you on board.
   I hear everything went well with your induction on Friday and you are now familiarising yourself with our systems and policies.

It's a shame the reception area is so separated from the rest of us here, but you know where we are if you need anything.
I hope you'll be very happy here.

Roger Lipton, Director of Human Resources, H&W, High Holborn WC2 6NP

FROM   Holly
TO   Roger Lipton

Dear Mr Lipton
Thank you for your email. I'm sure I'll be very happy, everyone has been so welcoming.
Kindest regards
Holly

Receptionist, H&W, High Holborn WC2 6NP

Subject: Reception experience

FROM   Patricia Gillot
TO   Holly

Holly
I told them to get me a receptionist I could work with, like the one I had before with lots of experience. Not having a go at you on your first day, but I feel like giving up I really do. Where've you worked again?
Trish

Patricia Gillot, Senior Receptionist, H&W, Holborn WC2 6NP

FROM   Holly
TO   Patricia Gillot

Hi Patricia
In 5* Hotels — on reception.
Holly

FROM Patricia Gillot
TO Holly

Great.

FROM Holly
TO Patricia Gillot

It was really busy there.

FROM Patricia Gillot
TO Holly

That's nice for you darlin. Just keep grinning at people for today and I'll do the rest. Hopefully by the end of the month you might know your arse from your elbow.
   Trish
   PS Stop trying to talk to me, this is a corporate bank. If you wanted to natter you should've taken a job in a salon. Email me when you have a problem.

Subject: A good luck message

FROM Alice and Matt
TO Holly

Holls
   Glad things are going so well again. It sounds wonderful there and you've got yourself a new start. Just what you wanted.
   Love
   Alice & Matt

FROM Holly
TO Alice and Matt

I hate the job and everyone's awful.

FROM Alice and Matt
TO Holly

Oh dear, by the way thanks for agreeing to bring out our parcel, it's really nice of you.
   xxxxxx

FROM   Holly
TO   Alice and Matt

No problem, what's in it?

FROM   Alice and Matt
TO   Holly

Oh, nothing, just a box of essentials.

FROM   Holly
TO   Alice and Matt

What — books and things?

FROM   Alice and Matt
TO   Holly

Yes, all that. I've given Ferret your number.
xxx

FROM   Holly
TO   Alice and Matt

Oh good

TUESDAY

Subject: A little advice from your Mum

FROM   Mum and Dad
TO   Holly

Holly
    Sorry to bother you again dear. Glad to hear you bumped into Jennie from school, you were always very fond of her, sounds like she's doing so well there.

I've given it some thought and the only way you're going to get as far as she has done, is by using any contacts you come across. My advice is; take her out for lunch as fast as possible. You never know what doors she could open for you.

What are you doing there at the moment again, PA work?

Mum xxx

FROM Holly
TO Mum and Dad

Mum

Jennie has been nice on the couple of occasions I've seen her, but I'm fine doing what I'm doing, which is RECEPTION work.

x

Holly

FROM Mum and Dad
TO Holly

That's what I said darling, it's the same thing.

Just make sure you eat properly, especially if you're going to be greeting all those people, you could pick up an infection from one of them.

Mum

Subject: A few pointers

FROM Patricia Gillot
TO Holly

Stop standing up when people come to the desk!

I'm off for a fag, I'll be on the other side of the glass doors and I'll be keeping an eye on you.

Got any problems — don't shout whatever you do, just think you're working in a library and you'll be halfway there.

FROM Holly
TO Patricia Gillot

OK Patricia, what time are toilet breaks?

FROM   Patricia Gillot
TO   Holly

Any time you can't hold on darlin — also it's just Trish, no one calls me Patricia.

Subject: School Friend!!!

FROM   Jennie Pithwait
TO   Holly

Hi Holly
    You went off the map for a few years? Where've you been??
    So glad you're working here, sorry about the misunderstanding yesterday. I should have told you what Mr Huerst looked like, lucky he was so forgiving even when you told him he needed an appointment.
    Jennie

Jennie Pithwait, Associate, Corporate Finance, H&W, High Holborn WC2 6NP

FROM   Holly
TO   Jennie Pithwait

Hi Jennie
    I felt like a real idiot, I even chased after him with his security pass.
    Holly

FROM   Jennie Pithwait
TO   Holly

He was fine, I said it was your first day.
    What's it like sitting with Trisha?

FROM   Holly
TO   Jennie Pithwait

Awful, rude, I can't stand her.

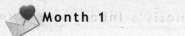

FROM Jennie Pithwait
TO Holly

Tough old girl, probably doesn't get laid much, great with clients but that's about it.
Jennie

FROM Holly
TO Jennie Pithwait

xxxx
Thanks Jennie.

Subject: Pretty P'Holly

FROM Jason GrangerRM
TO Holly

Hiya,
How's the job going? Is it OK to email you?

Jason Granger, Reception Team Leader, LHS Hotels, London,
W1V 6TT

FROM Holly
TO Jason GrangerRM

Emailing is good, the job stinks and I'm about to take a contract out, on my mum.
How are you?
xx

FROM Jason GrangerRM
TO Holly

I'm good.
Talking of stinky, guess what smelly celeb we've got staying here?

FROM Holly
TO Jason GrangerRM

Smelly?

FROM   Jason GrangerRM
TO   Holly

(Housekeeping told me she's got a few personal hygiene problems.)
   Who cares though — she's famous!!!

FROM   Holly
TO   Jason GrangerRM

That makes it OK then, does it?

FROM   Jason GrangerRM
TO   Holly

Of course? You don't like her though (she's a bit of a marriage breaker) — can't tell you who it is. If you were still working here I could, but I can't, it's a trust thing.
   Enjoy your nasty bank.

FROM   Holly
TO   Jason GrangerRM

JASON!!!

Subject: Totty

FROM   Jennie Pithwait
TO   Holly

Morning. Let me know if any hot guys are coming up so I can look out for them.
   Jen

FROM   Holly
TO   Jennie Pithwait

Will do.
   Holly

WEDNESDAY

Subject: Ferret

FROM Ferret
TO   Holly

Hi Hollsie
  Ferret here, Alice gave me your email.
  I've managed to get hold of more than she even wanted, just make sure you keep it in the freezer until you go.
  Chairman Mow once said 'Feel the rhythm'.

Subject: Bit slow

FROM Patricia Gillot
TO   Holly

Holly
  Speed it up a bit darlin. By now you should be getting two badges printed off, while calling the host to let them know their guests have arrived.
  It's all got to happen at once, otherwise the place'll start looking like Piccadilly station with nowhere for people to sit.
  Sorry to hassle you, but you're not picking things up fast enough.
  Trish

Subject: PARCEL

FROM Holly
TO   Ferret

Freezer? I don't understand?

Subject: Totty

FROM Jennie Pithwait
TO   Holly

Thanks for the heads-up on that one. Not strictly my usual type, I do like them a little taller, without the lurch, corduroys, rotting teeth and the smell.

Pref also for the future, can you prep them on first impressions; I like people who still have the ability to retain their spittle, the string from his shoulder wasn't working for me.

PS I'll get you back
Jen

FROM Holly
TO   Jennie Pithwait

Ooops sorry (I didn't actually think he was that bad).
Also where's good to eat around here?
xx
Holly

FROM Jennie Pithwait
TO   Holly

Out of here, turn left, there's a good sandwich shop on the other side, or up to the lights and turn right . . . nice arcade place up there.

. . . oh and to answer your question earlier, there's nothing worth chasing here.

By the way be careful about dumping on your own doorstep.

So come on then, give me some gossip, what's Holly been doing since school, I want to know everything. I heard you got yourself engaged, or married?

Jen

FROM Holly
TO   Jennie Pithwait

Nope, never married, love life's been much of a non-event. What about you?

FROM   Jennie Pithwait
TO   Holly

The odd one or two, quality guys, all prime beef.
   Xx

FROM   Holly
TO   Jennie Pithwait

You lucky thing!
   Holls

FROM   Jennie Pithwait
TO   Holly

Let's meet up for lunch, I'll give you a complete tourist guide, call you later.

FROM   Holly
TO   Jennie Pithwait

Thanks.
Holls

Subject: Hi Jason — I'm worried — it's Holly

FROM   Holly
TO   Jason GrangerRM

Jennie's asking questions.
   Holly

FROM   Jason GrangerRM
TO   Holly
PHOTOS Puppy-lickin

Just keep your cool, and keep yourself to yourself (well as much as you can on a main reception).
   xxx
   I'll call tonight

Subject: Team night out

FROM Judy Perkins
TO   Holly

Dear Holly
Being new, I think it would be nice if we welcomed you to the team by a few of us going for a drink in the next couple of weeks.
Let me know what night would be good for you.
Regards
Judy

Judy Perkins, Facilities Manager, H&W, High Holborn, WC2 6NP

FROM Holly
TO   Judy Perkins

Hi Judy
Thanks for the invite, any day next week would be OK.
Regards
Holly

Subject: Shella Hamilton-Jones — PA to Jane Jenkins

FROM Shella Hamilton-Jones
TO   Holly

Dear Holly
From looking at the schedule I can see you have booked meeting room 7 on Friday for Jane Jenkins. As you are aware from my previous call, this meeting is very important and Jane's preference is always ROOM 12.
I understand you are new here and it's difficult to begin with until you get your bearings; however, you should know Jane Jenkins has priority over other staff.
Please would you secure this room ASAP and then email me a confirmation when you have achieved this. You could also make a note that Jane Jenkins always has this room in future.
Yours sincerely

Shella Hamilton-Jones, PA to Jane Jenkins, MD Corporate Finance H&W, High Holborn WC2 6NP

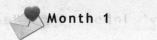

THURSDAY

Subject: Ferret

FROM   Holly
TO   Ferret

Ferret,
*   You haven't replied to me ... You told me to put it in the freezer,*
why the freezer???
*   Holly*

Subject: To Shella — Re Your Meeting Room Request

FROM   Holly
TO   Shella Hamilton-Jones

Dear Shella
*   I can only apologise for not booking meeting room 12 for you. I*
will make a note of Jane Jenkins' preference for the future, and
move James Lawrence's meeting now.
*   Yours sincerely*
*   Holly*

Subject: Important update

FROM   Mum and Dad
TO   Holly

Holly
*   I've set your granny up on a laptop, so she can email you. I think*
she's settling into the old people's home just fine.
*   Love Mum*

FROM   Holly
TO   Mum and Dad

Oh good, but I didn't think Granny liked it out there?
*   Holly*

FROM　　Mum and Dad
TO　　　Holly

Holly
　　She misses the rain, but apart from that she seems very happy.
　　Love Mum

Subject: Ordering Duty Free?

FROM　　Holly
TO　　　Alice and Matt

Alice
　　I've left two messages on your phone, I want to know what's in that parcel — if it's drugs you can forget it!?
　　Holly

FROM　　Alice and Matt
TO　　　Holly

Hi Holly
　　Don't be so crazy, what kind of sister do you think I am? I wouldn't ask you to bring drugs out?????? GOD NO!! No, these are just your common or garden rats.
　　Love you.
　　Alice xx

FROM　　Holly
TO　　　Alice and Matt

What???????

Subject: Alteration to my meeting

FROM　　James Lawrence
TO　　　Holly

Dear Holly
　　Just received your voicemail. I understand re: change in the

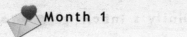

meeting, no problem at all and sorry I haven't stopped to introduce myself, it's been a hectic few days up here.
   Regards
   James
   PS You sounded shaken, don't let people get you down, people just get stressed here sometimes.

James Lawrence, VP Corporate Finance, H&W, High Holborn WC2 6NP

FROM   Holly
TO   James Lawrence

Dear James
   Thanks for that, it's kind of you. Have a fab day.
   Holly

Subject: A question for you Jennie . . .

FROM   Holly
TO   Jennie Pithwait

Who's James Lawrence?
   Hols

FROM   Jennie Pithwait
TO   Holly

— Why ?

FRIDAY

Subject: Rats

FROM   Holly
TO   Alice and Matt

Alice
   When I said, 'What?' that meant — what, are you crazy??? Rats?? Email me back or forget it!

Subject: Only just saw your reply

FROM   Alice and Matt
TO   Holly

Sorry Holly,
I didn't tell you, because I didn't want you to worry about them.
They're rats, but English ones, and you won't have to touch them,
they're all sealed up.
xxxx
Alice

FROM   Holly
TO   Alice and Matt

Oh, thank God they're English rats, they'll be so much more
refined????

FROM   Alice and Matt
TO   Holly

Don't tell Mum, you know how squeamish she is with these things.
We need to bring some rats into the country for the pythons to eat.
Here they cost 3 euros each, it's not economical and the quality is
poor.
Alice

FROM   Holly
TO   Alice and Matt

So these are quality-rats, that is good.
NO, I'M NOT DOING IT!!!

FROM   Alice and Matt
TO   Holly

If we don't feed them, the pythons will DIE, and Matt will be
devastated. There's nothing to worry about, they're not alive ...?

FROM Holly
TO Alice and Matt

They're not alive, oh that's fine then — so you want me to fill my case with DEAD rats? Fab, I'll just rearrange my packing; tuck them between my swimming cozzie and my knickers?!

FROM Alice and Matt
TO Holly

Please give it some thought. Remember breeding snakes is our only source of income.
*   Love Alice*
*   xx*

Subject: It's going to be a mad day — from Trish

FROM Patricia Gillot
TO Holly

... so get that smile ready, girl!

Subject: Help! — Aisha needs Holly

FROM Aisha
TO Holly

Hols,
*   Still not recovered from last weekend, think I ate something bad, feel terrrrrrrrrrrrrrrrible. Tell me something nice pleasssssssse Hols, I'm really depressed.*
*   Xxxxxxx ☹*

FROM Holly
TO Aisha

You didn't eat anything bad, it was the bottle of vodka you drank — where was Shona?

FROM   Aisha
TO   Holly

Mum's looking after her.
   x

FROM   Holly
TO   Aisha

Come on sweetie, get yourself together, you said you'd look for a job this week?

FROM   Aisha
TO   Holly

I went out last night, but I wasn't feeling good when I left the house, felt really weak. Also I'm worried about Henry, I texted him an hour ago, and he still hasn't texted back?

FROM   Holly
TO   Aisha

He's probably just busy, when someone's at work (try and picture this) — they don't have time to check their phone every 5 mins to see if they've been texted.
   From what I've heard working in Production can take you all over the place, he could be outside. Stop worrying!

FROM   Aisha
TO   Holly

He's not in Production.

FROM   Holly
TO   Aisha

Yes he is, you told me he was in TV Production.

FROM   Aisha
TO   Holly

That's Jimmy.

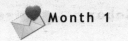

FROM Holly
TO Aisha

So who's Henry?

FROM Aisha
TO Holly

Henry is the guy I was with on Saturday.

FROM Holly
TO Aisha

So who's Jimmy?

FROM Aisha
TO Holly

He's the one in Production.

FROM Holly
TO Aisha

I know he's in Production, I mean who is he to you?

FROM Aisha
TO Holly

He's with me too. Look, you're not making me feel any better.
☹

FROM Holly
TO Aisha

Good, so you shouldn't. Stop feeling sorry for yourself and get a job.

FROM Aisha
TO Holly

Can I come over and stay next weekend? Let's have the whole weekend in, no drinks no partying???
xxxx

FROM Holly
TO   Aisha

Of course, although I might have someone called 'Ferret' popping in, not sure.

FROM Aisha
TO   Holly

Is he sexy?

FROM Holly
TO   Aisha

Goodbye.

Subject: You've got to keep an eye on people who are waiting!

FROM Patricia Gillot
TO   Holly

I'm sure that bloke with the yellow tie has been sitting there for 10 mins??

FROM Holly
TO   Patricia Gillot

He has, I've tried calling them upstairs three times, but can't get through to them. Sorry, I didn't know what to do.

FROM Patricia Gillot
TO   Holly

Then ASK, you need to go up and look for the host because the meeting could've started already without this one.
    Come on Holly, use your noddle.

Subject: Celebrity Pics

FROM Jason
TO Holly

Remember to ask the other receptionist for the directory of senior staff. Then you can take it home over the weekend and learn what they look like (hopefully they'll have pictures). Otherwise next week, it could be the other founding partner you ask to sign in.

FROM Holly
TO Jason

I hope not, he's dead.
    But thanks, I'll ask her about the directory at the end of the day.

Subject: You owe me

FROM Holly
TO Alice and Matt

OK, I'll do it, presumably it's legal.

FROM Alice and Matt
TO Holly

Oh, you're the best!!
    xxxx
    I'll remember this, thanks lots.

WEEK 2

MONDAY

Subject: I got a right ear bashing off them upstairs!

FROM Patricia Gillot
TO Holly

Because they want two receptionists on the desk when it's busy, lunch times usually. I'll go through it with you once we get some peace. They're doing my head in. So, one of us needs to go before the 12pm slot and one after the 2pm slot.

FROM Holly
TO Patricia Gillot

Sorry Trish, I didn't know, I'll be careful. I can go to lunch whenever you want.

Subject: Shootings

FROM Patricia Gillot
TO Holly

All these shootings, it gets worse every day. Even my youngest one says most of his classmates take weapons with them to school. It really gets to me.

FROM Holly
TO Patricia Gillot

How scary!!? That's awful.

Subject: Terrible news!

FROM Jason GrangerRM
TO Holly

Britney's had her hair cut off!!!!!!

FROM Holly
TO Jason GrangerRM

Yes Jason, thanks for the news alert, keeping me up to date with current affairs.
  xx

Subject: Lunch

FROM Patricia Gillot
TO Holly

I have to be somewhere at 2. Should be back within an hour but if it takes longer can you cover for me, while I'm gone?

FROM Holly
TO Patricia Gillot

No probs, I can cover, where should I say you are though?

FROM Patricia Gillot
TO Holly

Thanks. Just say I came back, you saw me, and you think I'm around somewhere?

FROM Holly
TO Patricia Gillot

OK.

Subject: Annoying calls

FROM   Patricia Gillot
TO   Holly

I just had an 'I'm so important' pr*ck on the line, spoke like I should know who he was, shouted the person he wanted twice (couldn't catch it either time) then had the cheek to leave me hanging while he took another call — that gets to me.

FROM   Holly
TO   Patricia Gillot

What d'you do when that happens?

FROM   Patricia Gillot
TO   Holly

I usually hang up on them, or ask them to call back and speak to Holly.

FROM   Holly
TO   Patricia Gillot

Thanks.

FROM   Patricia Gillot
TO   Holly

My pleasure darlin.

Subject: What's the name of that girl in *EastEnders*?

FROM   Patricia Gillot
TO   Holly

You know, the one who's been in all the trouble recently.

FROM Holly
TO Patricia Gillot

I don't know, which one?

FROM Patricia Gillot
TO Holly

If I knew I wouldn't be asking you now would I? Come on girl, that one who did something with Phil Mitchell. No, I mean The Bill, *PC something?*

FROM Holly
TO Patricia Gillot

Sorry I can't help.

FROM Patricia Gillot
TO Holly

DC June . . . someone?

FROM Holly
TO Patricia Gillot

Why d'you want to know anyway?

FROM Patricia Gillot
TO Holly

Sgt June Akland!!! That was her. See that girl on the couch with the brown hair? Forget it she's gone now. I'm off to lunch, see ya.

Subject: IMPORTANT REMINDER

FROM Holly
TO   Holly

SOAPS: remember to watch EastEnders and The Bill, oh and buy an alarm clock.

Subject: Sexy male porn

FROM Aisha
TO   Holly

I'm sending you some porn — you'll love it, pic of some guy I was with at the weekend.

FROM Holly
TO   Aisha

Please don't.

FROM Aisha
TO   Holly

I'm sending it.
   xx

FROM Holly
TO   Aisha

Don't.

FROM Aisha
TO   Holly

You'll love it.
   x

WEEK 2

TUESDAY

Subject: Allowances abroad

FROM   Holly
TO   GovernmentCustomsDept

Dear Sir or Madam
   Can you give me a list of what I can take or can't take when I go abroad to Spain please.
   Thanks.
   Holly.

FROM   GovernmentCustomsDept
TO   Holly

REF: 9222287

Dear Holly
   If you log on to our website there are details, including the laws governing export and import of goods to EU countries.

C&E

FROM   Holly
TO   GovernmentCustomsDept

REF: 9222287

Dear C&E
   I can't see anywhere on your list any mention of rats and I want to take some to Spain with me. Can you tell me where I stand with this?
   Hols x

FROM GovernmentCustomsDept
TO   Holly

REF: 9222287

Dear Holly
   Presuming you are serious, then the exportation of live animals should be listed there.

FROM Holly
TO   GovernmentCustomsDept

REF: 9222287

Dear C&E
   I am serious, but I intend to take only dead rats (frozen — like popsicles I believe), not the live variety. However, I have no intention of going to prison because of bunch of dirty rats.
   Hols

FROM GovernmentCustomsDept
TO   Holly

REF: 9222287

Dear Holly
   It might come as a shock to you, but I have never been asked about the exportation of dead rats. But from what I have discovered, the British Government doesn't mind how many dead rats you export, you can take the lot.
   The Spanish Government however might be more interested in their arrival. Best to contact the British Embassy in Spain.

Subject: Help Jason Help!

FROM Holly
TO   Jason GrangerRM

I still feel everyone's waiting for me to mess up hugely. Trish is ok with me but I think underneath it all she's just waiting for me to screw up. You know what I need to do ... I need to have a party and invite everyone from work?
   What do you think?????

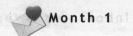

FROM Jason GrangerRM
TO Holly

Do NOT have a party, bad idea. You picked it up very quickly when you were here, just have some patience.
   xxxxx
   PS have you got that directory of staff yet??

FROM Holly
TO Jason GrangerRM

Got the book, then got in trouble with Trish for trying to take it home (security risk). Just trying to remember faces as they pass . . .

Subject: IMPORTANT QUESTION

FROM Charlie Denham
TO Holly

What d'you look for in a toilet?
   Charlie

CLUB SUBMISSION, London

FROM Holly
TO Charlie Denham

I don't look in toilets Charlie.

FROM Charlie Denham
TO Holly

What's important for you though?

FROM Holly
TO Charlie Denham

That I don't have conversations about toilets with my brother.

FROM Charlie Denham
TO Holly

OK, but apart from clean seats and some roll — what else is important for women?

FROM Holly
TO Charlie Denham

Go away Charlie.

FROM Charlie Denham
TO Holly

Have you told any of your hot receptionist mates that your brother owns a nightclub yet?

FROM Holly
TO Charlie Denham

No, because you don't, you own a building site.
    Holly
    PS we don't all hang out together in some kind of receptionist club, there's me and one other on the desk. That's all.

FROM Charlie Denham
TO Holly

Is she hot?

FROM Charlie Denham
TO Holly

Are you still there?

FROM Charlie Denham
TO Holly

What about the sign on the door? Lots of options ...

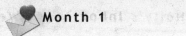

FROM Holly
TO Charlie Denham

Little girls room — sounds sweet.

FROM Charlie Denham
TO Holly

I think Rubber Ron has the casting vote, and he's gone for DOMS & SUBS.

FROM Holly
TO Charlie Denham

What on earth does that mean?

FROM Charlie Denham
TO Holly

Who knows? I daren't ask, some kind of kinky thing I think and that's trendy these days.

Subject: Totty??? Where is it?

FROM Jennie Pithwait
TO Holly

Come on, what's it like down there, anything on the horizon?

FROM Holly
TO Jennie Pithwait

It's manic, loads of meetings going on ... what's the big event?

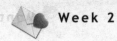

FROM   Jennie Pithwait
TO   Holly

Graduate recruitment day, fresh young blood, hot young men fresh off the press, cuties in their new suities, bless.
Why don't you take some pics on your phone and email them up?

FROM   Holly
TO   Jennie Pithwait

Not too keen, what would happen if I was caught?

FROM   Jennie Pithwait
TO   Holly

Instant dismissal, probably escorted off the premises.

FROM   Holly
TO   Jennie Pithwait

So my mobile stays in my bag. Some of them passing through have absolutely no social skills, they're so arrogant.

FROM   Jennie Pithwait
TO   Holly

Arrogant and suited. Tell me more!!!!

FROM   Holly
TO   Jennie Pithwait

Ooops, here comes another, got to go.

FROM   Jennie Pithwait
TO   Holly

Come what, one where? Don't leave me hanging . . . ???

FROM   Holly
TO   Jennie Pithwait

Sorry, you should have seen him. Yeeeeeeeeees indeedi, should be heading up to the fifth floor about now. Second time I've seen him too.

FROM   Jennie Pithwait
TO   Holly

I'm grabbing the lift now, I'm making a B-line, yabadabadooooooo.

Subject: Totty??? Where is it?

FROM   Jennie Pithwait
TO   Holly

Where'd he go??? He must have sneaked past me, the little bugger. What have they been teaching them at Uni — Ninja Warfare???

FROM   Holly
TO   Jennie Pithwait

If they are, then you're in trouble, you'll have to just set up your office in the lift.

FROM   Jennie Pithwait
TO   Holly

Fine, I'll move into the lift. But get some of them to use the stairs. I'm only one woman you know, I can't be riding it all day.

FROM   Holly
TO   Jennie Pithwait

I'm guessing you mean the lift.

FROM   Jennie Pithwait
TO   Holly

Nope.

Subject: Membership Approved — Fetish For Everyone!

FROM Fetish For Everyone SM
TO   Holly

Dear Holly
*   Thank you for your enquiry. We can now confirm you are a member of Fetish for Everyone SM. You will receive our regular updates, newsletter and event notifications.*
*   Admin*

FROM Holly
TO   Fetish For Everyone SM

No no no, I didn't want to be a member! I only wanted to know what a Sub or a Dom was, that was all I wanted to know. I DO NOT want to be a member, please remove me from the mailing list.

FROM Fetish For Everyone SM
TO   Holly

You have reached our automatic reply mailbox. We cannot answer your kinky question. Do not reply to us, you naughty pervert, as you'll only receive this message again and no slap on the wrist (unfortunately).
*   Happy spanking!*

Subject: MESSAGE TO MY BROTHER

FROM Holly
TO   Charlie Denham

I will kill you later for something ... please remind me!

Subject: Gucci bag lady

FROM Holly
TO   Patricia Gillot

Is she important?

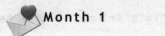

FROM   Patricia Gillot
TO   Holly

Only a bit . . . that was Mr Huerst's wife. She acts like butter wouldn't melt, but — I know different.

FROM   Holly
TO   Patricia Gillot

What???

FROM   Patricia Gillot
TO   Holly

It's only gossip, anyway I'd keep out of her way.

FROM   Holly
TO   Patricia Gillot

Like her boots though.

FROM   Patricia Gillot
TO   Holly

And it's all real, bag too.

WEDNESDAY

Subject: Meeting Room Mix-up AGAIN

FROM   Shella Hamilton-Jones
TO   Holly

Dear Holly
    Oh dear . . . Would you be so kind as to have a look at the room chart and tell me what you see in room 7 at 5pm?

Subject: Help Holly — Aisha Needs You!!

FROM Aisha
TO   Holly

Morning
    Have you got a minute? I need someone to talk to . . . actually if you've got a few minutes that would be more heading in the right direction.
    Aisha xx

FROM Holly
TO   Aisha

No, I'm busy.

Subject: Meeting Room Mix-up

FROM Holly
TO   Shella Hamilton-Jones

Dear Shella
    Yes, I see Jane Jenkins is booked in for a meeting. Is this OK?
    Kindest regards
    Holly

FROM Shella Hamilton-Jones
TO   Holly

Oh dear Holly,
    Do you not remember our little chat? I really can't believe you didn't bother to make a note of it.

FROM Holly
TO   Shella Hamilton-Jones

Yes, I did make a note of it, Jane Jenkins has a preference for room 12.

FROM Shella Hamilton-Jones
TO   Holly

Then why if she has a preference for room 12 is Jane Jenkins' name not in room 12?

FROM Holly
TO   Shella Hamilton-Jones

Because Mr Huerst also has a preference for room 12, and I've heard he's quite important.

FROM Shella Hamilton-Jones
TO   Holly

Then WHY HAVEN'T YOU PUT HIS NAME IN THE BOX!!???

FROM Holly
TO   Shella Hamilton-Jones

Because he's still standing in front of me, giving me details of the catering facilities he wants.
    Is there a need for capitals? (or are you meant to be shouting?)
    Feel free to come down and shout if you'd prefer?

FROM Shella Hamilton-Jones
TO   Holly

Out of Office AutoReply: Meeting Room Mix-up
Shella Hamilton-Jones is currently out of the office, please contact Jeremy Anderson in the case of an emergency.

Subject: Ferret Here Again

FROM Ferret
TO   Holly

Hiya there Hollsie,
    What time d'you want to see your little friends?

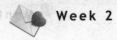

FROM   Holly
TO   Ferret

Preferably never.

Subject: URGENT URGENT Quickly Jennie — can you help me please!!!

FROM   Holly
TO   Jennie Pithwait

I think I made a boo boo. One of the MD's PA's Shella got upset with me, so I asked her to come down if she had a problem, now she's out of the office? I hope she's not actually coming down?

FROM   Jennie Pithwait
TO   Holly

I'm sure she is going down, but you won't want her to. Try not to mix it with her, she's a bit of a rockweiler, or rottweiler (not sure of spelling) but sure you get the message. She's like one of those big scary vicious dogs with the German names. Anyway love 'made a boo boo' — got to use it more instead of 'I f*cked up'. I'm sure my boss would appreciate the change.

Subject: HELP TRISH — it's urgent

FROM   Holly
TO   Patricia Gillot

Trish
Should I be worried? I think Shella is on her way down to have a go at me.

FROM   Patricia Gillot
TO   Holly

Sh*t!
What did you do to get her attention? I suggest you hide.

Subject: Sunday beers — your place

FROM   Ferret
TO   Holly

What about Sunday? And we can kick back and sink some bevies together (I've a few urban battle stories of my own to share).
   Ferret x
   Chairman Mow once said 'Free the force'.
   ☺

FROM   Holly
TO   Ferret

Sounds great.

Subject: Matthew McConaughey or a Mark Ruffalo?

FROM   Jennie Pithwait
TO   Holly

Any hunks on the horizon?

FROM   Holly
TO   Jennie Pithwait

Possibly Jennie, what d'you think of the swampy type?

FROM   Jennie Pithwait
TO   Holly

What — the type that are over-affectionate and clingy?

FROM   Holly
TO   Jennie Pithwait

No, the type that have strong political views and like to burrow?

FROM Jennie Pithwait
TO   Holly

Sounds good, put me down for two.

FROM Holly
TO   Jennie Pithwait

By the way, I was thinking of having a dinner party on Saturday. You know, just a few friends around, nothing special. Do you fancy it? I thought it would give us a chance to catch up on old times?
   Holly

FROM Jennie Pithwait
TO   Holly

Too right, a dinner do round at Hols in 'maida boo boo' — couldn't turn it down.

Subject: Reception Problems

FROM Shella Hamilton-Jones
TO   Holly; Roger Lipton

Dear Holly Denham & Roger Lipton
   I've included you on this email too Roger, because I feel our new receptionist isn't quite grasping how we operate here.
   I knew it wouldn't be an easy transition for her; making the step up into the corporate world, but there are a few things she needs to learn quickly.
   Holly mentioned to me that perhaps I would be better coming down to shout at her if something went wrong and I'd like to just point out that this is not how employees at Huerst and Wright like to operate. Every person in this building tries to pull together as a team. This is something she needs to understand, communication is the key to success.
   Maybe Holly could perhaps benefit from a training course on her communication skills and the booking of meeting rooms, just to get her up to speed. Holly has great potential, but a long way to go and I would like to offer my assistance to ensure her rapid progression.
   Yours truly,
   Shella

Subject: Dinner at mine

FROM   Holly
TO   Jennie Pithwait

Dinner definitely on.
   Holly

Subject: Quick break

FROM   Holly
TO   Patricia Gillot

Hi,
   I'm really sorry Trish, but can I go for a toilet break again?
   Holly

FROM   Patricia Gillot
TO   Holly

Of course you can sweetheart, you look white as a sheet — you OK?

FROM   Holly
TO   Patricia Gillot

I'm fine.
   Hols

FROM   Patricia Gillot
TO   Holly

Is it about that email?

FROM   Holly
TO   Patricia Gillot

Sorry Trish.

FROM　Patricia Gillot
TO　　Holly

You don't have to apologise, you're in a bad way aren't ya? Stay there, I'll get someone from facilities to cover the switch while you tell your aunty Trish all about it.
　x

Subject: Aisha

FROM　Holly
TO　　Aisha

Are you still on for Saturday?

FROM　Aisha
TO　　Holly

Hiya sweetie, of course! I'll bring bubbles — are you cooking?
　xxxxxx

FROM　Holly
TO　　Aisha

Of course, I've been preparing it all week, so don't be eating before you come!
　Holly
　x

Subject: Recipe suggestions please

FROM　Holly
TO　　Cooking Right Now

Dear Sir/Madam
　Can you recommend a recipe for a three-course dinner for 5 people?
　Kindest regards
　Holly

FROM Cooking Right Now
TO Holly

This week's gourmet suggestion is below:
A special roast with a regal cranberry and apple stuffing. The roast will make any dinner party into a sophisticated occasion and your guests will feel like royalty. Original recipe yield: 6 to 8 servings. Servings: 6

INGREDIENTS:
- 6 pounds crown pork roast
- 2 cups chopped cranberries
- ½ cup white sugar
- ½ cup butter
- 2 onions, chopped
- 2 cups chopped celery
- 2 teaspoons salt
- ¼ teaspoon ground black pepper
- 8 cups white bread cubes
- 2 apples — peeled, cored, and chopped
- ½ cup apple juice
- 1 egg
- 1 teaspoon poultry seasoning

DIRECTIONS:
1. Preheat oven to 375 degrees F (190 degrees C).
2. Season pork roast with salt and pepper to taste, then place on a rack in an open roasting pan, rib ends down.
3. Bake at 375 degrees F (190 degrees C) for 2 hours. Roast will be only partially cooked.
4. Meanwhile, in a medium bowl, combine cranberries and sugar and mix well; set aside. Melt butter or margarine in a large skillet over medium heat. Add onions and celery and sauté until tender, about 10 minutes. Add cranberry mixture, 2 teaspoons salt, ¼ teaspoon ground black pepper, bread cubes, apples, apple juice, egg and poultry seasoning. Toss well.
5. After the two hours, remove roast from oven. Turn rib ends up and fill cavity with cranberry/apple stuffing. Insert meat thermometer between two ribs in the thickest part of the meat, making sure that end of thermometer does not touch any bone.
6. Return stuffed roast to oven and continue roasting at 375 degrees F (190 degrees C) for about 1½ hours, or until internal temperature of meat reaches 175 degrees F (80 degrees C). (Note: If stuffing becomes too brown, cover it with aluminium foil.)
7. To Serve: Place roast on warm platter and let stand for 15 minutes for easier carving. Slice between ribs to carve, and serve with stuffing.

Subject: Dinner Party Enquiry

FROM　Holly
TO　　　GourmetFoodDeliveredToTheDoor

Hi
I am having a dinner party for 5 people. Can you tell me how much it would be to deliver food to my door? (Maida Vale)
Kindest regards
Holly

FROM　GourmetFoodDeliveredToTheDoor
TO　　　Holly

Dear Holly
We'd be delighted to help you, our prices start at around £400 for 5 people. We can email you a full price list if you can give us more details.
Regards
Francis

Gourmet Food, Delivered To The Door, London

Subject: Mum — can you give me some food advice please

FROM　Holly
TO　　　Mum and Dad

Hi Mum,
Can you tell me what I can cook for 5 people for a dinner party on Saturday, with a budget of about £20?
Love Holly

FROM　Mum and Dad
TO　　　Holly

What about Shepherd's Pie?

FROM Holly
TO Mum and Dad

I'm not sure Shepherds Pie is the answer this time. But thanks.
  Holly x

FROM Mum and Dad
TO Holly

Why only £20?

FROM Holly
TO Mum and Dad

Because I can't get to the bank on time.
  x

Subject: Saturday night

FROM Patricia Gillot
TO Holly

I've just checked with him indoors and we'd love to come to your dinner party. What kind of thing should we be wearing?

FROM Holly
TO Patricia Gillot

Anything — it's just a friendly get-together.
  x

Subject: Who's James Lawrence?

FROM Holly
TO Jennie Pithwait

Hey, just met that James for the first time, he's good-looking and seems really sweet.
  Holly

FROM   Jennie Pithwait
TO   Holly

Rumour has it, he's after half the girls in the company — so if your idea of sweet is a dose of crabs, then yes, I guess he's a real sweetie.
  Jennie

FROM   Holly
TO   Jennie Pithwait

That's a shame. Oh well, have a good night.
  Holly

THURSDAY

Subject: Get ready girl

FROM   Patricia Gillot
TO   Holly

It's another big day today . . . keep calm, keep smiling and we'll get through this lot together. Don't let anyone wind you up, if the Directors or VPs get stressed and shout, don't take it personal, keep that smile coming.
  Ship em in and ship em out!

FROM   Holly
TO   Patricia Gillot

Surf and Turf!

FROM   Patricia Gillot
TO   Holly

What?

FROM   Holly
TO   Patricia Gillot

I've no idea, I think it's from Top Gun, sorry. Had a bit of an Ice Man obsession when I was about 10.

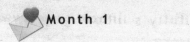

Subject: Life on the campo

FROM Mum and Dad
TO Holly

Holly

We were sitting on the terrace the other night, sharing a quiet sherry, talking about how when we made the move to Spain, everyone thought we'd be back within a month, but we weren't.

Your father was just saying something to me about how well we'd done and how beautiful the evening was, as the sun set behind the avo trees, and just then a huge tractor ploughed through the field next to us before disappearing down the hill the other side. Then another, and another.

Apparently they built our house on a right of way, a country highway apparently. So we'll be having quite a bit of traffic passing by.

Mum x

Subject: Bit of info about your friend

FROM Patricia Gillot
TO Holly

Shella (or Cruella, as Mags used to call her) can be a right cow, she's rubbed a load of people up the wrong way here. I take my hat off to you for standing up to her. I know at least two people she fell out with big time. But because she's a PA to an MD she gets away with it.

FROM Holly
TO Patricia Gillot

Does Jane know what she's like?

FROM Patricia Gillot
TO Holly

MDs like Jane want results and anything else is brushed under the carpet. Didn't you have any bitches like that in the hotel you worked at?

FROM   Holly
TO   Patricia Gillot

No, they were all really nice.

FROM   Patricia Gillot
TO   Holly

In four years you never came across anyone who was just pure evil?

FROM   Holly
TO   Patricia Gillot

How d'you know I was there 4 years?

FROM   Patricia Gillot
TO   Holly

Comes with the territory — you have to put up with so much cr*p sitting here, but we're the eyes and ears of the company — so yes, seen your cv, read it, think I even got a copy on me hard drive.

FROM   Holly
TO   Patricia Gillot

Oh, great.
   Re Shella — can I tell HR what's happening?

FROM   Patricia Gillot
TO   Holly

You could tell HR if you wanted, the other two did.

FROM   Holly
TO   Patricia Gillot

Did it help?

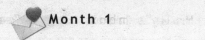

FROM Patricia Gillot
TO Holly

You could ask them, if they were still here.

FROM Holly
TO Patricia Gillot

Oh great.

FROM Patricia Gillot
TO Holly

She's a wrong un. If she were around my way, me and me sis would put our boots on and go round there.

FROM Holly
TO Patricia Gillot

Why, does she live on a farm?

FROM Patricia Gillot
TO Holly

What?

FROM Holly
TO Patricia Gillot

I just realised my guy over there is going to be late for his meeting, the one with the blue tie.

FROM Patricia Gillot
TO Holly

His meeting starts in two minutes. I'll take him up now, score us some brownie points, then I'll be off. See ya after lunch.

Subject: Are you around Jen?

FROM Holly
TO Jennie Pithwait

What does Trish mean when she says — she'll be around there in her boots? She's said it a couple of times?

FROM Jennie Pithwait
TO Holly

I didn't know what she meant either, until I went to an office party in Canary Wharf. I was drunk and a few of us ended up back at hers on the Isle of Dogs. She's got these boots, we're talking steel toe-capped boots, that they really do put on when they go around to sort out a neighbour.
Scary.

FROM Holly
TO Patricia Gillot

Oh Sh*t.

FROM Jennie Pithwait
TO Holly

Why?

FROM Holly
TO Jennie Pithwait

She said she'd go round to Shella's in them. I thought it was because Shella lives on a farm? (thought maybe it was muddy) ... oh dear.

FROM Jennie Pithwait
TO Holly

Classic, I'll be telling everyone.
Thanks!

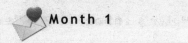

FROM   Holly
TO   Jennie Pithwait

No Jennie, please don't.
  x

FRIDAY

Subject: Charity People in Holborn

FROM   Holly
TO   Patricia Gillot

Are there charity people everywhere in Holborn?

FROM   Patricia Gillot
TO   Holly

Always outside the tube, you've just got to tell them where to go.

FROM   Holly
TO   Patricia Gillot

I find it difficult not stopping for them.

FROM   Patricia Gillot
TO   Holly

Is that why you were late?

FROM   Holly
TO   Patricia Gillot

I didn't think I was that late, I thought maybe a couple of minutes?

FROM Patricia Gillot
TO Holly

They watch the clock around here, they expect you to be here a while before you start.

FROM Holly
TO Patricia Gillot

Oh God! I'm so sorry, has anyone said anything?

FROM Patricia Gillot
TO Holly

No, not yet ...

Subject: Sophisticated Dinner — Are you coming Jason??

FROM Holly
TO Jason GrangerRM

You haven't let me know if you can make my sophisticated dinner do on Sat night. Some of my new friends from work are coming, I think you'll have a ball? ☺

FROM Jason GrangerRM
TO Holly

I've already told you. VERY VERY DODGY, HUGE MISTAKE, DO NOT HAVE A PARTY.
  Sorry I can't come, I've got a shift that night. Remember, I work on a reception desk which isn't just the place to park your coffee mug (wish you were still here).
  Can't believe you're partying with colleagues, cancel it fast.

FROM Holly
TO Jason GrangerRM

Why is it dodgy, why can't I?

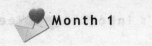

FROM   Jason GrangerRM
TO   Holly

RULE 1
Never get drunk with 'work people', ESPECIALLY ex-school mates who are now 'work people'. EVER EVER EVER (except if forced, at the Christmas party, but it's still wrong).

FROM   Holly
TO   Jason GrangerRM

OK but I don't intend to drink, so that's not a problem is it.

FROM   Jason GrangerRM
TO   Holly

RULE 2
Never under any circumstances invite 'work people' into your home. It's like offering a bunch of hungry cannibals your naked body on a plate and asking them to choose from a selection of forks.
    The people you think are your friends will be running around your flat, picking up evidence they can use against you. Skeletons in the closet ... porn on the computer ... really it's endless...
    Stop before it's too late...

FROM   Holly
TO   Jason GrangerRM

I don't have skeletons or porn??

FROM   Jason GrangerRM
TO   Holly

Skeletons... oh yes yes yes you do ... and you know it ...
    Porn — what about that naked strumpet you've got hanging up in the hall???!

FROM   Holly
TO   Jason GrangerRM

That's an oil painting of my granny?

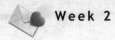
FROM Jason GrangerRM
TO   Holly

Really?? Saucy minx ...
    Anyway, you're an open book as it is.
    But, your flat is a library ... and you'll be judged from one glance inside your bathroom cabinet — and a sniff of that basket in your hall!

FROM Holly
TO   Jason GrangerRM

What's wrong with that basket in my hall?

FROM Jason GrangerRM
TO   Holly

It stinks, for heavens sake do some washing, anyway, got to go, love you hugely. BUT STOP THAT PARTY!!!

FROM Holly
TO   Jason GrangerRM

Wait wait, I can hide pictures, I can keep any reference to that time hidden. Surely????
    It is a bad idea isn't it, a terrible idea, but I've already invited people and it's nearly 5pm. I was feeling rotten Jason, because of that PA and wanted some friends on my side. Heeeeeeelp help help help help help help help help help help help help help help help help help help help help help help help help help help help help help help help help help help help help help help help help help help help help help
    Help me!!!!!!!!!!

FROM Jason GrangerRM
TO   Holly

Calm down, cancel it if you can. Grab them before they leave for the weekend and tell them your home's been flooded — that's what staff usually tell me when they're hung-over and don't want to come in.

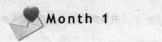

If not ... don't panic whatsoever, your sophisticated dinner party will, I'm sure, be a success.

(It's probably me just being silly and worrying too much because I haven't slept enough.)

xx Got to go,

I've got a 'room's too small' emergency on the fourth floor.

Subject: ORDER 2190007 Ace Internet Food Delivery CARD DECLINED

Thank you for your order. Unfortunately your payment was unsuccessful. Please re-order using a different credit card.

Thank you for choosing AceInternetFoodDeliveries — the easier way to do your shopping.

Subject: Saturday Night

FROM   Patricia Gillot
TO   Holly

Les just called, and he sounds really excited about tomorrow, we're both looking forward to it.

Thanks Holls.

Subject: Can't Cancel!!!

FROM   Holly
TO   Jason

It's too late, I can't cancel!

Subject: Change of plan

FROM   Ferret
TO   Holly

Hollsie
    Can't imagine you're still at work, but I tried calling you and your phone was off.
    I'm coming over a day early (not Sunday) so I'll be at yours around 7pm Saturday night.
    Look forward to seeing you.
    Ferret x ☺

WEEK 3

MONDAY

Subject: Sleeping with the enemy???

FROM Jason GrangerRM
TO Holly

Oh Holly,
  All I want to know is ... WHICH colleague did you go to bed with? (I got your message late Sunday.) Man or woman?

FROM Holly
TO Jason GrangerRM

Let me start at the beginning, because it's not fair to judge me till you've heard the state I was in!
  I got my hair done in the morning — no problem there, was quite pleased with it, got some streaks put in too.
  I was going to make a spicy chicken dish and I ordered the essentials off the web: milk, chicken, eggs and lots of other stuff — of course none of it arrived, at all ...
  My crappy old washing machine/dryer had broken down and apparently it'll be too expensive to repair therefore I had no clean clothes to wear and I had a dinner to make and an hour to do it in.
  Ferret came and went before anyone got there, he turned out to be quite funny actually. He brought a card for Alice and put the rodents in the freezer.
  While I was waiting for guests to arrive I managed to get through a bottle of wine while deliberating on how to explain the lack of food.
  By the time Jennie and Trisha had come I'd solved the food problem by filling up a large glass bowl with jellybeans which I thought at the time looked both colourful and trendy, for the modern dinner party guest. I think they thought I was only kidding and I had to dodge a few 'when's the real food coming' questions. In the end I heated up some frozen pizzas in the microwave ... I know, you don't have to say a word.
  By the time they'd finished their pizzas I was very drunk and I kept catching a strange smell, which was only ever there when I

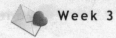

*turned around quickly (I came to realise it was coming from the top
I'd rescued from the dirty clothes basket you warned me about —
which no amount of perfume could help). About this point someone
then reached in the freezer for more ice and pulled out a frozen rat,
which seemed to really put a dampener on the evening, and it was
then that I decided people needed to hear me sing.*

FROM   Jason GrangerRM
TO   Holly

What did you sing?

FROM   Holly
TO   Jason GrangerRM

*What I always sing before I pass out — 'Over The Rainbow'.
   I woke up the next day in my bed.*

FROM   Jason GrangerRM
TO   Holly

*Holly
   You are the only person I know who could invite people for a
dinner party and not give them any bloody dinner.
   Without any doubt, you are, quite the most fabulously
entertaining sophisticated dinner party host in history.
   I feel this time your high point must have been offering rat ice-
cubes — genius! I'm duly devastated I couldn't witness it. Damn it.*

FROM   Holly
TO   Jason GrangerRM

*Spent the whole day on Sunday with raging hangover, worrying about
what I did, and what people are going to think of me today.*

FROM   Jason GrangerRM
TO   Holly

I can picture the scene — curtains drawn, too scared to leave the flat

or answer the phone, binging yourself on fatty foods and chocolate, Jalapeños, onion rings, chips, with side orders of Quality Streets, Love Actually, Bridget 1&2 and probably a couple more with Hugh Grant in.

FROM   Holly
TO   Jason GrangerRM

You think you know me.
*   I just wish I knew who put me to bed ... embarrassing.*

Subject: Extreme Weight Busters

FROM   ExtremeWeightBusters.com
TO   Holly

Course chosen: Standard
*   Thank you for registering for a free trial as a member of WeightBusters.com.*
*   You will now receive all our special messages of encouragement and daily dieting advice.*
*   Remember our methods are extreme, but we believe psychology to be the grounding in losing weight.*
*   So come on, let's beat this together!*
*   Your membership number is 7980*
*   Your password is TOOLARGE99876*

Subject: Celebrity news

FROM   Holly
TO   Jason GrangerRM

Noticed Helen Mirren did well at the Oscars.

FROM   Jason GrangerRM
TO   Holly

I've spent my life playing a queen and no one's given me diddly squat.

FROM   Holly
TO   Jason GrangerRM

Oh ... poor Jason.

FROM   Jason GrangerRM
TO   Holly

Actually that's a lie, I once got chased through Camden by a bunch of thugs who wanted to give me a 'f***ing kicking', bless.

FROM   Holly
TO   Jason GrangerRM

You've once again brightened up my day.
   xxxx
   (Not by the thought of you being chased across Camden — just because you're funny.)
   xx

TUESDAY

Subject: Your Party

FROM   Jennie Pithwait
TO   Holly

Nice party, thanks for the invite.

FROM   Holly
TO   Jennie Pithwait

What time can you do lunch today?

FROM   Jennie Pithwait
TO   Holly

Sorry, won't be able to make lunch today.

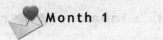

Subject: Meeting Room Request

FROM James Lawrence
TO Holly

Holly
I've scheduled a meeting with an important client today at 3pm.
I'd like one of the better rooms (for a change). Word on the street is that Holly takes bribes, is this correct?
James

James Lawrence, VP Corporate Finance, H&W, High Holborn WC2 6NP

FROM Holly
TO James Lawrence

Dear James
Bribery is essential (we run a mafia-style front of house down here).
If you don't pay us, we can make it very uncomfortable for you. No air-con, the wrong food, interruptions and faulty AV equipment.
Holly

FROM James Lawrence
TO Holly

Holly
Please forgive my previous ignorance in this matter. I'll pay like a good boy.
Can I have the gourmet menu for our guests, also — you think you could russle up a room with a view?
James

FROM Holly
TO James Lawrence

Not sure what you're expecting to see from a window in central London — the Egyptian Pyramids? Or the Hanging Gardens of Babylon?
You've got room 15, hope this suits your requirements.
Holly

FROM　James Lawrence
TO　Holly

Central London city smog will be fine (are we now in an episode of Faulty Towers?).
  Room 15 is perfect, please accept my thanks, oh and the offer of lunch sometime?
  J

FROM　Holly
TO　James Lawrence

Thank you, lunch some time could be nice.
  Holly

Subject: Thanks Aish!

FROM　Holly
TO　Aisha

Thanks for coming.

FROM　Aisha
TO　Holly

I know you probably hate me, and think I'm a useless friend, and I can understand it if you never want to talk to me again. But it wasn't my fault, I told you I was having problems.If it makes you feel any better I've been crying all weekend.

FROM　Holly
TO　Aisha

It doesn't make me feel better. I would have just liked you to have been there.

FROM　Aisha
TO　Holly

I was a mess Sat night — through to Monday afternoon. How did it go anyway?

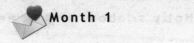

FROM   Holly
TO   Aisha

It went very well. You missed a classy night.
  X

Subject: Holborn Today

FROM   Holly
TO   Alice and Matt
PHOTOS *Rush-Hour*

Fab weather, (see photo attached). Forgot my umbrella, got a few bad looks from people for my hair looking like bush.
  Pooh.

FROM   Alice and Matt
TO   Holly
PHOTOS *Rush-Hour*

Rush hour in the campo — see attached.

  Alice
  xxx

Subject: Complaint

FROM   Maxi Hazier
TO   Holly

Holly
  Did you hang up on someone last week, because they were rude to you?

Maxi Hazier, VP Corporate Finance, H&W, High Holborn, WC2B 6NP, London

Subject: Not funny — in trouble again

FROM   Holly
TO   Patricia Gillot

This time for hanging up on a client. Any suggestions?

FROM   Patricia Gillot
TO   Holly

Why did you hang up on them?

FROM   Holly
TO   Patricia Gillot

They were gabbling, and being a bit offish.

FROM   Patricia Gillot
TO   Holly

A bit offish?? And you hung up on them? You can't do that!

FROM   Holly
TO   Patricia Gillot

But you told me to, only the other day!

FROM   Patricia Gillot
TO   Holly

I was having a laugh!
   You can't hang up on clients, there could be a shed-load of money waiting on that call. I know they're rude sometimes but you never know what's going on their end, so you've just got to grin and bear it.
   You messed up there babe, big time.
   Trish

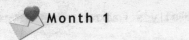

Subject: Got your urgent phone message!

FROM   Aisha
TO   Holly
PHOTOS *HELP-FOR-HOL*

HOLLY
I GOT YOUR URGENT PHONE MESSAGE about hanging up on a client.
See attached — this could be useful ...

FROM   Holly
TO   Aisha

That's great, thanks for that Aish, really helpful in my current state.
*   PS — what is he meant to be doing anyway?*

FROM   Aisha
TO   Holly

What d'you think — I'm lying on the bed.

FROM   Holly
TO   Aisha

What, underneath?

FROM   Aisha
TO   ·   Holly

Yes underneath.

FROM   Holly
TO   Aisha

And you're taking pictures????

FROM   Aisha
TO   Holly

I'll be honest, the view was better than the performance.
*   Anyway he didn't mind holding still for a couple of piccies, kept his hat on too. Yummie.*
*   xxx*

FROM   Holly
TO   Aisha

I would send you the pictures I took on my phone today, but they're probably too wild and wet for you.
*   xxx*

Subject: Miserable

FROM   Holly
TO   Jason GrangerRM

Jason
*   Do you have any friends who, without meaning to, remind you all the time how much of a non-event your love life is?*
*   x*

FROM   Jason GrangerRM
TO   Holly

Are we feeling a bit a low today? Don't worry about it, some people always have lots of partners, when the rest of us would just settle for one. There's probably one just lurking around the next corner.

FROM   Holly
TO   Jason GrangerRM

I'd like to think of them as waiting for me patiently. (Not keen on lurkers.)
*   xxx*

WEDNESDAY

Subject: Can you help me Trisha

FROM Holly
TO Patricia Gillot

Help, what should I do about Maxi?
I still haven't emailed her back about me slamming the phone down. What should I say?

FROM Patricia Gillot
TO Holly

It's your mess, sorry, you sort it out.

Subject: Advice needed please Mum

FROM Holly
TO Mum and Dad

I'm not sure, but I think since the party, people aren't very happy with me. I imagine I probably made a fool out of myself.
Trish, the other receptionist, is definitely annoyed with me. I'm just too worried to ask her why.
Oh and I think I messed up again here.
Not a great week so far Mum.
x

FROM Mum and Dad
TO Holly

Holly
Don't worry about them not speaking to you again.
Your father has spent a lifetime embarrassing me at parties, and it's all forgotten in the morning. Although the Petersons have never spoken to us since that night he swapped his clothes for their Christmas tree decorations and I was beginning to get some strange stares in Budgens, but then it all seemed to sort itself out in the end.
Love Mum

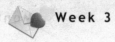
FROM   Holly
TO   Mum and Dad

Mum you emigrated, I don't want to have to emigrate.

FROM   Mum and Dad
TO   Holly

You won't have to, it'll all be fine. My advice is just keep being friendly, keep plugging away in life, keep smiling, and keep your clothes on. That's the advice I gave your father. Seems to have helped.
   Let me know if they talk to you again.
   Love Mum.
   x

Subject: Trouble at work

FROM   Holly
TO   Jason GrangerRM

No one's talking to me today. Saturday night could have been worse than I thought but the problem is I can't remember what I've done to upset everyone?

FROM   Jason GrangerRM
TO   Holly

Ask them what's wrong. I would, otherwise you'll never know.
   It could be just some misunderstanding from Saturday night — they mistakenly thought they were at a dinner party at Maida Vale, whereas you thought they were attending your stage debut at the Albert Hall. Misunderstandings happen.

FROM   Holly
TO   Jason GrangerRM

I would laugh ... but also I've messed up big time again; I cut someone off while they were talking and it's hit the fan.
   The worst thing is — I admitted doing it on purpose because I

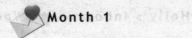

thought it was just some raving lunatic talking gibberish; turns out it was a private client talking about derivatives!? (whatever that means)

Subject: Sorry to bother you Holly

FROM Aisha
TO Holly

Are you there?

FROM Holly
TO Aisha

Yes, but quite busy, are you OK?

FROM Aisha
TO Holly

Yes, I'm just not sure I did the right thing, and want to ask your opinion.
   xxxxxxxxxxxxxxxxxxxxxxx

FROM Holly
TO Aisha

You can't keep juggling all these men at once and you said yourself Alex wasn't THAT hot in bed — and you certainly weren't with him for his personality!! Believe me, you did the right thing, he's gone and forgotten.
   xxxx
   got to work.
   Holly

FROM Aisha
TO Holly

He's in the other room sleeping.
   Sorry.
   ?

FROM Holly
TO Aisha

Oh, so you're back together, then I didn't mean he was that bad, I'm sure he's a fun, interesting guy, underneath it all.

FROM Aisha
TO Holly

I was going to end it, but ended up having sex with him instead.

FROM Holly
TO Aisha

Easy mistake to make, have you been to sleep yet?

FROM Aisha
TO Holly

No

FROM Holly
TO Aisha

Then go to sleep.
   x
   love you very much and you've got nothing to worry about, you're a fun crazy girl and everyone loves you.

FROM Aisha
TO Holly

Thanks, that's what I needed, I really should start paying you for lifting my downers.
   xxxx

THURSDAY

Subject: TEST TEST TEST

FROM   Elizabethontour
TO   Holly

TESTING

FROM   Holly
TO   Elizabethontour

Granny is that you?
    x

Subject: Granny online

FROM   Holly
TO   Mum and Dad

Mum, did you set Granny up as 'Elizabethontour' — if so that's really sweet, and I think she just emailed me.

FROM   Mum and Dad
TO   Holly

Holly
    Yes I set her up on Monday.
    She's so happy in Spain, she hasn't stopped smiling since she got here. We've been cleverly watering down her drink though.
    Other news; it turns out our land surrounding our finca is marked by white painted stones. This is the only way the town hall has of working out which is our land and which isn't.
    Fun Fun.
    All our love, Mum & Dad

Subject: Jason — your opinion please

FROM   Holly
TO   Jason GrangerRM

I feel more positive today with Trisha. I think just need to make more of an effort.

Subject: Watching my Soaps

FROM   Holly
TO   Patricia Gillot

Did you watch EastEnders Tuesday night? It was great!!

FROM   Patricia Gillot
TO   Holly

No, I've stopped watching it.

Subject: First a mobile phone — now you're on the
         internet?

FROM   Holly
TO   Granny

Hi Granny,
   I didn't realise it was you who had just emailed me.
   How are you? I hear you like the new country?
   Love Holls xx

FROM   Granny
TO   Holly

Dear Holly
   They've stuffed me into a home, like I needed it!
   I don't like the food, I don't like the weather, I don't like the people.
I would tell your mother, but my false teeth went missing in the

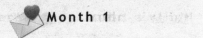

move and I won't speak again until I'm all dignified, so I just smile and nod. However, when I get hold of a new set, I'll tell them where they can stick their sangria. Incidentally they've started watering down me gin, they must think I'm stupid.

I am so glad you have found a new start. I'm so very proud of you Holly.

Missing you as always.
Love Granny
xxxx

Subject: Update

FROM Roger Lipton
TO Holly

Dear Holly,
Although you have been here just less than three weeks, I think it's time we had a review. Can you book a meeting room for next Wednesday around ten o'clock.
Yours sincerely
Roger

Subject: Extreme Weight Busters

FROM ExtremeWeightBusters.com
TO Holly

Standard Course.
Remember the old equation: Overeating = Overweight = No Friends or Partner
Today's menu:
Breakfast — Dry Toast and Tea
Lunch — Low Fat Natural Yogurt and Fruit Salad
Dinner — Sushi & Green Leaf Salad
Night Snack — Salad

Subject: Lunch

FROM   Jennie Pithwait
TO   Holly

You on for lunch today, I'm free around 2pm?

FROM   Holly
TO   Jennie Pithwait

I'd love to, but Trish always takes the 2pm slot, she has to go somewhere each day at that time.

FROM   Jennie Pithwait
TO   Holly

Where does Trisha NEED to go at that time???

FROM   Holly
TO   Jennie Pithwait

Don't know.

FROM   Jennie Pithwait
TO   Holly

Very suspicious. What d'you think she's up to???

FROM   Holly
TO   Jennie Pithwait

I don't know, but I guess it's her private business so I'm staying out of it.

FROM   Jennie Pithwait
TO   Holly

Private my arse, we should ask her.

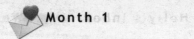

FROM   Holly
TO   Jennie Pithwait

I think I'll leave it.

FROM   Jennie Pithwait
TO   Holly

Well I won't, something's going on.

FRIDAY

Subject: Moving Mum

FROM   Mum and Dad
TO   Holly

Holly
  You think Granny is very happy out here then?
  Mum

FROM   Holly
TO   Mum and Dad

Of course she is, just give her some time and she'll come to love it there.
  xxx

Subject: Our emails

FROM   Holly
TO   Granny

Hi Granny.
  Quickly, can you delete our emails, I don't want Mum getting upset about what you've told me.
  Love Hols
  xxxx

FROM   Granny
TO   Holly

Dear Holly,
*   I was just watching The Last of the Summer Wine.*
*   You mum has got me the series, you see I can't get British telly out here in the sticks, that's another reason I miss England.*
*   What do you mean delete our emails?*
*   Love Granny*
*   xxx*

FROM   Holly
TO   Granny

If you highlight the email then press the delete button on the keyboard — that should do it. It's just that I told Mum we hadn't spoken to each other yet.
*   Holls*

FROM   Granny
TO   Holly

We haven't, this is email isn't it?

FROM   Holly
TO   Granny

I know but can you delete them, and from your deleted items?

FROM   Granny
TO   Holly

If they're deleted how can I delete them, and what am I deleting?

FROM   Holly
TO   Granny

Don't worry Granny, I love you very very much. I'll think of a way around this. Have a lovely day.
*   Love Hols*
*   Xxx*

Subject: Extreme Weight Busters

FROM   ExtremeWeightBusters.com
TO   Holly

Standard Course
   Remember:
   *If the mountain won't come to Mohammed, it could be because
mountains are big and heavy and don't move much.*
   Today's menu:
   Breakfast — Nothing
   Lunch — Chicken breast, on rice biscuits
   *Dinner — One of our special 'I'm a fatty' no-fat drinks (available
online)*
   Night Snack — Banana

Subject: Extreme Weight Busters

FROM   ExtremeWeightBusters.com
TO   Holly

*We are sorry you have cancelled your free trial membership of
ExtremeWeightBusters.com*
   **We wish you all the success in the future with your weight
problem.**

Subject: Room Checking

FROM   Patricia Gillot
TO   Holly

Rooms 6 & 8 need checking, I'll see you in 5.

FROM   Holly
TO   Patricia Gillot

Are you upset with me — have I done anything wrong?

FROM Patricia Gillot
TO   Holly

Don't worry about it.

Subject: CLUB SUBMISSION

FROM Charlie Denham
TO   Holly

We're running out of money to build this club, so I've sacked the builders and me and Rubber Ron are going to do everything.
  Charlie

FROM Holly
TO   Charlie Denham

You don't know how to build. You're rubbish at DIY. You can't even put up a shelf??

FROM Charlie Denham
TO   Holly

OK, if it was something technical like building the bar, or wiring the club, yes, that would probably be too much, but building walls — it's just bricks and cement.Unless you know any builders who could do it for free?

FROM Holly
TO   Charlie Denham

Sorry.

Subject: Your big mistake

FROM Jason GrangerRM
TO   Holly

So have you found out yet who put you to bed on Saturday?

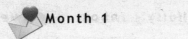

FROM   Holly
TO   Jason GrangerRM

Trish still isn't talking to me ... Maybe she saw something shocking...

FROM   Jason GrangerRM
TO   Holly

It's probably just your imagination.

Subject: Mad calls!

FROM   Holly
TO   Patricia Gillot

Trish
    You'll love this — you know when you ask someone where they're calling from, and they say something like 'Putney' instead of a company name ...

FROM   Patricia Gillot
TO   Holly

Yes.

FROM   Holly
TO · Patricia Gillot

Well I just got someone who stumbled — sounded confused and said 'The bath?' Funny when that happens isn't it?

FROM   Patricia Gillot
TO   Holly

Hysterical.

Subject: Jason — re Trish

FROM Holly
TO   Jason GrangerRM

Pretty sure it's not just my imagination.
  Atmosphere is stifling and I'm now embarrassed as hell ... I tried to get her to laugh, she didn't even crack a smile.

FROM Jason GrangerRM
TO   Holly

No she's fine, that's the normal reaction you get when you're telling jokes.

FROM Holly
TO   Jason GrangerRM

Up yours.

Subject: Hi, my best friend

FROM Holly
TO   Jason GrangerRM

Need a favour ...

FROM Jason GrangerRM
TO   Holly

Out of Office AutoReply
  Unfortunately no one is here to take your booking. If you would like to contact the reservations team, someone may be able to secure you a room.

FROM Holly
TO   Jason GrangerRM

Don't lie, I know you're there!!! It's only a small favour ...

FROM Jason GrangerRM
TO   Holly

I have one eye open, and a finger precariously close to the delete button.

FROM Holly
TO   Jason GrangerRM

Will you take my friend on ... as a receptionist?

FROM Jason GrangerRM
TO   Holly

Out of Office AutoReply
Unfortunately no one is here to take your booking. If you would like to contact the reservations team, someone may be able to secure you a room.

FROM Holly
TO   Jason GrangerRM

Stop it.

FROM Jason GrangerRM
TO   Holly

OK, who is he/she, what's he/she like, what is he/she to you? Why me? Why am I sitting here supervising children???

FROM Holly
TO   Jason GrangerRM

OK
Answers:
1: SHE's a good friend
2: Lovely
3: A good friend
4: Because you're a good friend
6: They're not children, you enjoy it, so stop being a woos (not sure how to spell it)
   Also — you should feel sorry for me, I'm likely to lose my job next week — you're not ... ☹

FROM   Jason GrangerRM
TO   Holly

*It's spelt wus, and fine, send her along for an interview on Monday.
It'll be quiet between 1pm-2pm so send her at 1 asking for me.
   And I'm not guaranteeing anything.
   x*

FROM   Holly
TO   Jason GrangerRM

*You are the best! She won't let you down.
And if she does, then it's nothing to do with me.*

FROM   Jason GrangerRM
TO   Holly

What ...?

FROM   Holly
TO   Jason GrangerRM

Out of Office AutoReply

Subject: You lucky girl

FROM   Holly
TO   Aisha

He said ... yes ...

FROM   Aisha
TO   Holly

You're lying.

FROM   Holly
TO   Aisha

BUT you have to PROMISE, you won't go out Saturday night, or I'll kill you. I mean it.

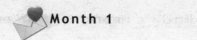

FROM Aisha
TO Holly

I promise, I promise ...

FROM Holly
TO Aisha

Make sure you dress appropriately, I'll call you later to go through some interview questions.

FROM Aisha
TO Holly

*Thanks honey, I won't be late don't worry, won't let you down.
What d'you mean 'appropriately' — like something slutty but not too revealing?*

FROM Holly
TO Aisha

Black suit, white shirt, tights, make up (not too much), stud earrings only, court shoes.

FROM Aisha
TO Holly

Tights — sick. What about nails?

FROM Holly
TO Aisha

Clear. NOT long, red and slutty.

FROM Aisha
TO Holly

Got it. Thanks for this, I owe ya. So Jason, is he straight?

FROM Holly
TO Aisha

*That is of no relevance to your interview.
Please be there ...
xx*

WEEK 4

MONDAY

Subject: A bit lost

FROM   Aisha
TO   Holly

Hi Holly
*   Still up from last night, havenx't gone to bedd, but I reckond I can still make it to the interviewx eitherway. Dont want to let you down,*
*   Where is it again?*
*   Aisha.*

Subject: What a small world

FROM   Mum and Dad
TO   Holly

Dear Holly
*   I said to your father only yesterday 'what a small world we live in' and it turns out I was right.*
*   A local farmer has been sneaking on to our land every night and moving those white painted rocks a yard closer to the house. If it carried on for much longer we'd have been in a negative equity situation. (Mummy joke)*
*   We've moved the rocks back where they were and on the other side of them there is a steep drop. So no more tractors coming through our land, how pleasant.*
*   Although your father's a bit concerned I've upset nearly everyone I've met since our arrival. Maybe I should invite the local farmers around for a wine and cheese party, what do you think?*
*   xxx Mum*

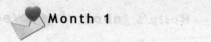

FROM   Holly
TO   Mum and Dad

Do you think I take after you Mum, or Dad?

FROM   Mum and Dad
TO   Holly

Me darling, really we're two peas in a pod.
    Mum.

FROM   Holly
TO   Mum and Dad

That's wonderful news.

Subject: A bit lost

FROM Aisha
TO   Holly

Holly
    It's me again, ok, if you're not going to react or talk to me, then I guess I'll have to admit I'm lying. I didn't go out on Saturday, you're making me boring already.
    Aisha

FROM   Holly
TO   Aisha

You could never be called boring.
    xxx

FROM   Aisha
TO   Holly

As I was off the partying I tried to call you on Saturday, but I couldn't get through to you?
    (I thought we could have been sad staying-in types together.)

FROM   Holly
TO   Aisha

I don't just sit there on my weekends waiting for you to call up drunk from some guy's house, I have a life.

FROM   Aisha
TO   Holly

Damn you! Where did you get this life from, were you on a date????

FROM   Holly
TO   Aisha

No.

FROM   Aisha
TO   Holly

Oh.

FROM   Holly
TO   Aisha

Doesn't mean I didn't have a great time.

FROM   Aisha
TO   Holly

Really.

FROM   Holly
TO   Aisha

Actually yes, I met up with pregnant Pam and spent the day in Guildford by the river.

Visited my school, then wondered why, and became incredibly scared I'd bump into old school friends who'd done much better than me. Ran away quickly with the secure intention of going back there once I was famous, thin and deadly in martial arts.

Then, I'd probably go there quite a lot, spend the days sitting outside the dark gates in a large, pink, open-top Rolls, growling at children.

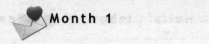

FROM Aisha
TO   Holly

Sweetie, you can get arrested for that stuff (it's happened to me before).

FROM Holly
TO   Aisha

Well anyway, it's a shame you missed out.

FROM Aisha
TO   Holly

Fun with pregnant Pam, I'll give it a miss.
   xxx
   Just being a bitch, I had a lovely time with Shona, we acted like kids (me more than her) and we were generally very childish and played tricks on Mum all day/night.

Subject: Psychic Readings

FROM StarsFutureWizard
TO   Holly

Dear Holly
   This is the week when a fabulous plethora of opportunities will arise. It's important to know which is the puppy wrapped in a pink bow and which is a wolf draped in sheep's clothing.
   Also why not take advantage of our Mad March offer on psychic readings? Find out if you're destined for love this March for just $2.99 for 3 mins.
   The Wizard

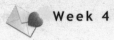

Subject: HOLLY DENHAM — IMPORTANT

FROM   James Lawrence
TO   Holly

My previous lunch offer — I feel it's important, to welcome you properly ... What about today?

FROM   Holly
TO   James Lawrence

James
    Thank you for the kind offer, I'd love to, but lunches are a bit difficult — we can't take the kind of lovely long lunches you chaps do up there,
        sorry.
        Holly

FROM   James Lawrence
TO   Holly

That's a shame.
    J

Subject: REMINDER James Lawrence ...

FROM   Holly
TO   Holly

James — wolf or puppy?

Subject: Hotel Employment / Job

FROM   Jason GrangerRM
TO   Holly

OK, just met with your friend Aisha. Before I go on, don't you have a friend called Aisha you said was a bit of a screw up??
    Jason

FROM   Holly
TO   Jason GrangerRM

Oh, I know the one, no that's not her (and I never said she was a screw-up, just a bit mad). But that's Teesha.

FROM   Jason GrangerRM
TO   Holly

OK. Eitherway, I thought she could have potential. She was bubbly, charming, charismatic and stylish (although she had the tendency to talk a lot, about herself, without being asked).

FROM   Holly
TO   Jason GrangerRM

Charismatic? Stylish? Why, what was she wearing?

FROM   Jason GrangerRM
TO   Holly

Black suit, white shirt, very professional, polished, pretty.

FROM   Holly
TO   Jason GrangerRM

That's all I wore when I was working for you, and you never told me I looked 'stylish!!' OR Charming or Charismatic, I can be Charismatic.

FROM   Jason GrangerRM
TO   Holly

I know you can be charismatic AND charming.

FROM   Holly
TO   Jason GrangerRM

You should see me here, you never exactly oozed charm when you were upset with everyone.

FROM   Jason GrangerRM
TO   Holly

*You don't know what compliments I've given you behind your back!
    Stop being a big sulky child, I thought you wanted me to like your
friend??*

FROM   Holly
TO   Jason GrangerRM

I did.

FROM   Jason GrangerRM
TO   Holly

*Well then?
    I didn't want to interview your messed-up friend anyway.
    GOODBYE!*

Subject: A huge thank you

FROM   Aisha
TO   Holly

*Just got home. I really hope I did OK, I held back on a few questions.
    Nice guy, good looking too! Let me know if you've got any news.
    xxx you're the best.
    Aisha*

Subject: Womens' problems

FROM   Holly
TO   Jason GrangerRM

Sorry

Bit stressed at the moment ...

Sorry ...

forgiiiiiiiiiiiiiiiiiiiiiive me

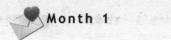

Pretty please???

(so ... did she get the job? xxxxx??)

☺

Holly loves you.

FROM Jason GrangerRM
TO Holly

You have issues and

stink

And have no friends

except me, because I know you're hormonal

So she can start on Monday.

FROM Holly
TO Jason GrangerRM

Love ya!
    She'll make me proud, I promise.
    But this doesn't mean she'll be like your new best friend??
    ... and you'll be hanging around with her, going to bars and being like all — 'Aisha said this' and 'Aisha said that ...'?

FROM Jason GrangerRM
TO Holly

No.

FROM Holly
TO Jason GrangerRM

Oh, and just one more thing. What compliments did you say about me behind my back? What did you say, was it nice, who did you say it to?

Subject: Hello — HELLO — Anyone there?

FROM   Holly
TO   Jason GrangerRM

Hello, did you get my last email? Hello?

FROM   Jason GrangerRM
TO   Holly

Hi
Sorry I was busy laughing at something funny Aisha said earlier, then I was planning what to wear when me and her go out clubbing together.
   xxx

FROM   Holly
TO   Jason GrangerRM

ha ha you're not funny.

TUESDAY

Subject: Holiday abroad

FROM   Holly
TO   Alice and Matt

Hiya Alice
   Looking forward to seeing you, not long to go!
   Seem to be upsetting everyone here, also got that meeting with HR tomorrow ...
   xxxx

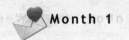

Subject: Trish please talk to me

FROM Holly
TO   Patricia Gillot

Please,
    I can't sit next to you without us communicating at all.
    It's bad enough that we can't speak and we always have to write, but now it's just murder, and we're meant to be going for a drink with the others tonight. Pleeeeeeease tell me what I've done. Is it to do with my work?

FROM Patricia Gillot
TO   Holly

No.

FROM Holly
TO   Patricia Gillot

Is it about the party?

FROM Patricia Gillot
TO   Holly

Yes.

FROM Holly
TO   Patricia Gillot

If it was my dancing, or singing, or food, I'm really sorry, I'm not the best host. I have been feeling bad for dragging you out for that.
    Please forgive me, everything just went wrong.
    Holly x

FROM Patricia Gillot
TO   Holly

I loved the party, it was great. Les did too, we were really enjoying ourselves, we haven't been out somewhere different for a while, and it was great. We even liked your jelly beans, and your singing wasn't that bad.

FROM   Holly
TO   Patricia Gillot

Then what was it?

FROM   Patricia Gillot
TO   Holly

I didn't appreciate you and that Jennie laughing about me.

FROM   Holly
TO   Patricia Gillot

I didn't laugh at you, ever??

FROM   Patricia Gillot
TO   Holly

You did, and I didn't think you were like that.

FROM   Holly
TO   Patricia Gillot

What did you think we said?

FROM   Patricia Gillot
TO   Holly

You know.

FROM   Holly
TO   Patricia Gillot

I honestly don't know what you think I was laughing about, but I can assure you I've been very grateful for how you've trained me, put up with my mistakes and been very patient.
     I know I haven't picked things up as fast as you thought I would.
     I wouldn't have said anything rotten about you — I promise!

FROM   Patricia Gillot
TO   Holly

I guess I should feel lucky you noticed I was there, you were spending so much time with your old school friend — little Miss 'look at my legs aren't they so young and smooth it's amazing how I never even have to shave them!' cow upstairs.

FROM   Holly
TO   Patricia Gillot

I don't know what you mean, I was very drunk very quickly, the night hadn't gone well with the food and everything, but I thought we'd all had fun ... I'm really sorry.

FROM   Patricia Gillot
TO   Holly

Also I hear you laughing about my 'island talk' as though I was from another planet, made me feel very small, gossiping about me.

FROM   Holly
TO   Patricia Gillot

Honestly I'm no gossip, we weren't doing anything like that at all!

Subject: Trisha's well-kept secret!!

FROM   Jennie Pithwait
TO   Holly

I've sussed it! I know why Trisha goes out at that time ... She's having an affair with one of the directors — must be!!

Subject: Trish please talk to me

FROM   Holly
TO   Patricia Gillot

You can't have heard the whole story, really it was me who felt stupid, I'll tell you when these two have gone.
    Honest, I'd never say anything bad about you, it was just about those boots you said you put on ... Really it's me being a dumb ass ... I thought they were for walking through the mud — it was about that farm comment I said (don't know if you remember).
    Holly.

FROM   Patricia Gillot
TO   Holly

You fool, I wondered what that was about.
    Tell me tonight, it just sounded bad, that's all, I felt hurt.

FROM   Holly
TO   Patricia Gillot

OK, it was just a misunderstanding, Trish.

FROM   Patricia Gillot
TO   Holly

PS also you were rambling drunkenly for a while about your night-mare life before in Canary Wharf. I know you lied about your CV, I did on mine too many years ago, but I wouldn't be telling Jennie.
    Also, when I put you to bed you woke up screaming.

Subject: Office girls

FROM   Charlie Denham
TO   Holly

This building thing is harder than we thought, the council are insisting on having both ends of the wall meeting the club ceiling at the same time, so Rubber Ron's gone out to buy a spirit level.
    Have you sorted me out yet with any of those tight-suited secretaries? Come on, there must be loads there, have you told them I own a club???
    Charlie

FROM   Holly
TO   Charlie Denham

Not the best time to talk to you but:
Stop being a pervert, you don't own a club, you own a building site, and neither of you have any kind of skill in this area at all, it's madness.
    You've got to find yourselves a handy man, please!

Subject: Job hunting?

FROM   Jason GrangerRM
TO   Holly

When's that HR thing then?

FROM   Holly
TO   Jason GrangerRM

Tomorrow 10am ... (don't like your subject box Jason) I think it probably will be an exit interview though.

FROM   Jason GrangerRM
TO   Holly

I'm telling you for certain — it WON'T be an exit interview!

Subject: Reminder! Suit

FROM   Holly
TO   Holly

Remember to wear best suit tomorrow!

Subject: Guildford — Saturday

FROM   Pregnant Pam
TO   Holly

Hi Holly
  Great seeing you on Saturday, we've got to do it again soon.
  xxxx

FROM   Holly
TO   Pregnant Pam

It was, I'm definitely up for doing it again later in month.
  xxxx

WEDNESDAY

Subject: Psychic readings, Stars and the Future!

FROM   StarsFutureWizard
TO   Holly

Stunts can only hurt your performance this week, so remember when ambiguity strikes at the heart of your consciousness, it's only a route to a blueprint that lurks behind mischievous gain, 'it's not the time of the moth' says the wizard, so keep one eye on Pluto and you'll know which side your toast is burnt.

Also why not take advantage of our Mad March offer on psychic readings? Find out if your destined for love this March for just $2.99 for 3 mins.
The Wizard

FROM   Holly
TO   StarsFutureWizard

To the Futures Wizard
What on earth does this mean??? Please explain???
I don't care about my lurking blue print, or any wizard's moth, I just want to know if I'm about to lose my job??
Or whether the guy on the 5th floor really likes me or is just keen to re-house a family of sea urchins?
Regards
Holly
PS Your 3 mins psychic reading was 2mins 50secs thanking me for calling, then telling me about other offers and 10secs explaining how little chance I had of love unless I stayed on the line and spent more money ????
Did I? No, your wizardness, I did not.

PPS I didn't use the work phone — this was at home — (in case this is being read by anyone from IT)

Subject: Team drinking night out

FROM   Judy Perkins
TO   Alvin Johnson; Dave Otto; Graham Kristan; Ralph Tooms;
   Samantha Smith; Patricia Gillot; Holly

Dear Team
   RE: Holly's Fabulous — welcoming night
   A good night was had by all, glad most of you could make it, let's do it again some time. Graham, you missed out.

Subject: Welcoming Night — xxx

FROM   Patricia Gillot
TO   Holly

To me that read RE: Holly is Fabulous. Welcoming night.
   Ha ha ... I think you've turned her head gal ...
   PS delete this immediately and from your deleted items!

FROM   Holly
TO   Patricia Gillot

She's not, is she?

FROM   Patricia Gillot
TO   Holly

Me: Hols is so innocent. Of course she is.

FROM   Holly
TO   Patricia Gillot

Oh great, and what are the chances — Judy was the one person here looking over my shoulder when I got that stupid email on my half day induction day — which shouted 'I'm a lesbian!'
   I'll kill my Brother!!!

FROM Patricia Gillot
TO Holly

That's funny, but I thought you knew.

FROM Holly
TO Patricia Gillot

No, not a clue. What should I do?

FROM Patricia Gillot
TO Holly

Nothing, unless you want to ...

FROM Holly
TO Patricia Gillot

Not really my type.

FROM Patricia Gillot
TO Holly

So am I still in with a shout then?

FROM Holly
TO Patricia Gillot

OH yes, I thought you'd never ask — let's get to it sexy!

FROM Patricia Gillot
TO Holly

Did you see I just spluttered over that woman's hand, don't make me laugh!

FROM Holly
TO Patricia Gillot

Hee hee ☺

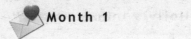

Subject: HR Meeting

FROM Holly
TO Patricia Gillot

Seeing HR soon, was it just because you were still angry with me that you said it was so bad that I cut that guy off?

FROM Patricia Gillot
TO Holly

I was joking when I said I just cut people off, I don't really, sorry.
That's the problem with email, you can't see when someone's having you on. It's like I said, that call could have been important. (important money-wise anyway) ...
Sorry babes ... xxx

Subject: HR Meeting

FROM Holly
TO Patricia Gillot

Meeting Roger Lipton very soon, I can feel the minutes ticking down. I'm really scared.

FROM Patricia Gillot
TO Holly

Don't you worry about them lot, I'll tell them that I told you to do it?

FROM Holly
TO Patricia Gillot

No don't be silly, it's my own fault.

FROM Patricia Gillot
TO Holly

If your meeting is anything to do with Cruella, I'll kill her!

FROM Holly
TO Patricia Gillot

I don't like the thought of them all having a go at me, especially if Shella's in there too. I'd die.

FROM Patricia Gillot
TO Holly

It'll be all very formal with HR, everything by the book. I call them office rozzas.

FROM Holly
TO Patricia Gillot

OK.

FROM Patricia Gillot
TO Holly

Don't you cry now, come on let's take a break.

FROM Holly
TO Patricia Gillot

But we can't leave the reception desk on its own.

FROM Patricia Gillot
TO Holly

I'm the senior receptionist here and I order you to leave your chair and come and give your Trish a hug! (Then go and get some fresh air and stop worrying! That's an order too)

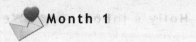

Subject: Washing Machines & Fridges

FROM HEM Machines
TO Holly

REF:9829833
Ms H Dinham
   Thank you for using H.E.M.
   We hope you are happy with your purchase and return to us again in the future for your home electrical items.

Paula, Customer Service

FROM Holly
TO HEM Machines

REF:9829833
   No I'm not happy with my purchase. I contacted your department twice last week. The washing machine you delivered was not functioning properly on arrival, so it has not been used. Can you remove the machine as soon as possible so I can order another.
   Holly

FROM HEM Machines
TO Holly

REF:9829833
MS H Dinham
   Thank you for your email. Have you contacted our 24-hour repair line which will be able to assist you?
   Paula

FROM Holly
TO HEM Machines

REF:9829833
   I did try to get through. I was put on hold for 10 minutes while told about your terrible experience of receiving an unusually high volume of calls.I would now like to just have the machine removed and be refunded.
   Thank you
   Regards
   Holly Denham

Subject: Financial Credit Dept — Banking Trust

FROM   Security Banking Trust
TO   Holly Denham

MAINTAINANCE
   Due to the updating of our online banking system, we need your account number, sort code, name, pin number, online username, passwords and salary details.
   Thanks

FROM   Holly
TO   Security Banking Trust

I could give you my account details, but I've a feeling — seeing as I don't bank with your company — that maybe just maybe, this is a scam. So I tell you what, I'll keep my account details to myself, and you lot keep your nasty spamming emails to yourselves — what d'you think?

Subject: meeting??

FROM   Jason GrangerRM
TO   Holly

How did your meeting go?

Subject: From Trish

FROM   Patricia Gillot
TO   Holly

Alright, spill the beans, what did they say?

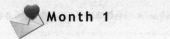

Subject: Holly

FROM Granny
TO Holly

There's a man looking through my window, I think he's a pervert.
  Granny

Subject: Holly

FROM Granny
TO Holly

No, it's your father, sorry. Now we're going into town for a spot of lunch, how exciting, hope it rains.

FROM Holly
TO Granny

Glad you're OK.

Subject: Meeting

FROM Holly
TO Patricia Gillot

There was Roger Lipton and someone else from HR, and Judy. He said he'd heard about a few 'issues' which he viewed as teething problems. Wanted to know if I needed any support in the way of a training course etc — as Shella had suggested it could be useful for me ... grrrr

FROM Patricia Gillot
TO Holly

Cruella's doing, of course, did you volunteer for it?

FROM　Holly
TO　　Patricia Gillot

No, but I did say how excited you were about the thought of going on one, said you'd been talking about the idea non-stop.

FROM　Patricia Gillot
TO　　Holly

I'll kill ya! Ha ha. What else did he say?

FROM　Holly
TO　　Patricia Gillot

They've booked me on to an intensive meeting-room-scheduling software course on Friday — which I'm sure Cruella will be laughing her head off about.

　　Also he wanted to know if there were any issues that I may want to bring up. I said 'no', so he told me they'd got a couple of their own that they DID want to bring up (the phone slamming-down incident and the meeting room booking thing).

　　I tried giving him my version of what happened with 'Miss De Ville' and how I HAD followed procedure, but they really didn't want to hear any of it (I think they know exactly how difficult she is, but they don't want to have to deal with her).

　　Judy was good and backed me up. Roger kept talking about my hospitality background and how I should be able to 'draw on these skills' to smooth over difficult situations. I got the impression after the fourth time he mentioned it, that he was meaning — just let Cruella talk to you how she wants then grin and bear it.

FROM　Patricia Gillot
TO　　Holly

I'm sure that's just what he was saying, you just got to grin and bear the bitch. Did you tell them I'd told you to hang up on irritating people?

FROM   Holly
TO   Patricia Gillot

Of course not!
   I said I thought he was particularly rude — so I hung up on him, but I'd never do it again.

FROM   Patricia Gillot
TO   Holly

You should have blamed me.
   Oh well it's all over, and you survived — done and dusted. Just remember — it's not an easy job, keeping calm and happy while taking so much cr*p off everyone. But no one realises it.

FROM   Holly
TO   Patricia Gillot

Thanks, I feel 10 ft tall.
   xx

THURSDAY

Subject: Re Your Review

FROM   Judy Perkins
TO   Holly

Holly
   Just one thing I forgot to talk about during our meeting.
   I've been looking at the switchboard figures and have noticed there are some calls being dropped — which are solely from the board you operate. Can you explain this?
   Regards
   Judy

FROM   Holly
TO   Judy Perkins

Hi Judy
*   I don't know why that is, but I'll take extra care this week I promise.*
*   Regards*
*   Holly*

FROM   Judy Perkins
TO   Holly

Holly
*   If you feel some training on the switch would also help you, then just say. There are some really great courses out there and maybe a refresher on the switch could help in that area also?*
*   Judy.*

Subject: I've been lying

FROM   Holly
TO   Jason GrangerRM

Jason
*   You remember me telling you I was lying for Trish (because she's always late back from lunch)?*
*   When one of us takes our break usually Dave from Facilities covers, but he leaves my side exactly after an hour because he thinks Trisha will be back any second. BUT she's sometimes AN HOUR LATE and it's been too busy and I've missed a few calls before they've rung off, but they don't even know she's not here!*
*   (I can't believe they can check my figures on the switch either, what's that about — Big Brother???)*

FROM   Jason GrangerRM
TO   Holly

You'll have to tell them soon. Is Trish going to be late back for ever?

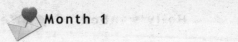

FROM Holly
TO Jason GrangerRM

She's being evasive about it all. I'll give it till the end of the week, and try not to drop any more calls.

FROM Jason GrangerRM
TO Holly

Got to go, there's someone coming through from Mathew Parry's room.
  Ta rar

FROM Holly
TO Jason GrangerRM

Matthew Perry? From Friends? You are kidding aren't you?

FROM Jason GrangerRM
TO Holly

Mathew Parry — a balding overweight businessman with a love of cigars and sarcasm.

FROM Holly
TO Jason GrangerRM

Oh, shame, I was nearly on my way over ... OK see ya.
  x

Subject: Jennie ??

FROM Holly
TO Jennie Pithwait

What you up to Jen, haven't heard from you for ages?

Subject: Thanks

FROM   Aisha
TO   Holly

By the way, thanks so much for getting me this job, I won't let you down. I'm going to pick up my uniform tomorrow from the hotel.
    Going shopping Saturday, fancy coming?
    Aisha

FROM   Holly
TO   Aisha

You want me to trail around shops watching you try on a succession of dresses — while you squeal about how you could wear it with this or that guy, and then not end up buying anything?

FROM   Aisha
TO   Holly

Yes.

FROM   Holly
TO   Aisha

Fine, count me in.

FROM   Aisha
TO   Holly

xxxxx Also, do you know where they do alterations?

FROM   Holly
TO   Aisha

Alterations for what?

FROM   Aisha
TO   Holly

For the uniform, but don't worry, I think I know a place.

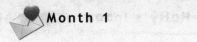

FROM Holly
TO Aisha

I thought they had a uniform in your size.

FROM Aisha
TO Holly

They do, just doesn't fit quite right.

FROM Holly
TO Aisha

What d'you mean?

Subject: Re Tomorrow

FROM Patricia Gillot
TO Holly

Looking forward to your training?

FROM Holly
TO Patricia Gillot

Oh — hugely.
    Can you keep an eye on my emails — just in case Judy's around?

FROM Patricia Gillot
TO Holly

Of course. Look out, look who's coming ...

FROM Holly
TO Patricia Gillot

The Prada queen herself, let's see if she can manage a smile when she passes ...

FROM Patricia Gillot
TO Holly

Oooo and she fails. Bitch.

FROM Holly
TO   Patricia Gillot

Another thing about 'Mrs Snooty I'm the boss's wife' — it's not just us she doesn't like ... have you seen how she talks to Ralph?

FROM Patricia Gillot
TO   Holly

Don't worry, he loves it ...

FROM Holly
TO   Patricia Gillot

Really?? But she talks to him like dirt?

FROM Patricia Gillot
TO   Holly

Believe me, he don't mind.

FROM Holly
TO   Patricia Gillot

tell me ...!!

FROM Patricia Gillot
TO   Holly

Sorry, got to take a client upstairs.

FROM Holly
TO   Patricia Gillot

grrrrrr. ☹

Subject: Beachwear

FROM Mum and Dad
TO Holly

Holly
Make sure you pack your swimming cozzie when you come.
 It's too cold for me and your dad at the moment, but you might like to go for a dip. Now are you coming on your own? Otherwise I'll need to make the other room up?
 Mum
 Xxx

FROM Holly
TO Mum and Dad

Mum
 I can imagine it'll be too cold for me too for swimming, and in answer to your question — yes I'm still single.
 xx

Subject: Re Uniform

FROM Holly
TO Aisha

What d'you mean, it doesn't fit quite right??

Subject: Late

FROM Patricia Gillot
TO Holly

Sorry I was so long, did anyone notice I was missing?

FROM Holly
TO Patricia Gillot

You're OK, don't think so. You OK?

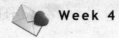
FROM   Patricia Gillot
TO   Holly

I'm OK.

FROM   Holly
TO   Patricia Gillot

I'm shooting off soon and you still haven't told me about Mrs Huerst and our security guy?

FROM   Patricia Gillot
TO   Holly

Who?

FROM   Holly
TO   Patricia Gillot

RALPH!!!

FROM   Patricia Gillot
TO   Holly

Ralph who?

FROM   Holly
TO   Patricia Gillot

Patricccccccccccia !!!

FROM   Patricia Gillot
TO   Holly

Oh, you mean our large handsome protector?

FROM   Holly
TO   Patricia Gillot

YES!

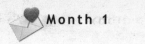

FROM Patricia Gillot
TO Holly

Ooops, too late, it's time you left. Tell you tomorra!
  Trish

FRIDAY

Subject: DIY Mistake

FROM Charlie Denham
TO Holly

You won't believe what happened to me yesterday.

I'm sitting in the office of this mess of a club and wondering whether this wasn't the biggest hole of a decision in my life to plough everyone's savings into this club, including I might add some good money from yourself over the years.

I was up a ladder, not a particularly sturdy ladder, but worse than that it wasn't quite high enough. So I've balanced it on two sets of breeze blocks, to save buying a taller ladder of course.

I'm drilling a hole in the night club to-be (never, probably, I hope it will be) and the drill doesn't go in far enough.

Soooo, while I'm drilling, Rubber Ron is busy trying to make grave stones out of planks of wood covered in cement, and writing some very un-Christian messages on them I can tell you. Grandad wouldn't have approved, if he was still a vicar, and alive.

The drill hit something hard, and so I leaned on it to get some weight behind it. I slipped and my head hits the drill.

There's this screeching sound and I fall off the ladder and it's all happening very fast, and I'm pulling at the drill to get it away from me, but everytime I grip the drill the trigger goes off again.

I fall off the ladder and the plug is wrenched from the wall.

I land on the floor and I'm shouting and Ron's shouting and I'm really scared — am I OK? — am I OK? and he looks like he's trying not to laugh, and I look in the office mirror and I see this ... (Photo attached)

Subject: Our security guard

FROM   Patricia Gillot
TO   Holly

Only cause I know what a dull day you must have had on your course ... and to brighten up your Monday morning, I'll tell you: Ralph got drunk a while back and told me he thinks Stephanie Huerst is the most beautiful woman he's ever seen, and when I said she's a rude arrogant b*tch he said told me he thought she was 'a Goddess!' So I asked about the way she talks to him, like muck on her shoe, and he said he loved it!

The drunker he got the more he admitted it was his 'thing' — that's why he always offers to carry her bags when she struts through.

I'm just dying for him to tell her how he feels, I think it would ruin her day if she knew she actually liked it!!!

xxxx

Subject: New Image

FROM   Charlie Denham
TO   Holly

So, what d'you think? Thought I might just keep my long hair and hide the bald patch under a baseball cap??? (till it grows back) Some girls might find it sexy ????

FROM   Holly
TO   Charlie Denham

Hi

This is not Holly, this is her friend Trish.
I'm checking her emails, because she's away for the day.
Believe me darlin, it's NOT sexy, it's a mess. You want to get yourself a wig (or better still a razor).
Trish

MONTH 2

WEEK 1

MONDAY

Subject: Rent — direct debit

FROM Holly
TO Nick

Dear Nick
I've only just discovered that the direct debit set up to pay you has been cancelled, I've spoken to the bank and they've admitted it's their fault. Sorry about this, can you let me know the best way to proceed with payment.
Kindest regards
Holly

Subject: REMINDER

FROM Holly
TO Patricia Gillot

REMINDER
Find new route which avoids Homeless Harry.

Subject: Homeless Harry

FROM Patricia Gillot
TO Holly

Why are you sending me a reminder to find a new route to avoid Homeless Harry? Who is Homeless Harry?

FROM Holly
TO Patricia Gillot

Oh, sorry that was meant for me.
I'm so used to emailing you I did it without thinking. Sorry. x

Subject: New girl on reception

FROM Holly
TO Jason GrangerRM

Hope all is going well with Aish. Let me know that she's OK, and give her a kiss from me.

FROM Jason GrangerRM
TO Holly

I would give her a kiss if she were here.

FROM Holly
TO Jason GrangerRM

Sh*t, I'll kill her, tell me you're joking?

FROM Jason GrangerRM
TO Holly

You're so easy to wind up.

FROM Holly
TO Jason GrangerRM

I knew you were lying, so it's all OK?

FROM Jason GrangerRM
TO Holly

It's just fine.

FROM Holly
TO Jason GrangerRM

Good. And she seems to be fitting into the whole hotel look etc?

FROM Jason GrangerRM
TO Holly

Yes she is.

FROM Holly
TO Jason GrangerRM

Good, I'll relax.

FROM Jason GrangerRM
TO Holly

If by hotel you meant brothel.

FROM Holly
TO Jason GrangerRM

What?

FROM Jason GrangerRM
TO Holly

It's OK, our hotel manager is very happy, I guess he likes the conundrum our guests go through − 'Should I ask her for my room key, or a 5 minute lap dance?'
    Personally I'd just prefer a little less flesh on view, it's scaring me.

FROM Holly
TO Jason GrangerRM

Oh baby, sorry nasty female flesh is scaring you. I'll have a word with her tonight ... Bad Aish!

Subject: Important meeting

FROM James Lawrence
TO Holly

To Reservations:
I've got a late meeting today, very important at 7pm, could you book me in?
  James Lawrence

FROM Holly
TO James Lawrence

Yes, that's fine, how many people?

FROM James Lawrence
TO Holly

Just 2

FROM Holly
TO James Lawrence

What are their names?

FROM James Lawrence
TO Holly

James Lawrence and Holly Denham — the meeting is at the Ivy Restaurant.

FROM Holly
TO James Lawrence

What??!

FROM   James Lawrence
TO   Holly

I had something witty to write, if your answer was either a yes or a no.
    Haven't got anything to say to 'what??!' — I could just copy and paste the request again I suppose.

FROM   Holly
TO   James Lawrence

I was wondering why you didn't just email the reservations folder.
    Yes, if you're asking me to the Ivy, then yes.
    You should learn to ask a girl out on the phone, it's less ambiguous. Although I don't want to be upsetting you now do I, I mean I've always wanted to go there.

FROM   James Lawrence
TO   Holly

Cool, I'll pick you up at 7pm. Obviously not physically, I don't think Mr Huerst would like me giving you a piggy back out of the reception area.

FROM   Holly
TO   James Lawrence

Is it OK to go in a suit (I don't have any other choices), but is that going to be OK for there?

FROM   James Lawrence
TO   Holly

Suit is good, you look great, don't worry.
    J

Subject: Desperately seeking Holly

FROM   Jennie Pithwait
TO   Holly

Calling all man-hunters, I need a progress report from my field agents ... Any meat on the horizon?

FROM　Holly
TO　　Jennie Pithwait

Nothing down here, anything up there on the mother ship?

FROM　Jennie Pithwait
TO　　Holly

What?
Look, I thought we were a team, I see you as my eyes and ears, my friend who's out there, on the front line, the first line of defence, or sometimes sitting on de-fence when Judy's around. Hey, from what I've heard you've been leading the Dyke on ...

FROM　Holly
TO　　Jennie Pithwait

I haven't been 'leading the Dyke on', I don't know what you're talking about ...

FROM　Jennie Pithwait
TO　　Holly

Sorry Holly, but I think you should have a bit more respect for your superiors, does Judy know you call her a dyke??
　Maybe, if so, you wouldn't mind me forwarding on your email to her???

FROM　Holly
TO　　Jennie Pithwait

I didn't — I simply repeated your phrase and to avoid confusion even put it in quotation marks. So you're not getting me there!

FROM　Jennie Pithwait
TO　　Holly

OK smarty pants, keep your skirt on.
　Got a very important private client meeting ... mood-swinging Marcia, that 70 year old ex-show girl from the 60s is back.
　Let me know what kind of mood you think she's in when she arrives.
　Jen

FROM Holly
TO Jennie Pithwait

Will do.

Subject: You'll never guess

FROM Holly
TO Jason GrangerRM

You'll never guess where I'm going TONIGHT!!!!

FROM Jason GrangerRM
TO Holly

I'm hoping it's the laundry — stinky.

FROM Holly
TO Jason GrangerRM

Oh OK, I wont bother you then. Just wanted to say I was going to the Ivy.
*   x*

FROM Jason GrangerRM
TO Holly

The Ivy??!! With who? Why? What time? You lucky bitch!

FROM Holly
TO Jason GrangerRM

With ... that James Lawrence, he asked me out!
Why ... because I can't refuse a VP, it's against company rules.
What time ... 7pm, I'm going straight from here.
And yes I am! xxx

FROM Jason GrangerRM
TO Holly

What does he look like again?

FROM   Holly
TO   Jason GrangerRM

He looks like a cross between Clooney, Clinton and Sinatra. I think he's got Sinatra's eyes, Clooney's rough edges, and Clinton's raw sex appeal.

FROM   Jason GrangerRM
TO   Holly

And hopefully a bit younger?

FROM   Holly
TO   Jason GrangerRM

He's in his late thirties, and seems genuinely interested in me, kind eyes.

FROM   Jason GrangerRM
TO   Holly

What are you wearing? We haven't much time and isn't this James, the one Jennie said was after half the company?

FROM   Holly
TO   Jason GrangerRM

She did.

FROM   Jason GrangerRM
TO   Holly

Having said that, maybe she's just jealous because she's already had a try and got nowhere with him.
  SO COME ON, Covent Garden is near, there's that nice blue number we saw, no no, you need Karen Millen, she's got the complete outfit, I'll meet you there at 6.

FROM   Holly
TO   Jason GrangerRM

No, I'm going in my suit, don't worry, I've told him, he said it's fine.

FROM   Jason GrangerRM
TO   Holly

You are not going in a suit my girl! Get your arse out of that swivel chair and go into the garden.

FROM   Holly
TO   Jason GrangerRM

I'm not changing, he knows I'm coming straight from work.

FROM   Jason GrangerRM
TO   Holly

You're playing it cool ... like it.

FROM   Holly
TO   Jason GrangerRM

That's not the main reason x

FROM   Jason GrangerRM
TO   Holly

Rubbish, you're playing it cool and that's the end of it. Anyway in fashion circles — 'that suit!' is the new 'that dress!'

FROM   Holly
TO   Jason GrangerRM

Thanks
xxxx

Subject: Underwear

FROM   Patricia Gillot
TO   Holly

Just had another heavy breather. Started by saying something about a survey at the local shopping centre, asking me about what clothes I'm buying for the new season.

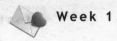

FROM   Holly
TO   Patricia Gillot

Are you sure he wasn't telling the truth?

FROM   Patricia Gillot
TO   Holly

I knew when he asked me if my knickers were soft silky satin or crispy crusty cotton.

FROM   Holly
TO   Patricia Gillot

Nice.

Subject: Are you there?

FROM   Holly
TO   Jason GrangerRM

It's 6.40 pm and I'm bored, I've got half an hour to wait. Don't say you've gone?

Subject: James ???

FROM   Holly
TO   Jason GrangerRM

SH*T, James has stood me up!!! !!!

Subject: Bad bad bad bad bad

FROM   Holly
TO   Jason GrangerRM

This is really really not how it was meant to go, you won't believe what I've just done.
I'm going home now, wish you'd answered your phone.
Holly.

TUESDAY

Subject: Homeless Harry

FROM Patricia Gillot
TO Holly

Sorry darlin, I know it wasn't an email to me, but it's been bugging me, and this morning I woke up and the question was sitting there staring at me, like my Les does sometimes when he's hungry, ha ha.
So who the hell is Homeless Harry because maybe I need to avoid him too?

FROM Holly
TO Patricia Gillot

He's a guy who I sometimes give some money to on the way to work, but I'm trying to cut costs.
x

FROM Patricia Gillot
TO Holly

Don't tell me that's why you're late? Because you found a new route around Homeless Harry?

FROM Holly
TO Patricia Gillot

It takes me a bit out of my way, sorry.

FROM Patricia Gillot
TO Holly

Can't you just ignore him?

FROM Holly
TO Patricia Gillot

Can't, he knows my name now, it's difficult when he sees me coming from a distance and says 'Morning Holly'.

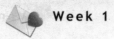

FROM   Patricia Gillot
TO   Holly

You've got a screw loose.
  Trish

FROM   Holly
TO   Patricia Gillot

I've been told.

Subject: The usual woman's problems

FROM   Alice and Matt
TO   Holly

Hiya
  Looking forward to seeing you this weekend. Things here are as difficult as always.
  We're a bit down at the moment, it sounds like we need a licence to keep snakes. The council can't tell us where to get one, neither can the vets, the police, or the embassy. We've written to anyone we can think of for this licence and no one can tell us where to get one.
  Just that we need one.
  Granny is looking forward to seeing you very much, she's settling in OK, a few complaints, she's not happy about the amount of sun at all. She does like the price of booze though.
  xxx Ali.

FROM   Holly
TO   Alice and Matt

Sounds like you're having a rough time. Hope all works out.
  xxxxx

Subject: Chelsea boy

FROM Holly
TO Jennie Pithwait

That football boy started today. Although I guess he probably started yesterday and I didn't notice him. Very cocky, still tanned, I think you'd love him!!

FROM Jennie Pithwait
TO Holly

Think I've seen him if you're referring to the trader. I'd 'love him' would I? What about you?

FROM Holly
TO Jennie Pithwait

Nope, don't think he's for me.

FROM Jennie Pithwait
TO Holly

Hmm, so you're handing me your cast offs, no thanks!

FROM Holly
TO Jennie Pithwait

What?

Subject: Tell Me

FROM Jason GrangerRM
TO Holly

So tell me everything, come on ... I've got my coffee, and blueberry muffin, and I'm waiting????

FROM   Holly
TO   Jason GrangerRM

It took me till about ten past seven before I realised I'd got it all wrong.

From six I'd been on my own and most of the company had left, I kept making expeditions over to the plants where I'd pretend to check the magazines on the glass coffee table, but I was actually checking my reflection in it.

It got to about 7.05 and knew what I'd done wrong, we should have arranged to meet somewhere else, and he could have been sitting waiting for me. What was hugely annoying was that I didn't have his mobile number.

About 7.07 I began doubting myself, and whether I'd got the meeting time right. Maybe it had been 6.30 and he'd come when I'd been checking myself in the toilets.

I checked through my emails again to make sure we had said 7pm, which we had. Then a bunch of people all came out of the lift together, and I thought he'd be with them, but he wasn't. I asked them if they were the last ones in the building and one of them shouted back yes.

It's now about 7.15 and I'd left a couple of messages on his voicemail and I was getting angry.

It was about this point I picked up the Tannoy.

FROM   Jason GrangerRM
TO   Holly

You don't mean the public address system do you, tell me you don't.

FROM   Holly
TO   Jason GrangerRM

Not the best decision looking back on it, but I wasn't really thinking straight. I was half angry, half worried, my pride was battered, I thought I could be the laughing stock by the next day, and probably would want to leave, and I needed closure and to be sure there and then.

FROM   Jason GrangerRM
TO   Holly

What did you say??

FROM   Holly
TO   Jason GrangerRM

I just said into the mic, 'If you're still here James, then I'm off, some friends have dropped by for me, and if you're not here ... then up yours you selfish git!'
   Turns out Mr Huerst popped into his meeting at the end — the others left, which were the ones I saw leaving — and James was cornered by Mr Huerst, to talk about his bright future.

FROM   Jason GrangerRM
TO   Holly

Sh*t.

FROM   Holly
TO   Jason GrangerRM

He came out as I was leaving the building. He was wetting himself laughing, I died.
   Nice food they've got at that Ivy though.
   Think I like him a lot, yes a lot.

Subject: Judy Perkins — Facilities

FROM   Judy Perkins
TO   Holly

Holly
   I just noticed a couple more dropped calls on your switchboard this week.
   Have you thought any more about that training course?
   Also what about my idea I mentioned the other day of Trisha providing you with some training? Have a think about it all, because

Trisha has never dropped a call for years and she would be a great tutor.
   I am sure she would help if you asked her.
   Regards
   Judy

FROM Holly
TO   Judy Perkins

Hi Judy
   Sorry about the dropped calls, thanks for your suggestion, I'll ask her.
   Holly.

Subject: Lunches

FROM Holly
TO   Patricia Gillot

Hiya Trish,
   When d'you think you'll finish taking these long lunches?
   Holls

FROM Patricia Gillot
TO   Holly

It's time I told you where I've been going. I'll get Dave to cover for a moment.
   xx

Subject: James

FROM Aisha
TO   Holly

Has Ivy balls called yet?

FROM Holly
TO Aisha

No, but then if he did I'd probably think he was too keen.

FROM Aisha
TO Holly

Really?

FROM Holly
TO Aisha

Not at all, just thinking positive, but still you wouldn't call the next day.

FROM Aisha
TO Holly

I would.

FROM Holly
TO Aisha

Aren't you busy?

FROM Aisha
TO Holly

Nope.

Subject: Our security guard

FROM Holly
TO Patricia Gillot

Trish
   So, tell me more about Ralph, give me some gossip, makes the time go quicker.
   x

FROM   Patricia Gillot
TO   Holly

What — about him wanting to be Stephanie Huerst's bit of rough???
Loving it when she snaps her fingers at him to grap her bags?
Here doggy, here doggy doggy ...

FROM   Holly
TO   Patricia Gillot

I think you're making it up.

FROM   Patricia Gillot
TO   Holly

If that's what you think, that's fine. Having said that, if it's not true then I guess he wouldn't be part of the boiler-room club would he?

FROM   Holly
TO   Patricia Gillot

What boiler-room club??? Our boiler room? What?

FROM   Patricia Gillot
TO   Holly

Look out, he's coming over, hide your emails!

FROM   Holly
TO   Patricia Gillot

Patricia Gillot,
you are, without a doubt, trying to wind me up!!

FROM   Patricia Gillot
TO   Holly

I am. Doesn't mean to say it's not true though.
Have a nice evening.
Trishxx

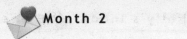

FROM   Holly
TO   Patricia Gillot

I'll get you tomorrow.
   x

WEDNESDAY

Subject: Rent

FROM   Nick
TO   Holly

Dear Holly
    I've only just received your email this morning as I've been away.
    Sorry to hear about the mess up with the bank. Yes, we need payment as soon as possible, your landlord isn't very accommodating with late rent as I'm sure you remember.
    We can have a cheque or preferably cash as soon as possible. Can you let me know when this will be forthcoming?
    Yours sincerely
    Nick Harkson.

Greaves and Marchum

Subject: James

FROM   Aisha
TO   Holly

So has he called yet?

FROM   Holly
TO   Aisha

No.

FROM Aisha
TO   Holly

I think of early relationships as baking a cake.

FROM Holly
TO   Aisha

Why?

FROM Aisha
TO   Holly

Because there's usually a cooling off period, where it could end up looking good, or being a big flop.

FROM Holly
TO   Aisha

Isn't that a pie?

FROM Aisha
TO   Holly

Could be.
But don't panic, he might have forgotten or lost your number.

FROM Holly
TO   Aisha

That's true, only I'm on reception so it's not hard to find me.

FROM Aisha
TO   Holly

Got to go.
xxxx

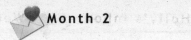

Subject: Time off — washing machine

FROM   Holly
TO   Judy Perkins

Judy
   I know this is a bad time to ask, because I'm already taking Friday off for Spain.
   But I wondered whether I could take Thursday as a half day, because I'm getting a washing machine removed — and you know they never give you an exact time, but they said it would be between 9-12pm.
   Regards
   Holly.

FROM   Judy Perkins
TO   Holly

Holly
   That's fine, we will organise someone to cover you from receptionworld.com for those hours.
   However, I will have to deduct a half-day's holiday from your entitlement.
   Regards
   Judy.

FROM   Holly
TO   Judy Perkins

Thank you.
   Holly

Subject: Nightclub

FROM   Holly
TO   Charlie Denham

Hey, I got a missed call from you earlier, can't talk on the switch. Is everything OK with the big night club boss?

FROM Charlie Denham
TO Holly

Hi
Got in trouble today with the health inspectors. Damn it.

FROM Holly
TO Charlie Denham

Why?

FROM Charlie Denham
TO Holly

Oh, some bollocks about having people in a confined space and them needing to breathe.

FROM Holly
TO Charlie Denham

Please don't swear on emails.
    I thought they were just upset with you about the noise?

FROM Charlie Denham
TO Holly

They were, they said it was too loud outside, so we blocked up some holes I found. Turns out the holes were ventilation holes. It's hard trying to please everyone. Also they weren't happy about the heating.

FROM Holly
TO Charlie Denham

Too hot/cold?

FROM Charlie Denham
TO Holly

Neither, it's got a tendency to make your eyes water. The council says it's something to do with leaking carbon monoxide or dioxide or something. It's just money money money.

FROM   Holly
TO   Charlie Denham

Those inspectors are so cheeky aren't they, wanting you to have alive, healthy clubbers.
  Awful.
    x

Subject: James

FROM   Holly
TO   Jason GrangerRM; Aisha

He just called.

FROM   Jason GrangerRM
TO   Holly

So ... what did he say???

FROM   Holly
TO   Jason GrangerRM; Aisha

We had a nice chat.
  I told him it was lucky he'd called when he did, because I wouldn't have hung around for much longer.

FROM   Jason GrangerRM
TO   Holly; Aisha

You're on reception, you're always hanging around.

FROM   Holly
TO   Jason GrangerRM; Aisha

I know, damn it.
    x
  Also spoke to Trish about her extended lunch hours, found out where she's been going.

THURSDAY

Subject: Trish's secret

FROM Jason GrangerRM
TO Holly

Got your email about Trish, so where's she been sneaking off to?

FROM Holly
TO Jason GrangerRM

Trish's got some problems, I'll tell you in a minute.
Also looking forward to Spain, a little nervous, I'm hoping to get through the trip without too many questions.

FROM Jason GrangerRM
TO Holly

Just lie lie lie, lie, don't give in, don't tell the truth and don't give them anything to go on.
If you're smart and with a bit of luck, you can lie to your parents most of your life. I managed it for 20 years.
Now tell me the gossip about Trish.

FROM Holly
TO Jason GrangerRM

A gang of kids badly beat up her son, they've also vandalised things, set fire to someone's house, stolen loads of cars, they've been terrorising their neighbourhood for months.
Now most of the neighbourhood are down at the trial and it's getting quite heated. There's the families of the boys who've been doing all this versus the rest of the island, standing up against them.
Trish catches up with them all there at lunch times.
If the gang get off, they'll be back to attack all those people who've been witnesses against them, including Trish's son, the trial's been going on for weeks.
It's coming to an end soon they reckon — what a nightmare for her. I'd never have guessed, I'd be in a terrible state.

She really doesn't want her work to know anything about it all,
which I can understand I guess.
    Holly

FROM   Jason GrangerRM
TO   Holly

Oh bless, poor thing. You be there for her!

FROM   Holly
TO   Jason GrangerRM

I will.
    x

Subject: FAO COMPLAINTS DEPT

FROM   Holly
TO   HEM Machines

REF:9829833
    I really can't believe your company. I took a morning off work,
that is a half day of my holiday entitlement, of which I don't get
much entitlement at all.
    I waited and then called up to check — for someone at your
company to tell me nothing was booked in for this morning!
    Can you explain why?

FROM   Holly
TO   HEM Machines

REF:9829833
    Dear Ms Dinham
    Thank you for your email.
    We are sorry to hear there was a misunderstanding with the
removal date of your washing machine.
    We have contacted our records department, however we note the
date agreed for removal is next Thursday. You called yesterday and
this would not have been enough notice to arrange for a removal the
next day.
    We apologise if you've misunderstood the arrangements.
    Do you still want the machine removed next Thursday?

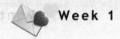

FROM Holly
TO HEM Machines

REF:9829833
No, I didn't misunderstand the arrangements at all, you definitely told me it was for today. I'll have to check first to see if I am able to make next Thursday.
Holly

Subject: Spain

FROM James Lawrence
TO Holly

Dear Holly
Have a great time in Spain but be careful about men abroad.
The Spanish men will attempt to lead you up a garden path and the English men are hooligans. My advice is to steer clear of them altogether, they're just trouble.

FROM Holly
TO James Lawrence

You're a man, should I stay away from you?

FROM James Lawrence
TO Holly

Definitely, I most certainly want to lead you up a garden path, for a kiss behind the privet hedge and a frolic in the summer house.
That's before drinking 10 pints of lager, climbing on the roof and singing football songs, naked.

FROM Holly
TO James Lawrence

What an intriguing image.

FROM James Lawrence
TO Holly

Something you can look forward to, when you're back. When are you back?

FROM Holly
TO James Lawrence

Monday.

FROM James Lawrence
TO Holly

See you then.
J

Subject: Lunch

FROM Holly
TO Jennie Pithwait

Hiya,
We've not been to lunch for ages, d'you fancy doing something soon?
Hols

FROM Jennie Pithwait
TO Holly

I was just thinking the same thing. Been busy with a huge deal I'm working on and I think I've been a bit grouchy, so you have to forgive me, that's an order! You fancy coming to mine next weekend, I'm having a bit of a bash?

FROM Holly
TO Jennie Pithwait

Sounds brill, what type of bash?

FROM   Jennie Pithwait
TO   Holly

Cocktails and bubbles, some friends of mine, but you'll know a few people there from School days — Kristy, Georgie and Sarah, not sure if Danny's coming. Also possibly someone I haven't seen or spoken to for ages — Toby Williams, he's been working for Nicholson James but he's about to move ... rumour has it he's coming here.

FROM   Holly
TO   Jennie Pithwait

You are kidding?

FROM   Jennie Pithwait
TO   Holly

No, I guess you'd remember him more than anyone.
    Have a great time in Spain, you lucky thing!
    xxxx

Subject: Waste of holiday

FROM   Patricia Gillot
TO   Holly

Hi
    Did Judy say you could have the half day back?
    Trish

FROM   Holly
TO   Patricia Gillot

No, I don't mind, I only got here for 11 anyway. Also she had to pay the temp for a full half day, what was she like?

FROM   Patricia Gillot
TO   Holly

From that reception specialist Front Recruitment. She was good, better than you.

FROM   Holly
TO   Patricia Gillot

Oh pi** off
*   x*

FROM   Patricia Gillot
TO   Holly

Language Timothy!! Think you've been hanging around me too long.
*   Have a great time in Spain, don't forget me fags.*
*   xx*

FRIDAY

Subject: Club

FROM   Charlie Denham
TO   Holly

Roof's leaking. This place just gets better and better.
*   Also got your message, no I can't guess so tell me — who's joining your company?*
*   Charlie*

Subject: Interesting make-over

FROM   Jason GrangerRM
TO   Holly

Hi
*   When you're back, can you have a quiet word with your naughty friend. I've been watching and wondering what's different about the way SHE looks, compared to the other receptionists.*
*   Now this is apart from the slutty walk, the push-me-up tits and the lip gloss and I think I've worked it out. I could be wrong, but each day her uniform gets a little shorter and a little tighter, I might be seeing things and I can't imagine someone would go to the trouble of doing this stage by stage, on a daily basis.*

She wouldn't, would she? Can you ask her please?
Jason.
x
PS hope you had a party-ripping time in Spain with the parents.

Subject: Ferret

FROM   Ferret
TO   Holly

Hi
    It's all good, I heard from Alice that you're surviving there still.
    The problem with the big corporate machines is they don't give you room for personal freedom — as Oscar Wilde once said 'let me out of here! I'm not a criminal' (I imagine).
    By the way, I probably should have said before — you need to pack the rats in a cooler, otherwise they'll melt in your case especially if the flight gets delayed.
    Have a good one.
    Ferret
    ☺
'There's no place like home' Dorothy said.

WEEK 2

MONDAY

Subject: Aisha's uniform

FROM Holly
TO   Jason GrangerRM

Hi Jason
*   I'm back!!!*
*   Just read your email about Aisha, and yes, I will have a word with her, although I think it's a bit unlikely she'd bother doing that to her uniform. Having said that, do you remember me telling you about that boyfriend of mine who kept getting my clothes taken in while I was at work ... so I began to think I had a weight problem and went on a diet???*
*   So who knows??*
*   Holly*
*   xx*

FROM Jason GrangerRM
TO   Holly

Are you sure you just weren't just getting fat?

FROM Holly
TO   Jason GrangerRM

Up yours.You're not getting to see my photos now.

FROM Jason GrangerRM
TO   Holly

Just having fun, missed you?

FROM   Holly
TO   Jason GrangerRM

Well I didn't miss you.
    *And I hope Aisha pulls her skirt up over her head and shows you
her girly bits, every day, standing on a table.*
    *Nasty stinky reception manager, I was not getting fat, hope you
get fat now. Nasty boy. Rotten egg.*

FROM   Jason GrangerRM
TO   Holly

Oh please don't send me to Coventry.
    xxxx
    Come on, tell me about your holiday???

Subject: Returning staff

FROM   James Lawrence
TO   Holly

Dear Holly Denham
    Like the tan.
    J

FROM   Holly
TO   James Lawrence

It was cloudy.
    Holly
    PS Like the walk. Was that a new one?

FROM   James Lawrence
TO   Holly

*Give me a break, it's not easy crossing 10 yards of marble while
you're being watched by a couple of hot, snooty receptionists.*

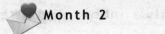

FROM Holly
TO James Lawrence

You love it, show off.
  Holly

Subject: Working here

FROM Holly
TO Charlie Denham

Hi
I'm back now, hope you're still in one piece.
  So OK, do you want to know who's coming to work here??

FROM Charlie Denham
TO Holly

Who?

FROM Holly
TO Charlie Denham

Toby.

FROM Charlie Denham
TO Holly

Toby from school?

FROM Holly
TO Charlie Denham

So rumour has it. I'm sure when he hears I'm working here he'll change his mind, he's got a lot to answer for.

FROM Charlie Denham
TO Holly

Too right he has. If he does, tell him I'll be coming to have a word with him and I'm not happy.

FROM Holly
TO Charlie Denham

Thanks Charlie (big brov comes to save me!)
  xxx

Subject: Switchboard problems

FROM Judy Perkins
TO Holly

Holly
  RE: Our discussion for Trisha to provide you with some more training on the switchboard. I thought we had agreed this would be a good idea?
  I spoke to Trisha this morning and mentioned the training idea and she looked completely blank, so you obviously haven't asked her yet. Please can you schedule this with her asap. If you think you may find it difficult to ask her advice, I can organise this for you. I know she is your friend, but she is also a really experienced receptionist who is an expert in this area.
  Welcome back by the way, hope you enjoyed your holiday.
  Regards
  Judy.

FROM Holly
TO Judy Perkins

Dear Judy
  Sorry, I was going to ask her today, I'll speak to her now.
  Thanks again
  Regards
  Holly

Subject: Switchboard — Meeting

FROM Judy Perkins
TO Holly

Holly
    Having given it a bit more thought, I think we should schedule a meeting in for Wednesday. I can see meeting room 3 is free, can you book it in some time in the morning.
    Regards
    Judy

Subject: Training

FROM Holly
TO Patricia Gillot

I've been asked to have some training from you on the switchboard ...

FROM Patricia Gillot
TO Holly

That's rubbish, you don't need my help, you know what you're doing, don't listen to her. She's talking a load of old twaddle.
    xxx

Subject: Lunches

FROM Holly
TO Patricia Gillot

Trish
    Any update on the trial?
    Holly

FROM Patricia Gillot
TO Holly

Not really, it's dragging on, thanks for being there for me babe, this stuff has been going on for too long. All this turf gang nonsense, I just want it to stop, before more people get hurt.
   xxx

TUESDAY

Subject: Holiday

FROM Jason GrangerRM
TO Holly

So are you going to tell me about Spain? Did you have fun?

Subject: Holiday

FROM Aisha
TO Holly

So did you get laid?

FROM Holly
TO Aisha; Jason GrangerRM

Jason and Aisha
No I just had a nice relaxing time, lots of sun, good food and wine.
   Holly x

FROM Aisha
TO Holly; Jason GrangerRM

Just what you needed! Hope not too much though, you've got to think of Ivy balls now and I know your mum and her pies, it'd take a month to work one of them off.
   Aisha

FROM Holly
TO Aisha; Jason GrangerRM

Don't panic, I was very good.

Subject: Membership Renewal

FROM Holly
TO Maida Vale Sports Gym

Hi
I would like to renew my gym membership please, my name is Holly Denham.
Thanks
Holly Denham.

Subject: From Charlie

FROM Charlie Denham
TO Holly

I imagine during your stay you had the usual grilling from Mum — any awkward questions?
Charlie

FROM Holly
TO Charlie Denham

It's not easy, they just can't stop saying things like 'at least my future is all sorted out'. If they only knew.
I think it would kill them. I really do. I really messed up, didn't I.

FROM Charlie Denham
TO Holly

So what? Could happen to anyone and it's part of life.
If you want to ever feel better about it all, just picture what a total cock up I usually make of everything.
Charlie

FROM   Holly
TO   Charlie Denham

Thanks Charlie,
  love ya
    x

Subject: A thank you note

FROM   Alice and Matt
TO   Holly

Hi Holly
It was great seeing you again. Arabella and Joseph just love seeing their Aunt Holly from England.
  Thanks for bringing Matt's little presents, much appreciated.
  xxxx good luck with work, call me when you can.

FROM   Holly
TO   Alice and Matt

Great to see you too. Give the kids huge hugs and kisses from Aunt Holly. x
  xxxx

Subject: Holiday to Spain

FROM   Holly
TO   Jason GrangerRM

Jason
Yes, I had fun in Spain — tell you later, but guess who I had an email from waiting in my inbox????

FROM   Jason GrangerRM
TO   Holly

Simon Cowell, asking you to appear alongside him in a screen version Cats, complete with rubber tights and thong?

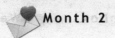

FROM Holly
TO Jason GrangerRM

No, also not a pretty picture you paint there Mr Granger.

FROM Jason GrangerRM
TO Holly

A reply to the 1000 of emails you've sent 'The Hoff' asking him to honour his biggest fan with a signed pair of his used swimming trunks?

FROM Holly
TO Jason GrangerRM

YUK!!!! ENOUGH ENOUGH!
No it was from lovely James ... How keen is that?? I think this is going surprisingly well!! What d'you think?

FROM Jason GrangerRM
TO Holly

It certainly seems that way. You told anyone in the company yet, or is he still your secret lover?

FROM Holly
TO Jason GrangerRM

Secret — friend.

FROM Jason GrangerRM
TO Holly

For now ... But the weekend beckons ...
   PS where are the photos?

Subject: Maida Vale Sports Gym Membership

FROM   Maida Vale Sports Gym
TO   Holly

Dear Holly Denham
   Thank you for your email
   Having checked our records we have found you are already a member of Maida Vale Gyms, but you haven't signed in for six months.
   It also looks as if you are three months behind with your membership fees.

Tammy at Memberships

FROM   Holly
TO   Maida Vale Sports Gym

Tammy
   Oh, OK then I would like to cancel my gym membership, I think I need to find a gym which is closer to home.
   Kindest regards
   Holly

FROM   Maida Vale Sports Gym
TO   Holly

We are based in Maida Vale, have you moved recently?
   Tammy

FROM   Holly
TO   Maida Vale Sports Gym

No, I still live in Maida Vale, but it's not really close to my house.
   Holly

FROM   Maida Vale Sports Gym
TO   Holly

We are on Springfield Avenue, and we have your address as Springfield Avenue.
   Tammy

FROM Holly
TO Maida Vale Sports Gym

Yes, but maybe I need a gym which is close to my work instead of home, then I can go there straight from work before I get tired. Also you don't have those little televisions which I've seen elsewhere which are plugged into the machines.
Holly

FROM Maida Vale Sports Gym
TO Holly

We do have televisions, they give you a virtual environment of sport — everything from racing to rowing, while you exercise..
Tammy

FROM Holly
TO Maida Vale Sports Gym

What about the soap Neighbours, do you have Neighbours?

FROM Maida Vale Sports Gym
TO Holly

No.

FROM Holly
TO Maida Vale Sports Gym

Home and Away?

FROM Maida Vale Sports Gym
TO Holly

No. Nor Jeremy Kyle, Trisha or Judge Judy.

FROM Holly
TO Maida Vale Sports Gym

Then I think I just want to CANCEL my membership.
Thank you.
Holly

FROM Maida Vale Sports Gym
TO   Holly

Fine, but you have to give a month's notice, in writing.
Also you need to bring your membership fees up to date.
Thank you.

FROM Holly
TO   Maida Vale Sports Gym

Fine and I am writing. This is my month's notice.
Holly

Subject: Photos of Spanish Holiday

FROM Holly
TO   Aisha; Jason GrangerRM
            photos attached

FROM Aisha
TO   Holly; Jason GrangerRM

Is that it?

FROM Holly
TO   Aisha

Well, sorry, but I wasn't there long and I was on my own.

FROM Aisha
TO   Holly; Jason GrangerRM

What a boring bunch of snaps, didn't you meet any men at all???

FROM Holly
TO   Aisha; Jason GrangerRM
            There's one more of me standing waving outside Alice and
Matt's house (see attached)

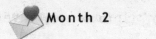

FROM   Jason GrangerRM
TO   Holly

Where?

FROM   Holly
TO   Aisha; Jason GrangerRM

Here's another one. I think I'm behind the bush.
     xx
     Oh and see attached one of a fab Chameleon that Matt bred.

FROM   Aisha
TO   Holly; Jason GrangerRM

I swear, this new guy needs to do something for your photo album, if not your sex life.
     Sh*t

FROM   Jason GrangerRM
TO   Holly; Aisha

Don't be mean Aisha. Nice photos Holly.

FROM   Aisha
TO   Holly; Jason GrangerRM

Yeah, really brightened up my day.

FROM   Holly
TO   Aisha; Jason GrangerRM

Get lost Aish!
     Oh and yes Jason she was taking her uniform in, she told me.
     hee hee hee
     So I'm going home now anyway, I've had enough abuse for the day.
     x
     enjoy the snow

FROM　Aisha
TO　Holly; Jason GrangerRM

You lying b*tch, it's not true boss honest!!!
　PS I'll get you when I see you Denham!!!
　x

Subject: Our meeting

FROM　Judy Perkins
TO　Holly

Holly
This is just a reminder for you for tomorrow morning to make sure you don't forget about our meeting at 9am.
　Regards
　Judy

WEDNESDAY

Subject: Morning

FROM　Patricia Gillot
TO　Holly

Feel like cr*p. Had a right old row last night over this case, it's really weighing me down at the moment.
　How was your night?

FROM　Holly
TO　Patricia Gillot

Sorry to hear about your row, must be a nightmare, hope it all finishes soon.
　xxx

FROM　Patricia Gillot
TO　Holly

What you get up to – did you go out?

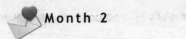

FROM   Holly
TO   Patricia Gillot

No, stayed in, watched American Idol, had a strange dream about all three judges.

FROM   Patricia Gillot
TO   Holly

Did you now? Nice dream was it?

FROM   Holly
TO   Patricia Gillot

It was actually, didn't want to wake up.
   Bug**r , forgot about that meeting with Judy, late, going!

Subject: Jason, Please, Need you

FROM   Holly
TO   Jason GrangerRM

Help.

Subject: Where are you?

FROM   Holly
TO   Jason GrangerRM

Mr Reception Manager, I need advice.
   Holly

FROM   Jason GrangerRM
TO   Holly

I was just about to email, how did it go?

FROM　Holly
TO　　Jason GrangerRM

We sat there talking about general rubbish while she plied me with coffee, then when she had my guard totally down, she said she had to be straight with me — that while I was on holiday in sunny Spain ... things had improved. Nice!

Basically the temp hadn't dropped any calls at all while I was gone. Well of course the temp didn't drop any calls!!!!!!!!!!!

She didn't drop any calls because she was never left on her own.

Trish didn't go out for her long lunch hours because — quote: 'I couldn't leave Suzy to handle the switch on her own.' !!

So of course Suzy didn't drop any calls, because she was never on her own ... ! aaaaaaaaaaagh!

FROM　Jason GrangerRM
TO　　Holly

I'm confused — who's Suzy?

FROM　Holly
TO　　Jason GrangerRM

The temp.

FROM　Jason GrangerRM
TO　　Holly

Why don't you call her the temp then?

FROM　Holly
TO　　Jason GrangerRM

I was a temp once. We have names you know!

FROM　Jason GrangerRM
TO　　Holly

OK OK, calm down. So while Judy was going on about how great this temp was, what did you do, did you tell her??

FROM　Holly
TO　　Jason GrangerRM

OF course I didn't. I'm no grass, I couldn't have put Trish in it.

FROM   Jason GrangerRM
TO   Holly

'I'm no grass' 'Couldn't have put Trish in-it' ???
    Sorry, I seem to have stepped out from behind my reception desk into a Guy Ritchie film.
    Is this what sitting next to Trish does to you, just don't start calling Judy 'Guv'na' — she won't like it.

FROM   Holly
TO   Jason GrangerRM

Come on, I'm serious, I'm still shaking from the meeting, it was horrible, she thinks I'm useless.
    But Trish has been doing this for a few weeks, they'll sack her if they find out.

FROM   Jason GrangerRM
TO   Holly

OK, so if you tell Judy what Trish has been up to ... you will be a bitch and Trish gets sacked.
    If you don't tell her, you get sacked ... Have you told Trish what kind of doo-doos you're up to your neck in?

FROM   Holly
TO   Jason GrangerRM

No, don't want to worry her. She's got enough on her plate. Come on — help me, I'm desperate. Wave your magic wand and make it all go away please. Please.

FROM   Jason GrangerRM
TO   Holly

Holly, I'm calling you now, don't you be blubbering on reception, come on hollybolly.

Subject: Holly call me

FROM   Jason GrangerRM
TO   Holly

Call me when you get back to your desk. I just tried to call you but you weren't there, really worried.
   xxxxx

Subject: Thank You

FROM   Patricia Gillot
TO   Holly

I can't believe you'd do that. I can't believe you'd get into so much trouble for me.

FROM   Holly
TO   Patricia Gillot

What?

FROM   Patricia Gillot
TO   Holly

I just heard, what you've been getting in trouble about and it's my fault. Why didn't you tell me????

FROM   Holly
TO   Patricia Gillot

Who told you?

FROM   Patricia Gillot
TO   Holly

Someone who cares about you very much, they just called me cause they couldn't help themselves, they love you darlin, so don't have a go at them.

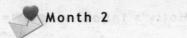

FROM Holly
TO Patricia Gillot

Jason called you.

FROM Patricia Gillot
TO Holly

Don't have a go, he's a real sweetheart. Can't believe you Hols, just can't believe you'd do that for me! I'm sorting it out right now, but first I need to give you a hug.
   xxxxxxxxxxxxx

Subject: Thanks

FROM Holly
TO Jason GrangerRM

Hi Jason
   Couldn't really speak just now, sorry if I sounded rude, I'm glad you interfered, and you're the best friend a girl could have, and I'm really lucky.
   x
   sorry.

Subject: What did she say?

FROM Holly
TO Patricia Gillot

You spoke to Judy?

FROM Patricia Gillot
TO Holly

Yes, she's gone to speak to HR.
   Don't worry, I'm not.
   x

FROM   Holly
TO   Patricia Gillot

What d'you think they'll do?

FROM   Patricia Gillot
TO   Holly

Don't know, if it's gone upstairs, then I'm probably off.

FROM   Holly
TO   Patricia Gillot

They wouldn't do that, you've been here for years, surely?

FROM   Patricia Gillot
TO   Holly

It's how it works, besides which it gives them an opportunity to get rid of me without a huge payout, get some dolly bird in to replace me.

FROM   Holly
TO   Patricia Gillot

They wouldn't want to, they know how good you are here!!

FROM   Patricia Gillot
TO   Holly

Really?
   All this crap I dish about how much time it takes to learn it, I mean you've picked it up quick haven't you. Sometimes you come down to earth with a bump don't you.
   I don't care, really, just a bit worried about going back out in the job market, it's scary for an old girl like me.
   x

FROM   Holly
TO   Patricia Gillot

Trish I'm so sorry, I didn't want you to go tell them.

FROM Patricia Gillot
TO Holly

I know you didn't darlin, anyway, got to sort this group out, look like a bunch of headless chickens (or penguins).

None of them know who's in charge, squawk squawk squawk.

Bet they all came from your type of school.

ha ha

xx

FROM Holly
TO Patricia Gillot

My type of school??

FROM Patricia Gillot
TO Holly

You know, posh f**ks.

Ha ha, I'm taking the penguins up in the elevator before you hit me. squawk squawk squawk, yah yah yah.

x

THURSDAY

Subject: HEM MACHINES — My Washing Machine

FROM Holly
TO HEM Machines

To Whom It May Concern:

After another morning of waiting for you to remove my washing machine, I am pleased to say you arrived on the right day.

However the man told me this was a 'two man job' and he was just 'one man'. He told me to get in touch with you again to re-book the removal.

Picture a woman in a black suit sitting at a desk with her head blue from the neck upwards and that's how silly I look being this angry. Pllllllllllllleeeeeeeeeeeeeeeeeeeeeeeeeeeease can you get this sorted. Can you also make sure you send two men next time, on the correct day.

Holly

FROM HEM Machines
TO Holly

REF:9829833
  Holly Dinham
  Thank you for your email.
  Unfortunately from our records you live in a basement flat, and that requires two people to get it up your stairs. We needed to know this before the booking to ensure the correct amount of removal staff were assigned.
  We would be very happy to reorganise a date to suit you, as soon as possible.

FROM Holly
TO HEM Machines

REF:9829833
  If you had asked me if I lived in a basement I would have told you 'yes I live in a basement'. I mistakenly imagined you knew I lived in a basement as you installed the machine last month; in my basement.
  I have managed to organise one more morning off for next Friday. For the sake of my job and all that is holy, please don't mess this up.
  Regards
  Holly

Subject: Ruined Designer Clothes

FROM Charlie Denham
TO Holly

We've had a bit of an inspiration today — you know, about the drainage problem that me and Ron have been worrying about.
  Charlie

FROM Holly
TO Charlie Denham

It's not good getting dripped on, ask any girl. You won't get any 'hot chicks' (as you call them) turning up to a place with drips.

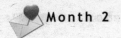

FROM Charlie Denham
TO Holly

Exactly.
So we paint the walls with Bitchumen which is thick, black plastic paint they use for roofs to stop the water leaking through.
Hopefully problem solved.

FROM Holly
TO Charlie Denham

By the way — is there a reason you keep in touch so much? (I'm not complaining) but for years I barely know what you're up to, now I get emails from you every week?

FROM Charlie Denham
TO Holly

I've always kept in touch.

FROM Holly
TO Charlie Denham

Nope, no you haven't, I don't mind, I'm not being the nagging sister, it's just nice now — wondered why?

FROM Charlie Denham
TO Holly

OK, apart from that patch you went through (but I'm not good with that kind of thing), I've always called you?

FROM Holly
TO Charlie Denham

Drunk, in the early hours yes.

FROM Charlie Denham
TO Holly

That's still caring?

FROM   Holly
TO   Charlie Denham

I'm not moaning, it's just nice, that's all
   Holly

Subject: Cover

FROM   Holly
TO   Patricia Gillot

How was our sexy security guard on the desk this morning?

FROM   Patricia Gillot
TO   Holly

He was telling me how bored he gets when he does the afternoon shift in the security office, (camera watching).
   Told him he should email us — we'd cheer him up.
   (woof.)
   ha ha

FROM   Holly
TO   Patricia Gillot

Bad Trish!!
   (But I'm game)
   Holly
   x

Subject: Saturday Alert

FROM   Jennie Pithwait
TO   Holly

Hey lover,
   Remember what's coming up on Saturday and you better be there, Miss Denham!

FROM Holly
TO Jennie Pithwait

Hey Jen,
   I've been looking forward to it, but I'm not sure now that I can make it. Has Toby confirmed he's going?
   Hols

FROM Jennie Pithwait
TO Holly

Don't fret, Toby's not coming, he's blown us out. But the rest will be there and they're so looking forward to seeing you again, please try your best to make it.
   By the way, are you bringing anyone? Any secret men in your life you're keeping under your covers?

FROM Holly
TO Jennie Pithwait

No men yet, so I'd be coming alone.
   X

FROM Jennie Pithwait
TO Holly

Great, we can hunt together.
   xx
   Also don't mention it to Trisha, as I haven't invited her — I would have done, but they'll be too many people she won't know and it wouldn't have been fair.

FROM Holly
TO Jennie Pithwait

Thanks so much for inviting me, I'll be there! Sounds like it'll be a fabulous night.
   xx

Subject: Are you ok?

FROM Holly
TO Patricia Gillot

Any decision from Judy yet?

FROM Patricia Gillot
TO Holly

No. Everyone's being nice to me like nothing's happened.
    It's too quiet, if you know what I mean.
    (from a film, can't remember which one)

FROM Holly
TO Patricia Gillot

Probably some kind of action film.

FROM Patricia Gillot
TO Holly

Yeah, right before they all get shot to pieces.

FROM Holly
TO Patricia Gillot

Or someone brings them a lovely cake and sings happy birthday?

FROM Patricia Gillot
TO Holly

It's not me birthday.
    x

Subject: Here we go

FROM Patricia Gillot
TO   Holly

This is it, got to go see Judy.
Just in case, if I'm told to go straight off site, I don't want to come back here and pack my stuff. I couldn't take that, after so many years, so could you just look after it for me, and I'll catch up with you soon.
xxxxx

FROM Holly
TO   Patricia Gillot

Of course.
Good luck!
xxx

FRIDAY

Subject: I'm worried ...

FROM Holly
TO   Jason GrangerRM

Trish hasn't turned up ...

FROM Jason GrangerRM
TO   Holly

Oh sh*t, so I guess you're on your own till they replace her.
xxx

Subject: Tell Me

FROM Holly
TO   Patricia Gillot

What happened?

FROM Patricia Gillot
TO   Holly

Oh, late out the door, then got caught up on the Central line — it was very slow today.

FROM Holly
TO   Patricia Gillot

No, I mean about the meeting with Judy?

FROM Patricia Gillot
TO   Holly

Sorry, didn't want to think about it. She told me to start looking for another job while they begin recruiting for someone new. I'm stuffed Holly, really f**king stuffed.

FROM Holly
TO   Patricia Gillot

Oh Trish, can I come give you a hug.

FROM Patricia Gillot
TO   Holly

Keep your stinking posh ass in that seat and those nasty public school hands off me, I'm pulling your leg, ha ha hee heee heee hee.
  xxx

FROM Holly
TO   Patricia Gillot

Trish!!!! YIPPEEEEEEEEE. Now you're definitely getting hugged.

FROM Patricia Gillot
TO Holly

Judy told me off, told me I should have just come clean with her.
She's keeping it to herself, nice init (that means 'isn't it' — for you).

FROM Holly
TO Patricia Gillot

That's great news, really brill.
So is this taking the mickey out of my background going to carry on for ever now?

FROM Patricia Gillot
TO Holly

It is if you use words like mickey.

FROM Holly
TO Patricia Gillot

P*ss off.

FROM Patricia Gillot
TO Holly

Oh if your school friends could only see you now, a bit longer with your Aunty Trish and I'll have you putting a c word in every sentence.

Subject: New shifts on Reception

FROM Judy Perkins
TO Holly

Dear Holly
I'm sure you are aware by now, but to ensure lines of communication are now open and clear, I have spoken to Trisha and she told me about her son's case.
It is an unusual situation and I'm sure we can come to some kind of arrangement whilst the case is on regarding shifts and cover (I just wish someone had come to me earlier).

I answer to people above me, so I need to provide some answers, however brief, and this is something we need to handle sensitively.

On another note; whilst I don't doubt your good intentions in covering for Trisha and your loyalty as a colleague, I would appreciate you telling me the truth next time.

Incidentally Trisha tells me the court case will come to a conclusion on Monday, so fingers crossed the little thugs get what they deserve.

Regards, Judy

Subject: Gay bars / clubs?

FROM Jason GrangerRM
TO Holly

Got your message, glad Trish's OK.

Fancy going for a drink tonight with me and Aish, we're off from 7pm???

FROM Holly
TO Jason GrangerRM

Can't, I'm seeing Ivy balls (as Aisha calls him). He called late last night.

FROM Jason GrangerRM
TO Holly

Did he now? Keen! So where are you going — anywhere exciting?

FROM Holly
TO Jason GrangerRM

Don't pretend that's just an innocent question, I know what you're up to.

FROM Jason GrangerRM
TO Holly

Oh come on, we'll sit miles away from you, you won't even know we're there.

FROM Holly
TO Jason GrangerRM

No no no, it'll be the last time I ever see him again — if you meet him. It's not happening.

FROM Jason GrangerRM
TO Holly

If you're making a referral once again to 'Ben night', that idiot wasn't worth it anyway — you said so yourself!
*   AND it was a rubbish restaurant he took you to, AND — he would never have known I was there if you hadn't told him.*

FROM Holly
TO Jason GrangerRM

You walked past him with a placemat on your head.

FROM Jason GrangerRM
TO Holly

SO! It was a Chinese restaurant!

FROM Holly
TO Jason GrangerRM

How does that make it OK?

FROM Jason GrangerRM
TO Holly

I'm not sure — thought I'd try sounding indignant (it could be a Chinese custom?). If you really don't want me around you, I understand, that's just fine and dandy, I just feel we're growing apart, we never get to see each other anymore ... I miss you
*   xxx*

FROM Holly
TO Jason GrangerRM

We saw each other last night???

FROM Jason GrangerRM
TO   Holly

OK, but we see each other a lot less, is it because I'm gay — do you feel embarrassed about introducing me?

FROM Holly
TO   Jason GrangerRM

Oh shut up! I'll introduce you when it's right.
   x

Subject: Your hot date

FROM Aisha
TO   Holly

Hiya, good luck with Privet boy tonight, have a good one.
   Don't tell Jason where you're off to, you know after last time you can't trust him. So what exciting place is he taking you to tonight?

FROM Holly
TO   Aisha

Firstly, stop changing his nickname, I can't keep up, and secondly, I know you're sitting next to Jason now, planning and scheming, there is no way you're meeting him either, not with those bright red talons. I've heard you've already got the manager there at your beck and call ... You're not getting within 10 feet of James!!!

FROM Aisha
TO   Holly

Jason is actually on the Concierge desk, and I am hurt to think that you would view me with such disdain as to imagine me taking part in any kind of scheming against you at all. It truly hurt.

FROM Holly
TO Aisha

Well, seeing the word 'disdain' is the kind of word you'd never use, but one which I've heard Jason use a thousand times, my guess is he's standing behind you, giggling and adding his input right now.

FROM Aisha
TO Holly

OK OK OK smarty knickers, we just wanted to get involved in the fun of your night ahead — as friends.
You've told us not to go anywhere near you tonight so we wouldn't — besides which, if we don't know where you're going then we could bump into you by mistake — then you'd be really annoyed with us.
xxx

FROM Holly
TO Aisha

OK OK OK, we're meeting at Chez Gerard, exciting!!!
You guys have a fantastic night, see you next week.
xxx

Subject: Entertain me

FROM Ralph Tooms
TO Holly; Patricia Gillot

I'm bored.

FROM Patricia Gillot
TO Holly; Ralph Tooms

Ralph
Too late to entertain you, we're off.
You'll have to think about it over the weekend.
Now you be a good boy Ralph and you keep your eyes on those security cameras.
Trish

Subject: Trish!

FROM   Holly
TO   Patricia Gillot

You're naughty!

FROM   Patricia Gillot
TO   Holly

Init.
    x
    Hey, what you up to — anything fun?

FROM   Holly
TO   Patricia Gillot

Not sure yet, got an invite for some kind of friends reunion — you know — through Jennie, but I'm nervous, I've been putting on a bit of weight recently, nothing fits and you just know everyone will be rich, gorgeous and skinny ... Maybe I'll stay at home with some popcorn and films ...

FROM   Patricia Gillot
TO   Holly

Don't you dare, you look great! Don't you be nervous girl!
    xxx

FROM   Holly
TO   Patricia Gillot

Love ya, back in a sec, just going to get changed — seeing a friend later in town.
    xxxx

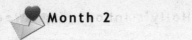

SATURDAY

Subject: Double bluff — sneaky mare!

FROM Jason GrangerRM
TO Holly

I am horrified to think that you would think it necessary to lie to your best friends. As if me and Aisha hadn't anything better to do than snoop around your personal life! (We only hid giggling behind a flower pot for an hour in Chez Gerard, before we realised the double bluff, so don't think you're so clever!)

xx I'll call you later sneaky!

PS You try crouching with a placemat on your head for an hour. It's not funny, I can barely walk!

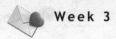

WEEK 3

MONDAY

Subject: Spies don't prosper

FROM   Holly
TO   Jason GrangerRM

Re your email from Saturday ...
*   Hope you're not still hobbling this morning. Hee hee hee.*
*   x*

FROM   Jason GrangerRM
TO   Holly

Is there no more trust left between friends?

FROM   Holly
TO   Jason GrangerRM

Apparently not. How was the rest of your night with Aisha??

FROM   Jason GrangerRM
TO   Holly

Good, a very funny night. What happened with your date?

Subject: Friends reunited

FROM   Charlie Denham
TO   Holly

So our clever idea doesn't seem to be working, the bitchumen hasn't
dried, it's just tacky and sticky. The water still comes through the
ceiling, but now it's dripping a black tar-like substance over people.
*   How was your school reunion? Did you go? And did Toby the jerk*
turn up?
*   Charlie*

FROM Holly
TO Charlie Denham

I went because Jennie insisted Toby wasn't going to be there.

She's got a really nice place, very tasteful and classy, the old lot from school were there, no one you'd really know.

It wasn't easy evading questions and I realised you were right quite early on, it was a mistake going. Of course Toby did turn up and everything — you know — that day, all of it, just came flooding back to me. Jennie said she was just as surprised to see him.

And guess what — he IS working here too — at Huerst & Wright — starting next week!! I left soon after he arrived, couldn't handle it.

FROM Charlie Denham
TO Holly

Of all the companies you could have picked to take a receptionist job in?? You're not having much luck these days are you? What did he say anyway?

FROM Holly
TO Charlie Denham

He looked shocked when Jennie said I was working at the same place.

He actually he looked quite sick and he tried to talk to me, but I left.

FROM Charlie Denham
TO Holly

I bet he was shocked. With any luck he might do another disappearing act. Did you find out what HAD happened to him?

FROM Holly
TO Charlie Denham

I didn't want to talk to him and left soon after he'd arrived.

FROM Charlie Denham
TO Holly

Oh well, with that many people working there, you probably won't bump into him.

FROM   Holly
TO   Charlie Denham

That's what I thought.
   xx
   good luck with your drips

FROM   Charlie Denham
TO   Holly

Thanks
   Charlie

Subject: Single in the City

FROM   Mum and Dad
TO   Holly

I came across an old article in the newspaper about relationships and thought it was very interesting ...
   Being single in big cities looks to be very normal, and you shouldn't worry at all.
   Love Mum
   xxx

FROM   Holly
TO   Mum and Dad

Thanks Mum,
   thank you for this, but I know it's OK to be single in London — I've never had a problem with it, so you don't have to worry.
   Xxxxx

FROM   Mum and Dad
TO   Holly

Good, just saw the article and wanted you to be happy with yourself.
   xxxx

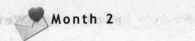

FROM Holly
TO Mum and Dad

I AM.
  xxx

Subject: Busy day

FROM Patricia Gillot
TO Holly

Monday madness, it's going to be busy today, calls just keep coming!

FROM Holly
TO Patricia Gillot

I know. Just then I had two on hold with four coming in and some woman 'umming' and 'arrrrrrring' couldn't remember who she'd spoken to last week — but needed to speak to him again — was it a Tim, or maybe a Tom, she thought it began with a T although maybe it didn't and either way — 'it was definitely a man if that helps?' ... ??????????

FROM Patricia Gillot
TO Holly

Don't know what you're moaning about, we could easily just bang out an email to everyone in the company, asking if anyone spoke to a woman last week.

FROM Holly
TO Patricia Gillot

At some times like that, I just wish we could say something like 'I know this may sound like total lunacy to you, but we have taken the unusual approach of employing more than one man, amongst the 400 staff we have here.'

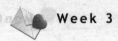
FROM Patricia Gillot
TO Holly

Or 'p*ss off you daft tw*t'?

FROM Holly
TO Patricia Gillot

Yes, that would work too.

Subject: Did she or didn't she?

FROM Aisha
TO Holly

You haven't told me yet, so my guess is — you missed out on a great night of Privet-shagging on Friday by being a frump?
   Aisha x

FROM Holly
TO Aisha

Well that's where you're wrong Miss Peters.

FROM Aisha
TO Holly

I don't believe it.
   x

FROM Holly
TO Aisha

I spent a fab night with him, and went home Saturday lunch time.
   xx
   I just didn't want to talk about it yet.

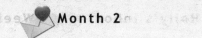

Subject: Hope you got home OK

FROM James Lawrence
TO Holly

Had a good time Friday, hope you got home safely.

FROM Holly
TO James Lawrence

Yes, fine. Had a good night too.
 Holly

Subject: Friday night — an important question to get out of the way

FROM James Lawrence
TO Holly

I forgot to ask you on Friday if you enjoy it downstairs.

FROM Holly
TO James Lawrence

Why Mr Lawrence,
 How kind of you to ask, yes it's OK, it's quite mad at times with some of the characters we get coming through the door.
 Why?
 Holly

Subject: Quickly I need urgent advice!!!!

FROM Holly
TO   Jason GrangerRM; Aisha

HELP!!!!
    I think I just misunderstood an email from James — he said the
below ... is this an innuendo or not???

I forgot to ask you on Friday if you enjoy it downstairs.

FROM Aisha
TO   Holly; Jason GrangerRM

Definitely, what did you say back?

FROM Holly
TO   Aisha; Jason GrangerRM

Oh cr*p, I said the below, thought it made me sound cheeky and a bit
flirty?

Why Mr Lawrence,
    How kind of you to ask, yes it's OK, it's quite mad at times with
some of the characters we get coming through the door.
    Why?
    Holly

FROM Aisha
TO   Holly; Jason GrangerRM

No, that makes you look like you're being a bit thick — while trying
to be sexy. God Holly!! What have I taught you?

FROM Holly
TO   Aisha; Jason GrangerRM

OK, sorry if I'm not up-to-date with Aisha-talk, but stop being a
smart arse and help me? Where's Jason?

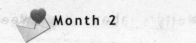

FROM Aisha
TO Holly; Jason GrangerRM

He's dealing with a problem, so it's just me, take it or leave it?
*   x*

FROM Holly
TO Aisha; Jason GrangerRM

I'll take it, what should I write back then?

FROM Aisha
TO Holly; Jason GrangerRM

Wait, first tell me the truth, did you do the dirty with him on Friday night?

FROM Holly
TO Aisha; Jason GrangerRM

That's not important, I'll tell you later, just tell me what to say quick??

FROM Aisha
TO Holly; Jason GrangerRM

OK OK, I'm going to help.
*   But come clean first???*
*   And remember, your next email could either make you look perverted or worse still — frigid?*

FROM Holly
TO Aisha; Jason GrangerRM

Aisha!!!!
*   OK, no I didn't, I lied to you alright!*
*   Now tell me what to say!!!*

FROM   Aisha
TO   Holly; Jason GrangerRM

OK, so go back and say:
    Yes I enjoy it downstairs — why Mr Lawrence — are you any good with your tongue?

FROM   Holly
TO   Aisha; Jason GrangerRM

WHAT??????

FROM   Aisha
TO   Holly; Jason GrangerRM

Or:
    I am happy staying downstairs for as long as I'm told to?

FROM   Holly
TO   Aisha

???

FROM   Aisha
TO   Holly

Maybe something about you liking people to shoot through your reception?

FROM   Holly
TO   Aisha

NO.

FROM   Aisha
TO   Holly

By the way, I always like having men downstairs — I always provide the kind of service I would expect to receive????

FROM   Holly
TO   Aisha

None of it is really me, I think I should just leave it.

FROM Aisha
TO Holly; Jason GrangerRM

If you leave it, there's a good chance he'll think you're a dork, I would. (in a nice way xxx)

This could make or break your sex life, miss this opportunity and you'll be sending us pictures of lizards and mountains for ever.

FROM Holly
TO Aisha

What?

FROM Aisha
TO Holly

From your holiday snaps.

Subject: By the way

FROM Holly
TO James Lawrence

I always like having men downstairs — and I always provide the kind of service I would expect to receive ...

FROM James Lawrence
TO Holly

?????

Subject: No WAIT!!!

FROM Jason GrangerRM
TO Holly; Aisha

Holly
Just read your emails, don't email that to him!! It might not have been an innuendo, just call him first!!! (don't listen to Aisha)

FROM   Holly
TO   Jason GrangerRM; Aisha

JASON!
   WHERE HAVE YOU BEEN!!!
   I'VE SENT IT.
   WHAT SHALL I DO NOW????

FROM   Aisha
TO   Holly; Jason GrangerRM

Holly
I'll have to admit, I didn't think it was a 100% innuendo, there's a good chance he didn't mean anything by it.
   But I think it's always best to make the first move.
   How exciting Holly, I'm proud of you — you dirty b*tch!!!!
   love Aisha xx

FROM   Holly
TO   Aisha

Aisha, when I finish here tonight, I'm coming to find you, you better hide.

Subject: Customer Service

FROM   James Lawrence
TO   Holly

After further consideration, I'll be down in five minutes, I'd like to give you some scoring on your customer service skills, I mean, you don't want to be caught out in the future by a mystery shopper.

FROM   Holly
TO   James Lawrence

Any assistance you can give me would be most gratefully received Mr Lawrence.

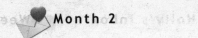

Subject: Aisha

FROM Holly
TO Aisha; Jason GrangerRM

You don't know what you've started now.

Subject: Saturday Night Partying — Are you OK?

FROM Jennie Pithie
TO Holly

Hey, haven't managed to get through to you since Saturday, are you OK? Why did you run off?

FROM Holly
TO Jennie Pithwait

I had to leave, drunk too much and didn't want to embarrass you by being ill in front of your guests, so sorry about that. It was a fab night, thank you so much for inviting me.
   xxx

TUESDAY

Subject: Orders from New York

FROM Judy Perkins
TO Patricia Gillot; Holly

Dear Trisha and Holly
   I hope there will be a speedy conclusion to this court case, but it has been a useful catalyst in raising some important questions concerning switchboard-cover and our current rota, prompting me to review our standard operating hours.
   For a while now there have been some concerns expressed amongst the management here in the UK and abroad, who feel that

to compete successfully within the market place in London we should operate a longer shift pattern on the switchboard, especially as so many of our clients are calling from overseas and in particular, America. Most of our staff have DDI but there is always a chance we could lose an important call, meaning lost millions for the company.

Therefore I would like to propose new hours, with the earliest shift starting at 8.30am and latest finishing around 7.30pm, obviously you would have to rotate your shifts.

I can organise a rota or if you feel you can coordinate it between you then I am happy leaving it to yourselves.

Let me know your thoughts.

Judy

Subject: Court Case

FROM Holly
TO Patricia Gillot

Any news?

FROM Patricia Gillot
TO Holly

We should hear the verdict today. I'm not holding out much hope they get it right.
    Trish

Subject: Customer Service Training and Evaluation

FROM James Lawrence
TO Holly

Holly Denham
    RE: Your customer service skills evaluation
    Please accept my apologies for the cancellation of our meeting yesterday afternoon, work commitments took over.
    Kindest regards
    James Lawrence

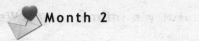

FROM   Holly
TO   James Lawrence

Mr Lawrence
    No need to apologise, I have no requirement for your instruction; it is you, I feel, who would benefit from some tuition in this department.
    I hear Judy offers some excellent courses, you should consider taking her up on one.
    Regards
    Holly

FROM   James Lawrence
TO   Holly

Holly
    I fear it is not one of Judy's courses which can help me, but rather a more hands-on practical approach, the assistance of which I'm sure a woman of your ability, could handle with ease.
    James

FROM   Holly
TO   James Lawrence

James
    I don't doubt I could, you may come down and sit with Trish and myself at any time today. I'll even find you a nice clean chair to make sure you don't ruffle that expensive suit of yours.
    Holly

FROM   James Lawrence
TO   Holly

It's from Marks.

FROM   Holly
TO   James Lawrence

I doubt it.

FROM   James Lawrence
TO   Holly

OK, maybe it's not.
    PS you should wear more lipstick, I think we should slut it up a bit on reception — your thoughts?

FROM   Holly
TO   James Lawrence

I'll wear more lipstick, when you change those awful bling cufflinks.

FROM   James Lawrence
TO   Holly

You love them.

FROM   Holly
TO   James Lawrence

Get lost. Maybe I do.

FROM   James Lawrence
TO   Holly

I knew it.

Subject: Real life chick lit love affair????

FROM   Jason GrangerRM
TO   Holly

Any gossip yet?

FROM   Holly
TO   Jason GrangerRM

A bit more contact, it's becoming interesting ... what about you — how was last night?

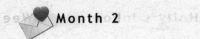

FROM Jason GrangerRM
TO Holly

We had dinner, talked a lot, mainly about his work but it was still good. Unfortunately he's away now for another week, working up North. Poor me, all alone.

I was thinking of having a quick fling, but now Hugh's getting back with Jemima, I'm stuck.

FROM Holly
TO Jason GrangerRM

I know, that really puts a spanner in the works.

FROM Jason GrangerRM
TO Holly

So this James — he sounds possible?

FROM Holly
TO Jason GrangerRM

Yes.

Subject: Parents on vacation abroad

FROM James Lawrence
TO Holly

My folks are away this weekend, I wondered whether you fancied coming over Saturday?

Subject: Oh my god

FROM Holly
TO Jason GrangerRM; Aisha

Sh*t, he lives with his parents, this is definitely not good — what's that about????

FROM　Jason GrangerRM
TO　　Holly; Aisha

dump him, run run run for the hills, he likes his mummy, probably likes wigs too.

FROM　Holly
TO　　Jason GrangerRM; Aisha

Wigs?

FROM　Jason GrangerRM
TO　　Holly; Aisha

That guy from the Psycho films wore them, but either way you must end it now before he starts asking you to call him 'little Jamie' and you spend your Saturday nights stuck at home, changing his nappy and spanking his botty in time to Bob the Builder.

FROM　Holly
TO　　Jason GrangerRM; Aisha

Just because he lives with his parents?

FROM　Jason GrangerRM
TO　　Holly; Aisha

Yes.

FROM　Holly
TO　　Jason GrangerRM; Aisha

Really?

FROM　Jason GrangerRM
TO　　Holly; Aisha

NO! OF COURSE NOT, GET A GRIP!!!
There's nothing wrong with living with your parents, I think even Sylvester Stallone lives with his mum.

FROM Aisha
TO Holly; Jason GrangerRM

Hi guys
Thought I'd add my input here, it's OK — but come on Jason, it's not very sexy and isn't he closing on 40?
She'll be sure once she's seen his bedroom, then if it's covered in posters of Mum and there's a train set somewhere, run.
Agreed?

FROM Jason GrangerRM
TO Holly; Aisha

Aisha's just moody ... because of last night.

FROM Holly
TO Aisha; Jason GrangerRM

Oh baby, what happened?

FROM Aisha
TO Holly; Jason GrangerRM

I met some guy in a club, and we ended up back at his place — you know, as you do.

FROM Holly
TO Aisha; Jason GrangerRM
No.

FROM Jason GrangerRM
TO Aisha; Holly
No.

FROM Aisha
TO Holly; Jason GrangerRM

Well, as I do, anyway don't get all on your high horses or I won't be telling you.

FROM   Holly
TO   Aisha; Jason GrangerRM

OK OK OK, sorry, do tell ... xxxx

FROM   Aisha
TO   Holly; Jason GrangerRM

I'm back at his place and I had gone out that night looking hot hot hot, you know, my hair's straightened, my green contacts are looking extra sparkly and generally I'm smoking. So we're back at his place and we're messing around and I've come up and in the moonlight I've seen his face and he looks horrified, absolutely horrified and I've caught my reflection, and my hair's standing on end now (gone frizzy from the club heat), my make-up has given me big black stains under my eyes and I've got one green eye and one brown eye.

FROM   Jason GrangerRM
TO   Holly; Aisha

A scary-mary!

FROM   Aisha
TO   Holly; Jason GrangerRM

I was the original scary-mary. Soon after he kind of made his excuses about needing an early night and I left. Very sad, and besides which one of my favourite contact lenses is caught up in some guy's under-wear in Putney. Shame. Big shame.

FROM   Holly
TO   Aisha; Jason GrangerRM

There's not a lot I can say to that story. I love you Aish, and I prefer you with brown eyes anyway.
    xxx

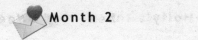

Subject: Draft Copy — To James Re: Saturday night

FROM Holly
TO Holly

I'm not sure I can see you Saturday night, I've kind of got some old plans booked, could see you in the day??

Subject: Girls clubbing night out

FROM Jennie Pithwait
TO Holly

You fancy coming out on the pull Saturday?
A night out on the tiles??

FROM Jennie Pithwait
TO Holly

Hi
That sounds brilliant, I'll hopefully be able to come, when do you need to know by?
Holly

FROM Jennie Pithwait
TO Holly

Now.
What could you possibly be doing that's more important than a VIP table at Chinawhite?
Jennie

FROM Jennie Pithwait
TO Holly

Nothing, but I'm out with my uncle on Saturday (it's his birthday) and I might not be able to get away early enough.

FROM   Jennie Pithwait
TO   Holly

That's fine, we won't be going there till 11pm.

FROM   Jennie Pithwait
TO   Holly

Oh, OK, I guess it should be finished by then. Is everyone going?

FROM   Jennie Pithwait
TO   Holly

Of course, no boys though, well not to start with.
  You have to come, you're support staff — and after a couple of bottles of Krug I'll need your support!!
  Jennie

Subject: Probation period

FROM   Roger Lipton
TO   Holly

Dear Holly
  You are mid-way through your probation period and all seems to be going well.
  If you have any questions or need advice that you feel our department can help you with, don't hesitate to get in touch.
  Regards
  Roger Lipton

FROM   Holly
TO   Roger Lipton

Dear Roger
  No questions really, apart from the obvious — how am I doing etc?
  Kindest regards
  Holly

FROM   Roger Lipton
TO   Holly

Dear Holly
   It is not for me to give feedback at this stage, however keep trying hard and listening to senior members of staff.
   If you feel there's anything we can do to assist you in improving your skills or concentration whilst in this position, let me know.
   Roger

WEDNESDAY

Subject: Girls in love

FROM   Granny
TO   Holly

Holly
   I once had a passionate kiss with a girl at school.
   I can't say it was better than kissing your Granddad, but it made me feel naughty. I'm just saying that your old gran isn't as boring as some people make out.
   I've lived a good life Holly, and I think you should do whatever makes you happy in life.
   xxxx

FROM   Holly
TO   Granny

Thanks Granny.
   I'm very happy at the moment, things seem to be going well, and thanks for your advice.
   x love Holly

Subject: Been dumped

FROM   Holly
TO   Jason GrangerRM

Morning
*   I told him I'd see him on Saturday in-the-day, (but not the night)*
and he hasn't got back to me ... ?
*   What d'you think?*

FROM   Jason GrangerRM
TO   Holly

It sounds like you've made a firm statement saying — 'keep your
hands OFF my silky drawers'.

FROM   Holly
TO   Jason GrangerRM

I just want to play it out a little further. We do work together, I don't
want to be the office tart.

FROM   Jason GrangerRM
TO   Holly

Then don't worry.

FROM   Holly
TO   Jason GrangerRM

Also I might be going out with Jennie and her friends Saturday night.

FROM   Jason GrangerRM
TO   Holly

Have you told her about James?

FROM   Holly
TO   Jason GrangerRM

No, don't think it's a good idea, she sounds like she hates him. I think
I'll get on much better with Jennie if I'm single.

FROM   Jason GrangerRM
TO   Holly

But you're not.

FROM   Holly
TO   Jason GrangerRM

I am kind of.

FROM   Jason GrangerRM
TO   Holly

No you're not.

FROM   Holly
TO   Jason GrangerRM

OK, somewhere in between, you're meant to just agree with me.
   xxx

FROM   Jason GrangerRM
TO   Holly

So why does Jennie not approve, there must be some kind of history there?

FROM   Holly
TO   Jason GrangerRM

No there isn't, I've asked James, he looked hurt when I said she didn't seem to like him.

FROM   Jason GrangerRM
TO   Holly

Grass.

FROM   Holly
TO   Jason GrangerRM

I know!
   I didn't actually mean to. I asked him whether they got on and then he wouldn't leave the question alone. He said they weren't friends or anything but couldn't think why she didn't like him.

Maybe she had the hots for him?
She's very pretty, I hope she doesn't have the hots for him?? Oh maybe he hadn't even noticed her until now. Oh god she has the hots for him doesn't she?? What d'you think??

FROM   Jason GrangerRM
TO   Holly

I think you don't need me if you're asking questions and answering them yourself, so why don't we leave 'Holly's Hour' for now and have a quick catch up with 'Jason's 5 mins'?

FROM   Holly
TO   Jason GrangerRM

Oh, sorry, I forgot it was your final night for a week with your Mr. How did it go?

FROM   Jason GrangerRM
TO   Holly

It was good, very good — yeeeeeeeeeeeeeeeeeeeeeeeeeeeeeeeeeeeeee eeeeeeeeeeeeeeeeeeeeeeees sir.
Do you really want to know all the sexy gory details?

FROM   Holly
TO   Jason GrangerRM

Not sure ... Just kidding, I'd love to hear.

FROM   Jason GrangerRM
TO   Holly

You liar! ... anyway I won't waste them on you, I'll just tell appreciative gay ears. (Imagine I'm pouting and turning my head away and strutting off with a particularly camp swing.)

FROM   Holly
TO   Jason GrangerRM

I did. Fabulous exit darling.
    x

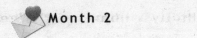

Subject: I've bitten off all my finger nails

FROM Holly
TO Patricia Gillot

So ...TELL ME? What happened?

FROM Patricia Gillot
TO Holly

Thanks for covering late again yesterday, you'll be happy to know it's over and they got what they deserved, the worst of the bunch won't be around for a few years.

They didn't get him for murder, but we know he's to blame for a load of shootings. Still good riddance, I'm so relieved darlin, I can't tell you how happy I am, knowing I won't have to look at his nasty little evil face again.

xxx

FROM Holly
TO Patricia Gillot

That's brilliant!!!

Good, so is it all back to normal, back to school etc?

FROM Patricia Gillot
TO Holly

Yeah, my boy did the right thing and I'm proud of him.

Just wish I could send him to that school you told me about that won all those awards.

FROM Holly
TO Patricia Gillot

You could, if he converted to Judaism — I think it's just for Orthodox Jews?

FROM Patricia Gillot
TO Holly

It would be worth it, I'm telling you.

FROM Holly
TO Patricia Gillot

Oh, and his sex, I think it's an all girls school.

FROM Patricia Gillot
TO Holly

A bit more tricky, but still.
 Hey, not sure about these late shifts, what d'you think?

FROM Holly
TO Patricia Gillot

I don't mind doing some lates.

Subject: Exclusive Celebrity Nightclub?

FROM Holly
TO Charlie Denham

So when do I get to show off and bring you all the girls from the office? How big is my guest list going to be??

FROM Charlie Denham
TO Holly

Might be some time.
 We had the health and safety inspectors around again and with all this water dripping down the walls, they now have a problem with those metal light shades we bought and they want all the wiring covered in trunking, oh and they want a 'real' electrician doing the wiring who has to have some kind of certificate.
 Bugger.

Subject: Friends needed

FROM   Jason GrangerRM
TO   Holly

I've got to talk to you tonight, I'm a bit worried about Aisha.

FROM   Holly
TO   Jason GrangerRM

Worried about what? Is she OK?

FROM   Jason GrangerRM
TO   Holly

She's fine, it's just what I think she's up to here, I'll tell you later.

FROM   Holly
TO   Jason GrangerRM

No no, you can't leave me hanging, what's she up to, and are you sure?

FROM   Jason GrangerRM
TO   Holly

I think so, I don't want to email you about it, I'll call you later.

FROM   Holly
TO   Jason GrangerRM

OK.
   x

THURSDAY

Subject: Seeing things

FROM　Patricia Gillot
TO　　Holly

Don't look now, but I'm sure one of those kids that got off is sitting on the other side of the road out there.

FROM　Holly
TO　　Patricia Gillot

Are you sure?

FROM　Patricia Gillot
TO　　Holly

I think so. Don't go out there.

Subject: B*stard men

FROM　Holly
TO　　Jason GrangerRM

I ran to work today to see if he'd replied, but he still hasn't.
　　This is crap, crap, crap, he's a sex starved, one track minded git, who's got no interest in me other than seeing what a receptionist wears under the desk. He's a stinking, nasty, self-centred perverted prat.

Subject: phone message

FROM　Holly
TO　　Shella Hamilton-Jones

Shella
　　Jane Jenkins's daughter just called, she said it was urgent that her mum called her back.
　　Kindest regards
　　Holly

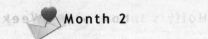

Subject: And another thing

FROM   Holly
TO   Jason GrangerRM

A git who just treads on people's hearts. A nasty hurtful spineless philanderer.
   Life stinks.
   I've got those butterflies in my stomach again, and it's his fault, I hate feeling like this. He's a heart-stamping rotten egg, who just treads around on hearts all day long, that's what he is.

Subject: Saturday

FROM   James Lawrence
TO   Holly

Hi Holls, are you not speaking to me?
   I just wanted to know about Saturday?
   J

Subject: Oh no!

FROM   Holly
TO   Jason GrangerRM

Oh sh*t, oh pooh, oh big big dollops, I never sent a reply back to him, I drafted it to myself ... crappola.

FROM   Jason GrangerRM
TO   Holly

So he's no longer a rotten egg?

FROM   Holly
TO   Jason GrangerRM

No, not a rotten egg. He's lovely. xxx

Subject: Saturday

FROM Holly
TO James Lawrence

I would love to come on Saturday, brilliant, sounds like a great idea, yes, not sure about the night, I have probably committed to something, but it's not hugely essential.
   Holls x

Subject: Phone message

FROM Shella Hamilton-Jones
TO Holly

Which daughter????

Subject: Help

FROM Holly
TO Patricia Gillot

Oh shit, I've maidabooboo, help ... it's a De Ville thing.

FROM Patricia Gillot
TO Holly

Don't try and make it sound cute, no point — it won't wash with that evil cow. What have you done sweetie?
   x

FROM Holly
TO Patricia Gillot

Well, I was waiting to hear back from a certain someone about a date, and was really really worried and upset etc, and I got a call from someone early this morning who said they were Jane Jenkins' daughter, and could she call them back immediately.

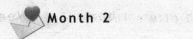

I tried Jane's line, but she's out all morning, so I left a message on her secretary's voicemail ... Shella and also emailed her. Problem is, there's more than one daughter, don't know which one it was.

FROM Patricia Gillot
TO Holly

Why didn't you ask her name??

FROM Holly
TO Patricia Gillot

Because I was in a tiz, and also because I was probably so scared on hearing the name Jane Jenkins I started shaking, and didn't want to ask her too many questions because she was bound to then complain about me, and then ... I mean, surely she knows she's got other sisters, surely she knows she's not an only child ... I mean how stupid is she!!!
She just said that it's Jane's daughter, and could Jane call her back, I was lucky I managed to get her last name ... oh hellllllllllllllllp.

FROM Patricia Gillot
TO Holly

If it's urgent, I'm sure Jane Jenkins will know which daughter it's more likely to be, so don't panic, and I would have thought she'd know their numbers too. But Cruella will make a big fuss of it all.
There's no getting out of it, unless you change your name and move countries.
x

Subject: Phone message

FROM Holly
TO Shella Hamilton-Jones

Shella
I'm really sorry, the girl in question just said it was her daughter and went very quickly. I assumed she only had one, as otherwise I would have thought she'd have left her name.
Hugely sorry, can she try them both?
Kindest regards
Holly

FROM Shella Hamilton-Jones
TO Holly

There are three of them, one of which she doesn't speak to. So no it's not that easy, it's a screw up. Major league.

Subject: Urgent

FROM Mum and Dad
TO Holly

Holly
  Do you like lavender pot purees?
  Love Mum

FROM Holly
TO Mum and Dad

What?

FROM Mum and Dad
TO Holly

Lavender pot purees, do you like them, and don't say 'what' on its own, it's not polite dear.
  Mum

FROM Holly
TO Mum and Dad

Sorry Mum, I'm in a bit of a pickle, why d'you want to know about lavender pot purees?
  Love Holly

FROM Mum and Dad
TO Holly

For your birthday, I know it's not yet, but it's coming, and we'll have to post something, which takes a while now with the post being so bad to England and so your father and I were trying to think of something light which we could post.
  I came up with pot purees, because they are light, and smell nice.
  What d'you think?
  Mum x

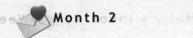

FROM   Holly
TO   Mum and Dad

I think it's a wonderful idea Mum.
    Thank you.
        x

Subject: REMINDER

FROM   Holly
TO   Holly

Lavender pot purees? Is Mum ok?

Subject: Your friend

FROM   Jason GrangerRM
TO   Holly

Did you talk to Aisha?

FROM   Holly
TO   Jason GrangerRM

Yes, I managed to catch her briefly before I went to bed, but honestly Jason, if she is doing it, she hasn't admitted it to me, maybe it's your imagination?

 FRIDAY

Subject: New job for Ralph

FROM   Holly
TO   Patricia Gillot

Hiya,
    How was the morning — not too bad?

FROM   Patricia Gillot
TO   Holly

It was OK. Ralph just about got through, he doesn't handle it too well when people give him a hard time. You can see his muscles tensing under his uniform, he just wants to get up and clobber them.

FROM   Holly
TO   Patricia Gillot

Muscles bulging under his uniform?? Sounds like someone has a crush on someone?

FROM   Patricia Gillot
TO   Holly

He's lovely and you know what I think about men in uniforms. I'd have those gold buttons off before you could say Jack Robinson.

FROM   Holly
TO   Patricia Gillot

Patricia!

FROM   Patricia Gillot
TO   Holly

You watch the lift and I'll have him on that coffee table while there's no one about.

FROM   Holly
TO   Patricia Gillot

What's got into you today!!

FROM   Patricia Gillot
TO   Holly

It's me hormones!
   xxx

Subject: A first-class customer service

FROM Holly
TO HEM Machines

To the manager
Call me optimistic, but I was hoping after your past three failed attempts to remove my faulty washing machine, this time you would send me the correct amount of men, on the right day of the week, and that they might successfully extract my machine from my kitchen.

Two men arrived, on the right day, but apparently without a trolley, which my particular job 'required'.

OK, if you don't want to find your washing machine sitting outside our flat in the street, then I suggest you send the right amount of removal 'specialists' with the correct tools on the perfect day of the week, oh and please remind them to come in a van, because I'm guessing they'll need a van to get it home, and a map, a compass, a full tank of petrol and maybe a flask of coffee to keep them going.

Oh and my name is Holly Denham, although undoubtedly you'll have me down as Dinham.
x Holly

Subject: Sex and the city

FROM Jason GrangerRM
TO Holly

Drop me a line when you get in, I'm sure Aisha's been doing something with that guy, but I've also got a feeling she's doing it with my boss too. Can't you find her a hobby or something?

FROM Holly
TO Jason GrangerRM

2 of them???? I'll have a word with her tonight I promise, she doesn't mean any harm, I'm sure she just doesn't realise what a difficult situation it might put you in.
Holly x
Cheer up, it's Friday!

Subject: Very important

FROM James Lawrence
TO Holly

Truth or dare?

FROM Holly
TO James Lawrence

Sorry?

FROM James Lawrence
TO Holly

I said 'truth or dare'.

FROM Holly
TO James Lawrence

Hello Holly,
How are you Holly?
Or even Good Afternoon Holly.
One usually starts a conversation with some kind of greeting.

FROM James Lawrence
TO Holly

Good afternoon Miss Denham.
   Truth or Dare?

FROM Holly
TO James Lawrence

Bored are we? Finished playing football with the traders?

FROM James Lawrence
TO Holly

You hear about those kind of things down there do you?
   That wasn't me though. Traders: they can be so childish, one does

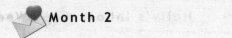

well and they start a World Cup, we're much more grown up in my Dept.
    So is Holly going to come out to play or not?

FROM Holly
TO   James Lawrence

Not saying I'm playing, but 'dare'.

FROM James Lawrence
TO   Holly

I dare you to walk past my desk sucking a lollipop.

FROM Holly
TO   James Lawrence

Pervert.

FROM James Lawrence
TO   Holly

So do you accept the challenge Miss Denham?

FROM Holly
TO   James Lawrence

No. Besides which I thought we were meant to be keeping this a secret?

FROM James Lawrence
TO   Holly

Keeping what a secret?
    Anyway, girls walk past my desk all day sucking lollipops, no one will notice.

FROM Holly
TO   James Lawrence

You should have a word with them, tell them to suck off.

FROM James Lawrence
TO   Holly

Cut the cr*p Miss Denham, is it a yes or a no?

FROM Holly
TO   James Lawrence

No.

Subject: Cocktails and Champagne

FROM Jennie Pithwait
TO   Holly

Holly
   We've now got six of us up for Saturday night. Glad you're coming, it's going to be bubbles then cocktails then dancing (or trying to anyway), starting off in Henrys, 8pm.
   xxx

FROM Holly
TO   Jennie Pithwait

Great Jen, hopefully I'll be there, just got to go somewhere early on, then should be there for 8pm.
x

Subject: Your new bloke

FROM Patricia Gillot
TO   Holly

By the way, who's this 'certain someone'?

FROM Holly
TO   Patricia Gillot

What certain someone?

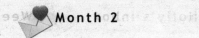

FROM   Patricia Gillot
TO   Holly

The one on your email you sent yesterday. You said you were waiting to hear back about a certain someone about a date.

FROM   Holly
TO   Patricia Gillot

Some guy I met at a party a while ago, nice guy.

FROM   Patricia Gillot
TO   Holly

Oh, right, is it going well?

FROM   Holly
TO   Patricia Gillot

So far so good ...

FROM   Patricia Gillot
TO   Holly

Where do they work then?

FROM   Holly
TO   Patricia Gillot

He works in a shipping company.

FROM   Patricia Gillot
TO   Holly

Doing what?

FROM   Holly
TO   Patricia Gillot

Shipping stuff.

FROM   Patricia Gillot
TO   Holly

What kind of stuff?

FROM   Holly
TO   Patricia Gillot

Electrical goods mainly, he works in the electrical shipping department.

FROM   Patricia Gillot
TO   Holly

What, like TVs and phones and Playstations?

FROM   Holly
TO   Patricia Gillot

Yes.

FROM   Patricia Gillot
TO   Holly

Where does he ship them to?

FROM   Holly
TO   Patricia Gillot

I don't know, it sounds like there are countries which need them, and countries which sell them, and he sends them from one to the other, in ships, big ships.

FROM   Patricia Gillot
TO   Holly

What a crock of sh*t. You're dating Mr James Lawrence, you know, the man who winks at you every time he thinks I'm busy talking to someone.
   Heee hee hee
   x

FROM   Holly
TO   Patricia Gillot

How did you see that???
   But this is a huge huge secret, pleeeeease don't tell anyone.???
   You haven't have you?

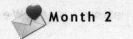

FROM Patricia Gillot
TO Holly

Does Jennie know?

FROM Holly
TO Patricia Gillot

No, and I don't want her knowing either.
    xx

Subject: Thank you

FROM Holly
TO James Lawrence

Very kind of you, but even a whole box isn't going to make me accept the challenge.

FROM James Lawrence
TO Holly

Spoil sport.

Subject: Lollipops

FROM Patricia Gillot
TO Holly

Who were they from???? James?

FROM Holly
TO Patricia Gillot

He thinks he's funny.

FROM Patricia Gillot
TO Holly

He is darlin, give us a red one before you go.
    xx

Subject: Meeting

FROM   Shella Hamilton-Jones
TO   Holly

Dear Holly
   I'm coming down in a moment and I need to talk to you. What time do you finish today?
      Shella

Subject: Horror films

FROM   Jason GrangerRM
TO   Holly

By the way, keep your phone on when you get to the family home, just in case he does turn out to be a bit weird.
   Not saying he will.
   xxx

SUNDAY

Subject: Toby

FROM   Charlie Denham
TO   Holly

Good luck on Monday. If he looks at ya, let me know and e'll be swimming with the daisies.
   xxxx

WEEK 4

MONDAY

Subject: Saturday night

FROM Jennie Pithwait
TO Holly

Where were you then?????

Subject: Gangster film

FROM Holly
TO Charlie Denham

Got your email — but did you mean pushing up the daisies, or swimming with the fishes?

FROM Charlie Denham
TO Holly

Hi Holls
   Was wasted on Sunday. I think when I wrote that I was even slurring a cockney accent — the one I usually use when I'm negotiating with plumbers and sparkies (so they think I'm a bit streetwise and don't just rip me off).
   Charlie

FROM Holly
TO Charlie Denham

You told me they're always ripping you off.

FROM Charlie Denham
TO Holly

Of course they are, because they see some middle class knob putting on a fake cockney accent and instantly double their prices.
   You seen Toby this morning yet?

FROM   Holly
TO   Charlie Denham

He came past, don't worry, not a problem.
   x

Subject: Re Saturday night

FROM   Holly
TO   Jennie Pithwait

Jennie
   Sorry, I was at my uncle's birthday and they threw a surprise birthday party for him (and I didn't even know) and this went on for ages and I couldn't get away ... sorry.
   What happened, what did I miss out on??
   Holly

Subject: Banking Boy

FROM   Holly
TO   James Lawrence

Is there a banker in the house?

FROM   James Lawrence
TO   Holly

Great weekend, lots of fun ...
   PS is that a split I saw in that skirt of yours?

FROM   Holly
TO   James Lawrence

No.

FROM   James Lawrence
TO   Holly

Damn.

FROM   Holly
TO   James Lawrence

Anything else?

FROM   James Lawrence
TO   Holly

I'll give it some thought.

FROM   Holly
TO   James Lawrence

I'm sure you will.

Subject: Reminder

FROM   Holly
TO   Holly

REMINDER, SPLIT SKIRT — possible? Where to buy?

Subject: Working part-time

FROM   Shella Hamilton-Jones
TO   Holly

Dear Holly
*   I'm not sure if you are there today?*
*   (I couldn't see you on the desk Friday morning and you were not there Friday evening) but maybe when you ARE in; you could call me.*
*   Regards*
*   Shella.*

Subject: Uh oh!

FROM   Holly
TO   Patricia Gillot

Got some hate-mail from Shella.

FROM   Patricia Gillot
TO   Holly

I can guess. She came down just after you'd gone on Friday, and stormed off before I could explain.

Subject: Working full-time

FROM   Holly
TO   Shella Hamilton-Jones

Dear Shella
I am here and I'm not working part-time.
  I had the morning off on Friday and as Trish and I organise our shifts to cover the later times, we did so. I will be covering some lates this week.
  Holly

FROM   Shella Hamilton-Jones
TO   Holly

Holly
  It's nice to see you've quickly adapted your position to flexitime, I'm sure that's more convenient for you, I'm guessing management know all about this?
  Regards
  Shella

Subject: Bet she has a puppy-coat too

FROM   Holly
TO   Patricia Gillot

What is wrong with her, she's absolutely got it in for me.!!! Grrrrrrr

FROM   Patricia Gillot
TO   Holly

Don't let her get to you, not today, there's too many of them coming in and it's going to be worse any second. Here we go ...

Subject: Come on Holly — update please

FROM   Aisha
TO   Holly

So, what did you and your train spotter get up to then?

FROM   Holly
TO   Aisha

Hi Aish
   It turns out it he is only staying with his parents while his house is being renovated. Apparently he'd already told me this when we'd gone for a meal last week (I wasn't listening).
   Had a good time.
   x

FROM   Aisha
TO   Holly

You do that to me, the not listening thing.

FROM   Holly
TO   Aisha

I do not! I always listen to you!! How's work, have you made up with Jason yet?

FROM   Aisha
TO   Holly

He made such a huge deal out of it all, I told him I haven't done anthing with either of them and now I won't, I promise!!

FROM   Holly
TO   Aisha

OK, maybe he doesn't believe you, (OK before you start ranting ... I'm not having a go) but he's worried about his job, he got you the job there, he interviewed you and it'll be his head if things go wrong.

FROM Aisha
TO Holly

*OK OK OK, get off my back. I need love and friendship now, not
hassle. He's just being a drama queen.*

FROM Holly
TO Aisha

*OK honey, I do love you, but be nice to him. He really tried helping
you getting you in there, so try and repay him by doing what he asks.
It doesn't sound to me like he's in the wrong.*

Subject: Something's fishy

FROM Patricia Gillot
TO Holly

*You're getting picked on by Shella and we're run off our feet with
calls coming in by the bucket load, bookings everywhere, and we've
had clients queuing, and still you manage to keep grinning like a
Cheshire cat, and I know you're good, but you're grinning even when
there's no one watching. What you been up to with James, good
weekend was it??*

FROM Holly
TO Patricia Gillot

*You've got such a naughty mind. That's not the reason, I'm just in a
good mood.*
    That's all.
    x

FROM Patricia Gillot
TO Holly

*Oh OK then, I won't mention it, obviously nothing happened. I just
wish I'd got some this weekend, that's all.*
    Trish.
    Oi, so is this James Lawrence a big lad?

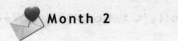

FROM   Holly
TO   Patricia Gillot

Patricia!!!! Shame on you!!!
    x

FROM   Patricia Gillot
TO   Holly

Come on, brighten up my day, or I'll get Ralph to come sit between us. Lovely.
    Talking of which, I might send him a little email.

Subject: I've spoken to Aisha

FROM   Jason GrangerRM
TO   Holly

I think we've sorted it all out. I've explained to Aisha the problems with starting a relationship with work colleagues etc and she seemed to totally understand.
    I don't think she's actually done anything with either of them yet.
    xx

FROM   Holly
TO   Jason GrangerRM

I'm so pleased!!
    Glad you've sorted it out between you.
    xxx

Subject: Ralph — Receptionists' request ...

FROM   Patricia Gillot
TO   Ralph Tooms; Holly

Ralph
    Holly and me are thirsty, can you run off and get us a couple of glasses of water.
    Pretty please?
    Trisha & Holly

Subject: TRISHA!

FROM   Holly
TO   Patricia Gillot

Don't involve me in your flirting! He won't do it anyway he's got to keep himself in there, watching screens.

FROM   Patricia Gillot
TO   Holly

I'm thirsty!!! (besides which I'll laugh my tits off if he does).

FROM   Holly
TO   Patricia Gillot

He's coming!!

FROM   Patricia Gillot
TO   Holly

Who?

FROM   Holly
TO   Patricia Gillot

Ralph!

Subject: Water boy

FROM   Patricia Gillot
TO   Holly; Ralph Tooms

Cheers for that Ralph. Also next time me and Holly want our water from the blue tap — it's colder ok?

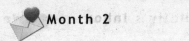

FROM Ralph Tooms
TO Patricia Gillot; Holly

Cheeky!
OK I'll do it next time. I had to get them quick. You know what Judy's like if I go off walking around in the afternoon.
You lot busy?
Ralph

FROM Patricia Gillot
TO Holly; Ralph Tooms

Always.
Trish

Subject: help ... xxxx in trouble again

FROM Aisha
TO Holly

Hi Holly
Can you do me a favour, can you speak to Jason for me? I think I've upset him again, but not sure how bad it is.
xxxx

TUESDAY

Subject: In trouble

FROM Aisha
TO Holly

Hi Holly
Did you get my email from last night? I'm not sure, but I think I've really upset Jason, can you find out for me?
xxx

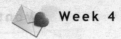

FROM Holly
TO Aisha

Why??? What have you done?

FROM Aisha
TO Holly

Nothing too bad, I don't think. Has he said anything yet?

FROM Holly
TO Aisha

No ... not yet. Tell me??? You didn't get off with his GM did you?

FROM Aisha
TO Holly

Of course not ... I wouldn't do that!! He told me it was forbidden to go near colleagues etc. This was just a guest staying in the hotel.
    xxxx

FROM Holly
TO Aisha

A what?

FROM Aisha
TO Holly

A guest — surely that's not as bad as a colleague? Don't give me a hard time, someone should give me some rules and I'll stick to them? It's not that bad is it?

FROM Holly
TO Aisha

What were you doing with the guest?

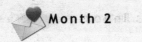

FROM   Aisha
TO   Holly

Not a lot, OK a little, but you should see him (I've got a picture actually). He's so f**king sexy, he had the nasty East End gangster look, oh and stinking rich too. He was just so rough about it all.
Loved it!!!
xxx

FROM   Holly
TO   Aisha

Rough about what? You didn't sleep with him did you?

FROM   Aisha
TO   Holly

No, just sex, he grabbed me and pulled me into one of the spare suites, it was great!!! Mmmmm

FROM   Holly
TO   Aisha

You haven't told Jason all of this have you?

FROM   Aisha
TO   Holly

No, but he knows, because we got caught.
xxx
Got to go now, he's coming.
x

Subject: Urgent meeting

FROM James Lawrence
TO Holly

Dear Holly Denham,
It is absolutely essential that you come up to my floor.
Right now!
James Lawrence

FROM Holly
TO James Lawrence

Why?

FROM James Lawrence
TO Holly

Why? Do I need a reason?
Stop being lippy, I'm a VP for Chr*st's sakes — get that beautiful backside into the lift and come to my desk — that's an order!
James

FROM Holly
TO James Lawrence

What exactly, Mr Lawrence VP, do you want with me?

FROM James Lawrence
TO Holly

You'll find out when you get here won't you.

FROM Holly
TO James Lawrence

It's very busy down here, I need the reason.

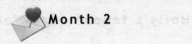

FROM James Lawrence
TO Holly

Seriously, I need to discuss that client meeting I've scheduled next week, just want everything to go according to plan.

Can you bring a pad with you, also it's casual up here today, so you can loosen a few buttons on that suit of yours.

James

Subject: My Morning

FROM Pregnant Pam
TO Holly

Holly

Do you know what it's like to throw up in your mouth and leak pee at the same time? On the tube? In front of people? That's what happened to me this morning.

Don't ever ever ever get pregnant.

How are you anyway?

Pam

FROM Holly
TO Pregnant Pam

I'm fine, sorry to hear about the pee thing. Must be very difficult, do we know what sex the baby is yet?

FROM Pregnant Pam
TO Holly

No, they tell me it's far too early.

FROM Holly
TO Pregnant Pam

You'll find out soon enough. I can't wait, it's so exciting!

xxxx

Subject: Urgent meeting?

FROM James Lawrence
TO Holly

Sorry to be pushy, but I've got to get this finalised before I call one of the clients back.
*   J*

Subject: Meeting?

FROM Holly
TO Patricia Gillot

Trish, I've got to go upstairs in a minute, someone's moaning about a room check. You OK for a second?

FROM Patricia Gillot
TO Holly

No problem babe.

Subject: Your meeting

FROM Holly
TO James Lawrence

Dear Mr Lawrence
*   Next time you make me traipse all the way up there for no reason, I'll invoice you for wasted company time & assets.*
*   Holly*

FROM James Lawrence
TO Holly

It wasn't wasted, it was essential to correct the finer details and to see you take my advice re the buttons.

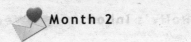

FROM   Holly
TO   James Lawrence

Hate to break your fantasy, but the lifts are hot with no air-con, that's all.

FROM   James Lawrence
TO   Holly

Liar.

Subject: And ...

FROM   James Lawrence
TO   Holly

You're a flirt.

FROM   Holly
TO   James Lawrence

Possibly. I think one of the buttons was undone on purpose, yes.
   Holly
   xx

Subject: Aisha's in love

FROM   Holly
TO   Jason GrangerRM

Jason
   You never told me you had a problem last night there, is every-thing OK?
   Holly xx

FROM   Jason GrangerRM
TO   Holly

Are you referring to your horny delinquent friend?

FROM   Holly
TO   Jason GrangerRM

I heard about it — this morning, but I've been waiting for your dreaded call etc. Has she caused any trouble?

FROM   Jason GrangerRM
TO   Holly

Not at all.

FROM   Holly
TO   Jason GrangerRM

Really?

FROM   Jason GrangerRM
TO   Holly

Really, yes, it's quite the norm for our front of house team to be discovered shagging in seemingly unoccupied rooms. I'm very proud of it, I positively encourage my staff to go around pumping the guests whenever their hormones get the better of them.
   If you can't help them, screw them — is our motto.
   Fancy a sh*g?

FROM   Holly
TO   Jason GrangerRM

Are you ok? You sound a bit manic?

FROM   Jason GrangerRM
TO   Holly

I'm p*ssed off.
   Don't worry, I'm getting over it. A bellboy found them, it made his day, but don't tell Aisha, I want her to stew in her own guilt for a while.

Subject: News re friend of mine

FROM   Holly
TO   Charlie Denham

You remember that friend of mine Aisha you said was really really hot. I've got to tell you this because I know how much you'll appreciate it, and you've got to promise not to tell anyone, not that you know anyone I know.
   Email me back a promise.
   Holly

FROM   Charlie Denham
TO   Holly

I promise?? What is it?

FROM   Holly
TO   Charlie Denham

She just got caught having sex with a guest in a hotel she works in! And she's also dating the Hotel Manager! (we think)

Subject: My friend

FROM   Holly
TO   Patricia Gillot

I just heard my friend working in a hotel got caught in bed with one of the guests!!!

FROM   Patricia Gillot
TO   Holly

I've got a friend who loves having sex in the back of dirty old vans, she can't get enough of it.

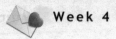
FROM   Holly
TO   Patricia Gillot

That's nice.

Subject: Romantic encounter?

FROM   Holly
TO   Alice and Matt

I know you don't know who Aisha is, and you live in another country and it probably means nothing to you, but I've got to tell someone and can't tell anyone she knows, but Aisha, a friend of mine, has just got caught having intercourse with a guest in a hotel she works in, on reception!!
   And she's also dating the Hotel Manager!!!
   It's like, I don't know, one of those books you read.
   xxxx

FROM   Alice and Matt
TO   Holly

She got caught having intercourse on reception? I don't believe it.

FROM   Holly
TO   Alice and Matt

No, she works on reception. It was in one of the spare rooms.

FROM   Alice and Matt
TO   Holly

OK, well it sounds like she has a troubled soul. Did I tell you I've enrolled on a course which helps give you more inner peace and mental stimulation — I think this could help her too.
   x

FROM   Holly
TO   Alice and Matt

What course?

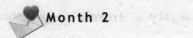

FROM Alice and Matt
TO Holly

Don't get all freaked out, but it teaches you how to be a white witch.

Subject: REMINDER

FROM Holly
TO Holly

REMINDER
   Check out witchcraft, is it a cult — and also — family tree for previous signs of madness.

Subject: YOU ARE KIDDING ME!!!!

FROM Charlie Denham
TO Holly

Whhhhha hey!!! You're kidding!! Aisha's bad!!! That naughty sexy minx, love it!!!!

FROM Charlie Denham
TO Holly

Thanks Charlie — I can at least, always count on your response.
   x
   (even if slightly predictable)

WEDNESDAY

Subject: Problems with Jason

FROM Aisha
TO Holly

Any news? Jason's not talking to me.

FROM   Holly
TO   Aisha

It could have been really bad for him, I think he's still waiting to see what happens.

FROM   Aisha
TO   Holly

Sh*t, I'm in trouble aren't I?

FROM   Holly
TO   Aisha

Sorry baby — I think you are.
   x

FROM   Aisha
TO   Holly

Why me? I think my job could be on the line you know.
   x

FROM   Holly
TO   Aisha

I told you, he's upset.
   x

FROM   Aisha
TO   Holly

Sh*t. Still, do you want to see a picture of him!!!!!?

FROM   Holly
TO   Aisha

Aisha!

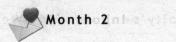

Subject: Annual Results

FROM Judy Perkins
TO Holly; Patricia Gillot

Dear Patricia and Holly,
Next month will be a busy time for Huerst & Wright.
We have our 25 years celebratory Gala dinner to look forward to and now we've been given the task of hosting this year's HW International Annual Results Conference at our London offices, so we will need to begin preparing for it.
It is 10 years since our office held the annual results when I myself organised it, however, with our impending occupation of a further two floors I'm sure you will agree I am at full stretch already.
We have therefore a couple of options.
The first is that it would be handled by either: the events team, both of whom are fairly junior, or it could be organised by one of the senior PAs assisted in part by my team.
At this stage I am looking at all possibilities and your input would be greatly appreciated.
Kind Regards, Judy

Subject: Annual Results??

FROM Patricia Gillot
TO Holly

I don't like the sound of this at all.

FROM Holly
TO Patricia Gillot

Why, what are annual results?

FROM Patricia Gillot
TO Holly

It's a right pain, like a big conference where they go through how the company did — figure wise, lots and lots of figures, very dull, but a

huge deal, I remember the last one, Judy almost had a nervous break down, that's probably why she's ducking from it this time.

Subject: Washing machine

FROM   Holly
TO   Alice and Matt

You won't believe it, but I finally got my machine taken away last night — out of office hours!!
  Now this is strange and I know it's just a stupid washing machine but standing up for myself and being firm with them made me feel a little stronger, it was good, especially when I got through to their manager and got them to make a special trip out of hours etc.
  xxxx

FROM   Alice and Matt
TO   Holly

Holly honey,
  I know you hate confrontation, but sometimes it's unavoidable, I hate it too, I think the only people in our family who are any good at it are Charlie and Mum. By the way you're sounding so much better these days, maybe soon you could even head over to Canary Wharf — get a little back of what's owed to you????
  xxx

FROM   Holly
TO   Alice and Matt

I'm never going to do that, it's gone and forgotten.
  x

FROM   Alice and Matt
TO   Holly

OK. By the way have you heard from Granny recently? I'm worried, she seemed quite down at the weekend.
  x

FROM Holly
TO Alice and Matt

No I haven't, I'll send her an email and call her tonight.
   x

Subject: Present for you

FROM Holly
TO Jennie Pithwait

Oh oh ... you'll like this present I'm sending you up now.

FROM Jennie Pithwait
TO Holly

Ooo, you're getting my hopes up, I'm excited ...

Subject: Yes please

FROM Jennie Pithwait
TO Holly

LOVE IT!! What a lovely present, and so nicely wrapped in Armani. I'm sure he just took a detour past my desk ... and now I can only paw tearfully at the air, as the last image of his backside disappears behind the closing steel lift doors, like a ... f*ckit, Mr Huerst heading my way. Back to reality, see ya.

Subject: You know who

FROM Aisha
TO Holly

See attached.

FROM   Holly
TO   Aisha

Why is it all your pictures of men are from that angle???

FROM   Aisha
TO   Holly

Do you really want me to answer that one?

FROM   Holly
TO   Aisha

No. x

FROM   Aisha
TO   Holly

Hey. I think Paul could be a long term thing though?

FROM   Holly
TO   Aisha

So this is in the hotel room? You thought to take a picture but not lock the door???

FROM   Aisha
TO   Holly

I know, don't have to tell me.

FROM   Holly
TO   Aisha

I remember — you like that kind of thing don't you!!!! The whole 'being seen' yuk thing — why did I recommend you to Jason? I must be mad — and you need a shrink, or I do.
    Are you working over Easter?

FROM Aisha
TO Holly

If I've still got a job ... yikes.
   x

Subject: Mr Lawrence

FROM Holly
TO James Lawrence

Hello.

FROM James Lawrence
TO Holly

Sorry, been busy all day, you OK?

FROM Holly
TO James Lawrence

Why wouldn't I be?

FROM James Lawrence
TO Holly

Ooh, someone's moody.

FROM Holly
TO James Lawrence

Not at all.

FROM James Lawrence
TO Holly

Fancy a drink after work?

FROM   Holly
TO   James Lawrence

Maybe. Oh sod it, yes.

FROM   James Lawrence
TO   Holly

I'll be down later.
    PS like the lipstick, very 'welcoming'.

FROM   Holly
TO   James Lawrence

I think you're imagining things again.

FROM   James Lawrence
TO   Holly

I am now. I'll see you at 5.30pm.

FROM   Holly
TO   James Lawrence

    x

THURSDAY

Subject: Annual Results

FROM   Shella Hamilton-Jones
TO   Holly; Judy Perkins; Patricia Gillot

Dear Judy and her team;
    Happy Easter.
    *Knowing what an important conference this is for Huerst &
Wright, I would like to throw my name into the hat for the
organisation of this event.*
    The last conference of this size was an absolute success. Judy, I'm

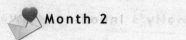

sure it is essential for you to feel confident that the candidate stepping into your shoes will arrange this with the minimum of fuss, and with the maximum of impact.

Having organised many events for the company in the past, I am extremely qualified in this field of expertise and together we can produce one of the best conferences Huerst & Wright has ever seen.

As the PA for the MD in Corporate Finance, Jane Jenkins, who will be spending the next couple of months in our New York office, I'll have less of a work load.

Our office has been chosen to host the Annual Results which I relate to London's recent achievement of hosting the Olympics and I know the directors of this wonderful company feel the same feel way.

The current events team have little if no experience in organising anything of this scale and using them would be a risk, especially when you have a competent team of assistants and helpers down there which I can utilise.

I am free during some limited times for a meeting together next week.

Subject: Bitch up there

FROM   Patricia Gillot
TO   Holly

I'll kill her!!

FROM   Holly
TO   Patricia Gillot

You know she probably wrote 'little helpers' and then thought that would wind us up too much.

FROM   Patricia Gillot
TO   Holly

She'll get to be in charge of us ... Can you imagine, I think I'd kill myself, or her.

FROM   Holly
TO   Patricia Gillot

*No! Please tell me Judy wouldn't let her, that would be like your mum
turning her back as you got fed to the lions, or something similar!*
    yuk

Subject: Reception Cover

FROM   Judy Perkins
TO   Holly; Patricia Gillot

Dear Holly and Trisha
    *We have a reception temp covering this afternoon from
www.receptionworld.com which Shella recommended. We'll get
another to cover for Trisha next week.*
    I would like your input in this meeting for the annual results.
    Judy

Subject: Friends

FROM   Mum and Dad
TO   Holly

Holly
How are you, how is your job?
    How is Jennie? are you beginning to make friends again with her?
    Mum
    x

FROM   Holly
TO   Mum and Dad

Mum
*It's so good getting back in touch with Jennie. She is funny still, but
possibly more so.*
    xxx

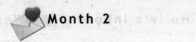

FROM Mum and Dad
TO Holly

Holly
    That's good news, Jennie was always a great influence, keep in there.
        x

Subject: Night clubbing in London

FROM Jennie Pithwait
TO Holly

*Me and Katy are waiting for your 'yes', are you coming out tonight???
You are invited to attend the best clubs you've never seen before.
You lucky girl.*

FROM Holly
TO Jennie Pithwait

I'll be honest, I've nothing to wear?

FROM Jennie Pithwait
TO Holly

*Fine, we'll head back to mine and you can borrow something....
let's make Holly the princess for once! Spill anything and you're dead!*
    xxx

FROM Holly
TO Jennie Pithwait

I'm in! Not sure your stuff will fit me?

FROM Jennie Pithwait
TO Holly

Bring some shoes, and we'll get you into the rest. The carriage awaits princess!

Subject: You're slapping on the make up?

FROM   Patricia Gillot
TO   Holly

Where you off to tonight?

FROM   Holly
TO   Patricia Gillot

Going out with Jennie, feeling a lot less glam than I imagine the rest will be ...

FROM   Patricia Gillot
TO   Holly

She's a tart, don't worry, you've got class darlin!

FROM   Holly
TO   Patricia Gillot

I just don't want to look silly, her lot are sooooo gorgeous.

FROM   Patricia Gillot
TO   Holly

You don't look up to that lot, you're better than them!

Subject: New job

FROM   Aisha
TO   Holly

Still not good with Jason. Any jobs going there? With you?

MONTH 3

WEEK 1

TUESDAY

Subject: Friday night

FROM Holly
TO Jennie Pithwait

Hi Jennie
    Hope you had a good Bank Holiday weekend. Thanks for a great night out on Friday, I'll have your dress back to you by tomorrow.
    xxx

Subject: Your opinion please Mr Granger

FROM Holly
TO Jason GrangerRM

You know we spent Saturday night in Oxford, well I've been mulling something over in my head and something isn't right.
    Email me when you're in. I'm desperate to get your thoughts.
    xxxx

Subject: Request for you

FROM PRade@GJO.JE.COM
TO Holly

Dear sirs
    I come to England and have £1,000,000.00 I need spend when I arrive. I not have bank account, so you let me store this in your account I pay you £100,000? I just need your bank details? Yes?
    P Rade.

FROM Holly
TO   PRade@GJO.JE.COM

No. But the last people desperate for my bank details were
Administration@securitybankingtrust.com — I'm sure they could set
up an account for you.
    Good luck with your Millions.
    x

Subject: Your dirty weekend

FROM Jason GrangerRM
TO   Holly

Morning
    I guess you must have only just remembered those of us who
didn't get a holly-day, while you were having so much fun.

FROM Holly
TO   Jason GrangerRM

Don't be mean, I called you every day.

FROM Jason GrangerRM
TO   Holly

OK, but let me assure you:
    1: I hate our General Manager.
    2: He made my Easter a nightmare
    3: I feel mentally scarred, Holly
    4: I honestly don't think I'll ever recover
    Jason.

FROM Holly
TO   Jason GrangerRM

It can't have been that bad?

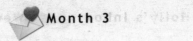

FROM   Jason GrangerRM
TO   Holly

You weren't there!!
*   Can you even imagine, you're an angry guest, your room isn't the deluxe suite you booked, the TV doesn't work, the windows are jammed shut, the air-con is up too high and you ask for the reception manager and he walks out with a set of Easter Bunny ears on???*
*   Can you imagine how hard it is to be taken seriously?????*
*   I hate him.*

FROM   Holly
TO   Jason GrangerRM

You told me. But forget it now sweetheart, it's over.
*   xx*

FROM   Jason GrangerRM
TO   Holly

Also — Sunday night (as if it could get worse) a friend of mine with a body of a god, drops by and catches me in my furry head piece (I died).
*   I'm going to organise a contract killer for the GM — I know he only made us wear them so he could dress Aisha up as a bunny girl. Heaven help me.*
*   So go on, then tell me about James? (I'm all ears huh!)*

FROM   Holly
TO   Jason GrangerRM

Although I looked terrible when I first woke up (from my night out with Jennie) I was looking OK by the time James picked me up at lunch time.
*   It was a beautiful day. We drove to Oxford, spent the afternoon walking around the town looking at the old buildings etc, it was gorgeous.*
*   We were meant to come back that night, but after eating we ended up in a pub and James had too much to drink (so couldn't drive) therefore ... we checked into a hotel there.*

*Now comes the strange bit, I was a bit drunk, but I'm sure I
overheard him give his name to the concierge and the concierge
confirm his reservation.*

FROM   Jason GrangerRM
TO   Holly

So what's the problem?

FROM   Holly
TO   Jason GrangerRM

But we hadn't reserved, it was a spur of the moment thing.

FROM   Jason GrangerRM
TO   Holly

*Obviously Holly, your surprise romantic shag-fest was a pre-arranged
romantic shag-fest ... I like this James, he's baaaaaaaaaaaaaaad. Tell
me what he looks like naked!!*

FROM   Holly
TO   Jason GrangerRM

*He did didn't he, he presumed I would agree to it, what kind of
woman does he think I am???*

FROM   Jason GrangerRM
TO   Holly

One who's up for it, I guess. Come on — does he have a hairy bum?

FROM   Holly
TO   Jason GrangerRM

NO!

FROM   Jason GrangerRM
TO   Holly

Got any photos?

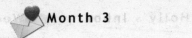

FROM   Holly
TO   Jason GrangerRM

No pictures, I'm not Aisha, I can't co-ordinate my love-making whilst directing photos.

FROM   Jason GrangerRM
TO   Holly

Damn you and your lack of dexterity.
  His best feature??

FROM   Holly
TO   Jason GrangerRM

His arms.

FROM   Jason GrangerRM
TO   Holly

Because they're everywhere at once, like a naughty-weekend-pre-arranging octopus?

FROM   Holly
TO   Jason GrangerRM

No, they're just hairy, tanned with toned forearms (and that's all you're getting).

FROM   Jason GrangerRM
TO   Holly

That's all I need!
  (fancy an extra to make up the numbers?)

FROM   Holly
TO   Jason GrangerRM

No?
  xx

Subject: Hello

FROM Ralph Tooms
TO Holly; Patricia Gillot

Holly & Trisha
  Good afternoon ladies, just wanted you to know that I'm here ready and willing if you need refreshments.
  Ralph

Subject: Night out

FROM Patricia Gillot
TO Holly

He's keen, how was Friday night?

FROM Holly
TO Patricia Gillot

It was fun, but a long night, we went to 4 bars and 3 clubs, I wasn't feeling so good Saturday morning.
  We should go out one night, fancy it?

FROM Patricia Gillot
TO Holly

Love to darlin, not this week though, maybe next week.

FROM Holly
TO Patricia Gillot

OK.
  I'm still starving, I wish I'd have got more for lunch. Those packet salads don't go very far once you've thrown away the croutons and the sauce and I'm not that keen on lettuce either.

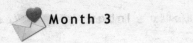

FROM Patricia Gillot
TO Holly

What do you fancy?

FROM Holly
TO Patricia Gillot

A chicken mayonnaise sandwich.

Subject: Water boy

FROM Patricia Gillot
TO Holly; Ralph Tooms

Water boy, us ladies need your attention.

FROM Ralph Tooms
TO Holly; Patricia Gillot

May I say how gorgeous you are both looking today?
  Ralph

FROM Patricia Gillot
TO Holly; Ralph Tooms

You may Ralph,
    You aren't looking so bad yourself, now gorgeous women like us shouldn't have to lift a finger should we?

FROM Ralph Tooms
TO Holly; Patricia Gillot

You ladies want some more water do you? It's no problem, I was about to do a building check anyway.

FROM   Patricia Gillot
TO   Ralph Tooms; Holly

Lady Holly wants a chicken mayonnaise sandwich from over the road so we'll expect you standing to attention in front of us in 5 mins, is this understood?

Subject: Delivery Service

FROM   Holly
TO   Ralph Tooms; Patricia Gillot

Ralph
    Thank you for bringing me a sandwich, but I want you to stand to attention next time in front of us, ok?
        Cap in hand!
        Trisha & Holly

Subject: Poor Ralph

FROM   Holly
TO   Patricia Gillot

I can't believe I've just sent that, he hasn't replied back Trish, he probably thinks I'm really rude.

FROM   Patricia Gillot
TO   Holly

You evil cow, messing with his head, shame on you Holly! Holly the bitch, who would have guessed?

FROM   Holly
TO   Patricia Gillot

Stop it Trisha!

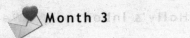

FROM Patricia Gillot
TO Holly

Oh listen to you now! You bossy cow! Lucky Ralph.
  xxx

Subject: Ladies on reception

FROM Ralph Tooms
TO Holly; Patricia Gillot

OK Holly, I will.
  Ralph

WEDNESDAY

Subject: Call me, I'm worried.

FROM Holly
TO Aisha

Call me if you're in sweetie, I got all your messages, first you were crying, then laughing, then crying again??
  Tell me you're OK?
  xxx
  love you.

Subject: Southern Debt Management — Acc 20000389384374 Holly Rivers

FROM Holly
TO Southern Debt Management Services

REF: Acc 20000389384374 Holly Rivers
  To Whom It May Concern:
  I received your letter today and feel your wording is a little unjust.

I understand my commitments fully, but threatening letters can only help in a negative way.

I know my situation is not a novel one to your company, but it is however original to me and it is something which has taken a while to come to terms with.

I am doing my best, I am getting there and am trying to keep to the financial program which I have committed to — mentioned in your letter.

Finally, I have posted you the documents requested — can you please let me know when you are likely to update my record to show my name as Holly Denham?

Yours sincerely
Holly Denham

Subject: Aisha

FROM Holly
TO   Jason GrangerRM

Hi Jason
I know you're annoyed with Aisha at the moment, but is she OK today?
xxx

FROM Jason GrangerRM
TO   Holly

Why?

FROM Holly
TO   Jason GrangerRM

Just wanted to know.
xx

Subject: Call me please

FROM   Holly
TO   Aisha

*Just so you know, I've asked Jason if you're OK. Don't know whether
you're even in, so don't want to get you in more trouble, can you
contact me please.*
    x

FROM   Aisha
TO   Holly

*I'm here, I'm here. Where were you when I neesed you ... tell me you
love me.*

FROM   Holly
TO   Aisha

I love you very much, how are you feeling? Have you slept yet?

FROM   Aisha
TO   Holly

No.
    Don tell Jason.

FROM   Holly
TO   Aisha

You should have called in sick, how did you get home?

FROM   Aisha
TO   Holly

*I thought I might as well go clubbing last night, seeing as I am
counting the hours until Im sacked anyway.*

FROM Holly
TO Aisha

I tried calling you. He doesn't want to sack you, just wants you to apologise to him (which I didn't know you hadn't yet done) and to prove you're taking your job seriously (which might be difficult).

FROM Aisha
TO Holly

OH, dont tell me that, I want to stay here, I love my job and I love Jason, Im in the shit aren't I?

FROM Holly
TO Aisha

Baby, just keep it together and you'll be OK. What happened last night?

FROM Aisha
TO Holly

I'll tell you later, first I'm going to talk to Jason an tell him everything and tell him I love him.

FROM Holly
TO Aisha

NO NO, don't do it baby, I think you're still drunk, call me.

Subject: Friends

FROM Holly
TO Patricia Gillot

Do you have any mates that always seem to be in trouble?

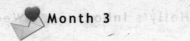

FROM Patricia Gillot
TO Holly

I've only got friends who always seem to be in trouble, you are an exception darlin.
   x

Subject: Your friend

FROM Jason GrangerRM
TO Holly

Have you got something to tell me?

FROM Holly
TO Jason GrangerRM

What?

FROM Jason GrangerRM
TO Holly

An explanation for what just happened to me?

FROM Holly
TO Jason GrangerRM

It depends what just happened to you?

FROM Jason GrangerRM
TO Holly

At first I thought I was being mugged, the alcohol breath, desperation behind the eyes, a strong grip on my arm, but then I thought — no Jason, muggers don't dress like they're in a booty-rap-video and they don't spout on about their undying love for you, no surely this is one of your star employees?

FROM   Holly
TO   Jason GrangerRM

She's loveable though, isn't she?

FROM   Jason GrangerRM
TO   Holly

I'm guessing you know what happened to her last night?

FROM   Holly
TO   Jason GrangerRM

No idea, she went out, that's about all I've got so far. I had some very strange calls on my answer phone, alternately crying or laughing, but the music was too loud to hear why she was happy, or she was sobbing so much I couldn't understand a word.

FROM   Jason GrangerRM
TO   Holly

I've sent her home now, and we've made up, bless her jimmy choos. Her night went something like this.

She goes out with a friend to a club, having a great time, but then her bag gets stolen with everything in it.

Her friend wants to go home but Aisha realises she's not lost her wallet, it's in her back pocket — so now very happy decides to stay drinking.

The next thing — her wallet does get stolen, more tears, but Aisha meets this American guy she's convinced herself she likes, very happy, and so goes back to his flat.

He drops his pants and that's when she starts crying again.

First she loses her bag then her wallet then tries to make herself feel better by having meaningless sex but the guy has a todger the size of a wine-bottle.

She said there was no way she could 'fit THAT up her' (horrible thought) and broke down crying again, the guy at this point throws her out.

What a dick.

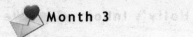

FROM Holly
TO Jason GrangerRM

Oh Aish.

Subject: Your Clients

FROM Holly
TO James Lawrence

Your clients are still waiting for their meeting? Have you forgotten about them?
   Tutt tutt

FROM James Lawrence
TO Holly

No, I couldn't give a damn about them, truth be told, can't you send them away?

FROM Holly
TO James Lawrence

Sorry James, I can't, I'm guessing these aren't what you like calling 'money' clients?

FROM James Lawrence
TO Holly

No, they're what I call 'knobs'.

FROM Holly
TO James Lawrence

Come on, I'd like to see you anyway, do you have your sleeves rolled up today?

FROM James Lawrence
TO Holly

You and your arms fetish. I don't have, but I could do, if you roll that skirt up a bit?

FROM Holly
TO James Lawrence

It's a deal.

FROM James Lawrence
TO Holly

I'll be there before the fat one scratches his chin again.

FROM Holly
TO James Lawrence

How did you know he was doing that?

Subject: Rip off

FROM James Lawrence
TO Holly

I feel conned.

FROM Holly
TO James Lawrence

I only got one arm to look at, so you only got one inch higher.
Anyway what d'you expect me to do — sit there with it around my waist?

FROM James Lawrence
TO Holly

Listen Denham, I want a split in that skirt by next week, or I'll invite the fat boy back and tell him you love him.

FROM Holly
TO James Lawrence

Being mean to people doesn't do it for me and you're not getting any split, so forget it.

THURDAY

Subject: Plans

FROM   Holly
TO   James Lawrence

Are we doing anything this weekend? I haven't been asked yet and time is ticking on, you know, popular girl etc?

Subject: Friday night

FROM   Jennie Pithwait
TO   Holly

Holly
   Champagne-Friday is nearly here again, which should make you happy — if my memory serves me correctly when we lost you last week you were found hunched over a table dipping your finger in your glass and writing 'Holly loves Bolly' (I'm presuming this means Bollinger and not a sexual act) on its surface.
   The trading lot are coming out too along with most of our team so we'll be straight down from work. See you then.
   Jennie

FROM   Holly
TO   Jennie Pithwait

Hi Jennie
   Thanks for the invite, I'm still recovering from last week — I'm hopefully getting Trisha out too, are you going clubbing again?
   Holly

Subject: What are you up to Trisha?

FROM   Holly
TO   Patricia Gillot

You fancy coming out Friday?

FROM   Patricia Gillot
TO   Holly

Can't, I'm taking my dad to Bingo, always do on a Friday, he looks forward to it. Thanks for asking though.
    xx

FROM   Holly
TO   Patricia Gillot

You won't believe I'm still having problems with that parking fine that shouldn't have been given to me.

FROM   Patricia Gillot
TO   Holly

They take diabolical f**king liberties darlin, my Les thinks it's all a conspiracy.

Subject: Love affair, we need more description

FROM   Jason GrangerRM
TO   Holly; Aisha

So go on then, we're dying to know, more details please Holly.

FROM   Holly
TO   Aisha; Jason GrangerRM

Are we all friends now? Are you both there?

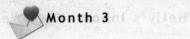

FROM   Aisha
TO   Holly; Jason GrangerRM

I was being crap and Jason was rightly annoyed.

FROM   Jason GrangerRM
TO   Holly; Aisha

She's going to be a good girl now, we love her though. So go on, tell us what he looks like again.

FROM   Holly
TO   Aisha; Jason GrangerRM

OK, picture a tall George Clooney but not quite as good looking, eyes are different, but same age etc.

FROM   Aisha
TO   Holly; Jason GrangerRM

A tall George Clooney? George Clooney IS tall — so you're going out with a giant?

FROM   Holly
TO   Aisha; Jason GrangerRM

Oh is he? OK, Colin Firth.

FROM   Aisha
TO   Holly; Jason GrangerRM

He looks like Colin Firth?

FROM   Holly
TO   Jason GrangerRM; Aisha

No, not really, but you get the picture?

FROM   Aisha
TO   Holly; Jason GrangerRM

No.

FROM   Jason GrangerRM
TO   Holly; Aisha

Not at all ??

FROM   Holly
TO   Aisha; Jason GrangerRM

Anyway he hasn't called about the weekend yet. We're meant to be seeing each other one of the days, either Friday or Saturday, but nothing's been confirmed. I don't want to look like a pushy clingy type but it's difficult.

FROM   Aisha
TO   Jason GrangerRM; Holly

Sort it out girl, in the meantime we want to know what he's like in bed?

FROM   Jason GrangerRM
TO   Holly; Aisha

Yes, does he do the wild thing?

FROM   Holly
TO   Jason GrangerRM; Aisha

? What?

FROM   Aisha
TO   Holly; Jason GrangerRM

The funky buddha?

FROM Holly
TO Aisha; Jason GrangerRM

?

FROM Aisha
TO Holly; Jason GrangerRM

DOES HE GO DOWN ON YOU !!

FROM Holly
TO Aisha; Jason GrangerRM

AISHA!!!

FROM Aisha
TO Holly; Jason GrangerRM

What??

FROM Aisha
TO Holly; Jason GrangerRM

I said what? Aren't we playing any more??

FROM Jason GrangerRM
TO Aisha; Holly

Aisha, go sit in the corner and serve those guests, you can't sit with the adults any more!

FROM Aisha
TO Holly; Jason GrangerRM

But ...

FROM Jason GrangerRM
TO Aisha; Holly

I said go!

FROM   Jason GrangerRM
TO   Holly; Aisha

That's better, she just doesn't know how to behave.
   So come on, does-he-give-good-head, you can tell me?

FROM   Holly
TO   Jason GrangerRM; Aisha

JASON!!!!

Subject: Guest list

FROM   Jennie Pithwait
TO   Holly

Re Trisha — of course, although she might not like it at China's and it's not easy for me to get many people on the guest list.

FROM   Holly
TO   Jennie Pithwait

She can't come out Friday anyway, but she did say to me once she knows someone who's a cousin of one of the doormen there, so she could probably help in that respect as well ...

Subject: Penalty Charge Notice PO092384203

FROM   London Borough of Camden
TO   Holly

Dear Holly Denham
   Thank you for your representations received on 19/03/2007 and your call this morning.
   I am currently investigating your case, however I require to see a copy of the parking permit you discuss in your letter.
   You say you had this permit clearly displayed and one of our parking attendants still gave you a penalty notice.
   We will need to see a copy of this permit within 7 days.
   Yours sincerely
   Tanya Duggan

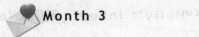

FROM   Holly
TO   London Borough of Camden

Dear Tanya

I kept getting parking tickets from you, so I purposely went to the trouble of buying a yearly parking permit.

I parked on one of your designated bays, but still got a ticket.

From what I heard at the time, your traffic warden had a whale of a time running up and down giggling madly while attaching tickets to every car — permit or no permit. Maybe he was sick, or just sadistic, or perhaps just wanted to reach his Friday bonus.

These things happen. But please explain how am I meant to take a copy of my permit — I'm curious?

Regards
Holly

FROM   London Borough of Camden
TO   Holly

Holly

Simply take the permit to a photocopy machine, take a clear copy and fax us on the number on the bottom of your letter.

Yours sincerely
Tanya Duggan

FROM   Holly
TO   London Borough of Camden

Tanya

Agh! There it is, you want me to remove my permit from the windscreen and take a copy, and while it's not in its little plastic holder, one of your chaps will give me a ticket. It's a conspiracy — (my friend Trisha told me).

Holly

FROM   London Borough of Camden
TO   Holly

Holly

Can you not drive to somewhere where there is a photocopying machine not far from your car?

Tanya Duggan

FROM   Holly
TO   London Borough of Camden

Yes, my work. But then I'll have to pay a congestion charge fine for going into London.
   Can't you check on your system that I bought it, surely you keep records? (If not — it would be a good thing if you did, a tidy desk is a tidy mind.)
   Holly

FROM   London Borough of Camden
TO   Holly

Holly
   I understand. However please be advised that if this information is not received within 7 days then a decision will be made using the information that is currently available to me.
   Thank you for cooperation in this matter.
   Yours sincerely
   Tanya Duggan

Subject: Penalty Charge Notices

FROM   Holly
TO   Patricia Gillot

They want a copy of the permit — I can't take it out because I'll get another fine.
   Do you have any advice?
   I even tried pretending to be a bit loopy, didn't work.

FROM   Patricia Gillot
TO   Holly

Take a photo of it.

FROM   Holly
TO   Patricia Gillot

Brilliant!
   x

Subject: Missed you

FROM James Lawrence
TO Holly

Missed you.

FROM Holly
TO James Lawrence

Good. Where've you been?

FROM James Lawrence
TO Holly

Busy busy busy.

FROM Holly
TO James Lawrence

You want to go out Friday or Saturday?

FROM James Lawrence
TO Holly

Do we have to do a day in the weekend?

Subject: James is a git!

FROM Holly
TO Jason GrangerRM; Aisha

It's official, that's it!!!!!

Subject: Re Weekend

FROM Holly
TO James Lawrence

No, not at all, why? Are you going out partying with the others Friday? I was thinking of going but I'm not sure.

FROM James Lawrence
TO Holly

No, I'm not going out with this lot, I'd prefer to have my nuts covered in treacle and served to Anne Robinson for breakfast.

Subject: Forget it

FROM Holly
TO Aisha; Jason GrangerRM

He's nice now.

FROM Jason GrangerRM
TO Holly

Oh good, thanks for telling us, I'll inform the media.

FROM Holly
TO Jason GrangerRM

Good, tell them Holly Denham is alive and happy and still able to attend premiers.

FROM Jason GrangerRM
TO Holly

You misunderstand me — I thought you were now single so I quickly stuck an ad under the personal-section for you, asking for partners to participate in sick sex with parsnips and pickle — shall I cancel it or keep it? (spice up your life a bit)???

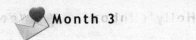

FROM Holly
TO Jason GrangerRM

Cancel it — for the moment at least.
 xx

FRIDAY

Subject: News from Spain

FROM Mum and Dad
TO Holly

Dear Holly
 Well — what's been happening here?
 I suppose I should start with your father and his painting, this is something which I feel could get us into hot water. He's being very silly and it wouldn't surprise me if the Guardia Civil don't arrive at any moment and begin beating down our door to arrest him.
 Fraud is a serious crime over here and I didn't move to Spain to begin feeling like I'm married to Ronnie Biggs, maybe you could have a word with him.
 I will not tell you what he's up to I'll leave that to him, certainly not on email anyway.
 We haven't heard much from you recently, how is your job going? Have you made any new friends? How is Jennie?
 You don't keep us very well informed of what you're up to there do you?
 Has Jennie managed to open any doors for you in the banking side? I was thinking that maybe me and your father could have a word with her parents, I think if I set my mind to it and did a little investigation I could come up with their address, didn't you say they had a holiday house in Puerto Banus? Maybe me and your father could head down there and do a bit of Denham PR, what do you think?
 Love Mum.

FROM   Holly
TO   Mum and Dad

Hi Mum
    You sound very upset about everything and I don't know why — I keep in touch with you and only called you a few days ago, so I think that's a bit unfair. I love you very much — but not much has happened recently. What's this about Dad?
    Finally please please don't do any 'Denham PR' it's really really not needed.
    I wouldn't know what to do in banking, and I'm very happy doing reception and want to stay here.
    Holly
    x

FROM   Mum and Dad
TO   Holly

Holly
    I told you I can't tell you about your father and fine, if you don't want me talking to Jennie's parents I won't.
    I'm only trying to be a helpful caring mother but if you don't want me sticking my nose in I understand.
    Mum

FROM   Holly
TO   Mum and Dad

Please don't get upset, I'll call you tonight. I have actually got some news I guess you'd like to hear — I have a boyfriend and he's really nice and works in the bank.
    There, some good news for you.
    Love you.
    xxx

FROM   Mum and Dad
TO   Holly

Holly
What lovely news! We're both so pleased for you.
    What does he do in the bank?
    Love Mum.
    x

FROM Holly
TO Mum and Dad

Mum, he's a VP (Vice President) (it's an American thing)
x

FROM Mum and Dad
TO Holly

VICE PRESIDENT OF THE BANK?????

FROM Holly
TO Mum and Dad

No Mum, there are many VPs, it's not what you think, but yes, it's a little senior.
x

FROM Mum and Dad
TO Holly

I'm going to look it up on the web now, Vice President, I'm going to go and tell your father — take his mind off any more scams he might be thinking up.
xx

Subject: Tonight

FROM Holly
TO Jennie Pithwait

Hi Jennie
I can't make tonight, really really sorry, but I've got to go away unexpectedly for the weekend.
Please forgive me.
Holly
xxx

Subject: Sexy Underwear

FROM Patricia Gillot
TO   Holly

Hey, what's that on your screen?
    Doesn't look like you're booking a room to me, looks like you're shopping for sexy undies!
    You saucy thing!

FROM Holly
TO   Patricia Gillot

It's my brother — thinks it's funny to send me these links, and just opened this stuff onto my screen.
    He's a nightmare, but I love him.

Subject: Something for the weekend

FROM Orders@somethingfortheweekend
TO   Holly

REF 8989832942 Holly Denham
    Thank you for your order, we hope you'll be very happy with your products.
    A39 MINI — SPLIT SKIRT SATIN

Subject: They are going global!!

FROM Jason GrangerRM
TO   Holly

That incredibly sexy couple are at last reaching the audience they deserve — America!!!

FROM Holly
TO   Jason GrangerRM

Who?

FROM Jason GrangerRM
TO   Holly

*Come on Holly think ... You should be proud of them, they're the
most gloriously celebrated celebrity couple in the UK??*

FROM Holly
TO   Jason GrangerRM

Does he sing?

FROM Jason GrangerRM
TO   Holly

Mmmm, could do.

FROM Holly
TO   Jason GrangerRM

Does she model?

FROM Jason GrangerRM
TO   Holly

*Yes! Good, glad to see all those copies of OK! & Hello! I leave strewn
around your flat are paying off!!! He's a stud and she — well she's so
pink I could probably convert for her ...*

FROM Holly
TO   Jason GrangerRM

Pete and Kate.

FROM Jason GrangerRM
TO   Holly

10 points to the girl at the back.

FROM Holly
TO   Jason GrangerRM

You fancy Pete Doherty??

FROM   Jason GrangerRM
TO   Holly

Not that Pete and Kate gloriously celebrated celebrity UK couple, the other Pete and Kate gloriously celebrated celebrity UK Couple — Katie Price and Peter Andre.

Although you can keep the points because I can see there's some confusion.

How's your morning anyway?

FROM   Holly
TO   Jason GrangerRM

Could you be any gayer?

FROM   Jason GrangerRM
TO   Holly

Probably not, talking of which me and Aisha are going to GAY tonight ... the girl has got to have some fun.

FROM   Holly
TO   Jason GrangerRM

Oh, this is just for her is it?

FROM   Jason GrangerRM
TO   Holly

Of course, I'm a happily married man.

FROM   Holly
TO   Jason GrangerRM

Great, so it's all 'Aisha and Jason' now is it, thanks for inviting me.

FROM   Jason GrangerRM
TO   Holly

Oh shut it hollysocks, I know you're spending the weekend with James.
   xxx

Subject: Dad's Oil Paintings

FROM   Holly
TO   Granny

Hi Granny,
   It was lovely to talk to you the other night, and I was really sorry — once again — that you were left a little in the dark about what to do with the computer. Hope your screen is now refreshing and you get my email. Also do you know anything about Dad and his painting?
   Holly
   X

FROM   Granny
TO   Holly

Holly
   You are wonderful. I feel like such a ninny sitting there staring at this computer for days on end, only to find out the thing needs refreshing and then I had the lovely feeling of seeing all these nice letters/emails waiting patiently for me.
   Your father and I have been up to mischief. He recently painted someone's baby as a commission and the word went around the town and everyone was talking about how super it was. So before he knew it he had people bringing their baby photos for him every day and he ended up with eight commissions for people's baby-portraits.
   Now your father paints because he likes painting oil landscapes, not oil babies, but your mother was so proud of him, she wouldn't let him refuse a commission.
   This is where I got involved Holly, because I told him to just paint the eyes, nose and mouth of one baby and then run off another eight copies. Then all he needed to do for each one was just add a little hair or baby clothes to make each one individual and no one would know.
   As it happens it all worked like a dream and your mother would never have twigged except for me and my big mouth.
   I was there on Monday with your parents while someone had come to pick up their painting.
   They were saying how wonderful the portrait was and how the little one had her father's eyes, and I said quietly to your dad, as I elbowed him and giggled that they actually had Jose's eyes from No10.

*This your mother overheard and I think that's when she became
upset. So that's the big news from Spain, it's really made my month.*

*I've thought of some good ideas for your father and me to get up
to new mischief in that bank of yours.*

(I'm just pulling your skinny leg, don't worry.)

Miss you so much

Love Granny

xxxx

Subject: Romantic Break

FROM   Jason GrangerRM
TO   Holly

So where is he taking you then?

FROM   Holly
TO   Jason GrangerRM

I don't know yet, he's not told me.

FROM   Jason GrangerRM
TO   Holly

So what time is he picking you up?

FROM   Holly
TO   Jason GrangerRM

Don't know — still waiting for a call etc ... ?

Subject: I just heard the news!

FROM   Aisha
TO   Holly; Jason GrangerRM

I just heard about you being stood up, the little sh*t.

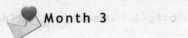

FROM   Holly
TO   Aisha; Jason GrangerRM

THANKS JASON!
I am not being stood up, I think he's just really busy today.

FROM   Aisha
TO   Holly; Jason GrangerRM

Yeah, busy today — I get that one too, they're all fuc*kers really they are. Come out with us.
  xxx

FROM   Holly
TO   Aisha; Jason GrangerRM

Aisha, please sort out your stars!! — Jason are you there??

FROM   Aisha
TO   Holly; Jason GrangerRM

He's coming back in a moment, I can see he looks really busy. So we're going to GAY, come with us??

Subject: The banker

FROM   Mum and Dad
TO   Holly

Holly
I've looked it up on the web in the Wikipedia and it says — In business vice-president refers to a rank in senior or middle management. Most companies that use this title generally have large numbers of people with the title of vice president with different types of vice president (e.g. vice president for finance).
So it sounds promising, doesn't it.
Love Mum

FROM　Holly
TO　　Mum and Dad

Yes Mum, it sounds promising.

Subject: James

FROM　Aisha
TO　　Holly; Jason GrangerRM

Hey, maybe he's going out with your friends upstairs?? and hasn't thought to break it to you yet, the Sh*tbag?

FROM　Holly
TO　　Aisha; Jason GrangerRM

Haven't you got work to do? Why don't you help Jason out?

FROM　Aisha
TO　　Holly; Jason GrangerRM

He looks like he's handling it, oh no he's not, I'm not getting involved.

FROM　Holly
TO　　Aisha; Jason GrangerRM

Involved, isn't that what you're meant to be doing as a receptionist for him??

FROM　Aisha
TO　　Holly

Don't have a go at me just because you've been stood up, it happens to me all the time!

FROM　Holly
TO　　Aisha; Jason GrangerRM

I have not BEEN STOOD UP!

Subject: The banker

FROM Mum and Dad
TO Holly

Middle management — I guess it depends how many VPs there are in your company. Do you know how many there are there?

FROM Holly
TO Mum and Dad

No Mum.

FROM Mum and Dad
TO Holly

OK, well it's all good news, I shouldn't keep you.
   I'm sure you're very busy there, your father and I are very proud of you.
   Love Mum

Subject: Strange but true

FROM Pregnant Pam
TO Holly

There's more discharge in my knickers today than I have even eaten, I can't hold anything down, have you got time to talk sweetie?
   Pam
   x

FROM Holly
TO Pregnant Pam

Sorry I can't Pam, I'll catch up on the mobile over the weekend and you can tell me all about it.
   xxx

Subject: The weekend

FROM   Holly
TO   James Lawrence

Not heard from you — can you please tell me what is happening???

WEEK 2

MONDAY

Subject: Spanish Life

FROM Alice and Matt
TO   Holly

Hi Holls,

Just got to tell you this, as I know how much you care about our snakes really.xx

We've just come back from the vets. Bobby (the snake) isn't very well. He's the biggest of all Matt's animals, 2 meters long and weighing in at 5 kilos of solid muscle so I went along to help Matt hold him while he had his jabs.

I think we'll now have to give him his antibiotic jabs ourselves because I don't think the vet is very keen on having him back.

Waiting their turn in the room outside were a lot of other people sitting with their pets (mostly English — reassuring their dogs/cats that a vet's surgery is a lovely place to be).

You see it's not the head that's the problem, you can pin that down, but while you're keeping your eye on his mouth, you tend to forget about the rest of his body — which began happily trashing the place (Bobby likes to thrash it about it bit).

We're all screaming at each other, a glass beaker has smashed on the floor, I stamped on Matt's foot in the havoc, and ended up being jabbed with the needle. 'It's only antibiotica, no worries' said the vet, whilst blood poured from my hand.

I can tell you those pets outside were not looking so keen any more.

When we came out you've never seen a row of faces so transformed, one woman gasped when she saw Bobby, and Matt points at her shitzu and says, 'you want to hang on to that love, he's only bite-sized and he's already swallowed the vet!'

(I was very embarrassed)

How we're going to manage to do these injections by ourselves every day for the next week, I don't know.

How's your morning?

Subject: You're in trouble

FROM Aisha
TO   Holly; Jason GrangerRM

You're in trouble young lady. I just called your work and your friend Trisha said you weren't in yet!!!

Subject: Meeting

FROM Judy Perkins
TO   Holly; Patricia Gillot

Dear Holly & Trisha
   I need to organise a meeting with you. I am thinking of some possible times next week, can you let me know if 6pm Tuesday can be confirmed?
   Regards, Judy

FROM Holly
TO   Judy Perkins

Hi Judy
   Yes, that's confirmed.
   Regards
   Holly

Subject: Meeting?

FROM Holly
TO   Patricia Gillot

Is this meeting about me? What's happened?

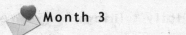

FROM   Patricia Gillot
TO   Holly

Sorry, I was miles away, don't panic, she thinks you were on the 5th floor doing room checks. This is about the annual results stuff.
    xxxx
    Tell me about your weekend?

FROM   Holly
TO   Patricia Gillot

It was great. You bad woman you ...

FROM   Patricia Gillot
TO   Holly

He made me promise darlin, I was dying to tell you Friday, but I didn't — I was a good girl and kept shtum!!

FROM   Holly
TO   Patricia Gillot

I thought he'd forgotten about it, I really did.

Subject: Dirty Stop Out

FROM   Jason GrangerRM
TO   Holly; Aisha

I've just heard from Aisha — you're not even in yet!!! And why didn't I get any more messages??? No update since Saturday? We need answers and we need them now!

Subject: My weekend break

FROM   Holly
TO   Patricia Gillot

What did he tell you then on Friday?

FROM   Patricia Gillot
TO   Holly

*He just turned up in that lovely motor and told me to make sure you
didn't get in a strop and walk out, silly b*gger — he's lucky, cause you
looked like you had the right hump until you saw him, wish I'd had
a camera.*

FROM   Holly
TO   Patricia Gillot

Guess where we went ...

FROM   Patricia Gillot
TO   Holly

Where?

FROM   Holly
TO   Patricia Gillot

He bought me a dress for it....?

FROM   Patricia Gillot
TO   Holly

I love this man!

FROM   Holly
TO   Patricia Gillot

and a hat ...

FROM   Patricia Gillot
TO   Holly

You lucky cow, he took you to the races?

FROM Holly
TO Patricia Gillot

Had just the best weekend. I wanted to bet on a horse, but after looking at them trotting around the start, I must admit — it was slim pickings.

FROM Patricia Gillot
TO Holly

Lucky you.

FROM Holly
TO Patricia Gillot

Get it, 'Slim Pickings?'

FROM Patricia Gillot
TO Holly

Yes, I got it darlin, funny.

Subject: My morning

FROM Holly
TO Aisha; Jason GrangerRM

Hi guys
*   It hasn't stopped since I got here, we've been rushed off our feet etc. I couldn't keep in touch on Sunday because I didn't have my phone any more (I dropped it down the toilet).*
*   I think I've had about 2 hours' sleep and it's really beginning to catch up with me.*
*   xxxx*

FROM Jason GrangerRM
TO Holly

I'm glad you didn't try and fish it out — tell me my classy friend — who was snooting it up with royalty at the Grand National ... you didn't have one arm of your dress half way down a Aintree bog on Saturday did you? Please say you didn't?

FROM   Holly
TO   Jason GrangerRM; Aisha

Of course not. I used a brush.

FROM   Jason GrangerRM
TO   Holly; Aisha

Oh Holly.

FROM   Holly
TO   Aisha; Jason GrangerRM

And a few bits of toilet paper.

FROM   Jason GrangerRM
TO   Holly; Aisha

I hope you didn't tell your escort of your adventures? Men have a thing about that, women's nails should be manicured to perfection, not dripping with pooh.

FROM   Holly
TO   Jason GrangerRM; Aisha

Of course I didn't! Anyway, where's Aisha, I need her advice?

FROM   Jason GrangerRM
TO   Holly; Aisha

Our happy little sex-pot has gone to lunch, I'll tell her when she's back you are in need of her services.

Subject: HOLLY DENHAM'S SUBSCRIPTION TO HOT NAKED GIRLS

FROM   Charlie Denham
TO   Holly

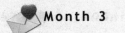

Got another inspection this Friday, so some praying might come in handy (if you can tell Alice).

Also managed to talk some local artists from the college into lending me their sculptures, and I got a bunch of old cages for hot girls to dance in — by the way do you know any hot girls who'd fancy spending a sweaty night in a cage — possibly wriggling????

Charlie

FROM   Holly
TO   Charlie Denham

No I don't — funny that isn't it?
PS re the subject box — ?!!

Subject: Monday blues

FROM   James Lawrence
TO   Holly

Miss you, honey pie sugar lumps squidgy fruit strawberry knickers.

FROM   Holly
TO   James Lawrence

You said we hadn't reached cutzie names-stage yet?

FROM   James Lawrence
TO   Holly

I know sweet pea, but I'm feeling reckless.

I called you just now and enjoyed a dirty conversation with a sex mad toilet attendant in Liverpool.

It was only after I'd agreed to a marathon bonking session over the back of a cistern, that I realised it wasn't you, but a chap named Doug, and it was me who was going to be over the cistern.

I politely declined.

How are you anyway?

FROM Holly
TO James Lawrence

Good. I still can't believe I did that with my phone. I'm really annoyed, I can't take the parking permit pictures now. Damn.

FROM James Lawrence
TO Holly

What interesting hobbies you have.

FROM Holly
TO James Lawrence

No, it's because of a fine — long story.

FROM James Lawrence
TO Holly

Is fumble bum tired?

FROM Holly
TO James Lawrence

Fumble bum?
   Not sure you've quite got the hang of this yet. Anyway it's not me — it's Aisha — my friend who likes nick names.

FROM James Lawrence
TO Holly

Oh I remember you mentioning your 'hot' friend — so when do I get to meet her?

FROM Holly
TO James Lawrence

When hell freezes over.

FROM James Lawrence
TO Holly

Is that a definite no?

FROM Holly
TO James Lawrence

I'm busy, and isn't there a deal somewhere that needs putting to bed or something?

FROM James Lawrence
TO Holly

I was going to suggest it myself, but glad you made the first move, come on can't you leave early?

Subject: Just got your message

FROM Aisha
TO Holly

Sorry, I've been busy here — you know how it is when you value your job and take it seriously ... How is the dirty stop-out feeling??????

FROM Holly
TO Aisha

Bad, I was going to ask your advice earlier — for how to get through the day when you've not slept.

FROM Aisha
TO Holly

Oh, it's quite easy, I usually go talk to a guy called Trevor, but you'll probably prefer just drinking a few espressos.

TUESDAY

Subject: Claim

FROM   Holly
TO   TOTALTFTIns-Claim-Dept

To whom it may concern
I took out insurance for my mobile phone and I now need a replacement please.
I dropped my last one as I was getting off a bus and it got flattened.
Can you let me know how I go about getting a new one.
Regards
Holly Denham

FROM   TOTALTFTIns-Claim-Dept
TO   Holly

REF 23400000000089888
Dear Holly Denham
Thank you for your email.
Arranging a replacement phone for you could not be simpler, simply send us the bits of the broken phone and we'll arrange for your new one to be posted out to you.
Thank you.
Yours sincerely
Frank Didman

Subject: Any Advice Welcome

FROM   Holly
TO   Aisha; Jason GrangerRM

Hi you two,
I'm trying to arrange for my new phone to be sorted out, but they want to see the bits. What should I do?

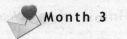

FROM   Jason GrangerRM
TO   Holly; Aisha

What bits, I thought you dropped it down the toilet?

FROM   Holly
TO   Jason GrangerRM; Aisha

I thought I might not be covered for toilet mishaps, so I lied.

FROM   Jason GrangerRM
TO   Holly; Aisha

What did your mother tell you about lying?

FROM   Holly
TO   Jason GrangerRM; Aisha

That it's OK to lie about three things: your age, a man's performance in bed, and the recipe for her steak and kidney pie — (it's a Denham secret). And I promise this is what she told me.
   I'm never likely to need to lie about the pie, so I'm swapping that one for insurance claims.
   ??? what do you think? ☺

FROM   Jason GrangerRM
TO   Holly; Aisha

You're swapping a lie about a pie, for major league insurance fraud? I'm not sure a judge would think it a fair swap, even with the added smiley face ...

FROM   Holly
TO   Jason GrangerRM; Aisha

You're not serious?

FROM   Jason GrangerRM
TO   Holly; Aisha

*Of course I'm not serious. Just get an old phone and run over it —
problem solved.*

Subject: Urgent Meeting Request

FROM   James Lawrence
TO   Holly

.Accept. .Tentative. .Decline. .Propose New Time.
   MEETING REQUEST FOR HOLLY DENHAM AT 3PM

FROM   James Lawrence
TO   Holly

.Tentative.
   *I remember the last meeting, to make sure it's a real meeting I
need to know —*
   A: What the meeting is about
   B: Where the meeting will be held
   Yours
   Holly

FROM   James Lawrence
TO   Holly

Holly
   To answer your questions:
   A: What the meeting is about
   ***Your lack of respect for senior members of staff and your
ability to communicate professionally***
   B: Where the meeting will be held
   ***In the lift at approx 3.03 pm — where I will be conducting a
thorough linguistic evaluation of our newest and naughtiest
receptionist***
   I will be sending the lift down for you at exactly 3.02pm.
   *I will expect you to be in there waiting for me when I enter at
3.03pm on the 4th floor.*

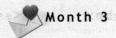
Any questions, email my secretary
James Lawrence
A very important person.
    PS. I expect the top three buttons of your suit and shirt to be undone — slutty look essential.

Subject: Prank Calls

FROM Holly
TO   Jason GrangerRM; Aisha

I'll get you both back for that one! Those in glass houses ...

FROM Jason GrangerRM
TO   Holly; Aisha

Oh hi Holly
    How's it going today, we've been really busy, what's up?

FROM Holly
TO   Áisha; Jason GrangerRM

Don't try that one!! I even heard Aisha laughing in the background!!

FROM Aisha
TO   Holly; Jason GrangerRM

HA HA HA HA
    That was so funny, did you actually say it out loud?

FROM Holly
TO   Aisha; Jason GrangerRM

Yes,
    Don't worry your time will come ... both of you!
    PS I just got an email from James asking me to meet him in the lift ...

Subject: What was that about?

FROM Patricia Gillot
TO Holly

What did you just say to them?

FROM Patricia Gillot
TO Holly

I got a call from someone saying they had an urgent message for one of the gentlemen in reception — a Mr Vingbender — they said his first name was Ray. SO I just asked our clients if any of them was a raving bender. Great.
   It turned out to be Jason and Aisha — of course.

FROM Patricia Gillot
TO Holly

Luckily they didn't understand you girl. Could have been bad, you should get them back for that.

Subject: How exciting — lift — meeting?

FROM Jason GrangerRM
TO Holly; Aisha

TELL US??? So are you going to go????

FROM Aisha
TO Holly; Jason GrangerRM

Of course she is!!

FROM Holly
TO Aisha; Jason GrangerRM

No, I'm not going.

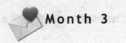

FROM Aisha
TO Jason GrangerRM; Holly

I'll go!!!

FROM Jason GrangerRM
TO Holly; Aisha

Unfortunately Aisha I don't think Holly was asking for a stand-in.
    James = Holly's boyfriend
    Dave, Peter, Paul, Matthew, Mark, Luke and any number of John's
= Aisha's boyfriends.

FROM Aisha
TO Jason GrangerRM; Holly

You're not funny Jason. So come on Hollysocks — are you going to go??????

FROM Holly
TO Aisha; Jason GrangerRM

NO.
    I don't know. Sh*t.

Subject: Someone Once Said ...

FROM Jason GrangerRM
TO Holly; Aisha

Time waits for no man.
    COME ON HOLLY. Tick tock tick tock, you've got 7 minutes to decide.

FROM Aisha
TO Holly; Jason GrangerRM

Come on Holly, do it do it do it do it!!!!!!!!

FROM Holly
TO Aisha; Jason GrangerRM

oohhhhhhhhhhhhhh don't know.

FROM Jason GrangerRM
TO Holly; Aisha

I'm sorry, I'm going to have to rush you on this one, I need your final answer, you have less than 2 minutes left!!!!

FROM Holly
TO Aisha; Jason GrangerRM

No.

FROM Jason GrangerRM
TO Holly; Aisha

30 seconds left, is that your final answer?

Subject: Meeting — sorry

FROM Holly
TO Patricia Gillot

Sorry Trisha, I completely forgot about a meeting upstairs, I've got to leave now, sorry.
  xxx

Subject: Romance or Filth, we need to know???

FROM Jason GrangerRM
TO Holly; Aisha

What's happening there? Don't leave us hanging????

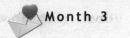

FROM   Holly
TO   Aisha; Jason GrangerRM

Out of Office AutoReply: Romance or Filth, we need to know???
   Unfortunately I am out of the office, if you require urgent assistance, please contact Patricia Gillot at PGillot@HuerstWright.com
   Otherwise I will be back soon.
   Kindest regards
   Holly Denham

Subject: What meeting?

FROM   Patricia Gillot
TO   Holly

I can't see a meeting in the diary, where've you been, and why you looking so flushed?

FROM   Holly
TO   Patricia Gillot

Sorry Trish, I didn't mean to be so long, I got grabbed as I was coming back by Judy who wanted to talk about this conference thing.

FROM   Patricia Gillot
TO   Holly

Coming back from where?

FROM   Holly
TO   Patricia Gillot

Coming back from my meeting.

FROM   Patricia Gillot
TO   Holly

With who?
   I know where you went first you saucy girl, you went up to see your fella again didn't you, oh I wish I could have an office romance, it's not fair.

FROM Holly
TO Patricia Gillot

Ralph?

FROM Patricia Gillot
TO Holly

I couldn't, I'd love to, but I couldn't, maybe I could enjoy setting him up with that stroppy cow.

FROM Holly
TO Patricia Gillot

Mrs Huerst? She'd eat him alive, poor Ralph.

Subject: Are you there?

FROM Holly
TO Jason GrangerRM; Aisha

I did it.
*   My heart is still racing — but mainly because I thought I was in trouble when I got collared by Judy, but then she just wanted to talk about work.*
*   I grabbed the lift and went to the fourth floor ...*

FROM Jason GrangerRM
TO Holly; Aisha

So????

FROM Holly
TO Jason GrangerRM; Aisha

We went down to the basement ...

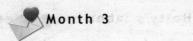

FROM Aisha
TO   Jason GrangerRM; Holly

Holly !!!
   Stop doing that dot dot dot thing, tell us everything, we want to know, did you shag him in the basement???

FROM Holly
TO   Aisha; Jason GrangerRM

I wanted to take my time to write this, OK.
From the beginning ...
   I took the lift to the fourth floor, he stepped into the lift and grabbed me and we kissed.
   But it was so passionate, he tugged my hair back and kissed me on the mouth, I was coming back up for another kiss and he held my hair for a moment and smiled, it was raunchy as hell! While he held me there he looked over to the buttons and pressed for the basement ...
   I never heard the doors open at all — I guess he must have blocked them open with his foot, but to be honest I wasn't really thinking about it, he had his hand squeezing my bum and I could feel him — (pressing against me).
   I won't go into more detail, we didn't do much more (OK I've got to tell you this bit because I know Aisha will be proud of me, at one point he was biting my breast hard, which drove me crazy).
   Help I want to start dancing around the reception area and singing, do you think I should sing???

FROM Jason GrangerRM
TO   Holly; Aisha

Don't sing, for the love of all that's beautiful DON'T SING!!
   Love you.
   x Jason.

WEDNESDAY

Subject: Jennie's party

FROM Toby Williams
TO   Holly

Holly
   Seeing as we're now working buddies, and you left so quickly when I arrived at Jennie's, I thought it would make sense to bury the hatchet if you like and go out for a drink this week.
   Toby

Toby Williams, VP Corporate Finance, H&W, High Holborn WC2 6NP

Subject: Toby

FROM Holly
TO   Charlie Denham

First contact has been made ... he just emailed me.

Subject: Kettle calling pot black

FROM Aisha
TO   Holly

So tell me Holly, how does it feels like to be such a slut????
   Shagging in the basement, coming to work without any sleep, whatever next? I guess it won't be too long before you're going at it on the front desk with Trisha pushing the passes out between your legs?
   Morning.

FROM Holly
TO   Aisha

Very funny, but not really fair — I didn't actually do anything much in the basement and I've NEVER had a go at YOU.

FROM Aisha
TO Holly

Never had a go??
    What about the half hour lecture when I got caught in the hotel room!!!!!
    'Aisha, you're not taking your job seriously, you're letting the side down, you're letting Jason down, Aisha can't you control your urges?????!'
    I was thinking, maybe you should wear a T-shirt when you get in that state again, something like 'holly's got the horn' so people know to steer clear of you, unless they want to be dragged into the lift for a gangbang holly-style ... oh and he fingered my buttons, oh and the doors were closing, oh and ... is it Holly Denham or Jackie Collins?
    Looks like you've changed over night.
    ha ha ha ha ha ha haa ha that's the last word, I'm going good bye horny holly
    xxxx

FROM Holly
TO Aisha

Aisha Peters! You think you're so funny, I'll just wait until you fall off that high horse and then we'll see, yes indeedy.

Subject: TW*T

FROM Charlie Denham
TO Holly

What did the sh*t bag say?

FROM Holly
TO Charlie Denham

Something about going for a drink!!!!????

FROM Charlie Denham
TO Holly

I'll kill him, tell him your brother still wants to talk to him, urgently.

FROM Holly
TO   Charlie Denham

Thanks, but I wouldn't want you to do anything.
  xxxx
  Hope your club's looking better, I think putting the art in there makes sense — the cages I'm not so sure about.
  x

Subject: No thanks

FROM Holly
TO   Toby Williams

I am on reception, you are in corporate finance. I am not your working buddy and — get lost.

FROM Toby Williams
TO   Holly

Like that is it?

FROM Holly
TO   Toby Williams

Yes.

Subject: HUERST & WRIGHT 25 YEAR BIRTHDAY

FROM Randolph Timothy Huerst
TO   Holly

Dear Holly
  As you are aware here in London, Huerst & Wright will be proudly commemorating their European Headquarters' 25th year in business next month.
  To celebrate this milestone achievement we are holding a gala dinner at the Dorchester and I wish to make it clear that I expect everyone to attend.

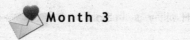

It will be a fantastic night and certainly a wonderful way to mark this auspicious day in the history books.
For this special occasion partners are also welcome.

Randolph Timothy Huerst, Huerst & Wright

Subject: Dating

FROM Holly
TO Patricia Gillot

I just got asked out on a date by randy old Randolph.

FROM Patricia Gillot
TO Holly

Me too at the Dorchester, to be honest I don't fancy it. I might ask him back to the wharf instead, we could have a pint in the Gun, followed by a knees up at the Watermans (there's usually a disco around 11). He'd want a puke in the bushes about 12 and he could catch a lift home with dangerous Dan after that.
Hey, you better be sitting with me, we'll have a right laugh.

FROM Holly
TO Patricia Gillot

Of course I will
xx

Subject: HUERST & WRIGHT 25 YEAR BIRTHDAY

FROM James Lawrence
TO Holly

Birthday b*llocks.
The only way I'm getting through that dribble is if I book us a suite, we can show our faces for the old man's speech then back upstairs for some interoffice bonding?
What say you Denham?
PS How's the nipple?

FROM　Holly
TO　　James Lawrence

Sore. You've made twisting very difficult.

FROM　James Lawrence
TO　　Holly

Don't twist then, you're on reception Holly, not Strictly Come Dancing.

FROM　Holly
TO　　James Lawrence

Anyway I'll be going with Trisha.

FROM　James Lawrence
TO　　Holly

So I'll be booking a bigger suite then.

Subject: Baby clothes, boy or girl?

FROM　Holly
TO　　Pregnant Pam

How did it go today, do we know yet whether it's a boy or girl?

FROM　Pregnant Pam
TO　　Holly

Hi Holly
　　Sorry, I forgot you couldn't talk earlier.
　　I went for the scan today and had a horrible journey on the way.
　　It seems like you give up your right to privacy when you're pregnant — everyone wants a touch of your tummy and grabs it before you can say no.
　　I was dying to find out the baby's sex today and I was in such a tiz you won't believe what I did Holly.
　　Are you alright to chat or are you busy?

FROM   Holly
TO   Pregnant Pam

Hi
   No I'm here I'm here, go on.
   xxx

Subject: Keep forgetting to ask you

FROM   James Lawrence
TO   Holly

Who's Toby?

Subject: Sister needs dating advice

FROM   Holly
TO   Charlie Denham

I go to lunch on top of the world, I come back and suddenly every-thing's going wrong.
   I need your help, did I tell you I've been dating someone at work?
   Actually I know I haven't told you, but there it is, I have and he's a really nice guy, but he's just asked me who Toby is.
   What should I say (Toby only happens to work on the same floor)?
   Holly
   PS don't worry if you have no advice at all, I know you are a guy and you find touchy feely problems difficult.
   x

Subject: Some wonderful news Holly

FROM   Granny
TO   Holly

Dear Holly
   It was so lovely to see you when you came here.
   I do wish you could come out to Spain more often even if it's only for the weekend. I know you say it's expensive but since your mother showed me how, your old gran has found she's a bit of a wiz at the computer.

I've found flights for just £20 on a site, imagine that! I've also given them your email address and name so they can send you their information on a daily basis.
   Love Granny
   xxxx

Subject: CHEAP FLIGHTS!!

FROM   BEST FLIGHTS AROUND
TO   HOLLY

Holly Denham
   BEST FLIGHTS AROUND
   FLY TO MALTA FROM £19!!!!!
   Simply log on to our site!!!!!
   OPEN 7 DAYS / 24 HOURS A DAY
   JUST CALL IN OR LOGON

Subject: Deals Deals Deals

FROM   Savings at You-Fly-We-Pay
TO   Holly

DEALS DEALS DEALS
   YOU FLY WE PAY!!!!!!!
   You're now registered with our NETWORK and will be receiving our UPDATES!!!!!!
   SIMPLY THE CHEAPEST FLIGHTS AROUND!!!!!!

Subject: Are you heading off?

FROM   CHEAP FLIGHTS FOR EVERYONE ALL THE TIME.COM
TO   Holly

Then you need look no further.
   We have cheap flights for everyone all the time, that's why we're called 'cheap flights for everyone all the time', crazy but true!!!
   If you book your flight today, we'll give you a free plane/hat.
   COOL !!!!
   BOOK TODAY BEFORE THEY'RE GONE!!!!!!

Subject: So ...

FROM   Pregnant Pam
TO   Holly

Holly
I went into the toilet with the sample cup, and I was so on edge because I was thinking, if it's a girl, then I can dress her up in lots of pink stuff and we can go out together and it'll be all girls together, but I'd probably worry more, so it might be better if it was a boy and that's when I dropped the cup down the loo!!!

YOu know what it's like because you told me about your phone-loo experiences and without thinking I've dived in and pulled it out full of what was left in the toilet bowl, and I'm thinking — it's alright it's alright, they'll never know, it's the same thing anyway.

So I've walked back with it, then realised what I'm doing, but she's caught me so I had to explain she couldn't have this one because it was toilet pee water, oh God Holly am I cracking up??

Subject: It's your lucky day

FROM   Flights To The Moon And Back
TO   Holly

FLIGHTS FLIGHTS FLIGHTS FLIGHTS FLIGHTS FLIGHTS
    AND
    FLIGHTS FLIGHTS FLIGHTS FLIGHTS FLIGHTS AND MORE FLIGHTS!!!!!!!!
    You can have a cheap holiday for less than £50!!
    You could be ...
    Eating Paella on the Costa del Sol from £20 (Spain)
    Eating Pizza in the Sistine Chapel from £29 (Italy)
    Eating burgers in Central Park from £80 (USA)
    Book now!! Before they've gone!!!!

Subject: Granny — Cheap Flights

FROM   Holly
TO   Granny

Thank you Granny,
*   it's very kind of you to register for me, I'll be sure to check out those deals.*
*   No need to put my name anywhere else though, I'm looking now with much hope. Thank you so much.*
*   Love you*
*   xxxxx Holly*

Subject: TOBY

FROM   James Lawrence
TO   Holly

Did you get my email about Toby?

Subject: Wait, before you do anything else ...

FROM   Flights To The Moon And Back
TO   Holly

... TAKE A FLIGHT!!!!!!
*   You know you want to !!!!*
*   You can have a cheap holiday for less than £50!!*
*   You could be ...*
*   Eating Paella on the Costa del Sol from £20 (Spain)*
*   Eating Pizza in the Sistine Chapel from £29 (Italy)*
*   Eating burgers in Central Park from £80 (USA)*
*   Book now!! Before they've gone!!!!*

FROM Holly
TO Flights To The Moon And Back

Thanks for your flight info but:

Those flights are just one way and the return flights are £200 plus £100 tax plus VAT.

So yes if I only had £50 then I COULD be in Spain, eating paella but without a return flight I'd be scraping it from the bottom of a beach bin and eating it from a hot flipflop.

SO PLEASE LEAVE ME ALONE

(and take me off your database)

Subject: Pregnant is Beautiful! YES IT IS

FROM Holly
TO Pregnant Pam

Don't worry about thinking you're mad, you're not honestly.

xxxxx being pregnant is a tough thing, but it's also such a beautiful thing too.xxx

So tell me, are you having a boy or a girl??

FROM Pregnant Pam
TO Holly

Beautiful?? Pregnancy??

You should see me, I'm a fat lump, my fingers have swelled up to size of burgers and my legs look like tree trunks.

I sweat, I ache, and Holly, I puke.

No I've no idea what the baby is, the nurse really winds me up, from what I've seen I'm giving birth to a small snow storm off Scotland. She keeps holding up this bit of plastic to the light and saying 'there's its little head, and there's its little body' and I've realised now she's mad.

She's probably been doing this for so many years she's lost it.

I bet other couples have their scans and they look at perfect pictures of their babies in clarity — my nurse had a machine which stopped working years ago and needs re-tuning, but no, she thinks she sees a baby.

At least it's only one.

Love Pam

FROM Holly
TO Pregnant Pam

Sorry I haven't been around for a while, can we meet up at the weekend, I'm sure you look lovely!
　xxx

Subject:Where are you?

FROM Holly
TO Charlie Denham

I've tried your mobile and I can't get through, you're the only one who knows about Toby, so just wanted to run it past you.xxxx
　Sh*t.
　I really like the guy I'm seeing — and I haven't emailed him back yet. I'll just have to make something up.
　x

Subject: Toby

FROM Holly
TO James Lawrence

Yes I heard Toby had come here, he was just some guy from my school, I didn't have much to do with him.
　xxxx

Subject: Are you sure???

FROM Patricia Gillot
TO Holly

You don't mind doing the later shift????

FROM Holly
TO Patricia Gillot

No, I'm fine, I'm happy doing 11—6 from now on.
　xxxx
　have a lovely evening

THURSDAY

Subject: Car problems

FROM   Holly
TO   James Lawrence

Morning James,
    Do you have your car here?

FROM   James Lawrence
TO   Holly

No Iain does, I'm sure he'd let you borrow it for a few minutes, where you going?
    J

FROM   Holly
TO   James Lawrence

Oh great, can I borrow it at lunch time, I won't be long, what car is it?

FROM   James Lawrence
TO   Holly

I think it's a Mini.

FROM   Holly
TO   James Lawrence

Oh, that's no good, do you know anyone else up there who could help me.

FROM   James Lawrence
TO   Holly

What's wrong with the Mini??

FROM   Holly
TO   James Lawrence

Not heavy enough, long story.
     xx

FROM   James Lawrence
TO   Holly

Why do women think putting a couple of x's at the bottom of their emails will stop men asking any more questions?

FROM   Holly
TO   James Lawrence

Don't know.
     xx

FROM   James Lawrence
TO   Holly

I know a jerk with a Chelsea-tractor up here, he's just a slap around the head away??
     Xx

FROM   Holly
TO   James Lawrence

OK, the reason a Mini is no good — I've got a Mini too, and I tried to run over my phone this morning but it didn't work, so I need a heavier car, long story.

FROM   James Lawrence
TO   Holly

There are other ways to get back at your phone you know, if it's been naughty, you could simply make it communicate in Japanese, put it on silent or even take away its battery privileges?
     Are you OK Holly, is the job getting to you?
     J

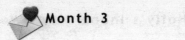

Subject: Flights — problem

FROM Holly
TO Alice and Matt

Hi
Granny's so lovely but she's beginning to think I'm cheap ... and doesn't understand why I haven't got the money to fly out more.
When I mentioned it being expensive she began looking for flights.

FROM Alice and Matt
TO Holly

Hi sweetie
Don't worry, I'll have a quiet word with her, without having to spill the beans.
xxx

Subject: Boredom

FROM James Lawrence
TO Holly

Holly
If it's simply a way of you girls getting through the boredom of a long lunch hour, I've heard backgammon is quite good, obviously it doesn't match the thrill of seeing your phone take a beating, but I dare say very little does, also if you put the pieces away afterwards and resist the temptation of setting fire to the board, you can use it again?
J

Subject: Help is never far away

FROM James Lawrence
TO Holly

I found this for you ...
Thought it might help

Do you sometimes feel everyone's against you?

Do you often get strange looks from co-workers?
Do your friends ever worry about your mental health?
Does blind rage sometimes take over?
If so then maybe you're suffering from stress and anger issues
Join our team of anger management classes today
You are not alone!!!
Anger&StressManagement-UK.CB

Subject: Toby

FROM James Lawrence
TO Holly

This Toby fella, are you sure you don't know him better than you say???

Subject: Help

FROM Holly
TO Charlie Denham

Help.
   I'm up a huge tree without a paddle and you're not answering your phone. Help Charlie help.

FROM Charlie Denham
TO Holly

Hi
   Just got your messages etc and email, sorry been up my own tree without a paddle with stuff here (whatever that means).
   The main thing I'd recommend is just not to lie, because guys talk, and you're bound to be caught out, but on the other hand don't tell him everything obviously.
   Charlie

FROM Holly
TO Charlie Denham

Too late, I lied already. Aaaaaaaaaaaaaa
   Holly

Subject: Earth to Holly ...

FROM Jennie Pithwait
TO Holly

Hi
   I haven't had a chance to call you back because the last few days have been crazy. So what have you been up to recently, where have you been, tell me everything???
   Jennie

FROM Holly
TO Jennie Pithwait

Nothing really exciting to tell you, we've got to go out again soon.
   Damn, lots of clients coming in, I'll call you later.
   xxxx
   Holly

Subject: Telling stories

FROM Holly
TO Aisha; Jason GrangerRM

Do you ever find days when all your lying seems to catch up with you at once???

Subject: Toby

FROM Holly
TO James Lawrence

It's manic down here at the moment, so can't get away, but I'll call you as soon as I can get a break. There's a bit more to explain.
   x

Subject: Lying

FROM Aisha
TO   Holly

Yes I once got caught with an ounce of dope up my snatch (wrapped in cellophane). I told them it was there because I just couldn't swallow any more.
  I know how you feel.
  x

FROM Holly
TO   Aisha

???

Subject: Aisha

FROM Jason GrangerRM
TO   Holly

She's a delight isn't she? Aisha just told me matter-of-factly what she emailed you. But don't worry Hollykins, people will forgive the odd lie. I'll call you tonight.
  x

Subject: Interesting ... So Toby was your childhood sweetheart???

FROM James Lawrence
TO   Holly

Don't bother calling me! You're obviously a lying, conniving harlot who has without any shadow of a doubt, previously kissed someone of the opposite sex.
  How can I possibly accept a dinner invitation to your flat tonight?
  J

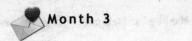

FROM   Holly
TO   James Lawrence

Are we having dinner tonight??

FROM   James Lawrence
TO   Holly

Of course, I love lying, conniving harlots.
If you can talk your scary gate keeper into nipping off for a fag we could roll around behind that unfeasibly tidy reception desk, that's if we don't get disturbed by any of your previous flings. Just interested — are there any more lurking in the building?

FROM   Holly
TO   James Lawrence

Not one — honest. Also she's not scary, she's lovely, and lastly I don't know what 'rolling around' involves.

FROM   James Lawrence
TO   Holly

Toby said you do ...

FROM   Holly
TO   James Lawrence

Toby is nothing buy a lowlife skank.

FROM   James Lawrence
TO   Holly

Really? I must admit he does strike me as the skanky type (if I've used the word correctly).

FROM   Holly
TO   James Lawrence

You have, perfectly.

FROM James Lawrence
TO   Holly

So tonight?

FROM Holly
TO   James Lawrence

Meet at the usual place down the road — 7.10PM?
  Holly
    x
    PS Talking of desks ... what is going on with your bombsite????

FROM James Lawrence
TO   Holly

Maid's been away, maybe you could get yourself up here with a duster?

FROM Holly
TO   James Lawrence

Maybe you could kiss my arse.

FROM James Lawrence
TO   Holly

Maybe I will.

FROM Holly
TO   James Lawrence

Maybe, oh, I've got work to do, see you later lover ...
  xxxxx

FROM James Lawrence
TO   Holly

Love the way you use your dots, makes your mind wander ...
  Oh talking of mind wandering, my desk, maids, uniforms, there is one thing that Toby has seen that I haven't and I feel this is totally unfair ...

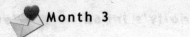

FROM Holly
TO James Lawrence

You can forget it! (It won't fit anymore anyway.)

FROM James Lawrence
TO Holly

No problem, I hear they've got replica rubber slutty school uniforms at most reputable sex shops?

Subject: Kinky

FROM Holly
TO Jason GrangerRM; Aisha

You two, not heard much from you today, hope you're having a ball, I'm muuuuuuuuch happier now.
    xxxx
    PS this relationship with James, it's quite intense.

FROM Jason GrangerRM
TO Holly; Aisha

Holly
    You can't put KINKY in the subject box then talk about it being intense????
    Come on Holly, has James been asking you to do things you wouldn't normally do?
    Jason x

FROM Holly
TO Jason GrangerRM; Aisha

In the past all this stuff wouldn't be something I'd even consider, but we just have so much fun together. I'm so happy at the moment.

FROM   Jason GrangerRM
TO   Holly

I KNOW YOU'RE HAPPY — I'm your best friend!!!!
    I say go for it and if I'm thinking what I'm thinking you're mean-
ing, then you'll probably love it.
    xxx
    (I've cut Aisha out of this email as I've sent her off on an errand
to another site for me anyway.)

FROM   Holly
TO   Jason GrangerRM

??? What is it you think he's asking?

FROM   Jason GrangerRM
TO   Holly

Whether he can do what I do a lot of, which is good, really it is, but
you want to make sure he uses plenty of KY, oh and you might want
to buy some poppers.
    xxx
    How exciting!!

FROM   Holly
TO   Jason GrangerRM

NO!!!! YUK!!! That's not what I was saying!!

Subject: Jason!

FROM   Holly
TO   Jason GrangerRM

Are you still there!!!! That wasn't what I was saying!!!!!!!
    Jason?????

Subject: Rain

FROM   Granny
TO   Holly

Holly
   Hello dear, they say it might rain again here later. I was asleep when it did it earlier this week, but let's wait and see shall we. Many years ago, during our honeymoon in Scotland, I posed for your grandfather like a ballerina while it rained. I don't know if you remember but your parents have a picture your grandfather took on their wall, I'd love to do that again.
   Love Granny x

FRIDAY

Subject: Rain

FROM   Holly
TO   Granny

Granny
   I'd left by the time you sent your email yesterday, but of course I remember the picture, you looked beautiful, and you should go out and be a ballerina if it rains!!!
   Love Holly

Subject: Late

FROM   Patricia Gillot
TO   Holly

Judy asked where you were, I said you'd called in — problems on the tube.

FROM　Holly
TO　　Patricia Gillot

*I'm so so sorry Trish, this new shift thing and I forgot it was 10.00
this morning, I just couldn't get it all together in time.*
　xx

FROM　Patricia Gillot
TO　　Holly

Don't worry darlin, you cover for me plenty.
　x

Subject: Sorry I was late

FROM　Holly
TO　　Judy Perkins

Hi Judy
　Sorry I was late this morning, I had problems on the Underground.
　Kind regards
　Holly

Subject: Marbella

FROM　James Lawrence
TO　　Holly

*Just found out that Marbella trip is on next Friday – I've definitely
got to go there for the weekend, I'll get you a ticket too if fancy
coming.*
　*I thought we could pop in for lunch down the coast and surprise
your family? What do you think?*
　J

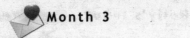

Subject: Gala dinner

FROM Jennie Pithwait
TO Holly

Are you coming to this Gala dinner next month — I'm guessing you'll be sitting with me??
  Jennie

FROM Holly
TO Jennie Pithwait

Of course!! We should all sit together in a big group of us, it'll be so much fun. I'm looking forward to it.
  What are you up to this weekend, how's work been this week?
  Holly

Subject: RE: Late

FROM Judy Perkins
TO Holly

Not a problem Holly, the tubes are always a nightmare, what trouble did you have?

FROM Holly
TO Judy Perkins

Judy
  It was a train caught in a tunnel, kept us there for ages, nightmare.
  Holly

FROM Judy Perkins
TO Holly

Oh dear, what line?

Subject: Trouble!

FROM   Holly
TO   Patricia Gillot

Shit, Judy wants to know which line now?

FROM   Patricia Gillot
TO   Holly

OK check the tube website, because I know that's what Judy'll be looking at, she's told me about it before.

FROM   Holly
TO   Patricia Gillot

I can't see any line having problems can you? There must be one line, THE ONE DAY YOU NEED THEM TO HAVE A PROBLEM FOR HEAVENS SAKE!!!!

FROM   Patricia Gillot
TO   Holly

Nothin darlin, not a fire, a fault, not even no one thrown themselves under one? Nothing?

FROM   Holly
TO   Patricia Gillot

Wait — minor delays on Circle Line!!! And some minor on the Hammersmith and City line too? Wait check out the Metropolitan line!!!

FROM   Patricia Gillot
TO   Holly

Severe delays on the Met Line! Bingo!!!
We have a winner, get that email sent darlin.
xxx

Subject: Tube nightmare

FROM Holly
TO Judy Perkins

The Metro Line, absolute nightmare.
  Holly

Subject: Marbella???

FROM James Lawrence
TO Holly

Need to know now, I'm booking the tickets — you fancy surprising your family??
  J

Subject: Kate or Britney?

FROM Jason GrangerRM
TO Holly

Where do you stand on the whole Kate or Britney debate?

FROM Holly
TO Jason GrangerRM

Are you bored?

FROM Jason GrangerRM
TO Holly

Very much.

FROM Holly
TO Jason GrangerRM

OK, what about helping me in the 'should Holly go to Spain with James' debate ?

FROM   Jason GrangerRM
TO   Holly

Has he asked you????

FROM   Holly
TO   Jason GrangerRM

Yes.

FROM   Jason GrangerRM
TO   Holly

Well of course the answer is YES YES YES!!!

FROM   Holly
TO   Jason GrangerRM

I'm not so sure.

FROM   Jason GrangerRM
TO   Holly

*He hasn't asked you to go dressed in some weird outfit has he?
     Tell me he's not making you sit on a plane in 10 kilos of rubber and a hose up your bum or something? If so then you should seriously consider the sweat implications when you touch down in Malaga, still, take an empty bucket and a couple of dry sponges and some more KY and you'll be fine. You might lose some weight too???*

FROM   Holly
TO   Jason GrangerRM

NO!! And stop talking about bums and KY, it's not nice, you've been hanging around with Aisha too much!!!
     x

FROM   Jason GrangerRM
TO   Holly

FINE!!!!!

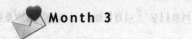

FROM Holly
TO Jason GrangerRM

I was only kidding.
    xxx

Subject: BUMS KY BUMS KY BUMS KY BUMS KY BUMS KY
BUMS KY

FROM Jason GrangerRM
TO Holly

BUMS KY BUMS KY BUMS KY BUMS KY BUMS KY BUMS KY BUMS KY
BUMS KY BUMS KY BUMS KY BUMS KY BUMS KY BUMS KY BUMS KY

FROM Holly
TO Jason GrangerRM

Have you finished?

FROM Jason GrangerRM
TO Holly

BUMS KY BUMS KY BUMS KY BUMS KY BUMS KY BUMS KY BUMS KY
BUMS KY BUMS KY BUMS KY BUMS KY BUMS KY BUBUMS KY BUMS
BUMS KY BUMS KY BUMS KY BUMS KY BUMS KY BUMS KY BUMS KY
BUMS KY BUMS KY BUMS KY BUMS KY BUMS KY BUMS KY BUMS KY
BUMS KY BUMS KY BUMS KY BUMS KY BUMS KY BUMS KY BUMS KY
BUMS KY BUMS KY BUMS KY BUMS KY BUMS KY BUMS KY BUMS KY

FROM Holly
TO Jason GrangerRM

You're being very childish Mr Granger. Where's Aisha?

FROM Jason GrangerRM
TO Holly

Not around, so why don't you want to go to Spain then?
    xxx

FROM   Holly
TO   Jason GrangerRM

Don't know, maybe I'm over-worrying, we would have to see my family and it's all a bit early ...

Subject: I'm very cross with you Holly

FROM   Mum and Dad
TO   Holly

Holly
   Did you suggest Granny danced in the rain today?
   Mum

FROM   Holly
TO   Mum and Dad

Yes, she told me about that time on her honeymoon when she danced like a ballerina in the rain.
   You know — that picture you have on your wall with her spinning around in that lovely long dress.
   Why, did it rain?

FROM   Mum and Dad
TO   Holly

No Holly, the picture in that long dress was taken years later.
   She was talking about that other one you have on YOUR wall in YOUR HALL, the one of her balancing on one leg on the grass by the lake, she is — as you will remember, without clothes, naked!!!
   I've never been so embarrassed, when we turned up for her usual lunch outing just now, we arrived to find your grandmother whirling around on the lawn, naked as a baby, with families coming to visit their relatives just standing around speechless. It scared the life out of them, I think one of the old boys is still in recovery.
   Can you please be careful what you encourage her to get up to.
   Mum

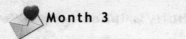

Subject: Marbella

FROM Holly
TO James Lawrence

Hi James
I think all my family are away unfortunately next weekend, so we won't be able to do that. But I'd love to go to Marbella!!!
xxxxx

FROM James Lawrence
TO Holly

Good, we'll have some fun.

FROM Holly
TO James Lawrence

PS I got me in trouble this morning ... for being late.

FROM James Lawrence
TO Holly

Not my fault. You started it.

FROM Holly
TO James Lawrence

So I did.
x

Subject: Lying to friends???

FROM Jennie Pithwait
TO Holly

I'm guessing at some stage you'll stop lying to me — I mean, as a friend this is something which is usually important to most genuine people. I'm going home now, goodbye.
Jennie

Subject: Granny

FROM   Holly
TO   Mum and Dad

Sorry Mum.
   Oh well, I'm sure there was no harm done and I'm sure it made her very happy.
   xxx

Subject: I just heard

FROM   Alice and Matt
TO   Holly

Holly
   I just talked to Mum and heard she's told you about Granny. What's so sad is they thought she was drunk and now they've banned her from drinking for the next month. Of course Granny never needs to be drunk to do that kind of thing, that's just how she is, lots of fun. From what we've heard she put on quite a show, with her own version of Swan Lake in front of a stunned audience in deck chairs.
   Could you give her a call tonight, and cheer her up though.
   xxx
   Alice

WEEK 3

MONDAY

Subject: Our trip to England

FROM   Mum and Dad
TO   Holly

Holly
   We're still coming in the Summer and your father and I have come up with an idea. We'd like to meet up with some of our old friends, the ones we haven't seen for a while, have a bit of a reunion night. Would it be OK to have this at your house? It would be really lovely to show them how well you've done and a few of them could stay over? What d'you think?
   Love Mum
   xxx
   PS How is James? We know so little about him, for instance you haven't even told us what car he drives or where his parents live?

Subject: Forgive me forgive me forgive me forgive me

FROM   Holly
TO   Jennie Pithwait

Have you forgiven me yet ... Pretty please?
   I tried calling you a few times over the weekend to explain.
   xxxx
   Holly

Subject: My weekend

FROM   Holly
TO   Jason GrangerRM; Aisha

Hi
   I saw James again (and pregnant Pam).

Are either of you there? I'm dying to tell someone about my weekend, how was yours?
xxxxx

FROM Aisha
TO   Holly

Hi
   Jason's somewhere upstairs sorting out problems, it's busy here, can we catch up after check outs?
   xx

Subject: Morning

FROM Holly
TO   Patricia Gillot

Morning, how was your weekend?

FROM Patricia Gillot
TO   Holly

OK, I spent Friday night in A&E with our Anthony. He'd been in a fight at school, turns out he's got a cracked rib.

FROM Holly
TO   Patricia Gillot

That's awful, is he OK?

FROM Patricia Gillot
TO   Holly

No, he's got a cracked rib? Then Saturday, you won't believe I wake up to find two hot battered fish on my front door step.

FROM Holly
TO   Patricia Gillot

Were they a present?

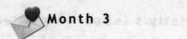

FROM   Patricia Gillot
TO   Holly

Yeah darlin, or course, that's what we do down the East End — didn't you know?

FROM   Holly
TO   Patricia Gillot

No, why?

FROM   Patricia Gillot
TO   Holly

Yeah of course we do, around our way we always give each other fish and chips as a thank you, not like you posh f**ks with your chocolates, a bag of chips left on someone's doorstep, yeah thanks mate, there's your chips, away you go.
  YOU MAKE ME LAUGH!!!

FROM   Holly
TO   Patricia Gillot

Sorry sorry sorry, OK so why the fish??

FROM   Patricia Gillot
TO   Holly

They were from our garden, Les' goldfish. Les reckons it's like a warning, or a revenge killing or something.

FROM   Holly
TO   Patricia Gillot

You mean — like the horse's head left in someone's bed in that film?

FROM   Patricia Gillot
TO   Holly

Something like that yes, why are you laughing again!!!

FROM　Holly
TO　Patricia Gillot

Fish?? In somewhere else it would probably be a child's prank, but in the East End it's a mafia killing — hand over the cash, or the fish gets it.
hee hee hee
I'm off before you can get me! Toilet break.
xxx

Subject: Weekend??

FROM　Holly
TO　Aisha; Jason GrangerRM

Anyone there? I STILL want to tell someone about my weekend???
xxxxxx

Subject: A truce ? xxxx

FROM　Holly
TO　Patricia Gillot

OK, so apart from that, how was the rest of your weekend?

FROM　Patricia Gillot
TO　Holly

Not good, Sunday we went to watch the London Marathon.

FROM　Holly
TO　Patricia Gillot

Oh so did I!! I went with James ...

FROM　Patricia Gillot
TO　Holly

I went with Les ... he got p*ssed up, had a fight, off to A&E (AGAIN)

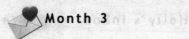

*came back, got angry about his fish, then he had a barny with the
neighbour and spent a night in the cells. I spent most the night trying
to argue him out of there.*
    How was your Sunday?

Subject: Be afraid, be very afraid

FROM   Holly
TO   Charlie Denham

Charlie
*Hide your strange friends, bury your dope, clean behind your ears
and say your prayers, MUM'S COMING TO ENGLAND.*
   xxx

FROM   Charlie Denham
TO   Holly

Hi Holly
   Yes I'd forgotten she was coming, also what strange friends?
   Charlie

FROM   Holly
TO   Charlie Denham

Strange friends — yes you have — what about Sticky Pete?

FROM   Charlie Denham
TO   Holly

It's Rubber Ron as you're well aware.

FROM   Holly
TO   Charlie Denham

*Also, guess what — Mum and Dad want a reunion party with their
friends ... at my lovely house???? ... Where they'll all be spending the
night!!!!????*
   Sh*t.

FROM   Charlie Denham
TO   Holly

That could be interesting, don't panic, we'll think of something.
  So — we had the inspection Friday.

FROM   Holly
TO   Charlie Denham

Sorry forgot to ask ... how did it go?

FROM   Charlie Denham
TO   Holly

Things didn't go too badly at first.
  BUT there was a sheet of metal (we've got a metal bar top) leaning against one wall and Ron thought he'd get it out the way. He began sliding it along the floor while I quietly spoke to the health and safety officers, but behind them I saw Rubber Ron slide the sheet over a radio cable, there was a huge bang (as the cable severed and made the sheet live) and just for an instant I saw him lit up and jumping through the air, then everything went black. They asked me what it was, I said we must have just blown a fuse, Ron moaned then in the darkness, but managed to drag himself off before the lights came up again, it was very close.
  He's OK, obviously a bit bruised, but the top news is ... I think we might have passed our health and safety inspection. Now we've finished, Rubber Ron said it would probably be a good idea to have done the whole safety dvds thing.

FROM   Holly
TO   Charlie Denham

That's what I've BEEN TELLING YOU ALL ALONG!!!

FROM   Charlie Denham
TO   Holly

No — he thinks we should MAKE a safety video. You know — show people how to steer clear of danger.

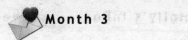

This week, we'll show you how Ron electrocuted himself, gassed 100 people and put a nail through his foot, next week you'll see how I lost my hair, an arm and why I can't have children?
What d'you think?
Charlie

FROM Holly
TO Charlie Denham

I think you're sick, but very funny. I would have thought Rubber Ron would have been insulated against this kind of thing??

FROM Charlie Denham
TO Holly

ha ha
  Charlie

Subject: Nice one

FROM Jennie Pithwait
TO Holly

Listen Holly, I don't care who you shag, but sneaking around so much, then telling Trisha all about it and not me, makes me realise how little you view our friendship.

FROM Holly
TO Jennie Pithwait

I couldn't hide it from Trish — she sits next to me and I didn't want to tell you because I thought you hated him so much.

FROM Jennie Pithwait
TO Holly

Oh come on, you even thought I'd had a fling with him, or at the very least had a crush on him, that's what you said on my answer-phone and THAT IS why you didn't tell me!!!!

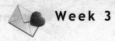
FROM   Holly
TO   Jennie Pithwait

I didn't really know what to think, I just knew it was going really well and didn't want it to go wrong, I'm so so so sorry, you're my friend and I'd never purposely upset you. Surely these kind of things can be forgiven between friends, pleeeeeeeeeeeeeeeeeeeeeeeeeeeeeeeeeease.

Subject: Tonight

FROM   Patricia Gillot
TO   Holly

Hate to be the bringer of bad news, but you know who we're seeing tonight.

FROM   Holly
TO   Patricia Gillot

Oh, I'd forgotten about her.

FROM   Patricia Gillot
TO   Holly

The dragon lady herself — lucky it's St George's Day, ha ha ha.

Subject: I'm in trouble

FROM   Holly
TO   Patricia Gillot

Jennie's really really upset with me ... Did you see that look she just gave me?

FROM   Patricia Gillot
TO   Holly

Yeah, she had a face on her like a slapped arse.

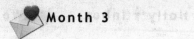

FROM   Holly
TO   Patricia Gillot

I shouldn't have lied to her.

FROM   Patricia Gillot
TO   Holly

You're better off without her, calling us 'support staff' the cow.
   So you ready for Shella Cruella?

FROM   Holly
TO   Patricia Gillot

No, she's bound to have a go at us about something, I'm just hoping
you brought those boots. TELL ME YOU BROUGHT THOSE BOOTS?

FROM   Patricia Gillot
TO   Holly

Steel-toe-capped ones? No, left them at home with me chips.

Subject: Coming to England

FROM   Holly
TO   Mum and Dad

Hi Mum
   I'm very excited about seeing you, and I know Charlie will be too.
   I would love to have your reunion-party at my house, however I
have decided to rent it out. It really is such a big place, and I could
live somewhere much smaller.
   I'd love to have you over though and we could have a lovely
dinner at my new place (I could possibly seat up to 8). The only
difference being they wouldn't be able to sleep anywhere. But you
and Dad could have my bed, and I've got a pull out sofa-bed.
   What d'you think?
   xxxx Holly

Subject: Charlie

FROM   Holly
TO   Charlie Denham

*I had an inspiration about the house thing, I told Mum and Dad I was
renting it out.*
    xxx

TUESDAY

Subject: What a night I had

FROM   Holly
TO   Jason

*I woke up in the middle of the night and guess who was lying next to
me?*

FROM   Jason GrangerRM
TO   Holly; Aisha

*Toby Maguire butt-naked except for a small amount of webbing over
his privates, which shimmered invitingly in the moonlight?*

FROM   Holly
TO   Jason GrangerRM; Aisha

Oh we are in a funny mood today aren't we Jason.
    *No, anyway you've ruined it now. I was going to say I woke up to
see that PA who hates me so much — Shella — lying next to me. I said,
what are you doing in my bed? And she said — 'Well Holly (she said
the H like she always does ... like she's coughing something up) you
forgot to book my meeting room, so I'm going to lie here until you
do.'*
    It was most disconcerting, I couldn't get her out.

FROM   Aisha
TO   Holly; Jason GrangerRM

Do you think this is some kind of fantasy you have about her?
   Aish

FROM   Holly
TO   Jason GrangerRM; Aisha

No Aish,
   it wasn't sexual, it's just because she makes me so nervous.

FROM   Aisha
TO   Holly; Jason GrangerRM

Where was James all this time?

FROM   Holly
TO   Aisha; Jason GrangerRM

Not there, we don't sleep with each other every night.

FROM   Aisha
TO   Holly; Jason GrangerRM

Maybe you should, I'd be banging his brains out every night if I was you.

FROM   Jason GrangerRM
TO   Holly; Aisha

Good point Aish, also if James was in your bed, there wouldn't be any room left for PAs? You should tell him.

FROM   Holly
TO   Aisha; Jason GrangerRM

I'm going now, thanks for your advice you two.
   PS — just remembered me and Trisha owe you a wind up — keep your eyes peeled!

Subject: Rent

FROM Nick
TO Holly

Holly
*   Just thought I'd send you an email to remind you about your rent this month, I know your landlord will be expecting it on time and I thought a reminder would help you.*
*   All the best*
*   Yours sincerely*
*   Nick Harkson*

Subject: Bitch from hell

FROM Patricia Gillot
TO Holly

That was fun last night.

FROM Holly
TO Patricia Gillot

Shella really hates me for some reason and I don't think she's about to make it easier for me here.
*   x*

FROM Patricia Gillot
TO Holly

Init, just watch your back.

Subject: Toby

FROM James Lawrence
TO Holly

Toby seems like a stand up kind of guy. If we're good mates will this make things awkward?

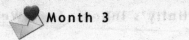

Subject: My lovely very cool sister

FROM   Charlie Denham
TO   Holly

What do you know about licensing laws?
   Charlie

Subject: Toby

FROM   Holly
TO   James Lawrence

What?

Subject: ?????

FROM   Holly
TO   Charlie Denham

I know nothing about licensing laws and now your cool sister is very suspicious.

FROM   Charlie Denham
TO   Holly

Don't worry, you don't need to know anything, just need to sign a few forms.

FROM   Holly
TO   Charlie Denham

What forms?

Subject: Toby

FROM   James Lawrence
TO   Holly

Yes, I invited him to Spain with us, hope that's ok?

FROM   Holly
TO   James Lawrence

Of course that's fine, I was thinking, why don't you invite your parents too, my mum is desperate to meet them and well, I just think it's time don't you?

Subject: Your weekend

FROM   Patricia Gillot
TO   Holly

Forgot to ask about your weekend, did you have fun with that pregnant friend of yours, you saw her this weekend didn't you? She still moaning?

FROM   Holly
TO   Patricia Gillot

She's finding it very difficult. She's always got a headache, always feels sick and she's single-handedly put me off having children. Her emails are like letter bombs, I'm scared to open them any more in case she attaches a picture of something nasty she feels like sharing with me.
  Being pregnant isn't that bad is it?

FROM   Patricia Gillot
TO   Holly

Why? Has that James been talking about having kids?

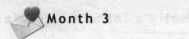

FROM Holly
TO Patricia Gillot

No, I was just thinking.

Subject: Your registration has been processed

FROM Totaljobs.co.uk
TO Holly

Congratulations
  Your job requirements have been entered onto our database.
  You will now receive job updates which match the criteria you have stipulated.
  Good luck in your employment search.
  Registration Centre

Subject: My belt

FROM Aisha
TO Holly

Lover girl — did you remember my belt?

Aish

FROM Holly
TO Aisha

It's under my desk, see you at 5pm.

Subject: What forms?

FROM Holly
TO Charlie Denham

Now I'm back from lunch — what do you want me to do?

FROM   Charlie Denham
TO   Holly

I'll come clean with you, we're having a few problems finding anyone without a criminal record to hold the licence, seems everyone's got one these days, in fact the only people I KNOW who don't have one are you and Granny.

    And I can't see Granny in rubber, luckily.
    xxxx

FROM   Holly
TO   Charlie Denham

I'm hoping you can't see me in rubber either you pervert. But anyway:

    1: I am not going to be held responsible for a club I don't even work in.

    2: Rubber? You said it was just a normal club with lots of strange artwork?
    Holly

Subject: SPAIN

FROM   James Lawrence
TO   Holly

OK, let's not take my parents or Toby OK? You're not getting wound up today, what's wrong with you?

    But I am very much looking forward to seeing the Denham clan — what did you say your sister does again?

FROM   Holly
TO   James Lawrence

Landscape gardening, with her husband.

FROM   James Lawrence
TO   Holly

Great, what does your brother do?

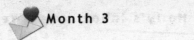

FROM   Holly
TO   James Lawrence

Runs a book shop.

FROM   James Lawrence
TO   Holly

Fab, where?

FROM   Holly
TO   James Lawrence

Israel.

FROM   James Lawrence
TO   Holly

Really?

FROM   Holly
TO   James Lawrence

Yes.

FROM   James Lawrence
TO   Holly

You're such a f*cking liar Denham.

Subject: Re normal club with strange artwork

FROM   Charlie Denham
TO   Holly

'Unusual artwork' is what I said, and it is, mainly naked bodies involved in kinky sex acts, but this doesn't detract from the fact that I need you to front the club and act as the licencee??
    Charlie

FROM   Holly
TO   Charlie Denham

What type of club is it then?

FROM   Charlie Denham
TO   Holly

A fetish club.

FROM   Holly
TO   Charlie Denham

You are kidding me — definitely not!

FROM   Charlie Denham
TO   Holly

Oh, come on, it's just like a normal club, only there's more to see, and you make friends a lot quicker?

FROM   Holly
TO   Charlie Denham

Go away.

Subject: My thoughts

FROM   Jason GrangerRM
TO   Holly

Holly
  I've given it a lot of thought today, and I don't think you should let James meet your family, not yet.
  xxxx
  Also have you had your legs waxed??
  Have you booked a tan?
  Have you booked your nails in? (if I remember they look awful).
  Finally what underwear have you packed, I'm worried.

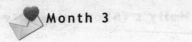

FROM   Holly
TO   Jason GrangerRM

Family — we're singing from the same hymn sheet.
    But the rest of it — you're making me nervous, I'm not worrying about all that, he's seen me naked, with the lights off. We've been together a while now, it's all fine.
    xx

FROM   Jason GrangerRM
TO   Holly

It is not all fine, you're about to set foot in a foreign land full of beautiful stylish women who know how to dress, walk, talk and eat lunch without spilling gravy down their fronts, and will be doing everything possible to get their manicured paws on your perfect marriage-material. And you don't even have a battle plan?
    But if you think it's all fine, then don't worry.
    Got to go.
    xxx

Subject: Wax Lyrical

FROM   Holly
TO   Jason GrangerRM

OK, I'm definitely having my bikini line doing. Right — I'm busy, places to go, people to see.
    xx

FROM   Jason GrangerRM
TO   Holly

... and somewhere in London there's a bunch of very scared wax strips making their way to the front of the queue.
    xxx

WEDNESDAY

Subject: Your house

FROM   Mum and Dad
TO   Holly

Holly
  Morning dear, it's such a shame you've decided to rent out your house before our reunion, but I've come up with a solution. Just rent it out initially on a short-let for about a month, your father can fly over next week and help you with interviewing potential renters. Then we can still hold our get-together at your place in June?
  Knowing how little time there is to get going I've put an advertisement on a couple of websites about it, and given them your phone number. I'll book your dad's flight now.
  Love Mum
  x

FROM   Holly
TO   Mum and Dad

Mum
  Just read your email.
  Thank you for being so concerned — and helpful, I've already begun to get a stream of calls to my mobile.
  But don't book Dad a flight! I can interview people myself and also having a 1 month let will mean the house is empty for a couple of weeks before you come, which is a waste of money.
  Regards Holly

Subject: REF: Acc 20000389384374 Holly Rivers

FROM   Southern Debt Management Services
TO   Holly

REF: Acc 20000389384374 Holly Denham
  Dear Holly Denham
  Thank you for your recent email. Our records have now been updated with your new surname: Denham.

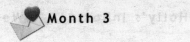

You will also be receiving confirmation via post.
Yours sincerely
Douglass Granger, Senior Collections Officer

Subject: Butt

FROM Aisha
TO Holly

Nice backside.

FROM Holly
TO Aisha

Why thank you Aish and you have a nice backside yourself.

FROM Aisha
TO Holly

Not yours — James'.

FROM Holly
TO Aisha

— ?

FROM Aisha
TO Holly

Nice strong hands too, I like hands.

FROM Holly
TO Aisha

So glad.

FROM Aisha
TO Holly

Like the uniform too. Soldier boys, hmmmmmm.

FROM Holly
TO Aisha

That was Ralph in the uniform, James was the guy I was talking to (although I am kind of grateful you haven't fantasized about him).

FROM Aisha
TO Holly

I know which one he was — I was joking about the uniform. James was the sexy one in the suit, very nice, very public school, confident rugby type, good suit.

Subject: Small favour

FROM Charlie Denham
TO Holly

So come on, I'm really stuck here and you know I wouldn't ask you if there was anyone else I could turn to? This is your brother asking you for a small favour.
   Charlie

FROM Holly
TO Charlie Denham

Small favour? You've got a club which is going to be full of rubber-dressed sex addicts (all probably on crack) doing goodness knows what, nasty, yuk, and you want my name on the front door????

FROM Charlie Denham
TO Holly

— yes.

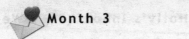

FROM   Holly
TO   Charlie Denham

NO!!!!

Subject: Hi

FROM   Pregnant Pam
TO   Holly

I just puked on my foot.
   Pam x

Subject: It's not a problem

FROM   Mum and Dad
TO   Holly

Hi
You don't need to sign off with 'Regards' darling, just 'Love Holly'
will do.
   Also it's a bit late, I'll email your father's details.
   Mum

FROM   Holly
TO   Mum and Dad

I know Mum — I was busy and wasn't looking what I was writing.
   What details?

FROM   Mum and Dad
TO   Holly

Holly
   His flight details of course and I do hope you make more of an
effort to watch what you're typing when you are writing to other
banks.
   Mum

FROM   Holly
TO   Mum and Dad

I don't write to other banks Mum — I'm not sure what you think I do here??

Also why have you got Dad coming here, this is utter madness, can you ask me first before organising things???

FROM   Mum and Dad
TO   Holly

He's coming to help you dear, to meet these people who wish to live in your house for the next month. It's very important you get the right type of people, I've read you can make yourself some good money if you choose wisely for short lets.

Anyway you clearly can't organise things yourself, otherwise you wouldn't have moved into a flat before renting out your house. Would you?
Mum

Subject: Service

FROM   Ralph Tooms
TO   Holly

Holly, can I get something from the shops for you please?
Ralph

FROM   Holly
TO   Ralph Tooms

No, but thank you.
Holly

FROM   Ralph Tooms
TO   Holly

Do you want me to report at your desk at 4pm sharp?

FROM Holly
TO Ralph Tooms

NOT Now Ralph I'm busy.

Subject: Organising

FROM Holly
TO Mum and Dad

Mum you really are unbelievable!!!!!!

FROM Mum and Dad
TO Holly

Thank you darling, so are you.
  xxx Mum
  PS Do make sure you have clean sheets on his bed and it would be nice of you to pick him up from the airport.

Subject: Service

FROM Holly
TO Ralph Tooms

Ralph, you're a good boy, sorry if I sounded mean. Just having a nightmare day.
  Holly

Subject: Your news

FROM Holly
TO Pregnant Pam

Hi Pam
  Sorry to hear about the sick. Do get better soon.
  Holly
  xx

Subject: Club

FROM   Charlie Denham
TO   Holly

So ?

Subject: Heeeeeeeeeelp

FROM   Holly
TO   Jason GrangerRM

Jason tell me your day is going as badly as mine, I feel I'm being attacked by mad people from every direction???

Subject: JASON!!

FROM   Holly
TO   Jason GrangerRM

WHERE ARE YOU???!!!!!!

Subject: Any jobs going?

FROM   Charlie Denham
TO   Holly

Any jobs going? I mean I'll be out of work soon, without a nightclub to build, not forgetting the huge debt I'll be in.
  Charlie x
  PS I've done you lots of favours.

FROM   Holly
TO   Charlie Denham

Name one!

FROM Charlie Denham
TO Holly

Toby.

Subject: You alright?

FROM Patricia Gillot
TO Holly

You don't look good?

FROM Holly
TO Patricia Gillot

Just seen a ghost.
  xxx

Subject: ???

FROM Jason GrangerRM
TO Holly; Aisha

To be honest Holly-I'd-prefer-to-let-a-sex-mad-nympho-meet-my-boyfriend-than-Jason, my afternoon hasn't been that good either.

FROM Holly
TO Aisha; Jason GrangerRM

Sorry Jason, but Aisha if you're there, please explain to Jason, you were just meant to be picking up your belt last night, that's all.

FROM Aisha
TO Holly; Jason GrangerRM

Grrrrrrrrrr

FROM Jason GrangerRM
TO Holly; Aisha

Is it a gay thing Holly? Is that it?

FROM   Holly
TO   Jason GrangerRM; Aisha

Of course, yes, that's exactly it.
    Stop being nasty, I've had a rotten day.

FROM   Aisha
TO   Holly; Jason GrangerRM

Grrrrrrr

FROM   Jason GrangerRM
TO   Holly; Aisha

Not being nasty, only teasing.
    Sorry, got to break off this banter for a moment ... Aisha do you want to join the conversation or are you going to continue to type grrrrrrrrrrrrr — hmm?

FROM   Aisha
TO   Holly; Jason GrangerRM

Grrrrrrrrrr

FROM   Holly
TO   Jason GrangerRM; Aisha

What's wrong with her?

FROM   Jason GrangerRM
TO   Holly; Aisha

She's been on heat all day, it's been like having a ravenous wolf sitting next to you, I'm considering sending her home before she attacks someone.
    What was James like then?

FROM   Aisha
TO   Jason GrangerRM; Holly

Nice, good butt.
    Yeah, I'd do him.
    Can I go home now Jason, if you don't let me I'll show you my tits?

FROM Jason GrangerRM
TO Holly; Aisha

Go!

THURSDAY

Subject: Monday's meeting

FROM Judy Perkins
TO Holly; Patricia Gillot

Dear Patricia & Holly
I thought our meeting on Monday night was very productive and I've been liaising with the HR department, Shella and management to finalise the best course of action.
I've taken on board your views in this matter and will be able to give you a clearer idea of who will be in charge of the conference within the next few days.
Do understand it won't ultimately be my decision.
Judy

Subject: Job Application

FROM Holly
TO ChezGerardCoventGarden

Dear Sir or Madam
Although having no recent waiting experience as you can see from my CV, I had a regular job as a waitress during the holidays whilst at university.
I am keen, presentable, enthusiastic, willing and feel this is an area where I could really excel.
Kindest regards
Holly Denham

Subject: Miss you

FROM   Holly
TO   Jennie Pithwait

Miss you.
   x

Subject: Your club

FROM   Holly
TO   Charlie Denham

OK, fine, you can put my name on the licence, but not because of any favour I owe you, just because you're my brother and I love you, even though you're a selfish git most of the time.
   x
   What do I need to do then?

FROM   Charlie Denham
TO   Holly

Holly, you're the best, you've saved my bacon.
   OK, all you need to do is answer a few questions on licensing laws.

FROM   Holly
TO   Charlie Denham

— OK.

FROM   Charlie Denham
TO   Holly

In court.

FROM   Holly
TO   Charlie Denham

Fine.

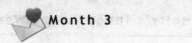

FROM   Charlie Denham
TO   Holly

Tomorrow.

FROM   Holly
TO   Charlie Denham

Oh please Charlie no!!

FROM   Charlie Denham
TO   Holly

Go on, you said you would help me.

FROM   Holly
TO   Charlie Denham

Yes Charlie,
*   next week — help you, next month — help you.*
*   I'm going to Spain tomorrow night??*

FROM   Charlie Denham
TO   Holly

There's no point helping next month, the court date is tomorrow, go on please? If you don't, there'll be a lot of very sad perverts with nowhere to go?

Subject: What about that then

FROM   Patricia Gillot
TO   Holly

You read Judy's email? 'Not my decision' — she says, don't like the sound of that, I reckon we'll have Shella sitting down here next week?

FROM   Holly
TO   Patricia Gillot

I think I can feel an illness coming on.

FROM   Patricia Gillot
TO   Holly

No you don't, if she's here, you're here, I'm not sitting with her alone!

FROM   Holly
TO   Patricia Gillot

I think it's glandular.

FROM   Patricia Gillot
TO   Holly

You're not sick.

FROM   Holly
TO   Patricia Gillot

Feel my forehead, it's very hot.

FROM   Patricia Gillot
TO   Holly

You'll feel my hand slapping your cheek in a second.

Subject: Not that cheek

FROM   Patricia Gillot
TO   Holly

I bet the clients would like it though. Where've you been on your holidays this morning then, anywhere nice?

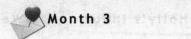

FROM Holly
TO Patricia Gillot

Tanning shop, Kilburn High Rd.

FROM Patricia Gillot
TO Holly

So what about Shella then?

FROM Holly
TO Patricia Gillot

I don't know, we'll have to watch our emails for a start. We need some kind of code.

FROM Patricia Gillot
TO Holly

*Yeah, if you see me raise my arm and bring it down on the back of her head — it means she's p*ssing me off.*

FROM Holly
TO Patricia Gillot

Like it.
x
   Anyway I don't think there's enough room not with my big feet and is it just me or are all the shops full of baby clothes? NOTHING FITS. EVER.

Subject: Shoes

FROM Holly
TO Jason GrangerRM

Got no shoes. ☹

FROM Jason GrangerRM
TO Holly

— So?

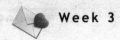

FROM   Holly
TO   Jason GrangerRM

Got no shoes. ☹

FROM   Jason GrangerRM
TO   Holly

Forget it.

FROM   Holly
TO   Jason GrangerRM

I hate it! None of them ever fit and I end up crying. ☹

FROM   Jason GrangerRM
TO   Holly

I don't like the looks I get when I'm searching for size nines. They think they're for me.

FROM   Holly
TO   Jason GrangerRM

I AM NOT A SIZE 9!

FROM   Jason GrangerRM
TO   Holly

OK, eight and a half, I'm still not doing it.
    I'll wait outside for you.

FROM   Holly
TO   Jason GrangerRM

☺

FROM   Jason GrangerRM
TO   Holly

OUTSIDE ONLY!

FROM   Holly
TO   Jason GrangerRM

☹

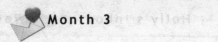

FROM Jason GrangerRM
TO Holly

Got to go, there's a pigeon on table five, the daft thing flew in and went straight for the restaurant, and of course pigeon catching is under my job description.

Subject: Drinks

FROM James Lawrence
TO Holly

Everyone from my floor is going for drinks later, you coming?

FROM Holly
TO James Lawrence

Would love to, but I can't.

FROM James Lawrence
TO Holly

Why not?

FROM Holly
TO James Lawrence

Studying.
*   I'll tell you about it another time.*

FROM James Lawrence
TO Holly

Sounds good. OK I'll catch you tomorrow.
*   J*
*   Hey, also I think your friend Toby is a sexist dork, a complete knob.*

FROM Holly
TO James Lawrence

Why? What's he done?

FROM James Lawrence
TO   Holly

Just saying things about you lot on reception. Don't worry, I had a word with him.

Subject: Gala Dinner

FROM Judy Perkins
TO   Holly; Patricia Gillot; Dave Otto; Ralph Tooms; Samantha Graham; Kristan

Dear all,
   The Gala dinner at the Dorchester to commemorate our UK office's 25 years in operation will soon be upon us, and I still haven't had your replies to who will be bringing a partner with them. I have put all your names down as attending because as you know it is an essential night in this year's calendar and I expect a full attendance from my department.
   So names please people, I need to know by Monday latest to ensure they're booked in.
   Yours
   Judy

FRIDAY

Subject: Spain

FROM Holly
TO   James Lawrence

Hi Babe
   Hope you had a good night last night and you're not feeling too rough.
   I'm packed and looking forward to Spain (although next time let's go somewhere cooler, where I can wear more clothes!!).
   Holly

Subject: Candles

FROM   Alice and Matt
TO   Holly

Hi Holly
*   Know anywhere I can buy candles from?*

FROM   Holly
TO   Alice and Matt

Spain (I don't think they're illegal Alice).

Subject: Battle plan

FROM   Jason GrangerRM
TO   Holly

How are you looking?

FROM   Holly
TO   Jason GrangerRM

In clothes — as good as I get.
*   Bikinis are another matter — the very thought is giving me goose-*
bumps.

FROM   Jason GrangerRM
TO   Holly

Get rid of the goose bumps, they're not helpful.
*   Right let's go through our check list:*
*   Legs ...*

FROM   Holly
TO   Jason GrangerRM

Waxed!

FROM Jason GrangerRM
TO   Holly

Eyebrows ...

FROM Holly
TO   Jason GrangerRM

Waxed!

FROM Jason GrangerRM
TO   Holly

Pits ...

FROM Holly
TO   Jason GrangerRM

Waxed!

FROM Jason GrangerRM
TO   Holly

Front bottom?

FROM Holly
TO   Jason GrangerRM

Waxed.

FROM Jason GrangerRM
TO   Holly

Good, Brazilian?

FROM Holly
TO   Jason GrangerRM

No — Hollywood, I thought — in for a penny in for a pound.

Subject: Witches

FROM Alice and Matt
TO Holly

I know you can buy candles here, but I need a lot of them — for my wicker witch nights.

I'm getting really into it, it's so enlightening Holly, really. I think you'd make a great witch, what d'you think?

xxx

FROM Holly
TO Alice and Matt

I think I have too many problems already — without being called a witch.

But I love you.

(not to be rude)

xxx

Look on the web for cheap candles.

Subject: Battle plan

FROM Holly
TO Jason GrangerRM

Where've we got to? Is that it?

FROM Jason GrangerRM
TO Holly

Only just started:

Feet ...

FROM Holly
TO Jason GrangerRM

Pedicured.

FROM Jason GrangerRM
TO Holly

Hands?

FROM   Holly
TO   Jason GrangerRM

Manicured.

FROM   Jason GrangerRM
TO   Holly

Back garden ...

FROM   Holly
TO   Jason GrangerRM

Cut the lawn and pruned the bushes.

FROM   Jason GrangerRM
TO   Holly

Good girl.
  (although I have no idea what you mean)
  Sunbed?

FROM   Holly
TO   Jason GrangerRM

Full body — spray tan, also massage, facial and cellulite buster.

FROM   Jason GrangerRM
TO   Holly

Like it.

Subject: Witches

FROM   Alice and Matt
TO   Holly

*Found a website just for witches and they sell everything I need, also
you get points every time you buy!*
  xxx
  Thanks for that.
  Alice

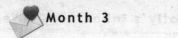

FROM   Holly
TO   Alice and Matt

That's great.
    Just a thought, when you say points — is it like air-miles?
    Because I can see that will be very useful. Instead of casting a spell from far away, you can go by broom, make sure it includes — broom tax?
    Holly

FROM   Alice and Matt
TO   Holly

You're not funny.

Subject: Battle plan

FROM   Jason GrangerRM
TO   Holly

What about phase two?

FROM   Holly
TO   Jason GrangerRM

Yes, clothing, I kind of ran out of money after phase one, so I'm mixing and matching ...
    Holly
    By the way, do you think my family are a little strange?

FROM   Jason GrangerRM
TO   Holly

Strange isn't the word. Phase three?

Subject: How's work

FROM   Holly
TO   James Lawrence

Didn't see you come through, are you in yet?

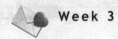

Subject: Phase three

FROM Holly
TO   Jason GrangerRM

Phase three???? Phase three??
   WHAT THE HELL IS PHASE THREE???
   Don't tell me I forgot one?

FROM Jason GrangerRM
TO   Holly

It's where you pretend that you completely forgot about the trip all together!!!!

FROM Holly
TO   Jason GrangerRM

Jason,
   Over the last couple of days I've been pushed, punched, plucked and preened. I've been sprayed, dyed, sponged and scented.
   More behind the scenes work has been carried out on this body than even my Mini, and that, I've discovered, used to be two different cars.
   I'm ready to go and I look good, I know this because Ralph keeps asking for orders ... so don't tell me I have to pretend I'd forgotten about it all, because I don't want to! I want to look forward to it. (Besides which it will never wash, I'll be lucky if he recognises me.)
   Agggh, sorry, it's all just a bit much, on top of all this I'm now the head dom at a fetish club, and I've still not heard from James.
   Holly
   PS I've emailed him already, twice and mentioned wanting to wear more clothes.
   PPS Don't bother saying anything, I know it wasn't a good move.
   PPPS I hate playing games anyway, you know that.

Subject: Jennie

FROM Holly
TO Jennie Pithwait

Are we still friends? I miss you???

FROM Jennie Pithwait
TO Holly

Sorry?
   Holly, I don't know what you mean, we've always been friends, there's no problem with me.
   Jennie

FROM Holly
TO Jennie Pithwait

Oh good! Have a great weekend then.
   Holly
   xxx

Subject: Spain

FROM Granny
TO Holly

Holly
   Would you like me to register your name with some more flight companies? I'm looking through them now and will get some more over to you in a jiffy.
   xxxx
   Love Granny

FROM Holly
TO Granny

Granny
   Please don't, I really have so many now, thank you so much.
   Are you still on meagre rations, since you entertained the troops?
   Holly

FROM   Granny
TO   Holly

Holly
*   I wasn't 'entertaining the troops' dear, I was stripping for the troops. It was so much fun, I danced and I danced, it was the first time I've really enjoyed myself here.*
*   They haven't put me on meagre rations, they've cut me off totally. I'm not a child, I don't like being treated like one.*
*   From your Granny*
*   x*

Subject: Spain

FROM   Jennie Pithwait
TO   Holly

I hear you're off to Spain — enjoy it won't you.
*   Jennie*

Subject: Afternoon

FROM   Jason GrangerRM
TO   Holly

Any news from him yet?

FROM   Holly
TO   Jason GrangerRM

Not a thing, I want some attention, there's no point looking this good if you don't have any.

FROM   Jason GrangerRM
TO   Holly

I could tell you something funny to cheer you up?

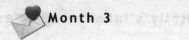

FROM   Holly
TO   Jason GrangerRM

Yes please do, I'm so bored. Even bossing Ralph around is becoming tedious, Trish had him standing facing the wall for a while, until Judy came by and told him off (he's meant to be checking passes).

FROM   Jason GrangerRM
TO   Holly

Knock knock?

Subject: Sorry I'm late

FROM   James Lawrence
TO   Holly

Terrible hangover, feel like crap. You look fantastic.

FROM   Holly
TO   James Lawrence

Thanks.

FROM   James Lawrence
TO   Holly

I got some gifts for your family. Got your old man some whisky.

FROM   Holly
TO   James Lawrence

That's nice, I thought we'd agreed we weren't seeing them.

Subject: Hey

FROM   Jason GrangerRM
TO   Holly

I said knock knock!

Subject: No, got that wrong ...

FROM   James Lawrence
TO   Holly

Got him some vintage champagne?

FROM   Holly
TO   James Lawrence

What?

FROM   James Lawrence
TO   Holly

You sound moody, so I thought that might swing it??

FROM   Holly
TO   James Lawrence

Sorry, not moody at all, I was just thinking about the whole you meeting the parents thing.
*   Very excited about Spain and it's very sweet of you to think about taking them presents, I'm just not sure.*
*   xxxx*
*   PS You still look good hung-over.*

FROM   James Lawrence
TO   Holly

Yeah, how good?

FROM   Holly
TO   James Lawrence

— Hot.

Subject: Hello??? IS ANYONE THERE???

FROM   Jason GrangerRM
TO   Holly

KNOCK KNOCK???

FROM   Holly
TO   Jason GrangerRM

James just arrived.
    What gets me is I spend two days making myself look perfect and he strolls in at ten to four with a hangover, not even bothering to shave and looks better now than he's ever done before.
    MEN HAVE IT EASY.
    Sorry, had to get that off my chest ... Who's there?
    PS Sorry if I sound self-obsessed, I really do definitely want to know who's there.
    xxx
    Sorry ...
    Who's there?
    AND he want's to see my family????
    SORRY, that's enough.
    Who is there?

FROM   Jason GrangerRM
TO   Holly

Who cares who's there?? (I was going to make it up as I went along anyway.)
    I think you should think long and hard about letting him meet any ANY of your family. EVER.
    xxx
    And that's meant in the nicest possible way.

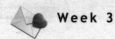

Subject: Am I hot enough to eat?

FROM　James Lawrence
TO　　Holly

Well?

FROM　Holly
TO　　James Lawrence

Don't push it Mr, you're late.

FROM　James Lawrence
TO　　Holly

I am, and I'm sorry, really really sorry.
　　James
　　PS Get your arse in that lift, I need an urgent meeting, Denham.

FROM　Holly
TO　　James Lawrence

Forget it.
　　You'll have to wait.
　　x

Subject: The problem is

FROM　Holly
TO　　Jason GrangerRM

He's just so rude, but ...
　　Anyway, back to what the choices are.
　　I've listed the pluses and minuses about surprising the family in Spain:

The Pluses
Great to surprise the family, also Mum would love James, and would get off my back about meeting men.

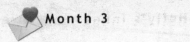

The Minuses
Matt and Alice could be in the middle of some weird snake hunt.
Mum is very difficult to handle.
   Alice and Matt could be in the middle of some weird snake hunt,
dressed as witches.
   The Guardia could be in the middle of taking Dad away for mass
producing babies.
   Granny could be in the middle of stripping again.
   I still haven't told James what I used to do for a living, he thinks
I've always worked in reception.
   Oh and he doesn't know I was once married.
   What d'you think?

FROM   Jason GrangerRM
TO   Holly

Do you think you love him?

FROM   Holly
TO   Jason GrangerRM

— Yes

FROM   Jason GrangerRM
TO   Holly

Then I would stay at home for the weekend, don't answer the phone,
preferably with a sheet over your head (he can go to Spain on his own
JUST IN CASE you bump into your family out there).
   xxx
   PS I think you've got to tell him the truth soon x
   PPS does your dad really mass produce babies?

FROM   Holly
TO   Jason GrangerRM

In picture form only.

FROM   Jason GrangerRM
TO   Holly

That's a relief, I thought your family had issues, but that takes the
biscuit even for you.

FROM   Holly
TO   Jason GrangerRM

Thanks. Why the sheet?

FROM   Jason GrangerRM
TO   Holly

Don't know, added to the image.
  x

SUNDAY

Subject: STOP

FROM   Jason GrangerRM
TO   Holly

I just got what I think was a drunken voicemail from you saying you were going to take him to surprise the family ... BAD BAD BAD idea, stop NOW. I have left four messages on your phone to stop you.

Having said that, if you don't check your emails till Monday, and you're now reading it on Monday, Hey sweetie, don't panic, it's not bad, it's all good and I'm sure he still loves you, nothing we can't sort out, don't worry xxx call me.

WEEK 4

MONDAY

Subject: HOLLY ARE YOU THERE?

FROM   Jason GrangerRM
TO   Holly

Did you get my email from the weekend????

Subject: My weekend

FROM   Aisha
TO   Holly; Jason GrangerRM

I've always loved Mondays, but usually because I'm still partying from the Saturday. This work thing really sucks.

Subject: Who we'll be working under

FROM   Patricia Gillot
TO   Holly

I spoke to Judy this morning.
    They'll be letting us know who's going to be in charge of organising the annual results later today.

Subject: Romantic weekend

FROM   Jason GrangerRM
TO   Holly; Aisha

Holly, if you're there can you email me, the suspense is killing me. (that and Aisha's perfume)

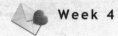
Subject: Romantic weekend

FROM Aisha
TO Holly; Jason RM

Yes Holly, please talk to us, Jason's sense of humour is killing me, he's so bloody funny.
    Aish

FROM Jason GrangerRM
TO Holly; Aisha

She's stunk the hotel out Holly.
    We've even had food returned in the restaurant because guests can taste cheap perfume on their eggs.

FROM Aisha
TO Holly; Jason GrangerRM

Oh, he's such a poof.
    I'm wearing no more than normal and it's bloody expensive too.
    Aish

Subject: Children Children

FROM Holly
TO Jason GrangerRM; Aisha

Just stop that now! Or you'll be split up and put on separate desks for the rest of the term.

FROM Jason GrangerRM
TO Holly; Aisha

We'll behave if you tell us about your weekend.
    Jason

FROM Holly
TO Jason GrangerRM; Aisha

So:

Saturday night I'd decided it was a fantastic idea, let's surprise the family, drive up there Sunday morning with James, introduce him to Mum.

The next day I barely knew where we were heading until we were half way to theirs — less than an hour away.

So when James got out to fill up the car with petrol, I got on the phone to Mum — told her not to mention anything work-related or husband-related and that's about all I could get out before he got back in.

FROM Jason GrangerRM
TO Holly; Aisha

Hold on, what happened on Saturday?

FROM Holly
TO Jason GrangerRM; Aisha

The trip up to that point had gone well. Stayed in a great hotel Friday and Saturday and I'd discovered his legs. Did I tell you his legs are lovely and hairy and tanned and he looks so good in shorts?

Subject: Your lot

FROM Patricia Gillot
TO Holly

Don't be skiving now darlin, you can do this lot.

Subject: Things in shorts

FROM Jason GrangerRM
TO Holly; Aisha

No you didn't tell us, I think you should.

FROM   Holly
TO   Jason GrangerRM; Aisha

Did I tell you when he came out of the shower in one of those soft white hotel towels — I threw myself back on the bed and had to cover my head with my book, because I was giggling like a school girl?

Did I tell you he uses one of those old shaving brushes when he shaves? He smells of Dunhill shaving soap and hair wax and it's intoxicating. Did I tell you this?

FROM   Aisha
TO   Holly; Jason GrangerRM

Am I reading a Mills and Boon?

FROM   Holly
TO   Aisha; Jason GrangerRM

Also that he crawled forward on the bed, took away my book and held my hands to the covers while kissing my neck?

FROM   Aisha
TO   Holly; Jason GrangerRM

I am, I'm reading Mills and Boon, can you spice it up a bit Holly, tell me how big his stiff cock was?

FROM   Jason GrangerRM
TO   Holly; Aisha

Ignore her Holly, this is quite enough for my pure mind.

FROM   Holly
TO   Jason GrangerRM; Aisha

Thank you Jason!!

FROM   Jason GrangerRM
TO   Holly; Aisha

So his balls, small and tight, or big and dangly?

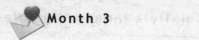

Subject: Laughing

FROM Patricia Gillot
TO Holly

Something funny?

FROM Holly
TO Patricia Gillot

Just booking this room and forgot to add the food.

FROM Patricia Gillot
TO Holly

I can imagine how funny that must be.
Liar.
x

Subject: More

FROM Holly
TO Jason GrangerRM; Aisha

I'm trying to write, but we're quite busy here.
x

Subject: Getting the sack

FROM Jason GrangerRM
TO Holly; Aisha

You were talking about his balls, come on.

FROM Holly
TO Jason GrangerRM; Aisha

Did I call anyone over the weekend?

FROM   Jason GrangerRM
TO   Holly; Aisha

You did, and sent a text saying 'remind me about this on Monday'.

FROM   Aisha
TO   Holly; Jason GrangerRM

OH, I just got Jason's joke about getting the sack, good, funny.

FROM   Jason GrangerRM
TO   Holly; Aisha

She's that slow with customers too.

FROM   Aisha
TO   Holly; Jason GrangerRM

I don't know if you called me Holly, although I got a call from someone on my answer-phone that sounded like a mobile had gone off in their pocket while they were walking, either that or they were having really slow dull repetitive sex — that wasn't you was it?

FROM   Holly
TO   Aisha; Jason GrangerRM

No, that wasn't me.

On the way out there, we'd sat in Business class, had champagne, had fab food.

He was joking around a lot which took my mind off the journey, — including a bit where we went through cloud and I thought the plane was on fire — until he pointed out it was the flashing red light under the wing colouring the white cloud and so everything was fine.

I had a lovely day by the hotel pool reading a book on the Saturday — while he was out at meetings, but by the time we were flying back I just felt weird.

Mum and Dad were OK, Alice and Matt couldn't make it, they were off up in Madrid buying tadpoles or lizards or something, and we popped by after to surprise Granny, who was so happy to see me, amazingly tactful, and wearing clothes.

So really I should be happy.

FROM Jason GrangerRM
TO Holly; Aisha

So nothing drastically went wrong then????

FROM Holly
TO Aisha; Jason GrangerRM

You said I should come clean with him Jason.
So I told him SOME things when I realised nothing was fitting.
After the meal with my parents, I took him to one side and told him that ... I used to be married (but that I don't like talking about it) and that my parents still thought I owned a big house.
I expected him to be shocked, but he didn't seem to mind.
He was his usual self, joking, but maybe a bit distant.
Could have been his work, maybe he just had a lot on his mind with deals going on or something.
Maybe he was tired.

FROM Jason GrangerRM
TO Holly; Aisha

Jekyll and Hyde, it's nothing, that's a typical Gemini trait.
Don't panic, just give him some space.
You haven't emailed him yet have you?

FROM Holly
TO Jason GrangerRM; Aisha

— No

FROM Jason GrangerRM
TO Holly; Aisha

Or called him?

FROM Holly
TO Jason GrangerRM; Aisha

Yes, didn't answer.

Subject: Lunch

FROM   Holly
TO   Jason GrangerRM; Aisha

Went to lunch, back. So what d'you think?

FROM   Aisha
TO   Holly; Jason GrangerRM

Honey, stuff him, I thought he was a jerk anyway and who lives with their mum at that age?

FROM   Holly
TO   Aisha; Jason GrangerRM

Not sure that's what I want to hear, but thanks.
   (He doesn't anyway — his house is being renovated.)

FROM   Jason GrangerRM
TO   Holly; Aisha

Don't worry, it's been half a day!!! He's probably still asleep!

Subject: Help

FROM   Patricia Gillot
TO   Holly

Can I get a hand here, are you going to help me or just type??? (Don't mean to be bossy, but it's getting busy.)

FROM   Holly
TO   Patricia Gillot

Sorry, I'll keep up
   xx

Subject: A wonderful day

FROM   Jennie Pithwait
TO   Holly

How was your weekend? I do hope it all went well.
   x

Subject: Jennie

FROM   Holly
TO   Jason GrangerRM; Aisha

I feel sick, I think Jennie knows something, she knows something's up with him. He must have said something upstairs.
   She just wrote 'how was your weekend? I do hope it all went well'.

FROM   Jason GrangerRM
TO   Holly; Aisha

What an evil bitch!
   How could she say these horrible disgusting things to you, wishing you well, that's just heartless!
   You're over-analysing everything. Get on and do some work and it'll all be fine.
   x

Subject: Surprise

FROM   Mum and Dad
TO   Holly

Holly
   What a wonderful surprise!
   It was so nice to see you and James yesterday. You looked so happy together, he's a great catch, very charming.
   I look forward to being invited to meet his parents, just give me a date and I'll pop it into my calendar.
   We love you so much Holly!
   Mum

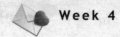

Subject: You're right

FROM　Holly
TO　　Jason GrangerRM

You're totally right, I think I was just being paranoid.
　　It's amazing how you can look at things that were said — and read them a hundred different ways.
　　Holly

TUESDAY

Subject: Your Spanish surprise

FROM　Granny
TO　　Holly

Holly
　　Lovely to see you and your new man.
　　Will you pass on my thanks for making an old woman very happy, by bringing you out here. What a lovely treat for me. Keep bringing me these young men.
　　All my love Granny

Subject: Annual results

FROM　Roger Lipton
TO　　Judy Perkins; Holly; Patricia Gillot; Ralph Tooms; Dave Otto; Samantha Smith

To: Facilities Department
　　Thank you for attending all the meetings concerning the organisation of the Annual Results.
　　We are very excited to be hosting this event in our UK office and it is essential that we chose someone to organise it who is committed, experienced, passionate and driven.
　　It is therefore our pleasure to confirm that Shella Hamilton-Jones

is taking charge of the conference, with full support from the facilities department.

Please ensure you offer her all the help and assistance she requires from you.

Yours sincerely, Roger

Subject: Leaving

FROM Patricia Gillot
TO Holly

That's it, I'm packing me bags.

FROM Holly
TO Patricia Gillot

Shella wont be that bad, surely. When we begin working with her, we'll probably all end up as friends.

Subject: My team

FROM Shella Hamilton-Jones
TO Holly; Patricia Gillot; Ralph Tooms; Samantha Smith;
Dave Otto

Dear Team

I am looking forward to getting my teeth stuck into this confer-ence, as I am sure you all are, however I will be very busy over the coming weeks.

If you have any suggestions or would like to ask me questions then please don't call, I have set up a new email account: ShellasAnnual Results@Huerstwright.com.

Commitment is important, team work essential; it's for the good of the company and at the end of it you can feel you've contributed to a wonderful event.

When I ask for assistance, I will not be pleased if I hear 'it's not my job' or 'that's outside my normal working hours'.

It's going to be very busy, so if you're one of those employees who is constantly taking time off all I can say just one thing: Shella will be watching!

Thanks again, and I look forward to working with my new energetic and helpful team.
Shella

Subject: Nice

FROM   Patricia Gillot
TO   Holly

I think that answers your question.

FROM   Holly
TO   Patricia Gillot

We're part of Shella's team, I'm thrilled.
  'Shella will be watching'?
  I wonder where the Big Brother cameras are hidden.
  You know she's probably already bugged us?

FROM   Patricia Gillot
TO   Holly

Well that's pointless because we're not allowed to talk.
  SHELLA STINKS, SHELLA STINKS, SHELLA STINKS.

FROM   Holly
TO   Patricia Gillot

Unless she means they've given her access to our emails???

FROM   Patricia Gillot
TO   Holly

Probably.

FROM   Holly
TO   Patricia Gillot

Oh God, I'd die if anyone could read my emails!

Subject: James

FROM   Jason GrangerRM
TO   Holly

Has he called yet?

FROM   Holly
TO   Jason GrangerRM

NO.

Subject: Toby

FROM   Patricia Gillot
TO   Holly

Come on then??

FROM   Holly
TO   Patricia Gillot

What?

FROM   Patricia Gillot
TO   Holly

You went to the same school?

FROM   Holly
TO   Patricia Gillot

Yes.

Subject: Fetish Queen

FROM   Charlie Denham
TO   Holly

Thanks for Friday, I owe you.
   So we're all pushing ahead, the big opening.
   Also Rubber Ron thinks you should have a stage name.
   Charlie

FROM   Holly
TO   Charlie Denham

Charlie
   Please don't put stupid things in the subject boxes like 'fetish queen'?? If someone was going through my emails looking for anything suspicious, this would stand out.
   Also — stage name?? What?

Subject: James

FROM   Jason GrangerRM
TO   Holly

Has he come in yet?

FROM   Holly
TO   Jason GrangerRM

No — got my eyes glued to the door.

Subject: Company restructuring and necessary
   redundancies

FROM   Charlie Denham
TO   Holly

Good Golly — it's Rubber Holly?
   OR
   I'll be Frank — it's Holly Spank?
   What d'you think?

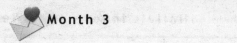

FROM Holly
TO Charlie Denham

I think you should stop trying to wind me up and do something constructive.

FROM Charlie Denham
TO Holly

Waiting for deliveries to show up. Also I've posted you some forms, just sign them and post them back.
    Cheers
    Charlie

Subject: Toby

FROM Patricia Gillot
TO Holly

So, you were Toby's girlfriend at school and now he's working here.

FROM Holly
TO Patricia Gillot

Yes, what's all that noise?

FROM Patricia Gillot
TO Holly

May Day protesters.
    So how long hadn't you seen him for?

FROM Holly
TO Patricia Gillot

12 years.

FROM Patricia Gillot
TO Holly

So what did you say when you first laid eyes on him here?

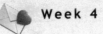
Subject: V exciting!

FROM   Jason GrangerRM
TO   Holly

BL**DY HELL!!! You should see this!

FROM   Holly
TO   Jason GrangerRM

WHAT???

FROM   Jason GrangerRM
TO   Holly

Naked male protesters — and he got it to spin.

FROM   Holly
TO   Jason GrangerRM

That's nice.

FROM   Jason GrangerRM
TO   Holly

Like a helicopter!

Subject: James

FROM   Holly
TO   Jason GrangerRM

Getting all stressed and confused.
*   All that shouting outside isn't helping. Grrrrrr.*
*   Waiting for him to arrive. Why isn't he here yet?*

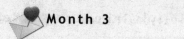

Subject: Toby

FROM Patricia Gillot
TO Holly

Come on darlin, you've left me hanging here. What did you say to him when you saw him after all that time?

FROM Holly
TO Patricia Gillot

I just told him to get lost. I don't want to think about Toby now, sorry Trish, will tell you one day.
  xx

Subject: I hate this

FROM Holly
TO Jason GrangerRM

Spent the night checking my phone every five minutes to make sure I hadn't missed any calls. Then when the phone did ring, it was Alice from Spain. Don't think I was very friendly.

FROM Jason GrangerRM
TO Holly

xx

FROM Holly
TO Jason GrangerRM

This is it!! Taxi, outside, he's paying for it.

FROM Jason GrangerRM
TO Holly

Don't bother looking up!!

FROM　Holly
TO　Jason GrangerRM

He's coming.

FROM　Jason GrangerRM
TO　Holly

Change of plan, LOOK, SMILE AND FLICK HAIR BACK.

Subject: What's happening?

FROM　Jason GrangerRM
TO　Holly

Tell me?? Is he still there?

FROM　Holly
TO　Jason GrangerRM

I saw a taxi pull up outside and I thought I could see him through the window, but we've got shaded glass, so it's not always easy to tell. But it was him.

He got out.

I tried to get myself looking good, I was going to shout over to Trish but she was dealing with clients who'd just arrived.

He opened the door at the end and I saw his face, but couldn't tell what his expression was, kind of just busy.

I looked down as he began walking towards us.

My heart was going so fast, I wanted to look nonchalant or even sexy, but I could feel the colour draining from my face and if he had talked to me, my voice would have been all squeaky because one of the clients decided she wanted to have her pass done by me and I hit some kind of top C when I spoke.

By the time I'd looked down to tear off the paper and fit it into the plastic wallet, he'd passed!!!!

Hugely frustrating, I hate this, I hate feeling like this.

Why didn't he stop??

FROM Jason GrangerRM
TO Holly

He's really late, what with the May Day thing, probably in trouble with his boss, got stuck in traffic.

Also he might have thought your relationship is so secure now that he doesn't have to try so hard?

There could be plenty of reasons. I thought you two were still trying to keep it a bit of a secret still anyway?

FROM Holly
TO Jason GrangerRM

I don't care about secrets any more.

I just want him to come over and hug me, take me to one side and show some love and tenderness, even a kiss on the cheek would do. Tell me that he's sorry he hasn't been able to call but he's been thinking about me constantly. Something like that.

FROM Jason GrangerRM
TO Holly

I wish I could tell you something to cheer you up.

Aisha's been working well today, handling lots on her own.

*I told her there wasn't any news from your man and she said to tell you — 'he's a d*ck anyway, she'd seen someone much better ... who looked like a cross between Clinton and Tyson'.*

Thought you might like that.

FROM Holly
TO Jason GrangerRM

How — how is that possible?

Subject: Our time together in Spain

FROM　Holly
TO　　James Lawrence

Hi James
　　Great holiday, lots of fun, thanks.
　　It's good knowing someone who you can have a laugh with, as well
as other stuff ... (talking of which ... I had a sexy delivery ... from
that shop you talked about ...) ☺
　　Just spoke to Judy, who asked me which table I wanted to sit on
for the Gala Dinner etc. I heard you've got a table for the boys and
are excluding wives and girlfriends etc, so I understand if that's the
case, but I've got to let her know today.
　　Holly xx

Subject: I emailed him

FROM　Holly
TO　　Jason GrangerRM

I sent him an email, tried to sound sexy and cool.
　　Regretting it now, could try recalling it. Won't bother.
　　I want to go home.
　　Now.
　　Wish you were here, wish we were sitting out in the sun,
somewhere abroad, on a beach, please don't email me back and say
I shouldn't have written to him. In fact, please don't email me back,
I'm going to sit on the internet now and look at holiday sites.
　　xxx
　　Wish you were here.

WEDNESDAY

Subject: Morning

FROM Jason GrangerRM
TO Holly

Morning,
How are you feeling?

FROM Holly
TO Jason GrangerRM

I was glaring at the phone last night for hours and hours before it finally rang.

I didn't see him pass for the rest of the day yesterday, so there was also a chance he was under a lot of pressure at work, working hard up in the office till very late. It's amazing how you begin analysing every minute detail.

So I had it stuck in my head that he was going to call me in the evening, but got stuck with loads of work that night in the office and horror upon horrors his mobile had run out of charge, or fallen out of the window etc.

I was going to call it from an anonymous number just to see if it rang.

I then started thinking he probably isn't calling me because he thinks I mentioned being married in the past for the sole reason of bringing up the subject of marriage and now he's run a mile.

I didn't hide my number, I just called his phone and it rang — it rang and I hung up before he even answered because otherwise he'd know it was me.

My phone then rang, and I knew it was him calling me back.

But it wasn't him it was you, hope I wasn't too short.

This morning I've tried thinking where I went wrong — maybe he didn't think I looked very attractive when we were in Spain.

I knocked my coffee off the seat on the plane back, and on to my lap and then later made a joke to security (because I was a bit drunk, and also noticing I wasn't getting any attention from James and thought saying anything could be better than getting no reaction from him at all) so I told the girl who patted my leg down that it

wasn't pee, then laughed and she just looked at James and then back at me, like, you've got a classy girl there haven't you?

But surely that's not right, I mean we've had lots of fun before, and he laughs with me at these kind of things and usually joins in. He probably didn't like me sitting by the pool in a jumper and thinks I'm insecure about my body (which I am) and he wants some ultra-confident girl. I do remember him noticing other women in the hotel who turned his eye.

It wasn't a jumper anyway it was like a baggy top. Maybe I shouldn't have giggled on the bed when he looked so hot in his towel, because then he knew how I wanted him so much and it probably ruined it. But surely you don't spend your whole life playing these games, surely you can one day say 'yes! I do fancy you, I do love you and I think you are fantastic and I want to give you my heart and soul because I trust you, love you and I want to spend the rest of my life with you and just stop playing these games!!!!!!!!'

I don't want to play these games any more Jason, I really don't, I've had enough, I don't want to, I'd prefer to be alone. Alone is fine, it's OK with me. I'll be alone.

Help

Subject: Just called him

FROM Holly
TO   Jason GrangerRM

Rang his mobile. It went to voicemail, so I didn't leave a message.

Then after a few minutes thought I should actually leave a message, so I rang again, and this time left one — 'just called to say Hi, but you're not there, so hope nothing's wrong and you're OK' — said something like that.

Nothing too clingy.

It's over isn't it?

FROM Jason GrangerRM
TO   Holly

That's fine, you checked whether he was OK, he could have been injured or something, you don't know do you?

Not clingy at all.

Jason

PS I wouldn't email him again though, unless it's abuse.

I could do it for you????

Subject: I'm here to help too

FROM Aisha
TO Holly

Sorry, not usually very good at this kind of thing sweetie.
How are you feeling?
Aish

FROM Holly
TO Aisha

OK.
What d'you think I should do?

FROM Aisha
TO Holly

I think you should forward on the below message to him:
You arrogant stuck-up shit bag, crap weazel, sleaze monkey, knob-jockey ...

FROM Holly
TO Aisha

Thanks.

FROM Aisha
TO Holly

Also ...
The only orgasms I had when we were going out, were ones when you weren't there.

FROM Holly
TO Aisha

xxxxx

Subject: Holly

FROM Patricia Gillot
TO Holly

You should check the mirror darlin.
  x

FROM Holly
TO Patricia Gillot

Got it, thanks for that.

Subject: Then

FROM Aisha
TO Holly

Big-arsed, small-dicked, hairy-backed, jam-rag-muncher.

FROM Holly
TO Aisha

Thanks Aish.

FROM Aisha
TO Holly

Then I'd make sure I had sex with all his friends. And told them how bad he was in bed. Then I'd stalk him for a while, and finally send him lots of pizzas he never ordered.

FROM Holly
TO Aisha

Does this ever work?

FROM   Aisha
TO   Holly

*When you're drunk, but when you sober up it's kind of worse.
   Sorry.*

Subject: Come on

FROM   Patricia Gillot
TO   Holly

*Come on there Holls, don't think about him and we'll get through
this bunch of idiots a lot quicker. Being busy will take your mind off
him and at the weekend I'll take you down the Island and you can
come out with me and Les, we'd love to have you over.*

FROM   Holly
TO   Patricia Gillot

*Thanks Trish, that sounds brilliant. I'll get myself together I promise,
I'll pull that smile out in a moment you'll see.
   xx*

FROM   Patricia Gillot
TO   Holly

*Course you will darlin, in a moment we'll have a word with Ralph,
get him on his knees barking at people when they come in.*

FROM   Holly
TO   Patricia Gillot

He'd like that.

FROM   Patricia Gillot
TO   Holly

*Course he would, I'll sit on his back and ride him around the coffee
table, you whip his arse with that ruler ...*

FROM Holly
TO   Patricia Gillot

I can picture it, what would we say to Shella if she decided then to do a spot check on us?

FROM Patricia Gillot
TO   Holly

We'd tell her it's what she asked for: team building. Ralph would agree with us (IF we let him take the horse's bit out of his mouth).

Subject: Nonce

FROM Patricia Gillot
TO   Holly

Can't believe he did that, gutless, that's what that was.

Subject: News

FROM Holly
TO   Jason GrangerRM; Aisha

Just saw him.

FROM Jason GrangerRM
TO   Holly

What happened?

FROM Holly
TO   Jason GrangerRM

He walked out. Then a few mins later he came back in, kept my eyes glued to him to make sure I didn't miss it, he didn't look though. It's over.

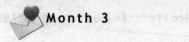

Subject: NO I'm not having it like that

FROM   Holly
TO   Jason GrangerRM

I'm not having that. I need to know.

FROM   Jason GrangerRM
TO   Holly

No, wait what are you doing?

FROM   Holly
TO   Jason GrangerRM

I'm going up there, back in a moment.

Subject: Important

FROM   Holly
TO   Patricia Gillot

Got to go somewhere, can you cover?
  x

FROM   Patricia Gillot
TO   Holly

— go!

THURSDAY

Subject: Any more news?

FROM　Jason GrangerRM
TO　　Holly

Have you seen him this morning??

FROM　Holly
TO　　Jason GrangerRM

No, oh, hold on.

Subject:　WONDERFUL WONDERFUL NEWS!!!

FROM　Pregnant Pam
TO　　Holly

The most amazing news in the world!!!
　IT'S A BOY!!!!
　xxxxxxx

FROM　Holly
TO　　Pregnant Pam

That's great, I'm so pleased for you, you must be very happy.
　Holly

FROM　Pregnant Pam
TO　　Holly

Really really happy, although I've already had his room done pink (I was sure I was having a girl).
　Still, you don't think it'll be too bad if I dress her up in lots of pink do you (just for the first few years)?

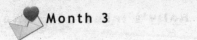

FROM Holly
TO Pregnant Pam

You said her — you mean him.

FROM Pregnant Pam
TO Holly

What?

FROM Holly
TO Pregnant Pam

Don't worry, but you'll have to paint it all blue now won't you?

FROM Pregnant Pam
TO Holly

No, there's no point. With any luck he could turn out gay???
   xxx
   I'm emailing everyone else now, talk later.

Subject: Him

FROM Holly
TO Jason GrangerRM

That was him came through. I was busy with some clients though.
   Holly

FROM Jason GrangerRM
TO Holly

Don't be going up there again, promise me ...

FROM Holly
TO Jason GrangerRM

Promise. I just stood there like a lemon last time, not going through that again.

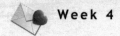

FROM Jason GrangerRM
TO   Holly

*People go up in lifts all the time without stepping out, no problem
there, you could have forgotten something.*
   xx

Subject: Time for baby clothes

FROM Pregnant Pam
TO   Holly

*You are totally right Holly, I need to dress him in blue, at least to
start with, so can you meet me later?*
   And we can go shopping together for baby clothes!!!!???

FROM Holly
TO   Pregnant Pam

I can't, sorry.

FROM Pregnant Pam
TO   Holly

Tomorrow then!

FROM Holly
TO   Pregnant Pam

I can't, really sorry Pam.
   x

FROM Pregnant Pam
TO   Holly

Why?

FROM   Holly
TO   Pregnant Pam

I just can't.
    Next week sometime.

FROM   Pregnant Pam
TO   Holly

Look, if you don't come shopping at the weekend, I'll come find you, I'll kick you out of his bed and if need be I'll drag you both with me!!!

FROM   Holly
TO   Pregnant Pam

Sorry it's very busy here, I can't chat.
    x

Subject: The Clients

FROM   Patricia Gillot
TO   Holly

Are you going to look after those clients darlin?

FROM   Holly
TO   Patricia Gillot

Sorry Trisha, forgot about them, I'll go and talk to them now.

TRISHA'S
INBOX

WEEK 4

THURSDAY

Subject: Does Trisha need service?

FROM Ralph
TO Trisha

Any new requests?

FROM Trisha
TO Ralph

Me and Holly were having a laugh yesterday about you Ralphy, we should get you crawling around this reception area!

FROM Ralph
TO Trisha

I wouldn't crawl for no woman really, I was just winding you both up.

FROM Trisha
TO Ralph

Funny, that's not what you said when you were drunk.

FROM Ralph
TO Trisha

Don't remember.

FROM Trisha
TO Ralph

So if we told you to kneel down in front of us, and be our little doggy, you wouldn't want to do that for us? Wouldn't you want to Ralphy???

FROM Ralph
TO Trisha

OK, but not in front of everyone.

FROM Trisha
TO Ralph

RALPH!!! That's great!

Subject: Screwdriver!

FROM Les
TO Trisha

Where did you leave the screwdriver?

FROM Trisha
TO Les

On the side, by the telly.

Subject: The Clients

FROM Trisha
TO Holly

Are you going to look after those clients darlin?

FROM Holly
TO Trisha

Sorry Trish, forgot about them, I'll go and talk to them now.

Subject: The screwdriver ...

FROM Les
TO Trisha

It's not here.

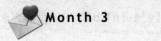

FROM Trisha
TO   Les

On the side, by the telly.

FROM Les
TO   Trisha

There's no point just repeating yourself, I'm telling you it's not here!

FROM Trisha
TO   Les

Tell me where you're standing.

FROM Les
TO   Trisha

What do you mean, where am I standing? I'm on the computer aren't I? What they feeding you there Trish, stupid pills?

FROM Trisha
TO   Les

No but you must have a prescription.
    When you aren't on the computer, when you're next to the telly — where are you?

FROM Les
TO   Trisha

In the lounge, oh, you mean the one in the bedroom.

FROM Trisha
TO   Les

GIVE THE MAN A PRIZE!

FROM Les
TO   Trisha

I'll give you more than a prize when you get home you cheeky cow.

FROM Trisha
TO Les

Saucy thing, alright, make sure you come home early then.

Subject: Our friend Holly ...

FROM Trisha
TO Jason

Jason
Do you mind if I email you? It's about Holly.
Sorry, but I'm worried for her.
Trisha

FROM Jason
TO Trisha

Of course not, is everything OK? Is she there?
Jason

FROM Trisha
TO Jason

She's sitting next to me, can't see my screen though.
She's not right, she looks like she's losing it. I know you're her friend, so hoped you could help. It's to do with James not calling, but surely that can't get to her this much?
She looks dreadful. She's my Holls, don't like to see her this way.
Trisha

FROM Jason
TO Trisha

Hi Trisha
I spent a hour on the phone to her last night, it's never nice being dumped especially when you think it's your fault and don't know what you've done wrong. We both know it's nothing she's done wrong herself (short of being TOO nice) but she's got that confidence thing, it's been knocked again.
Look after my little friend there please.
xxxx

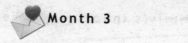

FROM Trisha
TO Jason

I'm doing my best, I've told her to go home sick, because if some of the management see her she'll get in trouble. She's barely talking to clients when they come in, her head's down, she doesn't look up and she mumbles to them.

Just want to know whether I should be that worried or whether she'll be fine soon?

FROM Jason
TO Trisha

If I tell you something, you promise not to tell Holly I told you — if she sees my emails she'll kill me.

I don't think it's a good idea for her to go home, I'd try to keep her there.

FROM Trisha
TO Jason

I think she should go home, take a couple of days off and she'll be fine.

FROM Jason
TO Trisha

I don't think that's a good idea.

FROM Trisha
TO Jason

Why?

FROM Jason
TO Trisha

I just don't.

FROM Trisha
TO Jason

If it's going to help, then tell me why, if it's gossip I don't want to know.

FROM Jason
TO Trisha

I DO NOT GOSSIP!

FROM Trisha
TO Jason

GOOD.

FROM Jason
TO Trisha

OK, sometimes I do, but not about friends!
OK sometimes about them too, but not about this sort of thing!

FROM Trisha
TO Jason

GET ON WITH IT! No wonder she's miserable, when it takes you both this long to get anything out, you're as bad as each other! Come on darlin, as Les would say — sh*t or get off the pot?

FROM Jason
TO Trisha

Who's Les? Doesn't matter, did Holly tell you she was married?

FROM Trisha
TO Jason

YES. But I don't know a thing about it.

FROM Jason
TO Trisha

OK, he was one of those men who had an opinion about everything, and his opinion was always right.
He (Sebastian) never admitted being wrong and whenever Holly did anything, it was always like 'I would have done it differently' which of course meant better.
She started being so scared about doing anything off her own back

— *because she didn't want to look like she'd got it wrong again, she started asking him first. t got worse and worse until she couldn't decide about anything herself, she gave up making any decisions at all. It got really bad.*

FROM   Trisha
TO   Jason

Like?

FROM   Jason
TO   Trisha

I caught her once asking him whether HE thought it was time she was hungry???? Seb-the-pleb I used to call him. The reason I'm telling you this isn't to gossip (and this sounds like I am). I just want you to know that she's such a sensitive girl underneath everything, after they split up she went into a huge depression. She didn't go out for weeks, I used to take her food around. She didn't open post, didn't do anything, so yes, I'd be very worried about her, as I am.

FROM   Trisha
TO   Jason

Bloody hell.

FROM   Jason
TO   Trisha

I don't want her going back to that.

FROM   Trisha
TO   Jason

Great!
    Hold on darlin, she's just emailed me, back to you in a minute.

Subject: I forgot

FROM Holly
TO Trisha

Sorry Trish, I think I forgot to tell Maxi's clients she was starting the meeting.

FROM Trisha
TO Holly

No you didn't, you spoke to them, they've gone up already.

FROM Holly
TO Trisha

Have they?

FROM Trisha
TO Jason

Yes darlin, you're fine.
x

Subject: Re: Our friend Holly ...

FROM Jason
TO Trisha

Also I want to pass some of the pressure over. Sorry to heap this on you, please don't tell her I told you anything. She could be fine with it all as you said, but it's best that you know this. I don't think it would be good to get her to go home, once she's out of the routine there's a small chance she won't go back there.
xxx
Hey, isn't it time we all met???

FROM Trisha
TO Jason

I've asked her to come out over our way — you fancy coming?

FROM Jason
TO Trisha

Love to, thanks Trish.
Jason

HOLLY'S
INBOX

WEEK 4

THURSDAY

Subject: Friends

FROM Pregnant Pam
TO Holly

Holly!!
  It's not fair, your friends should come first, especially when they're pregnant!!!

FROM Holly
TO Pregnant Pam

You do.

FROM Pregnant Pam
TO Holly

Seems like it's all James this and James that these days.
  If you were pregnant I wouldn't forget you.

FROM Holly
TO Pregnant Pam

James dumped me.

FROM Pregnant Pam
TO Holly

What??

FROM Holly
TO Pregnant Pam

  xxxxx

FROM Pregnant Pam
TO Holly

Oh sweetie.

Subject: I forgot

FROM Holly
TO Patricia Gillot

Sorry Trish, I think I forgot to tell Maxi's clients she was starting the meeting.

FROM Patricia Gillot
TO Holly

No you didn't, you spoke to them, they've gone up already.

FROM Holly
TO Patricia Gillot

Have they?

FROM Patricia Gillot
TO Holly

Yes darlin, you're fine.
    x

Subject: — ?

FROM Holly
TO James Lawrence

Is there a reason you're not talking to me?
    Is it just because we're over or because you are angry with me about something?
    If you don't talk to me I won't know and I'd at least just like to know?

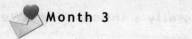

FRIDAY

Subject: Back pain

FROM Holly
TO Alice and Matt

Got your message last night. Sorry to hear about Matt's back, hope he's feeling better today.

FROM Alice and Matt
TO Holly

It's awful, he can't move at all, not a finger.
I managed to get him on to the bed last night and this morning he's absolutely stuck, the poor love.
I'm going off to the chemist now.
Alice

Subject: Flowers

FROM Patricia Gillot
TO Holly

Tell us, tell us, are they from who I think they're from???

FROM Holly
TO Patricia Gillot

Not sure, I don't think so.
Holly

Subject: Flowers

FROM Holly
TO Jason GrangerRM; Aisha

Did either of you two just send me some flowers?
Holly

FROM Jason GrangerRM
TO   Holly; Aisha

No, I didn't, did you Aisha?

FROM Aisha
TO   Holly; Jason GrangerRM

No.

Subject: Flowers

FROM Aisha
TO   Holly; Jason GrangerRM

Wait, do they look a little bit odd?
   Aish

FROM Holly
TO   Aisha; Jason GrangerRM

What d'you mean odd?

FROM Aisha
TO   Holly; Jason GrangerRM

Like not alive?

FROM Holly
TO   Aisha; Jason GrangerRM

You want to know if someone sent me dead flowers?

FROM Aisha
TO   Holly; Jason GrangerRM

Yes.

FROM Holly
TO Aisha; Jason GrangerRM

No Aisha, they're alive, I might not be looking great these days, but hopefully I haven't reached the stage when people start sending me dead flowers.

FROM Aisha
TO Holly; Jason GrangerRM

Oh dear, because I was hoping they were the ones I sent you when I didn't turn up to your party a few weeks ago.
    I've been hoping they'd arrive, must be still lost.
    Aisha

FROM Holly
TO Aisha; Jason GrangerRM

They aren't lost, they didn't arrive Aisha because you never really sent them.
    Love you though.
    SO who d'you think they're from then?

FROM Jason GrangerRM
TO Holly; Aisha

Very exciting, isn't there a message with them at all?

FROM Holly
TO Jason GrangerRM; Aisha

They're 'from an admirer'.

Subject: Our Brother Charlie

FROM Alice and Matt
TO Holly

I've never been so humiliated in my life.
    That brother of yours is in big trouble.
    Alice

FROM Holly
TO Alice and Matt

What's he done?

FROM Alice and Matt
TO Holly

He made me promise not to tell anyone.

FROM Holly
TO Alice and Matt

He hasn't got you involved in this stupid fetish club has he?

FROM Alice and Matt
TO Holly

What fetish club?

Subject: Him

FROM Holly
TO Jason GrangerRM; Aisha

So do you think they're from HIM then?

FROM Jason GrangerRM
TO Holly; Aisha

No, can't be, it said from an admirer ... so who d'you know who's hung like a horse in that place???

FROM Holly
TO Jason GrangerRM; Aisha

They could be from him? Maybe it's an apology?

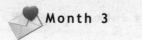

Subject: Charlie

FROM Alice and Matt
TO   Holly

Anyway, a month or so ago, he asked me to start buying him Viagra, because you can't buy it in England ... !

FROM Holly
TO   Alice and Matt

You are kidding me? You didn't say yes, did you?

FROM Alice and Matt
TO   Holly

YES.

FROM Holly
TO   Alice and Matt

Oh come on Alice???

FROM Alice and Matt
TO   Holly

You know what he's like, it's difficult saying no.
Anyway, that's not the worst bit, when I got him his Viagra last month, I got it from the village's ONLY pharmacist. Stupid thing to do, I know. I go there again today and my Spanish isn't great, and the shop is quite busy and I've begun explaining about Matt, and his back problem ... ?

FROM Holly
TO   Alice and Matt

And?

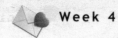
FROM   Alice and Matt
TO   Holly

I'm trying to explain to them in bad Spanish about Matt's back, the fact he's lying flat out, he's stuck there, stiff and it's painful and he can't get up.

The lovely little black-shawled Spanish women in the shop have shaken their heads in disgust and I've been given a bottle of pills I've only just realised are Viagra again!

I can't go back there, I'll have to find a new chemist.

Subject: It's over

FROM   Jason GrangerRM
TO   Holly; Aisha

Come on Holly, they won't be from him.
  Men are bastards and that's that.
  Apart from me.
  Jason

FROM   Holly
TO   Jason GrangerRM; Aisha

I think they could be???

FROM   Jason GrangerRM
TO   Holly; Aisha

Isn't there anyone else there you fancy???? Come on think?

FROM   Holly
TO   Jason GrangerRM; Aisha

No there isn't.

FROM   Jason GrangerRM
TO   Holly; Aisha

There must be someone else you want there, it's a big place??
  xx

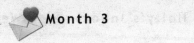

FROM Holly
TO Jason GrangerRM; Aisha

I don't want anyone else, I just want him.

FROM Jason GrangerRM
TO Holly; Aisha

But honey, you can't have him.

FROM Holly
TO Jason GrangerRM; Aisha

You sent those flowers didn't you.

FROM Jason GrangerRM
TO Holly; Aisha

*Yes sweetie, didn't think you'd imagine they were from him.
   Sorry.*

FROM Holly
TO Jason GrangerRM; Aisha

Oh.

FROM Jason GrangerRM
TO Holly; Aisha

*It seemed like a good idea to cheer you up.
All went a bit wrong.*

FROM Holly
TO Jason GrangerRM; Aisha

OK.

FROM Jason GrangerRM
TO Holly; Aisha

So just move on baby.

FROM   Holly
TO   Jason GrangerRM; Aisha

Just wanted him back.
   So much.

FROM   Jason GrangerRM
TO   Holly; Aisha

I know.

FROM   Holly
TO   Jason GrangerRM; Aisha

I don't want it to be over.
   Jason, I need to cry now.
   Got to go.
   love you both so much.
   x

Subject: Hi Holly

FROM   James Lawrence
TO   Holly

How are you?

FROM   Holly
TO   James Lawrence

OK, where've you been?

FROM   James Lawrence
TO   Holly

I've just been working hard. How have you been?

FROM   Holly
TO   James Lawrence

OK, a bit confused to be honest.

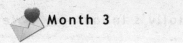

FROM James Lawrence
TO Holly

I know I've been a bit off recently. I didn't mean to upset you.

FROM Holly
TO James Lawrence

So, what are we doing?

FROM James Lawrence
TO Holly

How d'you mean?

FROM Holly
TO James Lawrence

Are we still together?

FROM James Lawrence
TO Holly

I care about you very much, but you know how hard it is having any kind of relationship.

FROM Holly
TO James Lawrence

What?

FROM James Lawrence
TO Holly

Any relationship is difficult, especially one with people at work.

FROM Holly
TO James Lawrence

No it's not, if it's secrecy you're worried about we can keep it secret. It can be our secret. Barely anyone knows?

FROM   James Lawrence
TO   Holly

Holly, it's not just a secrecy thing, it's just not good, having a relationship with people at work.

FROM   Holly
TO   James Lawrence

We can get through it.

FROM   James Lawrence
TO   Holly

Holly, we can't.

FROM   Holly
TO   James Lawrence

Please James, please don't do this. Call me now, let's go outside and talk about it for a few minutes.

FROM   James Lawrence
TO   Holly

No Holly, sorry.

FROM   Holly
TO   James Lawrence

I'm dialling you now, just pick up the phone please.
    For me, I need to talk about this.

Subject: PLEASE ANSWER YOUR PHONE

FROM   Holly
TO   James Lawrence

Please answer your phone, please James, I just need to talk to you, come on please, I just want to talk to you, I know you're saying it's over, but please.

Subject: HOLLY GO HOME

FROM Patricia Gillot
TO Holly

*Go home darlin, please go home, you can't sit there blubbering.
Come over here and give me a hug, then go.*
   xxxx

FROM Holly
TO Patricia Gillot

NO I'm NOT GOING ANYWHERE! NO.

FROM Patricia Gillot
TO Holly

Please darlin, you'll get yourself sacked, just go.
   xx
   I don't want to lose you.
   xx

MONTH 4

WEEK 1

BANK HOLIDAY MONDAY

Subject: Call me

FROM Alice and Matt
TO Holly

Give me a call when you get my email Tuesday, I've been trying to reach you all weekend.
    Alice

TUESDAY

Subject: News Update

FROM Jason GrangerRM
TO Holly

Did you hear about my poor love?

Subject: Morning

FROM Patricia Gillot
TO Holly

Nice to see you, fancy a coffee?

FROM Holly
TO Patricia Gillot

Hi
    Had some. How was your weekend?
    Holly

FROM Patricia Gillot
TO   Holly

Good.
  Interesting outfit you've got on, where's your jacket?

FROM Holly
TO   Patricia Gillot

Hi
  I forgot my jacket, sorry Trish.

FROM Patricia Gillot
TO   Holly

That's alright, get yourself the one from the cupboard the temp wore. It's just been cleaned.

Subject: Booking

FROM Jennie Pithwait
TO   Holly

Morning Holly
  Is there a problem with my meeting tomorrow?
  Jennie

FROM Holly
TO   Jennie Pithwait

Hi Jenny
  Everything fine with your booking, it's in the schedule all confirmed.
  Holly

FROM Jennie Pithwait
TO Holly

Sorry Holly,
But if you've already put it in the schedule, then why haven't you told me about it? How am I meant to know it's been organised?

FROM Holly
TO Jennie Pithwait

I never usually send you confirmation. You just know I'll do it?

Subject: News!!!

FROM Jason GrangerRM
TO Holly

Important French History was made this weekend.
It's the first time the words: 'Paris is going down' didn't refer to either a football team or a sexual act.
??

FROM Holly
TO Jason GrangerRM

????

FROM Jason GrangerRM
TO Holly

Paris Hilton — you know, she's going to prison — didn't you know????

FROM Holly
TO Jason GrangerRM

Sorry Jason, things here aren't going great.
Holly

Subject: Phone

FROM   Holly
TO   Alice and Matt

Got your email, I turned my phone off at the weekend, did you need me?

FROM   Alice and Matt
TO   Holly

Is everything OK?

FROM   Holly
TO   Alice and Matt

We've broken up.

FROM   Alice and Matt
TO   Holly

Oh honey,
    This is just totally unfair, you can't tell me something like that, how can I give my sister a hug when she's so far away.
    xxx
    What happened?

FROM   Holly
TO   Alice and Matt

It ended.

FROM   Alice and Matt
TO   Holly

I gathered that.
    Don't worry, you are beautiful and lovely and you've got a huge heart, and men are just crazy if they can't see that.
    Do you want to know my advice?

Subject: Bookings

FROM Jennie Pithwait
TO Holly

Holly
* I have client meetings all week and I simply need to know there won't be any hiccups.*

FROM Holly
TO Jennie Pithwait

No, don't worry, there won't be any hiccups.
* Regards*
* Holly*

Subject: Advice

FROM Holly
TO Alice and Matt

What's your advice then?

FROM Alice and Matt
TO Holly

Well, did I tell you that Matt now has bad diarrhoea? And he still can't move from his bed?

FROM Holly
TO Alice and Matt

No you didn't.

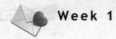

FROM Alice and Matt
TO Holly

Well, my advice is this:
When you look for a new man, don't go for a arrogant b*stard banker, who's obsessed with money.
But equally IF YOU DO go for a sweet, kind, gentle man, make sure he doesn't fill your house full of snakes, then cages full of rats so he can feed the snakes, then, now this is important to imagine Holly, it'll make you feel a lot better about your situation,
Make sure he then DOESN'T DO HIS BACK IN, and ask you to cover for him???!
So you spend you weekends cleaning up his shit, and feeding his rats.
AAAAAAAAAAAAAAAAAAAAAAAAAAAAGH
I think it's lucky I love him so much.

FROM Holly
TO Alice and Matt

I'll remember your advice.
Thanks Alice. xx
Holly

Subject: Outside

FROM Jennie Pithwait
TO Holly

Have you been out to lunch yet?

FROM Holly
TO Jennie Pithwait

Why — you fancy meeting up?

FROM Jennie Pithwait
TO Holly

No, can't, I'm too busy. I'm just going out for a sandwich and wondered — if it was cold, you'd wear a jumper whatever the weather was though.
x

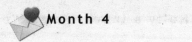

Subject: Tomorrow

FROM Patricia Gillot
TO   Holly

You going to be in tomorrow?

FROM Holly
TO   Patricia Gillot

Of course I will be.

FROM Patricia Gillot
TO   Holly

Good. I'm proud of you.

FROM Holly
TO   Patricia Gillot

I did the wrong thing on Friday didn't I, made a fool of myself.

FROM Patricia Gillot
TO   Holly

Listen, if you ever want to talk about anything, I'm here.

FROM Holly
TO   Patricia Gillot

I just really wanted it to work.

FROM Patricia Gillot
TO   Holly

I know.

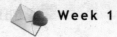

FROM   Holly
TO   Patricia Gillot

I thought we went well together, it's been so much fun.
  I thought it was fun for him too.

FROM   Patricia Gillot
TO   Holly

It would have been darlin, don't worry about him.

FROM   Holly
TO   Patricia Gillot

Have a great evening.
  xxxxxx
  I'm not usually this wet, promise.

WEDNESDAY

Subject: My daughter

FROM   Mum and Dad
TO   Holly

Holly
  We haven't heard from you for a while, what's the news, you don't keep us very informed do you?
  Love Mum

Subject: Meeting

FROM   Jennie Pithwait
TO   Holly

My meeting this morning was missing a continental breakfast, we had to reorder. If this is the amount of care you put into your relationships, it's no wonder they have a limited shelf life.
  Jennie

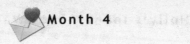

Subject: JASON AND AISHA! GET YOUR ARSES HERE

FROM Holly
TO   Jason GrangerRM; Aisha

You two WILL NOT BELIEVE THE CHEEK OF THIS BITCH.
  HATE HER HATE HER
  I'm going up there now.

Subject: Your email??

FROM Aisha
TO   Holly; Jason GrangerRM

Darling, who are you talking about? And are you sure you want to do this?
  Aish

FROM Holly
TO   Aisha; Jason GrangerRM

Jenny or Jennie stupid spelling anyway bitch, she just emailed me and said 'if this is the amount of care you put into relationships no wonder they have a limited shelf life'!!!!!!!!!

FROM Aisha
TO   Holly

GO UP NOW AND KILL HER.
  I'll take the blame, do it Holly.

FROM Holly
TO   Aisha; Jason GrangerRM

I'm going to.

Subject: Morning

FROM Patricia Gillot
TO Holly

Where are you off to?

FROM Holly
TO Patricia Gillot

Upstairs, got to go, back soon.

FROM Patricia Gillot
TO Holly

SIT DOWN.

FROM Holly
TO Patricia Gillot

You don't understand Trish, I'll tell you later.

Subject: Jennie

FROM Aisha
TO Holly

She's laughing about your break up, the slut, isn't she?

Subject: SIT DOWN!

FROM Patricia Gillot
TO Holly

Subject: READ YOUR SCREEN!!! MRS TYSON SIT DOWN NOW!!!

FROM Patricia Gillot
TO Holly

FROM Holly
TO Patricia Gillot

It's Jennie, she's so, you won't believe — Trish I just need some fresh air now.

FROM Patricia Gillot
TO Holly

I know, that's it, now go and get some air and then do your make up. Give us a hug first.

Subject: All sorted babe

FROM Aisha
TO Holly

I've been speaking to an ex-shag of mine and he knows one of the Adams family, so don't you worry.

FROM Patricia Gillot
TO Aisha

This is Trisha — Holly's nosy friend sitting at her desk.
Don't start with all that Aisha, let her decide if she wants to do it. There's other ways of dealing with this.
Trisha.
Please delete this email.

Subject: Flight back to England

FROM   Mum and Dad
TO   Holly

Holly
  Will you reply to my emails when I write to you!
  Your father is getting better, better enough to travel again, so I think we should go about booking his flight back to England.
  It's very difficult to arrange anything with you these days.
  What day is best for you, so you can pick him up from the airport?
  Mum

Subject: Booking

FROM   Holly
TO   Jennie Pithwait

Dear Jennie
  If you know anything about what we do down here, then you'd realise how much care we do take to book a room's facilities. However, if the catering staff don't follow our instructions to the letter, then mistakes can happen; as in this case, I booked the room accurately, the catering staff didn't deliver.
  So maybe you should take your head out of your arse and check these things before pointing the blame??
  I would have thought they'd have at least taught you that up there?
  Also for your information, my relationships only have a short shelf life with those people I decide to push off the shelf.
  Holly

Subject: Just Heard

FROM   Jason GrangerRM
TO   Holly; Aisha

You OK?

FROM Holly
TO Jason GrangerRM

I am now. Tell me something happy.

FROM Jason GrangerRM
TO Holly

I'm going to GAY Saturday, and you can come???

FROM Holly
TO Jason GrangerRM

Sorry, I can't this weekend. Just found out I got a job I went for and I'm working that night. (I'm starting to do some evening waitressing in a restaurant in Covent Garden.)

FROM Jason GrangerRM
TO Holly; Aisha

Which one, we'll come and see you!

FROM Holly
TO Jason GrangerRM; Aisha

Like that's happening. No telling nothing.

FROM Jason GrangerRM
TO Holly; Aisha

Does your work know?

FROM Holly
TO Jason GrangerRM; Aisha

No, we can't have two jobs.
 dan dan dahhhh. I'm a rule breaker, sue me.

FROM Jason GrangerRM
TO Holly

You're going to be shattered.

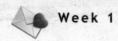

FROM   Holly
TO   Jason GrangerRM

I know, but bills need paying, things aren't great in that area.

Subject: The news you've been waiting for!

FROM   Charlie Denham
TO   Holly

Spread the word ...
  Holly Denham is now ...
  The official licensee for one, dirty and depraved, club of filthy perverts!!!
  You lucky lucky thing, spread the news!!
  We passed everything, ready for business.
  Charlie

Subject: Money

FROM   Jason GrangerRM
TO   Holly

I didn't know you had any money problems, you always look like such a princess!

FROM   Holly
TO   Jason GrangerRM

You're the best.
  But a bad liar — like when you suggested that 'suits were the new dresses' when you realised I didn't have the money for shopping so I didn't feel crap about it all.
  That was nice.
  x

FROM   Jason GrangerRM
TO   Holly

Oh, you're making me all emotional, I'm going to go and hug a stranger.

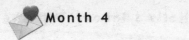

Subject: Your club

FROM Holly
TO Charlie Denham

I'm not going to be spreading the news around, because it's not anything I'm proud of. (So please don't you tell anyone, that's the last thing I need at the moment!)
    (Sorry Charlie, I'm pleased for you though.)

FROM Charlie Denham
TO Holly

Ooops, your name is on our headed paper.
    But don't panic, no one you know will know. Unless you know anyone who's likely to go to these kind of things.
    Charlie
    PS Opening Night not far away!

FROM Holly
TO Charlie Denham

HEADED PAPER!!! I can't talk about this now, but no, Charlie, this is not good.
    I won't be going to your Opening Night either, SORRY.

Subject: Apologies from Jennie

FROM Jennie Pithwait
TO Holly

Sorry for the misunderstanding I've checked into it, and I was wrong about the booking,
    Jennie.
    PS I was right about the shelf life though, James wasn't exactly pushed? Was he now?

Subject: Jennie

FROM Holly
TO Patricia Gillot

Did you see Jennie just then???

FROM Patricia Gillot
TO Holly

Yeah, she's just doing it to wind you up.

Subject: Friends you don't need

FROM Holly
TO Jennie Pithwait

Maybe he wasn't pushed.
But you certainly were,
pushed,
dumped,
and thankfully now in the bin.
Enjoy it there won't you.
Holly

FROM Jennie Pithwait
TO Holly

Such a pity.
Going out clubbing with you was really like going out with a younger sister:
one who never wore the right thing,
never said anything grown up,
and never had any money.
Oh well.
xxxx

FROM Holly
TO Jennie Pithwait

Isn't there a bone to chew somewhere?

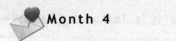

Subject: CV BANK

FROM   ReceptionWorld.com
TO   Holly

Dear Job Seeker
    Thank you for registering your CV with ReceptionWorld.com
    Your CV will now be available to many employers across the world looking for experienced receptionists.

    ADMIN

Subject: Re your last message

FROM   Jennie Pithwait
TO   Holly

No bone to chew, but there's your ex-boyfriend to screw.
    Ooh yes, I think I'll go do that.
    xxx

Subject: Embarrassing

FROM   Jennie Pithwait
TO   Holly

If you didn't get that ... he wasn't pushed, he was stolen.
    Oh and please don't get your mother writing to my parents again, it was so embarrassing to hear they were begging to have my help.
    To be honest, receptionists don't make it in the banking world.
    Oh except meeting and greeting.
    Go Holly.

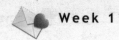

Subject: Need to go

FROM Holly
TO   Patricia Gillot

*Can I go home please trisha, just can't be here any more.
   sorry.*

FROM Patricia Gillot
TO   Holly

What's wrong darlin???

FROM Holly
TO   Patricia Gillot

*Can't be here,
   sorry.*

FROM Patricia Gillot
TO   Holly

What's she done to you now?

FROM Holly
TO   Patricia Gillot

*Don't worry,
   Bye.
   xxxx*

Subject: MORE NEWS!

FROM Jason GrangerRM
TO   Holly

*Got some more news about Paris and Britney, might cheer you
up ... ??!!!*

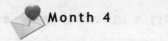

FROM   Holly
TO   Jason GrangerRM

Hi Jason
This is Trisha, Holly's just gone home. Can you look after her.

FROM   Jason GrangerRM
TO   Holly

Why? What's happened???

FROM   Holly
TO   Jason GrangerRM

She read something, her face went, shoulders went.
    Emailed me, told me she had to go. Then got up and walked out into the rain. Didn't take her coat or nothing.
    Trisha
    Look after her Jason. You know what it's about — Jennie.

FROM   Jason GrangerRM
TO   Holly

OK, thanks.

THURSDAY

Subject: Can I have an answer please?

FROM   Mum and Dad
TO   Holly

Holly
    I'm getting a little bit annoyed with you Holly.
    It's become very frustrating, especially when I need to organise so many important things.
    Firstly, your house.
    We've begun sending out invitations for our reunion party

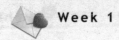
in England, they have your address on them so I really do need your father to meet with whoever will be staying there over the next month; now he's well enough to travel.

Secondly I'd like to invite the Lawrences. I think it would be a great way to meet them and I'm dropping them an email now, can you ask lovely James whether they're likely to be staying over?

Mum

Subject: Attention Trisha — from Jason, Holls' friend from the hotel

FROM Jason GrangerRM
TO Holly

Trisha
I don't think Holly will be back there again, so I'm hoping you're still reading Holly's emails.
If so, can you delete her inbox etc?
I've sent this to what I think will be your email address too.
Thanks for this.
Regards
Jason

Subject: From Trisha — to JASON

FROM Holly
TO Jason GrangerRM

OK darlin, didn't think she would be really. I'll tell everyone. Pass on my kisses to her, poor love.
I'll tell Judy and I'll delete all her messages now, can you get her pass back off her and her uniform.
Trish

Subject: This might be a nice thing for us to do?

FROM   Pregnant Pam
TO   Holly

I was thinking of something nice we could do together, what about going to feed the ducks? There's some in St James' Park and they're so sweet?
   Pam

Subject: Service

FROM   Ralph Tooms
TO   Holly; Patricia Gillot

Haven't heard much from you two.
   If you want I'm around to get drinks or like if you want food.
   I'm here to be used, I mean not used I mean here to be helpful, but you know if I'm not too busy and everything. Then I could. If you needed anything. If not then that's cool.
   Ralph

Subject: Jennie

FROM   James Lawrence
TO   Holly

I heard Jennie's been having a go.
   Hope you can take it all on the chin, you know her cutting dry wit, it's just the way she is.
   Makes for an entertaining day though, she drives everyone nuts up here, you should see her.
   Hope we can be friends soon and all go out together.
   Sorry about the way things turned out. I'm sure the bank's full of nice guys though, better than me.
   James

Subject: Fabulous sunny day!

FROM   Holly
TO   Patricia Gillot

Hello
   xxx

FROM   Patricia Gillot
TO   Holly

Where've you been??????
   Trish

FROM   Holly
TO   Patricia Gillot

You told me today to come at 12pm?? The late client meeting??

FROM   Patricia Gillot
TO   Holly

I did darlin, I did, I forgot.
   You look great. Really gorgeous, glad you're in, I wasn't sure you'd turn up.

FROM   Holly
TO   Patricia Gillot

Yes, I'm back, and happy.
   Sorry about yesterday, things will be different today though, I promise you. I'm going to have some fun.
   Let's see, who's first? I see I have an email from my mum, that should be enlightening.

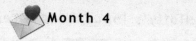

FROM   Patricia Gillot
TO   Holly

Jason sent you an email, I answered it for you.
    I think he was worrying about you.
    Trisha
    Are you sure you're OK, you're not on drugs are ya?
    It's not sunny out there you know?

FROM   Holly
TO   Patricia Gillot

Isn't it?
    Oh, I'm sure it was when I left home, maybe it's just my mood.

FROM   Patricia Gillot
TO   Holly

Yeah, or the prozac.
    xx

Subject: Getting it up

FROM   BEAUTY MAKE-UP FROM TRACEY
TO   Holly

Sorry to be sending this you but;s
    (*%$Sex life getting you down?
    (*&)
    Then maybe you need Viagra
    $10 x 2 pks
    $20 x 4 pks
    $40 x 10 pks

Chemist online

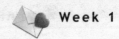

FROM　Holly
TO　　BEAUTY MAKE-UP FROM TRACEY

Thank you ever so much for your kind offer of Viagra, however, I am a single lady, so I can choose to make myself happy with something which doesn't have the option of being limp or small.

I do know a couple of people who may be interested however:
One is CharlesDenham@Artnightclub.com
And the other is JLawrence@huerstwright.com

Oh and I think the latter would probably be interested in any diverse sexual toys you might stock, plastic sheep, adult baby kits (if they exist), you know the type of thing.

Also I believe JLawrence is also keen to find a bride, if you have any suggestions. Possibly a kennel too.

And I know this is a long shot, but if you have any information on cheap flights or real estate, then he's your man.
Yours
Holly

Subject: House and renting etc

FROM　Holly
TO　　Mum and Dad

MUM
　　DO NOT WRITE TO ANYONE, UNTIL YOU'VE SPOKEN TO ME.
　　HOLLY

Subject: MUM WHERE ARE YOU?

FROM　Holly
TO　　Mum and Dad

?????????????????????????????
?????

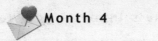

FROM　Mum and Dad
TO　Holly

I don't know, we hear nothing from you for ages, then you're on the phone leaving urgent messages and emailing demanding attention.
　I suppose now you need US we have to be here.
　Yes Holly, what is it?
　Mum

FROM　Holly
TO　Mum and Dad

Mum
Just don't email anyone for the moment, you haven't have you?

FROM　Mum and Dad
TO　Holly

Why?

FROM　Holly
TO　Mum and Dad

Mum,
picture this: I'm typing by stabbing the keyboard and I'm gritting my teeth because you're not answering my question.
　Please, oh lovely mother of mine, have you or have you not emailed JAMES' PARENTS YET?

FROM　Mum and Dad
TO　Holly

No!

FROM　Holly
TO　Mum and Dad

Good!
　Now just stay by the computer, we need to talk, but first I have to deal with a friend of mine who seems to have a duck fixation.
　Love Holly

Subject: Ducks?

FROM   Pregnant Pam
TO   Holly

There may be some ducks closer to you, if you're interested?
   Pam

FROM   Holly
TO   Pregnant Pam

Ducks??? Pam, are you OK?
   Holly

FROM   Pregnant Pam
TO   Holly

Hi Holly
   Doesn't have to be ducks. We could just sit and eat some sandwiches? Just thought it might be nice?
   Pam

Subject: Service

FROM   Holly
TO   Ralph Tooms

Ralph,
   Thank you for your kind email.
   xx
   Yes you can run off and get me some lunch if you'd like, you can report to my desk at 1500 hours.
   From your boss.
   Just joking!

FROM Ralph Tooms
TO Holly

Sorted, I'll be there, cheers.
Oh with or without the cap?
Ralph

FROM Holly
TO Ralph Tooms

With, definitely with!!

Subject: Lunch — sorry

FROM Holly
TO Pregnant Pam

I'm sorry, can't do the duck thing.
Holly

FROM Pregnant Pam
TO Holly

That's OK.
Pam

FROM Holly
TO Pregnant Pam

Don't like ducks. But please please please can we meet up and do some baby shopping?? Isn't it time you got some clothes that weren't pink? Seen some lovely pooh bear jammies???

FROM Pregnant Pam
TO Holly

Yay.
Great, yes yes, this is going to be so much fun. I promise it won't be dull. Oh great, I'll start planning where we can go.
Pam

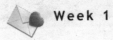
FROM Holly
TO Pregnant Pam

Great, and you can fill me in with everything I've missed.
  xxxx

FROM Pregnant Pam
TO Holly

Everything??

FROM Holly
TO Pregnant Pam

Yes, even the yukky bits.
  Holly

Subject: MUM

FROM Holly
TO Mum and Dad

I really really really really didn't appreciate you sending a letter to Jennie's mum and dad, to ask them if she could get me into banking.
  You will never know how utterly humiliating that was. I told you not to — and you still did, it was really hurtful.
  I am very happy on reception and don't know a thing about finance, as you'll no doubt find out soon.
  I wouldn't ever ever want anything from Jennie, I can make my own way.
  Love you.
  Holly

FROM Mum and Dad
TO Holly

Dear Holly
  I'm sorry if what I did upset you.
  Jennie's lovely, I'm sure she would have understood all I was doing was looking out for you, so don't worry (I must add I think you're being a little over-dramatic about it all).

It sounds to me like someone's fallen out with their best friend from school. What have you done to upset Jennie?

You didn't get drunk and sing again did you? I've told you about the dangers of social drinking, it's best to stay at home on your own if you're going to get drunk.

Love Mum

FROM Holly
TO Mum and Dad

Mum

No I didn't get drunk!!! And sitting at home drinking on your own is an awful thing to be encouraging people to do.

Sorry, but I'm very busy now, lots of people coming in.

x

FROM Mum and Dad
TO Holly

OK, so let's forget about all that, but when are we going to meet with lovely James' parents?

FROM Holly
TO Mum and Dad

You won't be meeting with lovely James, lovely Jennie or either of their lovely lovely parents, because James dumped me. That's right, he dumped me because he thought I was too keen, or too fat or maybe it was meeting the weird parents, who knows. But the fact is he's decided he'd prefer to be shagging lovely Jennie, and Jennie's decided she'd like to make me feel well and truly sh*t about it all.

So no I can't think I'll be entertaining the happy couple Mum.

Oh, PS, and also I lost my house.

xxx

Subject: You OK?

FROM Patricia Gillot
TO Holly

You OK there?

FROM   Holly
TO   Patricia Gillot

Couldn't be better thanks.
  Holly

FRIDAY

Subject: Parents

FROM   Holly
TO   Jason GrangerRM

A bright and crispy morning to you Jason.
  I want to know — have you ever told your mum exactly how you feel? I did that yesterday and it felt great. Probably won't ever speak to me again, but it was at least very relieving.

FROM   Jason GrangerRM
TO   Holly

Yes, I told my mum how I felt when I was sixteen — (that I was gay), she took it pretty hard at first.
  I think she convinced herself it was all just in my head, then she blamed society for making me gay. We had a huge row where things were said which neither of us meant, then it was all over. I didn't talk to her again for a few years, which was sad, because she's actually alright.

FROM   Holly
TO   Jason GrangerRM

I like your mum, she is great.

Subject: Her upstairs

FROM Patricia Gillot
TO Holly

Morning
   Didn't tell you yesterday, petrol and flames came to mind, but she came down looking for you yesterday.

FROM Holly
TO Patricia Gillot

Jennie?

FROM Patricia Gillot
TO Holly

No darlin, the bleedin' queen?
   She came down before you got here, looking all pleased with herself. She must have thought you weren't coming back.

Subject: Men

FROM Aisha
TO Holly

I haven't been in touch for a bit, because I guessed you were feeling a bit bad. You better now sweetie?
   Aish

FROM Holly
TO Aisha

Yes. I know you're not good at the whole consoling thing. But I'm fine, how are you?

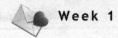
FROM Aisha
TO   Holly

I thought you'd never ask.
*   I've been lying to Jason for a while now, about a few different*
things, and I'm still seeing his boss ... Also do you think it's too early
to ask for holiday???

FROM Holly
TO   Aisha

Aisha???
*   Please tell me you're joking?*

FROM Aisha
TO   Holly

No, and I'm seeing his boss above his boss. I know, I know. But there's
no good giving me a lecture now.
*   Also, I'm kind of pregnant.*

FROM Holly
TO   Aisha

Pregnant??????

Subject: Problems with our Front of House

FROM Jennie Pithwait
TO   Holly

Holly
*   RE Delivery of accurate messages*
*   Can we revert to the standard company rules when it comes to*
passing on important client information.
*   I object to being called over in the reception area and having a*
Post-it note rudely jammed into my hand.
*   Jennie*

Subject: Throwing the towel in

FROM Mum and Dad
TO Holly

Dear Holly

I've given a lot of thought to your last email.

It's not our fault you split up with James but of course we both feel for you greatly and you must be going through a difficult time.

But I want to know if you feel this isn't just another 'Sebastian-type situation', all over again?

Mum

FROM Holly
TO Mum and Dad

What exactly is a 'Sebastian-type situation' Mum????

FROM Mum and Dad
TO Holly

You know, giving up at the first hurdle, letting a good one slip away. Don't have a go at me when I suggest this, but have you thought it could be something to do with you?

Mum

Subject: Pregnant

FROM Aisha
TO Holly

I just don't want a lecture, I need a shoulder to cry on, and to talk about it all.

Are you around tonight, for an Aisha chat?

xxxxxx

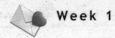

FROM Holly
TO   Aisha

Of course I'm not going to give you a lecture?? I'll be around to chat tonight, come over.
Love you
Holly

FROM Aisha
TO   Holly

Oh good.
OK then I'm not really pregnant, I just didn't want to get the lecture about shagging the bosses.
But I honestly do really want to ask Jason for time off to go on holiday ... to Ibiza for a week!!! How lucky am I???
All paid for ...
xxxxx

Subject: Fridays

FROM Patricia Gillot
TO   Holly

Busy init?

FROM Holly
TO   Patricia Gillot

Do you have the sort of friends who would lie about being pregnant?

FROM Patricia Gillot
TO   Holly

Oh God yeah, sometimes you got to, to get your man.
I've never done it though.
Trish

Subject: Ex-husbands

FROM Holly
TO Mum and Dad

Mum,
I can't believe you've just written that? I don't think you realise how bad he actually was.
Dad knows, why don't you ask Dad about Sebastian before you write this stuff?
Holly

FROM Mum and Dad
TO Holly

Listen, I'm not trying to point the blame, only get you to look at it from our side darling.
Mum

FROM Holly
TO Mum and Dad

Great time to talk to me like this. While you're in the mood Mum, why don't you go out and kick a kitten or burst a child's balloon?
I'm really trying to hold it together here Mum. Can you get off my back today.

FROM Mum and Dad
TO Holly

I don't think me getting off your back will help you at all.
Now on top of all this, you tell us you've lost that lovely house? What happened?

FROM Holly
TO Mum and Dad

I'm not talking about this now, I've just split up with a someone I really liked, and I thought my mum would be the last person I'd need to hide from.
Can you go away Mum, please.
Holly

FROM   Mum and Dad
TO   Holly

OK Holly I will.
    But tell me first, just what exactly did YOU think was so wrong with Sebastian anyway?

FROM   Holly
TO   Mum and Dad

I was frightened of him Mum and I don't think you're meant to be frightened of your husband OK?
    No I don't think you should be.
    Now please Mum, get lost!

Subject: Hello

FROM   Jason GrangerRM
TO   Holly

Hey
    What's the news?
    Jason

FROM   Holly
TO   Jason GrangerRM

Wish I was working there with you.

FROM   Jason GrangerRM
TO   Holly

Come on, it's amazing how you're doing. Love this new napalm-spitting, revenge-battling you!!

FROM   Holly
TO   Jason GrangerRM

It's not really a new me to be honest.
    It's the same me, but really battered, really nearly very beaten,

the me which wants to hide and hide and hide and never come out to play again.

Each day I get up and I really do fight Jason I do, I fight to get him out of my head, because I always wake up thinking of him and my mornings are spent just staring into space remembering things, trying to work out what I said wrong, what I did wrong to f*ck it all up.

I come to work hoping Trish can get me out of it, but it takes a while, she's really wonderful and I fight, I fight to put it all at arm's length, like try to imagine I'm someone else, like it never happened, like he doesn't work on the floors above me, and that bitch isn't there too, I push it away, and sometimes I win, I do, and I share a joke with Trish and by the time I go home at night I'm feeling better, I've covered it all over, I've bluffed myself and I go to bed, I fall asleep and the fighting is over. I wake up the next day and guess what?

I dreamt about being back with him of course, I was back with him and it was all so perfect and brilliant and wonderful, then slowly the hammer comes down and I remember, IT'S OVER !! — and it's all fresh again!!

And why did it happen, what did I do to mess it up??

I repeat this cycle of absolute sh*t each day and I HATE IT! I hate it so much Jason.

FROM   Jason GrangerRM
TO   Holly

Call me as soon as you can, I'll come and meet you outside your office for lunch, my treat?? I'll bring you ice cream, and smarties and all things fun and bad.

I'll just wear a thong — nothing else???

Singing the Macarena? Juggling bananas?

xx

FROM   Holly
TO   Jason GrangerRM

Would the thong be in leopard print?

FROM   Jason GrangerRM
TO   Holly

Of course.

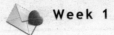

FROM   Holly
TO   Jason GrangerRM

I don't want the red Smarties.

FROM   Jason GrangerRM
TO   Holly

I'll remove them all.

FROM   Holly
TO   Jason GrangerRM

OK.
 See you lunch time.
 xxx love you

Subject: Our fun night together!!

FROM   Aisha
TO   Holly

What time do you want me there tonight?
 Aish

FROM   Holly
TO   Aisha

I don't.
 xxx

Subject: Cruella

FROM   Patricia Gillot
TO   Holly

She's on her way down.

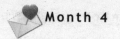

FROM Holly
TO Patricia Gillot

Now?

FROM Patricia Gillot
TO Holly

Yes now, she just called.

FROM Holly
TO Patricia Gillot

Sh*t, I'm going for a fag.

FROM Patricia Gillot
TO Holly

You don't smoke!

FROM Holly
TO Patricia Gillot

Then I'm going for a herbal joss-stick praying session.

FROM Patricia Gillot
TO Holly

Before she gets here, you want to delete any messages calling her Cruella.

FROM Holly
TO Patricia Gillot

Why, because she'll see what you call her Trisha? THAT YOU CALL HER SHELLA OLD BAT FROM HELL CRUELLA?

FROM   Patricia Gillot
TO   Holly

OK, stop that now, when she finishes talking to him she'll be able to see my screen!

FROM   Holly
TO   Patricia Gillot

OK, I won't call Cruella anything else, she's lovely.
   Lovely lovely Cruella. Who doesn't smell bad at all.

FROM   Patricia Gillot
TO   Holly

You are so wrong, you stop giggling.

Subject: STINKS, CRUELLA STINKS, IT'S TRUE

FROM   Holly
TO   Patricia Gillot

This is like Russian Roulette, it's so much fun!!

FROM   Patricia Gillot
TO   Holly

You wait till after school, I'm going to pull your hair.

FROM   Holly
TO   Patricia Gillot

ha ha ha ha

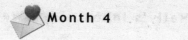

Subject: I'm dying

FROM Aisha
TO Holly

I'm dying.
It's true, I didn't want to tell you that before, but there it is. I have two more weeks to live. Poor me.
xxxx boo hoo.

FROM Holly
TO Aisha

That's awful.
Oh well.
Holly

Subject: OK OK OK

FROM Aisha
TO Holly

I'm not really dying, I admit it.
Aisha

FROM Holly
TO Aisha

Good.

FROM Aisha
TO Holly

But I am being followed!

FROM Holly
TO Aisha

I've told you before, you are not being followed. This is just another good reason to stay off the drugs.
x

Subject: Friends

FROM Holly
TO   Patricia Gillot

Hey
> *Do you have any friends that think they're being followed?*
> *Holly*

FROM Patricia Gillot
TO   Holly

What's with all the 'do you have friends' questions?
> *I don't have any friends who think they're being followed, no.*

FROM Holly
TO   Patricia Gillot

OK.

FROM Patricia Gillot
TO   Holly

I do have a friend called Mystic Sam though — tells everyone he can look into the future.
> *Hears voices in his head, telling him about stuff.*

FROM Holly
TO   Patricia Gillot

Do you believe him?

FROM Patricia Gillot
TO   Holly

Yeah, but you'd hear voices too if you smoked as much weed as he does, he's off his nut most of the day.
> *Actually he thought he was being followed, but he was, got nicked for dealing. I'm off, goodnight.*
> *xxx*

WEEK 2

MONDAY

Subject: Gay clubbing in London

FROM　Holly
TO　　Jason GrangerRM; Aisha

AISHA AND JASON
After thinking long and hard about my life, I've decided I might give it a go at being gay. Alright, maybe not gay, but I thought I'd try hanging out in the odd gay club with you Jason, get my mind off men.
xxxxx
Sorry to just talk about myself, hope you both had wonderful weekends and are bubbling with exciting news.

FROM　Aisha
TO　　Holly; Jason GrangerRM

Get your mind off men, yeah good one, so you're going to start hanging out in places which are packed with hunky, muscular, oiled, beautiful men, who know how to dance?
Yes that'll take your mind off men.

FROM　Jason GrangerRM
TO　　Holly; Aisha

I hate to agree with Aisha, about anything actually, (and not that I wouldn't welcome you with open arms).
But Aisha's right, the guys do look good, and sensitive too ...
Which is a bummer for you.
Jason

FROM　Aisha
TO　　Holly; Jason GrangerRM

Yeah, what's a bummer is how full of crap you are Jason.

FROM   Jason GrangerRM
TO   Aisha; Holly

Aisha's upset because after I took her to GAY she got kicked out of an after party. Two men were kissing, she threw herself underneath them and screamed 'take me I'm yours!'
    Neither of them did and we had to leave, it was really embarrassing.

FROM   Aisha
TO   Holly; Jason GrangerRM

They were really rude Holly.
    Anyway, I think you should seriously consider the lesbian thing.
    Aisha

FROM   Holly
TO   Aisha; Jason GrangerRM

The lesbian thing?

FROM   Aisha
TO   Holly; Jason GrangerRM

Yes. It could be a nice change for you?
    I've tried and it's lots of fun, I know a lovely Chinese girl actually, I met her last week.
    She'd sit on your face for you?

FROM   Holly
TO   Aisha; Jason GrangerRM

I'm OK. Very kind of you though Aisha.

FROM   Jason GrangerRM
TO   Holly; Aisha

Now I've just finished being sick, (thank you Aisha) we're agreed that Holly shouldn't worry about guys, immerse herself in quality magazines, OK!, Hello! etc, think lovely thoughts, and just enjoy being single for a while?
    Jason

Subject: James Lawrence

FROM Alistair Moffett
TO Holly

Hi
I hope this isn't inappropriate, but I recently heard the news that you are no longer dating James Lawrence from IBD. I was hoping this may mean you would now accept a dinner invitation from me, Alistair Moffett.
Regards
Alistair Moffett

Alistair Moffett, Legal and Compliance, H&W, High Holborn WC2 6NP

Subject: Annual results

FROM Shella Hamilton-Jones
TO Holly; Patricia Gillot; Samantha Smith; Dave Otto;
Ralph Tooms

RE Annual Results
Dear Conference planning committee,
We have a mammoth task ahead of us. With over 500 delegates descending upon our shores, we will need to avoid a minefield of potential disasters, all of which I am confident can be avoided, providing we first ensure we have enough planning and preparation.
Owing to the late withdrawal of our Brussels office as a venue we have just two months to get this right.
A budget has been set and unlike the Jubilee extension which was £1.2 billion over-budget and 2 years late and the Channel Tunnel which was £5.2 billion over-budget and 5 years late, this conference will be within budget and on time.
A great deal of research will need to go into achieving the best value for all areas of the conference, and I will be emailing you over the next few days with details of which areas will be covered by which team member.
Yours sincerely
Shella

Subject: Hot stuff

FROM Gavin Oliver
TO Holly

Holly
　Fancy a beer after work?
　Gav

Gavin Oliver, Equity Derivatives, Emerging Markets, H&W, High Holborn WC2 6NP

Subject: News!!!!

FROM Holly
TO Jason GrangerRM; Aisha

I've been asked out by two guys, so I think I'm going to go out with both of them?
　Holly

FROM Jason GrangerRM
TO Holly; Aisha

Yes, that was always the other option — go out with as many men as humanly possible, at the same time.

FROM Holly
TO Jason GrangerRM; Aisha

I'm going to be a slut!

FROM Jason GrangerRM
TO Holly; Aisha

Good. Well that's settled then.

FROM Aisha
TO Holly; Jason GrangerRM

Oh, goodie we can be sluts together!!
  How exciting. Oh oh and we could charge for it??

FROM Jason GrangerRM
TO Aisha; Holly

Tell Aisha your problems and suddenly the world seems that little bit rosier.

FROM Aisha
TO Jason GrangerRM; Holly

Stop being so grumpy Jason.

FROM Jason GrangerRM
TO Holly; Aisha

You split up from someone, and Aisha's way of cheering you up is to offer you a life of prostitution. I admire the way she can find a nugget of gold in any bad situation.

TUESDAY

Subject: Bet you're glad

FROM Toby Williams
TO Holly

Hi Holly
  I heard what happened with James, glad you realised what he's like.
    Toby

FROM   Holly
TO   Toby Williams

I also know what you're like too. So do me a favour and stop emailing?
    Holly

Subject: Re your email

FROM   Holly
TO   Alistair Moffett

Hi
    Do you know James then?
    Holly

FROM   Alistair Moffett
TO   Holly

Dear Holly
    No, I've never met him.
    Alistair

Subject: Legal & Compliance

FROM   Holly
TO   Patricia Gillot

Hey, would the Legal and Compliance lot know the IBD lot?

FROM   Patricia Gillot
TO   Holly

Not really.

FROM   Holly
TO   Patricia Gillot

So if someone chats me up from Legal & Compliance because he's heard I'm now free, there's no reason he'd know, other than ...

FROM   Patricia Gillot
TO   Holly

It's gone around the whole bank.

FROM   Holly
TO   Patricia Gillot

Good, that's what I thought, nice to know.

FROM   Patricia Gillot
TO   Holly

You lucky cow, all that attention! Come on, give me the goss, who are they then???

FROM   Holly
TO   Patricia Gillot

Someone called Alistair Moffett?

Subject: Clients waiting

FROM   Jennie Pithwait
TO   Holly

Dear Receptionist
    Tomorrow I'll have quite a few clients coming in for meetings, be a dear and run them up for me. I don't think I'll be able to come down and collect them myself (unfortunately).

Subject: Dinner invitation

FROM   Alistair Moffett
TO   Holly

Holly
    Does this mean you would be accepting my invitation or not?

Subject: I know Alistair

FROM   Patricia Gillot
TO   Holly

Alistair Moffett, no, you don't want to go near him, he's half your height darlin.

FROM   Holly
TO   Patricia Gillot

That's not so bad?

FROM   Patricia Gillot
TO   Holly

He has a beard.

FROM   Holly
TO   Patricia Gillot

Short and trendy or big and scary?

FROM   Patricia Gillot
TO   Holly

Big. And he's a groper.

FROM   Holly
TO   Patricia Gillot

Come on, you're making that up?

FROM   Patricia Gillot
TO   Holly

No, honest.

FROM Holly
TO Patricia Gillot

I guess that's it for Alistair then.

FROM Patricia Gillot
TO Holly

I think he's married too.

FROM Holly
TO Patricia Gillot

Enough Trish, I get the picture.
    xxx

FROM Patricia Gillot
TO Holly

Yeah I wouldn't go near him. Some of the secretaries complained about him last year.

Subject: Dinner Invitation

FROM Holly
TO Alistair Moffett

I'm going to have to say no to your invitation but thank you.

FROM Alistair Moffett
TO Holly

Any reason?

FROM Holly
TO Alistair Moffett

Yes, I don't go out with married gropers.
    Holly

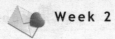

Subject: Alistair

FROM   Patricia Gillot
TO   Holly

Thinking about it, I think he got sacked last year.

FROM   Holly
TO   Patricia Gillot

How can he be here still then?

FROM   Patricia Gillot
TO   Holly

Looking at the directory I got it wrong, different Alistair.
Oh darlin, your one is lovely, get in there quick.

WEDNESDAY

Subject: Chat up lines

FROM   Holly
TO   Jason GrangerRM

I was called 'hot stuff' on an email from a trader, what d'you think?

FROM   Jason GrangerRM
TO   Holly

Very cheesy, depends what he looks like.

FROM   Holly
TO   Jason GrangerRM

Quite nice, but in a cheeky chappy laddie kind of way.

FROM Jason GrangerRM
TO Holly

Like the opposite of anyone you'd usually like.

FROM Holly
TO Jason GrangerRM

We've got this company dinner at the Dorchester next Friday ...

Subject: Lying to friends

FROM Holly
TO Aisha

So have you told them you can't go out with them any more?

FROM Aisha
TO Holly

I've talked to them yes.

FROM Holly
TO Aisha

Not just talked to them.
HAVE YOU TOLD THEM BOTH you won't be able to see them any more (without wearing your uniform).

FROM Aisha
TO Holly

YES.

FROM Holly
TO Aisha

and that doesn't mean having sex while wearing it either.
(I just want to make this completely clear.)

FROM   Aisha
TO   Holly

You're like my mum! Yes I've told them I won't, OK?

FROM   Holly
TO   Aisha

Good.

FROM   Aisha
TO   Holly

Stop stressing. Just cool it, hot stuff.

FROM   Holly
TO   Aisha

Very funny. Tell Jason he's dead.

Subject: Attention: Receptionist

FROM   Jennie Pithwait
TO   Holly

Re Clients
    I heard your message about my clients having arrived down there.
    I believe they allow support staff to use the company lift, so if you could run them up to me that would be just fab, meeting room 20. And try not to dillydally.
    Jenns x

Subject: HER UPSTAIRS — HELP TRISH

FROM   Holly
TO   Patricia Gillot

Don't tell me I have to do this, I'll die, please Trish.
    See below what she emailed me:

Re Clients
I heard your message about my clients having arrived down there.
I believe they allow support staff to use the company lift, so if you could run them up to me that would be just fab, meeting room 20. And try not to dillydally.
Jenns x

FROM   Patricia Gillot
TO   Holly

Oh I wanna kill her.
Go back to the manual and do what it says there.
And try smiling, you look like you're going to puke.
Trish

Subject: Attention: Jennie

FROM   Holly
TO   Jennie Pithwait

Unfortunately, owing to your recent request to 'revert to the standard company rules' I have reverted to the reception manual which states that it is a security risk for us to be taking clients up whenever we feel like it.
It is a shame, because I'd love to help, but company policy clearly states the host of the meeting should come down to collect their visitors.
Have a lovely day 'Jenns'??
Holly xx

Subject: Your useful Gran

FROM   Granny
TO   Holly

Holly
I've been using the worldwide web once more.
I have registered your name with some new companies.
It's been quite exciting.
xxx

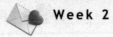

FROM   Holly
TO   Granny

Thank you Granny, but you haven't registered me on any more cheap flight sites have you?

Subject: I'm a bit lost

FROM   Jason GrangerRM
TO   Holly

Why are we now looking at barrow boys and what's the Dorchester got to do with it?

FROM   Holly
TO   Jason GrangerRM

Oh, nothing, I've got this cr*ppy company cr*ppy do next Friday.
   Jennie and James will be there, probably sitting together.
   I didn't want to go without a partner but I haven't got long if I'm going to find someone (need to give Judy a name by Friday).
   Therefore — thinking about the two dating offers I had.
   No! This is stupid, I'm not letting her get to me. I'll go alone

---

Subject: Reception

FROM   Jennie Pithwait
TO   Holly

Hi
   Are you sure you want to play it like this?
   I'm very worried you could end up with egg on your face?
   Jennie

Subject: JASON!!!

FROM   Holly
TO   Jason GrangerRM

Changed my mind!!! Need a date! ASAP!

Subject: Exciting

FROM   Granny
TO   Holly

Holly
   Have you received anything there yet?
   Love Granny

FROM   Holly
TO   Granny

No Granny, maybe it didn't work.
   Don't worry though, what is it you wanted to send me?
   Holly

Subject: SO YOU ARE SINGLE??? THEN HELP IS ON THE
   WAY!!!

FROM   UKSingles
TO   Holly

Thank you for registering with UK Singles, Dating Online.
   ***Registration Name** Hollylookingforlove*
   ***Password** Denham*
   ***Registration Account number** 92482374*

Subject: DATING ON LINE — IT COULDN'T BE EASIER

FROM DatingDirect.com
TO   Holly

Dear Holly
  Thank you for registering with Dating Direct.com.
  You will soon receive an email with more details.
  Admin

Subject: Thank you Granny

FROM Holly
TO   Granny

Hi Granny
  I think they're coming through now. Thank you for putting my name on dating sites, that's very sweet of you.
  Holly

FROM Granny
TO   Holly

You are very welcome.
  Granny
  xxx
  He wasn't good enough for you anyway.

FROM Holly
TO   Granny

Thank you for saying that.
  xxxx

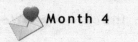

Subject: — Hi

FROM SwingersLife
TO Holly

SWINGING SEX RULES!!!! SO MANY COUPLES SO LITTLE TIME!!!
   !!!SEX AND THE SINGLE SWINGER !!!
   ENJOY YOUR REGISTRATION

Subject: One thing though Granny ...

FROM Holly
TO Granny

Please don't register me on any swinging sites.
   xxx
   Holly

FROM Granny
TO Holly

Ooops sorry darling, they were something I had been looking at.
   Love Granny

Subject: Conference planning committee

FROM Shella Hamilton-Jones
TO Holly

RE Annual Results
   Dear conference planning committee,
   After some careful consideration I have decided it would be fairer to discuss which areas of research would be most suited to which committee member before delegating these responsibilities.
   Do keep in mind when volunteering that quite a bit of this work will need to be achieved during your free time.
   We have use of meeting room 13 at 7pm and I expect everyone to be there, I can only apologise for the short notice, but I too will have to make sacrifices.
   Shella

Subject: Working in the restaurant

FROM   Holly
TO   Patricia Gillot

I can't go to Shella's thing, I've got to be in the restaurant by 7pm tonight!

FROM   Patricia Gillot
TO   Holly

Haven't they sacked you yet?

FROM   Holly
TO   Patricia Gillot

No. It may surprise you Patricia, but I'm actually very good!

FROM   Patricia Gillot
TO   Holly

It does flipping surprise me.
   ha ha
   You can't miss Shella's 'planning committee meeting'.
   And my Les wont be happy, you know what he's like, he likes his dinner around 8.

FROM   Holly
TO   Patricia Gillot

I've got to work tonight. What can I tell Shella then?

FROM   Patricia Gillot
TO   Holly

I'll tell her you've got the trots?

FROM Holly
TO Patricia Gillot

Great, why not start another rumour about me?

FROM Patricia Gillot
TO Holly

I'll stand up for you.
I'll tell her clients have been complaining, and we had to keep the front door open all day. It's something to do with all that posh food you eat.

FROM Holly
TO Patricia Gillot

Don't you dare! I'll get you Patricia Gillot!

FROM Patricia Gillot
TO Holly

You could have some illness which needs dealing with?
I'll just say it's too personal to say, so she won't ask?

FROM Holly
TO Patricia Gillot

Sounds good.
Thanks
Holly

THURSDAY

Subject: Wake up!

FROM   Jason GrangerRM
TO   Holly; Aisha

Come on, we've got work to do ...
   You need to find a man and we have 24 hours to do it.
   You need to be psyched and pumped?

FROM   Holly
TO   Jason GrangerRM; Aisha

After sleeping on it, I'm not sure I want the added pressure of finding someone. It's all not necessary.
   Jennie's obviously got it in for me and I don't want to come to work everyday thinking about arguments and bitchiness, so I've been looking on www.receptionworld.com and think I'll apply to a few positions.
   xxxx

FROM   Jason GrangerRM
TO   Holly; Aisha

Necessary ???
   Necessary??? No of course it's not necessary, but you don't always do things because they are necessary?
   You can't just give up!

FROM   Jason GrangerRM
TO   Holly; Aisha

Do you think Aisha broke down and cried when she realised everyone in that flat (apart from me) wanted her to leave?
   No, she stood up with pride, put her dress back on, slurred a few insults and stormed out.

FROM   Holly
TO   Jason GrangerRM; Aisha

OK, fine, so what d'you want me to do?
    (Like the pep talk, very inspiring.)

FROM   Jason GrangerRM
TO   Holly; Aisha

I'll be back in two minutes with a plan.

Subject: Meeting last night

FROM   Holly
TO   Patricia Gillot

How did it go last night?

FROM   Patricia Gillot
TO   Holly

I told Shella you couldn't make it cause you had a problem. She wanted to know what it was. So I said it was a really personal problem, you had an appointment with the doctor, but she still wanted to know.
    That girl has got one cheek on her I'm telling you.
    How did it go in the restaurant last night??

FROM   Holly
TO   Patricia Gillot

So what did you tell her?

Subject: List of potential candidates

FROM   Jason GrangerRM
TO   Holly; Aisha

OK, so we need to draw up a short-list of potential candidates.
    Had any luck with Granny's dating sites yet?

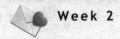

FROM Holly
TO Jason GrangerRM; Aisha

No. Not too keen on the dating site thing.

FROM Jason GrangerRM
TO Holly; Aisha

OK what about the two who emailed you on Monday?

FROM Holly
TO Jason GrangerRM; Aisha

I didn't reply to the 'hot stuff' email, and the other one is probably out of the question now.

FROM Jason GrangerRM
TO Holly; Aisha

Yes, I think you need to get back in touch with both of them.
  A sexy well-placed email could bring Alistair back on board.
  What d'you think Aisha?

FROM Aisha
TO Holly; Jason GrangerRM

I think he sounds like a knob.

FROM Jason GrangerRM
TO Holly; Aisha

Not particularly helpful Aish.
  Go on Holly email him something, you can get around him.

FROM Holly
TO Jason GrangerRM; Aisha

Oh, OK I'll give it a go, I suppose there's nothing to lose.

Subject: Trisha, you haven't answered my question

FROM   Holly
TO   Patricia Gillot

What did you tell Shella when she wanted to know what my personal problem was?

Subject: Sorry

FROM   Holly
TO   Alistair Moffett

Dear Alistair
   I have just realised what a huge mistake I've made, I am truly sorry, please forgive my rude email.
   I sent it to the wrong Alistair.
   I would love to have dinner with you.
   Holly

FROM   Alistair Moffett
TO   Holly

Holly
   I don't understand, you know another Alistair at Huerst Wright?
   Alistair

FROM   Holly
TO   Alistair Moffett

Yes.

FROM   Alistair Moffett
TO   Holly

One who gropes people?

Subject: Dating update

FROM   Holly
TO   Jason GrangerRM; Aisha

It's going to take some time I think. This could be harder than I thought.
*   Holly*

FROM   Jason GrangerRM
TO   Holly

You don't have time, are you working tonight?

FROM   Holly
TO   Jason GrangerRM

No, night off.

FROM   Jason GrangerRM
TO   Holly

Then you need to see them both tonight, so you can decide whose name to give Judy tomorrow.

FROM   Holly
TO   Jason GrangerRM; Aisha

You are joking?

Subject: Hot stuff

FROM   Holly
TO   Gavin Oliver

Hi
*   Thank you for your email, sorry it's taken me so long to get back to you. A beer might be nice sometime, yes.*
*   Holly*

FROM   Gavin Oliver
TO   Holly

Sounds good, let's go out next week some time.

Subject: Trisha answer please!!

FROM   Holly
TO   Patricia Gillot

What did you tell Shella?

FROM   Patricia Gillot
TO   Holly

You've got haemorrhoids darlin.
    Love Trish

FROM   Holly
TO   Patricia Gillot

TRISH!!!!!

FROM   Patricia Gillot
TO   Holly

That's why you walk funny.

FROM   Patricia Gillot
TO   Holly

??

FROM   Holly
TO   Patricia Gillot

Just kidding. She didn't ask — just said you were sick.

Subject: Communication problems

FROM   Holly
TO   Alistair Moffett

Hi Alistair
  It really is a long story, do you fancy just having a quick drink after work, and I can explain everything?
  Holly

Subject: Annual Review

FROM   Shella Hamilton-Jones
TO   Holly

Dear Holly
  RE: Annual Results Conference.
  It was a shame you weren't able to make our meeting last night, but I understand you were not feeling well etc.
  Although I would be the last person to wish ill of anyone, I do hope it was nothing trivial (in the nicest possible way). We are trying to organise this event in half the usual time scale.
  Organisational and research sectors were allotted to committee members last night and I'm sure Trisha would have told you by now which one will now be your responsibility.
  As you are one of the newest employees in facilities and also the one who has needed so much help in achieving a relatively average level of success in their position, I personally would have given you far less involvement.
  The decision though was achieved through a unanimous vote of the members and therefore until you prove yourself incapable — the result stands.
  I will expect the information provided in Excel with formulas calculating the various packages and offers available.
  As I'm sure you will appreciate you have the largest area to cover in terms of research, so please begin as soon as possible.
  I wish you all the best.
  Yours truly,
  Shella

Subject: TRISHA

FROM   Holly
TO   Patricia Gillot

Is there anything you forgot to tell me about last night?

FROM   Patricia Gillot
TO   Holly

I'm off, see you tomorrow.
  Lots of love
  Trisha
  xxxxxxxx

FRIDAY

Subject: Fun fun fun Friday!!!!

FROM   Holly
TO   Jason GrangerRM; Aisha

Today is going to be a fantastic day!!!
  Hello London.

FROM   Jason GrangerRM
TO   Holly; Aisha

What happened last night???

FROM   Holly
TO   Jason GrangerRM; Aisha

I went out with both of them!!

FROM   Jason GrangerRM
TO   Holly; Aisha

You didn't!!!!!

FROM   Holly
TO   Jason GrangerRM; Aisha

No I didn't.
    I called them both, apologised for the ridiculous emails sent —
under pressure (thank you Jason).
    And cancelled it all, thanking them for being nice.
    AND NOW I'm going to have a fab day, because I'm lucky just to
be alive and healthy and yeeeeeeeeeeeeeeeeeeeeeeeeeeees.
    xxxxxxxxxxxxxxxxxxxxxxxxxxxxxx

FROM   Jason GrangerRM
TO   Holly; Aisha

Aisha!!!!
    Have you given Holly one of those special mints of yours??

FROM   Aisha
TO   Holly; Jason GrangerRM

Do you mind!
    I'm being a responsible mother these days. Talking of which are
you two still coming over at the weekend? Shona is looking forward
to it.

FROM   Holly
TO   Jason GrangerRM; Aisha

Of course, I'm coming.
    Now I have to find out what my lovely colleague has been up to.
    xxxx

Subject: Morning

FROM   Holly
TO   Patricia Gillot

Trish my good friend and colleague, is there anything you wish to tell me?

FROM   Patricia Gillot
TO   Holly

Yes, I've been doing this for 20 years and I'll never get used to people saying 'Hi Trish' as they go past.
*   They never hang around long enough for you to see who they are. I spend all day looking up for no reason.*

Subject: About that meeting last night ...

FROM   Holly
TO   Patricia Gillot

Is there anything else apart from that, which may have slipped your mind?

FROM   Patricia Gillot
TO   Holly

Love to talk, but I've got to shoot off for a break.
*   Love ya*
*   Trisha*

FROM   Holly
TO   Patricia Gillot

I'm not going anywhere, I'll be here when you get back!

Subject: Client

FROM　James Lawrence
TO　　Holly

Hi honey
Last minute call, I'm rushing off to see a client in Birmingham, so tonight's out, we can go Saturday?
James

FROM　Holly
TO　　James Lawrence

Hi Honey
I think you emailed the wrong woman.
If you wanted Jennie, she's the one dressed like a slut at the far end on the left. I can forward her your blow-out though if you want?
Holly
(you're such a knob)

FROM　James Lawrence
TO　　Holly

Hi
Sorry I'm trying to get out of the door quickly and made a mistake.
Hope you're OK.
James

Subject: Meeting

FROM　Holly
TO　　Patricia Gillot

What did you sign me up for last night???

FROM　Patricia Gillot
TO　　Holly

Nothing happened last night.

FROM   Holly
TO   Patricia Gillot

OK, the night before, stop being evasive.

FROM   Patricia Gillot
TO   Holly

I'm sorry darlin, I tried to help. Don't think it'll be so bad.

FROM   Holly
TO   Patricia Gillot

It was a unanimous vote!!!!!

FROM   Patricia Gillot
TO   Holly

I know, I was going to vote against them, then I thought it actually might be good for you?

FROM   Holly
TO   Patricia Gillot

WHY????

FROM   Patricia Gillot
TO   Holly

To be honest, keep your mind off things.

FROM   Holly
TO   Patricia Gillot

*The second job is doing that fine, I don't have much time left.
    What am I meant to be doing then?*

FROM   Patricia Gillot
TO   Holly

You're doing accommodation.

FROM   Holly
TO   Patricia Gillot

What?

FROM   Patricia Gillot
TO   Holly

Like hotels etc.

FROM   Holly
TO   Patricia Gillot

You mean where everyone stays?

FROM   Patricia Gillot
TO   Holly

Yes.

FROM   Holly
TO   Patricia Gillot

Where 400 delegates stay?

Subject: Gifts

FROM   Alice and Matt
TO   Holly

What would you do if you had a queue of people bringing jam jars full of creepy crawlies into your flat every day?

Subject: Annual results

FROM   Holly
TO   Patricia Gillot

When do I have to do this by??

Subject: Night of the Naughty Nurses v Rubber Ron's Running Bottoms

FROM Charlie Denham
TO Holly

It's an idea for the opening night? I'm not sure myself?

FROM Holly
TO Charlie Denham

Go away.

Subject: Annual results

FROM Holly
TO Patricia Gillot

I said when do they need this by?

FROM Patricia Gillot
TO Holly

Not for a couple of weeks.

Subject: Conference planning committee

FROM Shella Hamilton-Jones
TO Holly

Hi Holly
    As we need to begin finalising which hotels can offer us the best packages as soon as possible, I'd like your initial offering to be handed in by next Friday.
    Hope this is OK with you?
    Regards
    Shella

Subject: Leather Mistresses from Pangea VS The Naughty
   Knights from Ikea

FROM   Charlie Denham
TO   Holly

Maybe we could get sponsorship from Ikea??
   Charlie

Subject: It's one week

FROM   Holly
TO   Patricia Gillot

I have one week, not two.

FROM   Patricia Gillot
TO   Holly

Sorry babe, I'll help you.
   xxx

Subject: Witches

FROM   Holly
TO   Alice and Matt

Sorry Alice
   *Are you OK? Why do you have a queue of people outside bringing
you creepy crawlies? It's not something to do with that Witch thing
you've started is it?*

FROM   Alice and Matt
TO   Holly

*No Holly, that's voodoo, and I'm not practising voodoo. The witch
thing is just a hobby, like stamp collecting or chasing buses.*

FROM Holly
TO Alice and Matt

Who chases buses? I know you live out in the sticks, but you must know those people you see chasing buses in London are trying to get on them — to get to work?

FROM Alice and Matt
TO Holly

Ha ha, you know I mean counting them or whatever those people do — train spotters etc.

FROM Holly
TO Alice and Matt

OK, but train spotters don't turn people into frogs then fly away cackling on broom sticks.

FROM Alice and Matt
TO Holly

Neither do I?

FROM Holly
TO Alice and Matt

Oh, good. So why all the creepy crawlies in jam jars?

FROM Alice and Matt
TO Holly

It's to do with the snakes — because Matt has become such a revered figure out here, for his knowledge of reptiles and insects, people think he'd be interested in whatever they can trap and stuff in a jar. Actually he just likes snakes, but we haven't got the heart to tell them.

So about every other day we get one excited visitor or another coming to the house, and there they sit on the other side of the table from Matt and between them ...there's usually a musty old jam jar with a sad creature looking out from behind the glass.

One woman comes at least once a week with something she's

spattered inside a jar. There's also this guy who keeps giving Matt lumps of sh*t he thinks are pupai. I mean, how would you like it if people brought you their sh*t all day?

FROM   Holly
TO   Alice and Matt

They do — I'm a receptionist — I get to hear everyone's problems all day long and because I've got to stay at my desk, I can't escape.
    (I know I've taken what you've said as a metaphor, but I can't get my head around being brought the real thing.)
    xxxxx
    Good luck with it all. I'll call you over the weekend.

WEEK 3

MONDAY

Subject: Party at the Dorchester

FROM   Holly
TO   Patricia Gillot

Morning Trish
  Are you going with Les to the dinner thing on Friday?
  Holly

FROM   Patricia Gillot
TO   Holly

No darlin, I don't want him there, I thought we'd have fun together.
  Trish

FROM   Holly
TO   Patricia Gillot

I love you Trisha and I want your children.
  xxxx

FROM   Patricia Gillot
TO   Holly

Take em darlin.
  But they're a handful I'm telling you.

FROM   Holly
TO   Patricia Gillot

Thanks Trish.

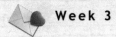

FROM Patricia Gillot
TO Holly

So are you going to tell me what happened with Toby?

FROM Holly
TO Patricia Gillot

When?

FROM Patricia Gillot
TO Holly

You know when, at school. There's got to be a good reason you spit each time you say his name.

Subject: Procedure

FROM Jennie Pithwait
TO Holly

Holly
I've spoken to a senior director here and she said there's no reason you shouldn't walk our clients up, it's part of your job, so next time get your skates on eh Hols???
x

FROM Holly
TO Jennie Pithwait

Dear Jennie
Unfortunately as previously emailed, this is against company policy, so until company policy changes, it is really out of my hands.
Kind regards
Holly

TUESDAY

Subject: Story time

FROM   Patricia Gillot
TO   Holly

So you're at school and?

FROM   Holly
TO   Patricia Gillot

I didn't really fit in.

FROM   Patricia Gillot
TO   Holly

Was it your hair or your singing?

FROM   Holly
TO   Patricia Gillot

Thank you Trish.
   I think because the school started at 13 and I came from a comprehensive when the others came from prep schools.
   That could have been one reason, the other reason was my skirt.

FROM   Patricia Gillot
TO   Holly

Below the knee?

FROM   Holly
TO   Patricia Gillot

Ankle length.

FROM   Patricia Gillot
TO   Holly

Your mum cracks me up.

FROM   Holly
TO   Patricia Gillot

She's hysterical. I was also very unconfident.

FROM   Patricia Gillot
TO   Holly

What about sport?

FROM   Holly
TO   Patricia Gillot

I used to hide. Sometimes I hid behind the chapel during matches and smoked cigarettes.

FROM   Patricia Gillot
TO   Holly

You dirty smoker!
I'd never have guessed, so where was Jennie?

FROM   Holly
TO   Patricia Gillot

What — while I was smoking? Probably winning tennis matches, surrounded by boys.
She invited me to a party at her house, I was so excited (she was popular) but it turned out she invited most of our year.
They had this amazing place, a pool, they even had waiters serving us drinks — alcoholic drinks.

FROM   Patricia Gillot
TO   Holly

Nice responsible parents.

FROM Holly
TO Patricia Gillot

It was amazing, they had a dance floor and bar in a marquee!
 So I had a party at mine, I thought it might help me make friends.

FROM Patricia Gillot
TO Holly

Dance floor?

FROM Holly
TO Patricia Gillot

My dad in a chef's hat cooking burgers on the barby in the garden, we had Top-deck Shandy — you know the non-alcholic stuff for kids, (unless you drink about 100 of of them).
 And when Jennie arrived with some other girls, they went straight up to the off-licence and brought alcohol back.
 Of course my dad confiscated it.
 Everyone seemed to leave after that.

FROM Patricia Gillot
TO Holly

So where was Toby?

FROM Holly
TO Patricia Gillot

He was this recluse, I actually met him smoking behind the chapel.
 I wasn't inhaling, just doing it to make myself feel better about things. Mostly I think I did it because it was something my Mum hated, and she'd have killed me if she'd found out.
 He was there, smoking. He was very cool, very bad.

FROM Patricia Gillot
TO Holly

Bad boy Toby, like the sound of him … so come on.

Subject: Important reminder

FROM   Holly
TO   Holly

3 DAYS LEFT TO GET FUNERAL DRESS!!!!

Subject: You lucky boy

FROM   Holly
TO   Jason GrangerRM

I got all your messages!!! So pleased you're back together.
    xxxxx

FROM   Jason GrangerRM
TO   Holly

It's great.
    You still worrying about Friday?

FROM   Holly
TO   Jason GrangerRM

It's going to be one huge massive unbelievably huge chance for Jennie to rub my face in it all.
    Can you think of how I can avoid utter embarrassment and the desire to plunge a stake knife into her back?

FROM   Jason GrangerRM
TO   Holly

Don't go?

FROM   Holly
TO   Jason GrangerRM

Can't not go, no way, can't do it.
   I was thinking about asking Aisha to go in my place, what d'you think? Obviously in a mask?

FROM   Jason GrangerRM
TO   Holly

I think they'd notice.
   Apart from the fact it's NOT a fancy dress party (so she might stand out a little) she's also got black hair, oh and in case you'd forgotten, black skin too (you haven't).

FROM   Holly
TO   Jason GrangerRM

So I guess that idea is out???

FROM   Jason GrangerRM
TO   Holly

Yes it is, so stop mulling over it — Oh and don't imagine for one instance that she could wear a full costume either, not even if you get permission to wear one.

FROM   Holly
TO   Jason GrangerRM

How do you always know what I'm thinking??

FROM   Jason GrangerRM
TO   Holly

I know you.
   Also from what I've heard Aisha only goes to fancy dress parties dressed as a bunny girl, and that's not a full costume, that's a thong and a bit of fluff taped to her backside.
   The other obstacle is she'll be on a plane to Ibiza.

FROM   Holly
TO   Jason GrangerRM

You've let her go???

FROM   Jason GrangerRM
TO   Holly

Yes, don't ask.
   xx

Subject: Birth

FROM   Aisha
TO   Holly

Did you tell Pam not to worry about the birth?
   Aish

FROM   Holly
TO   Aisha

I did, thank you for that, she sounded much less scared after I spoke to her.

FROM   Aisha
TO   Holly

People just like to wind everyone up about it.
   If giving birth was that bad, the tubes wouldn't be so packed would they?
   Aish

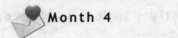

Subject: Story time

FROM Holly
TO Patricia Gillot

*He was kind of the opposite to me, people wanted to be his friend,
but he didn't want it.*

The first time I saw him, he didn't say anything to me.

*I was sitting up on a water barrel and he just kind of nodded, that
was all. It was just the two of us, smoking quietly.*

*I could faintly hear the shouts of the girls from my house, playing
hockey, I always knew when I had to run back, when I heard the final
whistle.*

FROM Patricia Gillot
TO Holly

What did he look like then?

FROM Holly
TO Patricia Gillot

*Not much different, same build, slim, at first the other boys didn't
think much of him. He came from a comprehensive too, that's how
we first started talking.*

FROM Patricia Gillot
TO Holly

Go on, I'll do this lot, you just write!

FROM Holly
TO Patricia Gillot

Aren't you going to lunch?

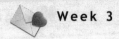

FROM   Patricia Gillot
TO   Holly

I'm going nowhere, neither are you, we'll get Ralph to get us something, he's been desperate for orders.
   So what happened next?

FROM   Holly
TO   Patricia Gillot

I was always the substitute, it was so rare that they ever needed me for games, I think they used me once in about a month.
   So when I heard this voice shout my name, I nearly jumped out of my skin.

Subject: Judy

FROM   Holly
TO   Patricia Gillot

Sorry, I'm so late back, I got collared by one of the directors who wanted to know why it was such a problem taking clients up to meeting rooms.

FROM   Patricia Gillot
TO   Holly

We do it as a favour to the host IF we can't get hold of them, but it's THEIR responsibility to come down and collect THEIR guest.
   We're not skivvies for that bitch Jennie, she's just doing this for power play. She'll get her comeuppance one day.

FROM   Holly
TO   Patricia Gillot

Judy told me to ignore him anyway.
   So, where'd we got to?

FROM   Patricia Gillot
TO   Holly

You were behind the Chapel ...

FROM   Holly
TO   Patricia Gillot

I used to sit under this tree where I had my cigarettes buried in a plastic bag, watching the game, well not really watching the game, I'd begun watching the path to the Chapel.

I got the timing right on a couple of occasions, I used to pick up my hockey stick and run like the wind, stand for a couple of minutes catching my breath behind the building, doing my hair, then saunter nonchalantly around the side.

FROM   Patricia Gillot
TO   Holly

Oh you're such a tart!!!

FROM   Holly
TO   Patricia Gillot

I was not a tart Patricia, I was just very keen.

So after I'd put some lipstick on, lip liner, mascara, eye shadow etc ... I walked around the side.

FROM   Patricia Gillot
TO   Holly

TART!!!!

FROM   Holly
TO   Patricia Gillot

I'm joking, we weren't allowed any of that there (OK I smuggled lipstick in, but that's all).

SO the path to the Chapel split in two, one path took you to the Chapel and the other off to one of the other houses.

I couldn't see him there, so guessed he'd gone to the house.
   I swore and then I remember seeing his legs on the ground next to me, he was sitting with his back against the chapel looking right at me.

FROM   Patricia Gillot
TO   Holly

Sh*t, what did you say?
   You could have been swearing about anything.

FROM   Holly
TO   Patricia Gillot

Exactly, so I didn't say anything, this was the third time I'd been there with him without saying a word.
   Then this girl appeared from our house, someone had been injured and they'd been searching for me.
   She made some bitchy comment about being from a comprehensive and smoking then ran off to get me in as much trouble as she could.

FROM   Patricia Gillot
TO   Holly

Was this girl Jennie?????

FROM   Holly
TO   Patricia Gillot

No, one of her friends, but she had lots (and I can't blame her for that). After she ran off to tell them, I remember getting my things together to go back and Toby said something like 'From a comprehensive too?'
   And I nodded and then — he smiled.
   But that smile, to me, meant a lot, it meant, it's all sh*t and don't worry about it, and you'll get through it, and I respect you because I'm also from a 'comp' and lots of lovely things like that.

FROM   Patricia Gillot
TO   Holly

He just smiled!
  He was probably thinking I can't wait to get her clothes off.
  ha ha ha
  Look out!!!!

FROM   Holly
TO   Patricia Gillot

What?

Subject: Nasty

FROM   Holly
TO   Patricia Gillot

I can't believe Shella!!!!

FROM   Patricia Gillot
TO   Holly

What did she do??

FROM   Holly
TO   Patricia Gillot

She ripped off my cutsie bunny picture and threw it in the bin!!!
  And worse ... my picture of Mr Big!!
  Told me to grow up!
  Clients can't see it from their side!!!!!
  grrrrrrrrrrrrrrrrrrrrrrrrrrrrrrrrrrrrrrrrrrrr

FROM   Patricia Gillot
TO   Holly

Shella's a class act.
  Don't worry, I'll plaster rabbits and Mr Big all over the desk tomorrow.

FROM   Holly
TO   Patricia Gillot

Are you OK?

FROM   Patricia Gillot
TO   Holly

Cramps, had them years, they just come on, sometimes are worse than others.

FROM   Holly
TO   Patricia Gillot

You should have that looked at??

FROM   Patricia Gillot
TO   Holly

I will.
    So where did you and Toby do it then?
    I want all the details, want the colour of the moon, where the snooty girls were playing hockey, where the naughty boys were filming it from. I want the full story.

WEDNESDAY

Subject: Trisha is off today

FROM   Judy Perkins
TO   Holly

Holly
    Unfortunately Patricia called in sick this morning, but instead of arranging a temp, Shella will be covering for her during the busy period — from 11am to 3pm.
    I've looked at the meeting-room schedule and it does look like a

*fairly busy day, so it will be good to have someone working alongside
you who understands our systems here etc.*
  Any problems, give me a call.
  Regards
  Judy

FROM Holly
TO Judy Perkins

Hi
  OK Judy, I was thinking, couldn't Ralph cover, I'd look after him?
  Holly

FROM Judy Perkins
TO Holly

It's not his shift today and Neil is too new to know what's going on.
  Judy

Subject: TRISHY!!!

FROM Holly
TO Patricia Gillot

Trishy
  Just heard you're sick today, so this is a get well soon email.
  *Of course hopefully you'll read this when you're back to work and
I'm praying it will be Thursday, because I've got to work with Cruella
today and that's just not fair!*
  *I can picture you'll be laughing yourself silly when you read this,
yes that's right you've made me have to work next to that viper all
day!*
  *Oh and I'm worried about you too (not just thinking of myself),
please be better.*
  Xxxxxxxxxxxxxx Xx

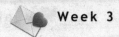

Subject: Passwords

FROM Judy Perkins
TO   Holly

Holly
   Do you know Trisha's password?
   Because Shella will need to check her emails to make sure there aren't any about bookings.
   I know they should go to the main booking email address but sometimes Trisha emails PAs who are friends of hers directly.
   Judy

Subject: EMERGENCY HELP HELP HELP

FROM Holly
TO   Jason GrangerRM

Sh*t! I need you urgently, where are you?
   Why don't you keep your mobile on??
   How d'you recall email, I need to know — if you don't know yourself, then can you let me know someone who does know?
   This is really really really urgent.

Subject: URGENT HEEEEEEEEEELP

FROM Holly
TO   Charlie Denham

URGENT
   How do you recall emails? I'm in deeeeeeeeeeeeeep shit.

Subject: Reception Assistance

FROM Shella Hamilton-Jones
TO Holly

Holly
    I'll be working with you on the desk today, some of my tasks here needed completing, but I'm on my way down now, so don't panic.
    I'm probably not as easy-going as Patricia normally is, so be prepared for that.
    Essentially, today our front of house will perform like a well-oiled machine.
    Yours
    Shella

Subject: nok nok

FROM Joseph
TO Holly

Hellow Arnty Holly
    nok nok

Subject: Your son

FROM Holly
TO Alice and Matt

I guess you've given your son my email address, because Aunty Holly just got an email from him.

Subject: Passwords

FROM Judy Perkins
TO Holly

Holly
    I can't get through to Trisha's mobile so I've contacted IT and

they're cancelling her password, and reissuing a new one, so don't worry. If Trisha calls, just let her know it's nothing important now and I wish her a rapid recovery.
   Regards
   Judy

Subject: nok nok

FROM   Joseph
TO   Holly

arnty nok nok

Subject: YOUR EMERGENCY

FROM   Jason GrangerRM
TO   Holly

I don't have my mobile on for the same reason you don't, because you can't have them ringing on reception.
   Now calm down, what's the problem.

FROM   Holly
TO   Jason GrangerRM

It's OK now, Trisha's off sick and so they've got Shella (Cruella) to cover, so I sent Trisha a jokey email for when she gets back which wasn't exactly complimentary towards Shella, then I find out Shella's using Trisha's login name, to keep track of any stray bookings.
   I don't know what Trisha's passcode is to delete my message, so I called her, but she's not answering.
   Then I got through to Pam who told me how to recall the email, so I've done that, so it should be OK now.
   xxxx
   PS she's sitting here now, grrrrrrrr, what a day I'm going to have.

Subject: nok nok

FROM   Joseph
TO   Holly

nok nok

FROM   Holly
TO   Joseph

Sorry Joseph,
*   I was busy, but it's nice to hear from you — how is school?*
*   Oh and 'Who's there?'*
*   Love Holly*

FROM   Joseph
TO   Holly

Im App

FROM   Holly
TO   Joseph

I'm App Who?

Subject: WAIT NO NO NO

FROM   Jason GrangerRM
TO   Holly

Sorry sweetie, just found out, that recall thing doesn't work.
*   It just sends them another email after the first message, showing you're desperate to recall it.*
*   It's pointless, if she opens the RECALL message first and agrees, then you're OK ... chances are though she'll open the other one first, THEN see you're trying to get it back ...*
*   Sorry.*
*   Xxxx*

Subject: ha ha ha ha ha ha

FROM   Joseph
TO   Holly

You just sed Im a poo
    ha ha ha arnty holly is a poo
    arnty holly is a poo

Subject: Help!

FROM   Holly
TO   Jason GrangerRM

OH GOD
    She's opened up the system now, and is reading through things, how will I know if she clicks on the RECALL first or the other one first?????

FROM   Jason GrangerRM
TO   Holly

From what I gather, you either get a message saying Recall Success
    Or
    Recall Failure ...
    good luck.

Subject: Recall failure

FROM   Patricia Gillot
TO   Holly

Your message
    Subject: TRISHY!!
    Could not be recalled

Subject: Holly

FROM   Joseph
TO   Holly

arnty holly is a poo
arnty holly is a poo
arnty holly is a poo
arnty holly is a poo
HA HA HA
Love Joseph
xxxxxxxx

FROM   Holly
TO   Joseph

I get it Joseph, that's very funny.
Thank you.
Love
Holly

Subject: Oh No!

FROM   Holly
TO   Jason GrangerRM

Crapola.
It got opened.
?

Subject: Holly

FROM   Patricia Gillot
TO   Holly

Holly
I'll be working from both my email and Patricia's today, therefore
I may email you from either, just in case you get confused.

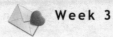
Also there seem to be an awful lot of people that aren't down in the schedule arriving for meetings, is this because Patricia hasn't bothered updating the system?
Regards
Shella

FROM   Holly
TO   Patricia Gillot

Nothing to do with Trisha.
Sometimes it's because the secretaries or PAs don't give us all the names, but mainly it's just because there are new additions to the original meetings.
And no one's bothered letting us know (so the first we know about it is when they are standing in front of us demanding a badge).
Holly

FROM   Patricia Gillot
TO   Holly

Holly
But how do you fill in their details on the badges program whilst making the appropriate changes in the scheduler?
Shella

FROM   Holly
TO   Patricia Gillot

You have to flip between screens, by using CTRL and the tab button. (It's easier if you keep all five screens open at once.)

Subject: an email sent

FROM   Aisha
TO   Holly

I hear you're about to be sacked again — what's naughty Holly been up to now?
Aish

FROM   Holly
TO   Aisha

I'm not about to be sacked!

FROM   Aisha
TO   Holly

If you are though, fancy coming to Ibiza on Friday?

FROM   Holly
TO   Aisha

I'm not going to be sacked!!!

Subject: Clients

FROM   Holly
TO   Shella Hamilton-Jones; Patricia Gillot

That couple on the second couch, I think they've been there a while, is it all sorted?

FROM   Shella Hamilton-Jones
TO   Holly

Holly
    Of course it is, you don't have to watch over me, I've informed the host so it's their responsibility now.
    Shella

Subject: Justin Tanworth

FROM   Shella Hamilton-Jones
TO   Holly

Justin Tanworth just blew his top at me, because I had left his guests sitting around down here, but I informed his secretary, so surely it's her fault?

FROM   Holly
TO   Shella Hamilton-Jones

It should be, but we get the blame, because ultimately his secretary has a better relationship with him than we do, and the PAs and secretaries are used to relying on us to continually remind them to inform the host.

They might call the host and say their guests are waiting for them down here, but if the Director forgets this and the PA thinks they've done their job, if the guests are still down here it's our fault for not telling them again.

FROM   Shella Hamilton-Jones
TO   Holly

But the director was already in the meeting?

FROM   Holly
TO   Shella Hamilton-Jones

Then we can text him, or call the phone in the meeting, or if we can't leave the desk and his secretary is not around, then we have to get someone else to go into the meeting etc.

FROM   Shella Hamilton-Jones
TO   Holly

Well this has got to change, it's just not right.

Subject: REMINDER

FROM   Holly
TO   Holly

ONLY 2 DAYS LEFT TO GET FUNERAL DRESS!!!

Subject: what'sziz name

FROM Holly
TO Jason GrangerRM

*I've just thought, what kind of idiot signs his name off as 'J'
anyway??*

FROM Jason GrangerRM
TO Holly

Hiya
   Only complete tits do that.
   xx
   *PS we are talking about James aren't we, I don't think I've ever
done it?*

FROM Holly
TO Jason GrangerRM

No you haven't.
   xx
   No feedback yet from my email, she can't have read it.

FROM Jason GrangerRM
TO Holly

Something else on your mind?

FROM Holly
TO Jason GrangerRM

*Yes, I still haven't got a dress for Friday, because there is nothing in
the shops ever which fits me.*
   *The shops are just full of TINY CLOTHES FOR TINY PEOPLE and I
don't think any of these people exist, the clothes are just put in
shops to upset me!!!!!*

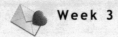

FROM   Jason GrangerRM
TO   Holly

Do you want me to come with you?

FROM   Holly
TO   Jason GrangerRM

I bet SHE will be going to the Gala in something which makes her nasty vindictive, evil, heart-stabbing, boyfriend-robbing body look great, and it's not fair! I bet she goes windsurfing too.

FROM   Jason GrangerRM
TO   Holly

Windsurfing?

FROM   Holly
TO   Jason GrangerRM

That's what HE likes doing, because HE wanted a sporty girlfriend, and SHE's always in the gym.
    I bet she does sky hopping, wind surfing, river bashing crappy pooh fart yuk.

FROM   Jason GrangerRM
TO   Holly

Are we being childish?

FROM   Holly
TO   Jason GrangerRM

Yes.

FROM   Jason GrangerRM
TO   Holly

Do you want to meet me tomorrow to find something?

FROM Holly
TO Jason GrangerRM

Yes. Please Jason.
  xxx
  Sorry for being childish.

Subject: Assistance please

FROM Holly
TO Alice and Matt

Can you put a spell on someone for me?

FROM Alice and Matt
TO Holly

I can give it a go? Are they sick?

FROM Holly
TO Alice and Matt

No, not yet. I was hoping you could make them sick??

FROM Alice and Matt
TO Holly

I'm studying to be a white witch.
  That means we help people get better, not the other way around.
  Sorry xxx
  (I can pray for her?)

THURSDAY

Subject: Catering

FROM   Shella Hamilton-Jones
TO   Holly

Holly
I think it would be quicker and make a lot more sense if we simply called up the catering team, to let them know if there are extra meals needed.
Shella

FROM   Holly
TO   Shella Hamilton-Jones

No, you have to update the scheduler too, otherwise the wrong costs are allocated to the host etc.

FROM   Shella Hamilton-Jones
TO   Holly

What happens if you fail to update the scheduler?

FROM   Holly
TO   · Shella Hamilton-Jones

There's a chance you'll get shouted at, the host or the catering team will be on your case.
Best to do it right first, also it keeps a record that you've done it, so there can be no arguments.
Holly

FROM   Shella Hamilton-Jones
TO   Holly

They can't really shout?

FROM   Holly
TO   Shella Hamilton-Jones

Not in front of clients, but they do.

Subject: RE your email

FROM   Charlie Denham
TO   Holly

Just picked up your message from yesterday.
    No I wouldn't bother recalling it, it'll look worse.
    Charlie

FROM   Holly
TO   Charlie Denham

Thanks Charlie, for your rapid response, I know this NOW.
    Regards
    Holly

Subject: She's still here

FROM   Holly
TO   Aisha; Jason GrangerRM

I've got to work with Shella again!
    Trish is still poorly.
    ☹
    Poor Trish.

Subject: Sick

FROM   Les Gillot
TO   Holly

Hey there darlin. You doing OK without me?

FROM   Holly
TO   Les Gillot

Why Leslie, I never thought you'd ask ... Does Patricia know you're emailing me?
  Holly

FROM   Les Gillot
TO   Holly

You think you're so funny!
  Leslie! I'll tell him.
  I hear we've got a new girl on reception.

FROM   Holly
TO   Les Gillot

Yup,
  Sitting next to me right now.
  Dan dan daaaaah
  How are you feeling?

FROM   Les Gillot
TO   Holly

Bit better, sitting up in bed now. So how bad is she? Tell us?

FROM   Holly
TO   Les Gillot

She's actually quite good. She's introduced a lot of new procedures which seem to be working out well etc. It's been a breeze.

FROM   Les Gillot
TO   Holly

What new procedures????
  Don't like the sound of this one, what's she after?

FROM   Holly
TO   Les Gillot

Sorry.
   Really bad thing to wind up a sick person.
   heee heee
   It's so so so bad here, you won't believe it, really missing you!!

FROM   Les Gillot
TO   Holly

Oh thank god for that.
   I was hoping you would miss me ... and I was sitting here thinking the bitch was after me job!!!
   You're a cruel girl Holly, you wait till I get back.

FROM   Holly
TO   Les Gillot

Are you back in tomorrow?

FROM   Les Gillot
TO   Holly

Yes, then I want to know about Toby and you better make it good, I've been looking forward to story time with Holly.
   xxxxx
   Trisha (keep smiling)

FROM   Holly
TO   Les Gillot

Promise I'll tell you everything.
   ☺
   I hope you really are in tomorrow, I can't go to that thing on my own ...
   xx

Subject: Ibiza

FROM   Aisha
TO   Holly

How's your day going?
   Did I tell you I'm going to Ibiza with a millionaire?

FROM   Holly
TO   Aisha

Yes you did.
   I can't email much today, Shella keeps watching my screen.
   Have a lovely time in Ibiza you lucky thing.
   xxxx

FRIDAY

Subject: She's back!!

FROM   Holly
TO   Patricia Gillot

Nice to have you back, what did the doctor say?

FROM   Patricia Gillot
TO   Holly

They don't know what's wrong with me.
   What was she like then the new girl, don't tell me she did well?

FROM   Holly
TO   Patricia Gillot

She started off the day with a quick meeting.
   She sat me down and told me she wanted to improve the company's 'front of house' with some new procedures.

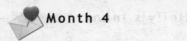

She said I had to keep my wits about me, because SHE wouldn't be as 'easy going' as you are.

FROM Patricia Gillot
TO Holly

What were these new procedures??????

FROM Holly
TO Patricia Gillot

When people come in and the phone rings, instead of answering it, and smiling at the clients to let them know you've seen them ... She wanted to let the phone ring continually while tutting at the clients and saying 'hold on hold on, can't you see I'm trying to do two things at once!!'

FROM Patricia Gillot
TO Holly

Ha ha ha, oh that's cheered me up, did she lose it?

FROM Holly
TO Patricia Gillot

It was her first time.

FROM Patricia Gillot
TO Holly

Flipping marvellous!!! I've wanted this for years ... for her to see what it's like, don't ruin it for me by saying you got on with her — remember this is the woman who screwed up your little rabbit picture!
    Did she lose her rag with anyone?

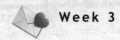

FROM Holly
TO Patricia Gillot

*She did, it was actually quite satisfying, you would have loved it ...
at one point she was shouting at a PA, and I had to remind her where
we were.*

FROM Patricia Gillot
TO Holly

OH OH OH YES YES YES

FROM Holly
TO Patricia Gillot

OK, anyway, I need a toilet break, are you OK for a moment?

FROM Patricia Gillot
TO Holly

*I think Shella's right about one thing though, I'm too easy on you ...
this place is going to be run more professional from now on, so sit
your arse down, I'm off for a f**king fag.*
   Trisha ha ha ha ha
   Oh, then after your break it's story time!

Subject: Holly Denham, star of the show ...

FROM Jason GrangerRM
TO Holly

*Good luck tonight — and remember, go easy on the booze and try and
keep this in mind for when you're staring out drunkenly across the
room. The sea of faces glaring back at you, their expressions are not
of 'wonder' but are in fact of 'fear', they are scared, so sit down.*
   *This is NOT, I repeat NOT the Albert Hall/Stars in their
Eyes/Opportunity Knocks/The Royal Variety Show/X Factor, and
although your singing is quite good you are a receptionist called
Holly Denham, NOT one called Leona Lewis.*
   xxx love you xxxx
   Jason

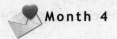

FROM   Holly
TO   Jason GrangerRM

Please have some faith in me, I will be a picture of grace and decorum.
   xxxx

Subject: Ibiza

FROM   Holly
TO   Aisha

Have fun in Ibiza, don't do anything you don't want to just because it's a nice boat or villa or whatever and you feel grateful ... call me if you need me.
   Love you
   xx

FROM   Aisha
TO   Holly

Yes Mum, I promise Mum.
   Re your night tonight, I know you don't often listen to my advice, but sometimes I can help—?

FROM   Holly
TO   Aisha

Tell me???

FROM   Aisha
TO   Holly

OK, well this is how I got a bit of revenge once. Are any men making speeches there tonight?

FROM   Holly
TO   Aisha

Yes.

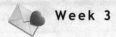

FROM　Aisha
TO　　Holly

Good, when you get there, find out who's going to be making a speech, choose the best looking of the bunch. And simply do a little flirting.

FROM　Holly
TO　　Aisha

That's it?

FROM　Aisha
TO　　Holly

Yes ... when I did it and he was called to make a speech, he was under my table giving me head!!!
*　You should have seen it, there was a spotlight looking for him and everything!!*
*　Xxxxxx enjoy.*

FROM　Holly
TO　　Aisha

Thanks Aish, I'll take your advice on board.

Subject: Story time!

FROM　Patricia Gillot
TO　　Holly

Why was Toby bad then?

FROM　Holly
TO　　Patricia Gillot

OK, when I first began talking to him we were both 15, but I'd known OF him since we'd both started there.
*　There's kind of an unwritten law which says the new boys joining*

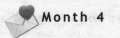

the school are the lowest of the low — it's easier for the girls, but that first year is really tough for the boys.

They do all the cleaning chores, sweeping and keeping the house and dorm spotless etc, and the older boys talk down to them.

A year later and it's their turn to pick on the new boys — it's kind of a tradition in private schools.

FROM   Patricia Gillot
TO   Holly

What nice traditions you lot have, so Toby went for one of them did he?

FROM   Holly
TO   Patricia Gillot

I heard he had about three fights with the older kids when he started, he just wouldn't accept it. In the end they all left him alone and he kept this bad boy reputation.

He wasn't a trouble maker though, he just didn't like the school much.

FROM   Patricia Gillot
TO   Holly

Good for him.

FROM   Holly
TO   Patricia Gillot

I got in lots of trouble after I was caught smoking and then the teachers knew where everyone had been going to smoke, so then that was out.

It was a couple of weeks before I saw him again, I was just sitting on a bench in the sun outside the school library and he sat down next to me. He started chatting about the school and the cliques and everything, and he told me they had a new secret place for smoking.

I had decided smoking wasn't really for me by this time, but I wanted to go there anyway.

FROM Patricia Gillot
TO Holly

I bet you did, you naughty tart.

FROM Holly
TO Patricia Gillot

We went to the chapel, but this time inside it.

I remember thinking, it must be some kind of awful joke and there's going to be my classmates there laughing and it would be a set up or something.

We worked our way along a pew and sat down. Then he reached down and pulled up this wooden hatch in the floor. It was dark and he jumped down, and disappeared.

I waited for a moment and then, asking God to watch me, I went in after him.

FROM Patricia Gillot
TO Holly

Holly Denham, you surprise me.

FROM Holly
TO Patricia Gillot

I surprised myself. Down in the dark I sat until he lit a light.

It was this whole passage network of kind of tunnels, in the foundations. You couldn't stand up, but he'd set the place up with cushions and bean bags, drinks and there was a Walkman, I couldn't believe it.

He said he went there to get away from everyone.

It was so good, I began meeting him there regularly and we'd read, chat, or listen to music, I kissed him on my second time under the chapel.

I didn't do any more smoking, but I'd found something much better.

FROM Patricia Gillot
TO Holly

What? What had you found … and I bet your mum would have been just as annoyed.

FROM Holly
TO Patricia Gillot

More, when she found out. More later, got to go.
  Xxx

FROM Patricia Gillot
TO Holly

Oh Holly!!!

WEEK 4

BANK HOLIDAY MONDAY

Subject: Toby

FROM　Alice and Matt
TO　　Holly

About Toby.
*　　I've been thinking about it over the weekend, and you need to speak to him, find out why he never wrote to you.*
*　　There might be a reason, it can't have been easy for him either, you were both very young.*
*　　xxx*
*　　Alice*

TUESDAY

Subject: The reason he never wrote

FROM　Holly
TO　　Alice and Matt

He never wrote to me Alice because he's a bastard.
*　　I'm sorry, but he broke my heart and it's taken a long long time to get over him and now I've done it.*
*　　If he'd have cared at all, even a little bit, he'd have got in touch and I don't think being young is an excuse.*
*　　xxxx*

FROM　Alice and Matt
TO　　Holly

OK.
*　　I didn't mean to sound pushy.*
*　　Also I think Joseph is playing up more and more. Today I couldn't find my favourite shoes, I asked Joseph if he knows anything about*

them, because I saw him holding them yesterday. He gave me an innocent explanation, filled with so much detail (a real epic) that I know he was lying, but he won't admit it.

   Happy days.

   Alice

Subject: Toby

FROM   Patricia Gillot
TO   Holly

Can't believe what happened at the party. You've got to talk to him now?

FROM   Holly
TO   Patricia Gillot

No thanks.

FROM   Patricia Gillot
TO   Holly

You told me the good bits about when you two were young, so I can't see what the problem is, until you tell me what went wrong?

FROM   Holly
TO   Patricia Gillot

I missed my period, and for him, that was that.

FROM   Patricia Gillot
TO   Holly

You were pregnant?

FROM   Holly
TO   Patricia Gillot

I didn't get my period for weeks, it was a boarding school so these things aren't easy to keep quiet and our school was in the country, so no way of getting to any shops, so no pregnancy tests either.

In the end I was so scared I told Toby.

We had an argument, the next thing I knew was he'd done a runner and never came back to school.

Finally, I discovered I wasn't pregnant, but with typical school gossip, everyone thought I'd had an abortion.

I was really in love with him, head over heals, you know what it's like with first love.

I never heard from Toby again though.

FROM   Patricia Gillot
TO   Holly

Oh.

Subject: Conference

FROM   Shella Hamilton-Jones
TO   Holly

Dear Holly
  Organising a conference is not an easy feat; I need to have everything prepared as soon as possible.
  Have you managed to get some of the research started for the hotels?
  If not can you get yourself in gear and get it done ASAP?
  Regards
  Shella

FROM   Holly
TO   Shella Hamilton-Jones

Shella
  Yes, I've finished it, let me know when you want it?
  Regards
  Holly

FROM Shella Hamilton-Jones
TO Holly

Holly
If you honestly think you are ready to show me a professional project-managed production of the information requested, then I need to see it ASAP.
Therefore I have requested you work upstairs with me tomorrow afternoon to go through your presentation; we've organised a receptionworld temp to help cover the desk with Trisha.
Regards
Shella

Subject: It's so exciting ...

FROM Jason GrangerRM
TO Holly

Let me know the gossip, (like if he says anything else).

FROM Holly
TO Jason GrangerRM

I'll never forgive him for dumping me at my hour of need — so drop it!

FROM Jason GrangerRM
TO Holly

SORRY.

FROM Holly
TO Jason GrangerRM

Didn't mean to sound grumpy, just had everyone ask me this morning.
He's always been a strange boy, it doesn't change a thing.

Subject: Dorchester

FROM Patricia Gillot
TO Holly

*Sounds like you're right then, he's not worth thinking about darlin.
    You fancy going for a drink some time this week?*

FROM Holly
TO Patricia Gillot

*That sounds good,
    Re Shella — I can't believe she's still such a bitch, what is wrong
with that woman??*

FROM Patricia Gillot
TO Holly

Maybe she did read your email slagging her off?

FROM Holly
TO Patricia Gillot

*No, she couldn't have done, she would have crucified me happily if
she had.*

FROM Patricia Gillot
TO Holly

*Looks like she is anyway — presentation?? Project managed??
    I'd take the day off sick, sounds like a ritual killing to me.*

FROM Holly
TO Patricia Gillot

Thanks.

FROM Patricia Gillot
TO Holly

Also, you haven't heard from Jennie or James yet???

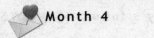

FROM Holly
TO Patricia Gillot

Not yet, d'you think I'm going to be in trouble?

FROM Patricia Gillot
TO Holly

For doing what? They were acting like idiots.

FROM Holly
TO Patricia Gillot

I'm sure I'll hear something from Jen soon though, she reminds me of a shark who's gone back down below to lick her wounds — before she comes back up for an even worse attack.

FROM Patricia Gillot
TO Holly

Can I at least say I like Toby's style?

FROM Holly
TO Patricia Gillot

He's got a way with words, always had.
   But that's about it.
   xx

WEDNESDAY

Subject: Your brother

FROM Alice and Matt
TO Holly

I'm not happy with Charlie.
   When you next talk to him, you may want to tell him how unamusing he is.

FROM   Holly
TO   Alice and Matt

*No, I'm not being blamed for anything he does, he's OUR brother.
(What's he been up to now?)*

Subject: It's all about me!!

FROM   Aisha
TO   Holly

Guess where I am?

FROM   Holly
TO   Aisha

Ibiza?

FROM   Aisha
TO   Holly

OK yes, but where exactly??

FROM   Holly
TO   Aisha

Having sex with someone??

FROM   Aisha
TO   Holly

*No actually Miss Holly-pants, although I think I might later.
   I am on a lovely boat!!*

FROM   Holly
TO   Aisha

You're not on a boat, how can you be emailing me from a boat?

FROM Aisha
TO Holly

It's a big one, and the guy who owns it has let me shower in his place, and use his stuff.
I think he said I could use his stuff, cause I am.
Holly my bestist bestist friend, this is going to surprise you, but I was thinking about you, and and the party seems to have got a bit dull anyway and I wanted to know what happened, at that party.

FROM Holly
TO Aisha

You want to know what happened to me???

FROM Aisha
TO Holly

No. Not really, I'm going back upstairs.
bye
x

Subject: Office party thing last Friday

FROM Aisha
TO Holly

I do really want to know, ☺
Tell me please Holly pants, before I get kicked off his computer (I might look at some dirty pictures in between your emails if you don't mind) (men on this ship aren't much to look at) (all old and fat)
(and some with beards) But tell me because I realy want to know!!!!!
xxxxx

FROM Holly
TO Aisha

Are you OK?

FROM　Aisha
TO　　Holly

Why wouldn't I be?
　　I'm on holiday having just the best time, it's all fab.
　　xx Tell me

FROM　Holly
TO　　Aisha

It was really strange and I don't know what to make of it yet.
　　The Gala all began as expected.
　　I was nervous the whole day, I only managed to eat breakfast and a bag of crisps for lunch.
　　I wore that dress I wore to your party, the black and white one and I added some long white gloves and my new shoes.
　　Not looking too bad.
　　It was raining, so I purposely made sure I'd ordered a cab with plenty of time to spare.
　　Kept my hair out of the rain between cab and Dorchester and followed the signs down to the function room — massive place, people were arriving as I went in.
　　I was one of the first few and the others were in small groups of their own (people I didn't recognise), so I thought about heading back out and going to a bar until everyone else arrived, but then Trish and the boys from the post room turned up.

FROM　Aisha
TO　　Holly

Had you seen her yet?

FROM　Holly
TO　　Aisha

No.
　　The place began filling up and I began to hope that maybe she wasn't going to come at all, that she'd be too scared of confrontation, and they'd both decided to boycott it out of a sense of proportion or kindness or something.
　　I got a couple of drinks down me and then of course Jennie did turn up.

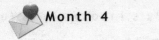

FROM Aisha
TO Holly

What was she wearing?

FROM Holly
TO Aisha

A tight red slinky dress of course — it was as if the nightmares I'd had were premonitions. Everyone was looking at her while she pranced around like some kind of princess, both of them together, him in a black tux.

FROM Aisha
TO Holly

She's a dirty whore.

FROM Holly
TO Aisha

Thanks Aish.
   After watching this for a while I realised I had to leave, I couldn't be there.
   I thought they'd at least have kept their relationship a little secret.
   I mean when I was with him it was oh so important no one knew, bastard, but they walked around the place arm in arm, her like the cat that got the cream.
   That's when I first began feeling sick.

FROM Aisha
TO Holly

You didn't puke did you??? No Holly, not in front of everyone?

FROM Holly
TO Aisha

... I remember, thinking, this is it, I'm going to throw up over myself, all over my dress and everyone's going to laugh.
   The more I thought about it the worse I got, I felt myself turn cold.

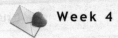
I got to the bathroom and locked myself in a cubicle shaking like a leaf and fighting the urge to throw up.

I wanted to go home, I couldn't picture even being able to make it to the exit door of the building.

I remember thinking I'd happily spend the rest of my life locked in there, with food and water passed under the door — as long as I didn't have to go out and face everyone.

FROM Aisha
TO Holly

Poor baby, I would have saved you, if I hadn't been on a plane drinking champagne.

FROM Holly
TO Aisha

Trish found me in the end and insisted I come out (or she was going to 'kick the f***ing door in').

She's so lovely, I owe her, I hope one day I can be there for her.

She made me down four drinks she'd got waiting for me and put more make up on, luckily Jennie didn't come in while I was wiping mascara off my cheeks.

I avoided her until we were all seated — and that's when it all began to go wrong.

I could still see them through a gap in peoples heads — their table was on the other side of the room and although there were about a hundred people in between us, I could see them, kissing, laughing and all over each other.

I tried not to think about them and at first managed to get involved in conversation — and alcohol.

Problem was — I couldn't eat anything because I was so worked up, so food came and went and I kept drinking and by the time the dessert had been served I was well on the way.

FROM Aisha
TO Holly

I've a feeling someone wants to use this room (I've locked the door). Who cares, so you're sitting there drunk?

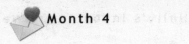

FROM Holly
TO Aisha

I remember thinking as I approached them that they needed to be told — so they both could know what heartless bastards they were.

I was going to appeal to their better instincts and I thought I had something worked out, which would make them feel really small about their behaviour. But as I began getting closer to them, squeezing through past people's chairs etc, I bumped into someone who knocked a drink (luckily) down themselves. After I'd apologised and began heading off again towards Jennie and James, I'd forgotten everything I'd planned to say.

James had now noticed me so I couldn't exactly turn back, I carried on till I got to their table.

He nudged Jennie and then she looked up and whatever I had left to say, went. She looked me in the eyes and immediately that smirk began building on her lips. I began saying something and from recollection it went — 'I think — you two — well people think — I think you are', and that's as far as I got before Jennie said:

'Sorry — Holly is it? I think you're at the wrong table, you're over there with support staff.'

At which point I felt myself go red and things seemed to wobble. I heard her laugh, I must have garbled something and just then I heard a voice say:

'I think what Holly's trying to say is "James, if you want a bed, rent a room, this is an office party, not a brothel, so scrape that whore off your arm and go find one!!!"'

It was Toby and he was standing next to me and then him and James seemed to launch themselves at each other.

At that point I was being led away by Trisha and it all seemed to fizzle out. I went home soon after. No one's said anything yet from upstairs, but I'm waiting ...

What d'you think?

FROM Aisha
TO Holly

Go Toby!!

I think I would have punched the bitch, or poured a drink over her, or thrown food in her lap.

So you getting back with Toby?

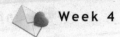

FROM Holly
TO   Aisha

No, definitely not.

FROM Aisha
TO   Holly

He needs bagging quickly, got any pictures of him?
*   No, go back to your party. Wait, scratch that, GO TO BED!*
*   xxxxxx*
*   (for sleep)*

FROM Aisha
TO   Holly

Might need to talk to you later.

FROM Holly
TO   Aisha

Bed bed bed, Aisha needs to sleep.
*   Say night-night to everyone Aishy*
*   (I'll be here if you need me)*

THURSDAY

Subject: Envelopes

FROM Shella Hamilton-Jones
TO   Holly; Judy Perkins; Patricia Gillot

Dear Judy,
*   Having now spent some time on the reception desk myself, I know that both Holly and Patricia are very busy, for most of their time.*
*   However during the quieter times eg; at the beginning and end of each day, I was hoping to utilise their able dextrosity in communi-cating an urgent message to employees and delegates.*
*   If this is OK, I'll have the envelopes which need stuffing delivered to them now.*
*   Yours*
*   Shella*

Subject: Shella

FROM   Holly
TO   Patricia Gillot

Able dextrosity???

FROM   Patricia Gillot
TO   Holly

Hand me my boots, I need to pay her a visit.

FROM   Holly
TO   Patricia Gillot

If she's always this rude to everyone in the company, how come she hasn't been sacked years ago??

FROM   Patricia Gillot
TO   Holly

They're too scared.

FROM   Holly
TO   Patricia Gillot

But she's a PA, it's not like she's bringing money into the company or anything?

FROM   Patricia Gillot
TO   Holly

That's not why they're scared, it's not a money thing.

Subject: Mum

FROM   Alice and Matt
TO   Holly

Don't you think it's time you called her? She really is feeling bad about everything.
    Alice

FROM   Holly
TO   Alice and Matt

I'm not calling her yet. Maybe I will soon.
    So tell me what did Charlie do?

FROM   Alice and Matt
TO   Holly

Our delightful brother called up on Monday night around 7pm, drunk, and I know he feels awkward when my children answer the phone because he doesn't know what to say to them, but I really do think he should work on something — anything except telling little Joseph how to make a magic sweet tree ... ????
    Do you know how to make one?

FROM   Holly
TO   Alice and Matt

No, but I'm guessing it's fun?

FROM   Alice and Matt
TO   Holly

Apparently you need to empty a bag of sugar and a slab of butter into one of mummy's shoes and bury it in the garden, (or so Uncle Charlie told him).
    You know how my son looks up to Bad Uncle Charlie, he'll do anything Charlie tells him.
    Can you have a word with Charlie for me? He just laughs when I tell him, and then gets upset when I don't find it funny.

FROM Holly
TO Alice and Matt

Sorry, I tried not to laugh, I did maybe a teeny bit.
But I guess not funny when it's your shoes full of butter, I'll have a word with him I promise.
xxx
Haven't actually heard from him in a while.

Subject: And as if by magic ...

FROM Holly
TO Patricia Gillot

The desk was swamped in envelopes!
Grrrr

FROM Patricia Gillot
TO Holly

We should get Ralph to help, he'd love doing this for us.

FROM Holly
TO Patricia Gillot

No he wouldn't.

FROM Patricia Gillot
TO Holly

He would if we made him do it kneeling in the middle of the reception??

FROM Holly
TO Patricia Gillot

☺
Funny, and when Judy catches him, I can picture her face now, utter confusion??? (Followed by rage.)
Best not.
So tell me why people are frightened of Shella (apart from her charming persona)?

Subject: Where are you these days?

FROM Holly
TO Jason GrangerRM

Not heard a squeak from you?
   xxx

Subject: Envelopes

FROM Patricia Gillot
TO Holly

Pass me some more.
   And answering your question, when I joined, Shella had already been here a while, there was a lot less of us back then, and she was the PA for Mr Wright, before he died ...

FROM Holly
TO Patricia Gillot

So?
   So what are you saying??????

FROM Patricia Gillot
TO Holly

That she knows that Mr Huerst killed Mr Wright!

FROM Holly
TO Patricia Gillot

?

FROM Patricia Gillot
TO Holly

And Shella and Randy Randolph Huerst have been having an affair, for 20 years!!!

FROM   Holly
TO   Patricia Gillot

??

FROM   Patricia Gillot
TO   Holly

Stop sending over those flippin question marks, it's true!

FROM   Holly
TO   Patricia Gillot

Sorry Trish but I feel this may be just your imagination?

FROM   Patricia Gillot
TO   Holly

It's true, Randolph Huerst and Shella Hamilton-Jones have been sharing the same bed for years, and they killed Mr Wright.

FROM   Holly
TO   Patricia Gillot

They did, did they?

FROM   Patricia Gillot
TO   Holly

They did, and they had a kid, and this is the best bit, it's my job to tell you darlin, it's you.

FROM   Holly
TO   Patricia Gillot

I am the love child of Shella and Mr Huerst?

FROM   Patricia Gillot
TO   Holly

Yes.

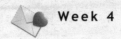

Subject: WORK WORK WORK

FROM Jason GrangerRM
TO Holly

Haven't had much chance to gossip, been busy, since Aisha's away, also got two more off sick.
    xxx

Subject: The truth is

FROM Patricia Gillot
TO Holly

OK, I'm lying.

FROM Holly
TO Patricia Gillot

That's a shame, I was going to ask Daddy for some cash.

FROM Patricia Gillot
TO Holly

Anyway Shella must know something big, some dark secret they don't want coming out.
    Also, I thought you said James lives in Richmond?

FROM Holly
TO Patricia Gillot

He does (please refer to him as scumbag — makes me happier).

FROM Patricia Gillot
TO Holly

But then who lives in Islington — his parents?

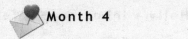

FROM Holly
TO Patricia Gillot

No, his parents live in Chelsea — I went there once — nice house, scumbag parents (didn't meet them).
(But probably are.)
Why, who lives in Islington?????

FROM Patricia Gillot
TO Holly

I've got his letter here, Mr James Lawrence — 140 Elgin Drive, Islington.

FROM Holly
TO Patricia Gillot

Are you sure?????

FROM Patricia Gillot
TO Holly

Yes. I think he's been telling you porkies?

Subject: When you come back

FROM Patricia Gillot
TO Holly

Hope you and Shella had fun together. I've been thinking about this address thing, and there must be a reason he's been a lying little toe rag.

FRIDAY

Subject: Bite Marks

FROM Patricia Gillot
TO Holly

How did yesterday with Shella go?
    You look happy, why aren't you missing some teeth?
    Can't see no bite marks on your arms either?

FROM Holly
TO Patricia Gillot

We talked about everything I'd put together. Shella looked at it.
    Didn't pass any comment at all, said she'd review it and get back to me this morning.
    So ... aaaaaaaaaagh viper email at any moment.

Subject: A bright sunny Friday to you Miss Hilton

FROM Jason GrangerRM
TO Holly

Looking forward to meeting Trisha tonight.
    Where are we going then?

FROM Holly
TO Jason GrangerRM

Don't know, I was thinking about Henry's bar in Covent Garden?

Subject: Nightclub

FROM Holly
TO Charlie Denham

I haven't heard from you for a while, is everything going OK with the club?
   Holly

Subject: I'll pray for you darlin

FROM Patricia Gillot
TO Holly

Tell me when Shella sends that hate email and I'll go pick us up some chocolate cake from catering.
   Now more important things:
   Mr James Lawrence
   140 Elgin Drive
   Islington
   that's Islington NOT Richmond
   What's that about then?

FROM Holly
TO Patricia Gillot

He definitely lives in Richmond, with half the house covered in tarpaulin, massive extension on the back.
   Maybe this is a friend's place?

FROM Patricia Gillot
TO Holly

How d'you know he lives in Richmond?

FROM Holly
TO Patricia Gillot

He told me.

FROM Patricia Gillot
TO   Holly

Yeah but he could be lying.

FROM Holly
TO   Patricia Gillot

OK, but why would he lie?

FROM Patricia Gillot
TO   Holly

That's what we need to find out.
   *So you never saw this huge house in Richmond or any pictures of
it with this amazing extension?*

FROM Holly
TO   Patricia Gillot

*No, I wanted to go one night but James said something about it being
too far out of town to bother — in Richmond? So do you think he lives
in a tiny flat in Islington and he made the other one up?*

FROM Patricia Gillot
TO   Holly

I hate to bring her up, but where does Jennie live?

FROM Holly
TO   Patricia Gillot

No, she doesn't live in Islington.

FROM Patricia Gillot
TO   Holly

*Richmond's too far, but if he said it was in Islington, you could have
been over there in a shot.*
   *I think he's lying. He tells girls he lives in some swanky palace in
Richmond, while really he's slumming it in some rat hole in Islington?*

FROM Holly
TO   Patricia Gillot

Islington's still quite expensive though?

FROM Patricia Gillot
TO   Holly

Still might be a hole.
    He might even be putting on a fake accent, my guess is he speaks more like me.
    When he's with you he's all 'just a gin and ha ha yar'? and back home he's 'gizza pint an some scratchins you muppet!'

FROM Holly
TO   Patricia Gillot

Stop making me laugh, I need to pee!

FROM Patricia Gillot
TO   Holly

It's probably not even his real name, he's probably called Jimbo, he's probably got a mark 2 Escort hidden somewhere.

FROM Holly
TO   Patricia Gillot

What's that?

FROM Patricia Gillot
TO   Holly

Ask him, when he walks past say:
    'Oi Jimbo! Next time I'm in yer mannor give us a butches at yer mark 2 you can't.'

FROM   Holly
TO   Patricia Gillot

That's it — you've done it — I've got the giggles — I'm off, before I have an accident.
  xx

Subject: Wanted to talk

FROM   Toby Williams
TO   Holly

Hi.

Subject: Why I've been quiet

FROM   Charlie Denham
TO   Holly

I lost the club.
  Charlie

FROM   Holly
TO   Charlie Denham

What? Why didn't you tell me — are you alright?

Subject: Annual Review: Your research

FROM   Shella Hamilton-Jones
TO   Holly

Holly
  I'm keen to get together for another meeting some afternoon next week, let me know when would be suitable for you.
  Having had time to study your submission for longer I found myself considerably impressed and you've left me rather intrigued,

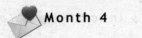

because I can't see anywhere on your CV the mention of any training at all in events or project management?
   Regards
   Shella

Subject: Talk

FROM   Holly
TO   Toby Williams

Why are you emailing me?

FROM   Toby Williams
TO   Holly

I want to talk to you.

FROM   Holly
TO   Toby Williams

No, Toby please.

FROM   Toby Williams
TO   Holly

I know you were married.

FROM   Holly
TO   Toby Williams

What?

FROM   Toby Williams
TO   Holly

I know he was a bastard and you've no reason to trust men, but please Holly.
   I just need to get everything straight, can I see you tonight?

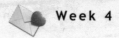

FROM Holly
TO Toby Williams

Toby, don't do this. Please. I don't want to go back. Please Toby, just leave it all alone.

FROM Toby Williams
TO Holly

Come out tonight and let me explain. Please.

Subject: Pain

FROM Patricia Gillot
TO Holly

My arse is killing me on this seat. I'm going for a fag, you alright?

FROM Holly
TO Patricia Gillot

Fine.
    x

FROM Patricia Gillot
TO Holly

Looking forward to seeing your Jason tonight — back in a mo.

Subject: Annual Review: Your research

FROM Holly
TO Shella Hamilton-Jones

Shella
    I'm fine any day next week — it's just Judy and Trisha who I would need to check with etc.

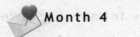

Re — events & project management training — I just looked on the internet etc.
Kindest regards
Holly

FROM Shella Hamilton-Jones
TO   Holly

Holly
   Let me get this straight; you went on to the internet and you learnt all that in a week?
   Shella

FROM Holly
TO   Shella Hamilton-Jones

Yes.

Subject: Shella

FROM Holly
TO   Patricia Gillot

Is it likely that Shella could have a copy of my CV?

FROM Patricia Gillot
TO   Holly

Of course. Why? Also you decided what we're going to do about James' dodgy address thing?

FROM Holly
TO   Patricia Gillot

I'm not going to do anything about his address thing — what's there to do?

Subject: Tonight

FROM   Toby Williams
TO   Holly

You haven't answered me, I'm not going to push this for ever, I'd really like you to come out so I can talk to you.
*   If not then that's fine and I promise this will be the last time you will hear from me.*
*   Toby*

Subject: Internet

FROM   Shella Hamilton-Jones
TO   Holly

Holly
*   I find this very difficult to believe, but the work is very good, which is the most important thing.*
*   I will email you a time for us to meet up again next week.*
*   Shella*

Subject: Hello

FROM   Holly
TO   Toby Williams

Are you there?

FROM   Toby Williams
TO   Holly

Yes.

FROM Holly
TO Toby Williams

I just didn't want to write something which could be read by everyone up there, while you were at lunch or something.

FROM Toby Williams
TO Holly

No, I'm here, no one's around, I think most of them are in the bar still.

FROM Holly
TO Toby Williams

Thank you for last Friday night.

FROM Toby Williams
TO Holly

You're welcome.

FROM Holly
TO Toby Williams

I wasn't doing so well.

FROM Toby Williams
TO Holly

You were doing fine.

FROM Holly
TO Toby Williams

No I wasn't.
  I thought that kind of thing would get easier, but it's got harder the older I've got. I've lost a lot of what I used to have.

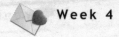

FROM   Toby Williams
TO   Holly

I don't think you have.

FROM   Holly
TO   Toby Williams

I have. You remember when we'd take on all the cliques and gangs, and give them as good as we got?

FROM   Toby Williams
TO   Holly

Of course.

FROM   Holly
TO   Toby Williams

When I was standing there last Friday, I suddenly felt like I was back in that cafeteria, and you were there with me, and we were giving as good as we gave. It was weird. Very strange.

FROM   Toby Williams
TO   Holly

For me too. I just want you back Holly, give me a chance.

FROM   Holly
TO   Toby Williams

I can't.

FROM   Toby Williams
TO   Holly

Holly
     I've never stopped loving you, ever. Just give me a chance.
     Please.

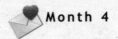

FROM Holly
TO Toby Williams

I loved you too, so so much.
I can't go back though, please understand this.
When you left, it was so difficult. Too difficult. I want to get myself stronger now and I don't want to lean on your shoulder, or anyone else's ever again.
Too many ups and downs, I can't cope with it all, sorry Toby.
xx

FROM Toby Williams
TO Holly

I'm coming down Holly, I'm not giving up.

Subject: Going out

FROM Holly
TO Patricia Gillot

I'm going out, if you see Toby tell him no.
Sorry.
x

FROM Patricia Gillot
TO Holly

No what? What's going on, do you need me babe?

Subject: Me

FROM Aisha
TO Holly; Jason GrangerRM

got very drunk, got married.
picture attached

FROM   Sara

TO   Toby, William

Have a won... ... ... party

... you'll ... ...
... ...
... ...
... ...

... ...

FROM   Lisa Wingate

TO   Brittany

... ...

Subject: Coming out

FROM   Bob

TO   Patricia Blank

... ...

FROM   Rebecca Joel

TO   Holly

... ...

Subject: Me

FROM   Lisa

TO   Will, ...

... ...

MONTH 5

WEEK 1

MONDAY

Subject: Wedding??

FROM   Holly
TO   Jason GrangerRM

Hiya
   Tell me when our lunatic friend gets in!!!
   xxx

FROM   Jason GrangerRM
TO   Holly

She's not coming in.

FROM   Holly
TO   Jason GrangerRM

So you've spoken to her???

FROM   Jason GrangerRM
TO   Holly

She called in sick, of course.

FROM   Holly
TO   Jason GrangerRM

So? What was our naughty sparrow doing in a wedding dress?

FROM   Jason GrangerRM
TO   Holly

The question is was it a wedding dress?

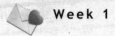
FROM   Holly
TO   Jason GrangerRM

Stop teasing me, do you know or not?

FROM   Jason GrangerRM
TO   Holly

No.
   Didn't speak to her myself, now she's not answering the phone, I'll keep you updated on Mrs — whoever.
   At least this is the kind of thing I can imagine her wearing to her wedding.

FROM   Holly
TO   Jason GrangerRM

Yes, totally inappropriate, looking a complete trollop and the kind of thing I could only dream of being able to get away with (at a fancy dress party).
   Love her.

Subject: Rent

FROM   Charlie Denham
TO   Holly

Unless we come up with the back-rent they're not going to let us back in the club.
   Charlie

FROM   Holly
TO   Charlie Denham

I heard. How long have you got?

FROM   Charlie Denham
TO   Holly

Maybe a few weeks, I hope.

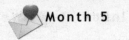

FROM   Holly
TO   Charlie Denham

If I could help you, I probably would (as much as I'd fight against doing it). Sorry, Charlie.
  xx

Subject: Friday night

FROM   Holly
TO   Patricia Gillot

Morning you drunkard. Had a great time Friday night, thanks.
  xxxxx

FROM   Patricia Gillot
TO   Holly

I was in a right old 2n8 when you left.
  Good weren't it and we love gorgeous Jason.
  He's so funny, he had me and Les in stitches the whole night. Me Vikki was after him and she wishes she could change him!

Subject: Your ex

FROM   Patricia Gillot
TO   Holly

So what are we going to do about James' address thing?

FROM   Holly
TO   Patricia Gillot

Nothing?

FROM   Patricia Gillot
TO   Holly

Don't you want to know why he lied?

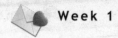

FROM   Holly
TO   Patricia Gillot

I'm happier not thinking about either him or Jennie at all.

FROM   Patricia Gillot
TO   Holly

Well I'm not leaving it, I'm a right nosy so-and-so and I want to know.

Subject: Reference for you

FROM   Jason GrangerRM
TO   Holly

A Hillary just called from 'the HR dept at Huerst & Wright' wanting a reference for you.
   When I tried to give them one, they didn't sound too impressed, like they wanted to check it with our personnel dept etc.
   I gave them all this months ago?

FROM   Holly
TO   Jason GrangerRM

I bet that's something Shella's stirred up, she sounded very suspicious last week.

FROM   Jason GrangerRM
TO   Holly

That's your own fault then, I told you not to be such a smarty-pants.

FROM   Holly
TO   Jason GrangerRM

I wasn't being a smarty-pants, just doing my best, anyway that's not helpful. What will your HR say if they go directly there for a ref?

FROM   Jason GrangerRM
TO   Holly

They'll probably confirm the dates, that you were here two weeks and not two years ...

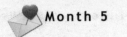

FROM Holly
TO Jason GrangerRM

Oh joy. Fab, that's just great.

FROM Jason GrangerRM
TO Holly

You should probably come clean now.

FROM Holly
TO Jason GrangerRM

I can't do that, they'll definitely sack me then.

FROM Jason GrangerRM
TO Holly

*If you'd told Trisha the truth you could ask her.
(Holly! Stop glaring at me.)*

FROM Holly
TO Jason GrangerRM

*It's a bit late now, but I know, I know.
Got to go, conference stuff with Shella again.
x*

TUESDAY

Subject: I've been thinking

FROM Jason GrangerRM
TO Holly

I want a baby.

FROM   Holly
TO   Jason GrangerRM

I'm not ready for them Jason, besides which I'm not your type (I have nasty breasties).

FROM   Jason GrangerRM
TO   Holly

I know, quite repulsive.
   I'm feeling blue.
   ☹

FROM   Holly
TO   Jason GrangerRM

Are you getting paternal again?

FROM   Jason GrangerRM
TO   Holly

Yes.

FROM   Holly
TO   Jason GrangerRM

OK, I found this in our receptionists' magazine, you could sponsor a child, you get letter from them and school reports and everything, check it out. http://www.frontofhousemagazine.co.uk/loveachild .asp
   If that doesn't work I could get pregnant Pam to give you a call, that should put you off?
   xxxxx

FROM   Jason GrangerRM
TO   Holly

Thanks.
   x

Subject: Holly

FROM Shella Hamilton-Jones
TO Holly; Judy Perkins

Dear Judy
Is it possible to borrow Holly for another couple of afternoons this week? I'd like to get her involved in other areas of the planning of this conference. (I've copied Holly into this email.)
Regards
Shella

Subject: Granny

FROM Alice and Matt
TO Holly

Hi Holly
I spoke to Mum today, she was telling me how Granny has been going to church more and more these days.
Mum says it's because Granny's thinking about the next life, and what it might have in store for her.
☹

Subject: Dad's army

FROM Holly
TO Granny

Hi Granny
How are you? Everything here much the same.
Also did you get those tapes I sent you of Dad's Army?
Love Holly xxx

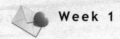

FROM Granny
TO Holly

Holly
Thank you so much for the tapes, I haven't received them yet, but you know what the post is like.

Have you spoken to your mother?

I know she has a tendency to put her foot in her mouth whenever she opens it, but she usually means well.

It's best not to let these things dwell, or one day you'll find it's just too late to make things up.

It's your decision of course and you can tell your nosy grandmother to bog off if you want.

Love Granny
xxx

FROM Holly
TO Granny

Thanks Granny, I'll get in touch today.

Of course I love her lots, just wanted to punish her a bit first.

Also that comment you emailed — about needing to get things straight before it's too late. You're not having any morbid thoughts are you — Alice mentioned you've been going to church a lot?

Holly

FROM Granny
TO Holly

Holly
I'm not having any morbid thoughts dear, I just don't think arguments should go stale.

Yes I am going to church a lot, not so I can get closer to God as your mother thinks, but to get closer to the communion wine, as I can get quite sozzled on the port if I'm left to hold the chalice long enough. Unfortunately the parish priest, at some stage, snatches it back and offers it to the next poor sinner. Still I guess he has a job to do.

If I was treated as an adult instead of a child I wouldn't have to go to church.

Your Gran as always
Elizabeth
xxx

FROM   Holly
TO   Granny

Granny,
*   you have an amazing way of always making me smile!*
*   xxxx*

TRISHA'S
INBOX

TUESDAY

Subject: I'm waiting

FROM Les
TO Trisha

So what's the news?

FROM Trisha
TO Les

I'm still waiting Les, he hasn't emailed yet.

FROM Les
TO Trisha

Tell me when he does won't you.

FROM Trisha
TO Les

I said I would didn't I?

Subject: Hello

FROM Les
TO Trisha

Any news?

FROM Trisha
TO Les

No Les.

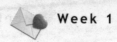

Subject: So?

FROM Les
TO   Trisha

Any news?

FROM Trisha
TO   Les

Les, can't you p*ss off and leave me alone? Find something else to do?

FROM Les
TO   Trisha

Alright, I'm only asking, do you think I should go with him?

FROM Trisha
TO   Les

I don't know, I'll find out when he emails OK!

Subject: Tests

FROM Dr Goth
TO   Trisha

Dear Patricia
  We still need to organise a time for you to come in again for further tests. Please can you contact the surgery when you have a spare moment.
    Kelly C
    Admin

Subject: Psssssssssssssst are you there?

FROM Jason GrangerRM
TO   Trisha

All set, I'm going there from 6pm ... waiting ... How exciting!

FROM　Trisha
TO　　Jason GrangerRM

At last, I thought you were going to bottle out on me. Did you sort yourself out with everything you need?

FROM　JasonGrangerRM
TO　　Trisha

The essentials required for any modern agent or gay spy (we like to be known as WAGS).

FROM　Trisha
TO　　Jason GrangerRM

Darlin that spells MAGS.

FROM　Jason GrangerRM
TO　　Trisha

I know, just realised but who cares, I just want to be a WAG. Anyway, I got our chef to rustle us up a great selection of food and drink which I've packed into a cooler, there's enough there for when Les swaps over.

FROM　Trisha
TO　　Jason GrangerRM

Oh he will be happy, does he need to take anything with him?

FROM　Jason GrangerRM
TO　　Trisha

I'm hoping I'll have seen it all by the time he does a handover (although I saw diddly squat for 2 hrs last night so who knows).

I have: a camera, digital with Zoom, of course, and lastly I'm not only a super cool agent, I'm also the master of disguises!!!

I've found the perfect outfit, it's a kind of Lily Savage meets Inspector Clueso …(basically a moustache, a raincoat and a red wig I borrowed from a tranny friend of mine).

I'm so excited, I can't breathe.

FROM   Trisha
TO   Jason GrangerRM

James doesn't know what you look like does he?

FROM   Jason GrangerRM
TO   Trisha

No?

FROM   Trisha
TO   Jason GrangerRM

So what you doing?

FROM   Jason GrangerRM
TO   Trisha

You've got to do it right Trisha. You can't sit in a car watching someone's house dressed as you are, it's no fun at all.

FROM   Trisha
TO   Jason GrangerRM

Babes, if you go dressed like a clown, you'll get arrested.

FROM   Jason GrangerRM
TO   Trisha

You're right, damn, OK I'll go as I am.

FROM   Trisha
TO   Jason GrangerRM

You spoken to Holly?

FROM   Jason GrangerRM
TO   Trisha

Yes, to throw her off the scent I've been pretending to be moody all morning, said I wanted a baby.

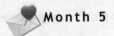

Five minutes later she's sent me something for sponsoring a child, bless her — might do it too.

This has been so much fun!! Shame Aisha's going to miss it.

FROM Trisha
TO Jason GrangerRM

Holly wouldn't let us do it if we mentioned it to her.

FROM Jason GrangerRM
TO Trisha

Don't tell her, whatever you do.

FROM Trisha
TO Jason GrangerRM

What time are you heading off?

FROM Jason GrangerRM
TO Trisha

In about 3 hours ... My heart's already going.

FROM Trisha
TO Jason GrangerRM

Don't get caught, you want my Les to meet you there? You might be better off with some muscle behind you.

FROM Jason GrangerRM
TO Trisha

Oh Trisha, if you'd said that in a gay club ... I AM fighting the urge to make any number of innuendos.

If nothing's seen by the morning, then he can take over, I've got your number.

FROM Trisha
TO   Jason GrangerRM

OK darlin, call me as soon as you see anything, whatever time it is.
xxxx

FROM Jason GrangerRM
TO   Trisha

I will mon pretty Island conspirator.

Subject: Why so happy?

FROM Holly
TO   Trisha

Why are you looking so pleased with yourself?

FROM Trisha
TO   Holly

No reason.

FROM Holly
TO   Trisha

Come on now Trisha, tell me, why do you keep giggling?

FROM Trisha
TO   Holly

Can't a girl giggle to herself sometimes, isn't it allowed now?

FROM Holly
TO   Trisha

Smiling's OK, but being genuinely happy probably isn't allowed, I'll check the manual.

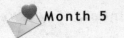

FROM Trisha
TO Holly

Fffrrrrrrrrt

FROM Holly
TO Trisha

Patricia Gillot, did you just blow a raspberry at me????

FROM Trisha
TO Holly

YES Ha ha.
Oh and I'm not happy you keep getting stolen off my reception desk by Shella, it's not fair, I don't want to work with a temp.

FROM Holly
TO Trisha

Sorry.

Subject: News

FROM Trisha
TO Les

He's got everything sorted, he even had a moustache and wig.

FROM Les
TO Trisha

What's he want that for?

FROM Trisha
TO Les

He's just getting excited about it, he got you some food an' all, but he doesn't need you there tonight, you go along in the morning if he's seen nothing.

FROM   Les
TO   Trisha

OK OK, what we having for dinner?

FROM   Trisha
TO   Les

Lobster with orange sauce, followed by coconut truffles, happy?

HOLLY'S
INBOX

TUESDAY

Subject: Why so happy?

FROM Holly
TO Patricia Gillot

Why are you looking so pleased with yourself?

FROM Patricia Gillot
TO Holly

No reason.

FROM Holly
TO Patricia Gillot

Come on now Trish, tell me, why do you keep giggling?

FROM Patricia Gillot
TO Holly

Can't a girl giggle to herself sometimes, isn't it allowed now?

FROM Holly
TO Patricia Gillot

Smiling's OK, but being genuinely happy probably isn't allowed, I'll check the manual.

FROM Patricia Gillot
TO Holly

Fffrrrrrrrrt

FROM Holly
TO Patricia Gillot

Patricia Gillot, did you just blow a raspberry at me????

FROM   Patricia Gillot
TO   Holly

YES Ha ha.
   And I'm not happy you keep getting stolen off my reception desk by Shella, it's not fair, I don't want to work with a temp.

FROM   Holly
TO   Patricia Gillot

Sorry.

Subject: Truce?

FROM   Holly
TO   Mum and Dad

Do you want to be friends again?
   Holly

FROM   Mum and Dad
TO   Holly

Yes Holly, I'd like that very much.

FROM   Holly
TO   Mum and Dad

I don't like falling out with you Mum, I really don't.

FROM   Mum and Dad
TO   Holly

I don't like it either, these last few weeks have been truly horrid.

FROM   Holly
TO   Mum and Dad

Then you must stop meddling, please Mum.
   I know it's all done with the best intentions, but it doesn't usually work out well for anyone.

FROM Mum and Dad
TO Holly

Will you call me please?
 I just want to talk to my daughter again.
 Please can you call me now?
 Mum

FROM Holly
TO Mum and Dad

I'll just ask Trisha and call you from a meeting room.
 love you
 xx

WEDNESDAY

Subject: The Post Room??

FROM Jennie Pithwait
TO Holly

Holly
 I couldn't help but noticing you down there madly folding envelopes on Friday, as I passed.
 Your mother must be so proud of you!
 I bet you can fold twenty a minute if you really try hard!!
 I hear these are for the Annual Review which I will be attending, so please make sure you get my letter out on time dear.
 x
 J

Subject: Oi Part Timer!

FROM Patricia Gillot
TO Holly

Do I get you for the rest of the day?
 Or are you off gallivanting upstairs again?

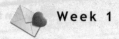

FROM   Holly
TO   Patricia Gillot

Sorry Trish, how was your morning?

FROM   Patricia Gillot
TO   Holly

Cr*p, to be honest darlin. I've got used to your face, as sad as it sounds.

FROM   Holly
TO   Patricia Gillot

I got an email-nasty from Jennie, she is the most despicable bitch ever! I thought she'd changed since school but ...

Holly
   I couldn't help but noticing you down there madly folding envelopes on Friday, as I passed.
   Your mother must be so proud of you!
   I bet you can fold twenty a minute if you really try hard!!
   I hear these are for the Annual Review which I will be attending, so please make sure you get my letter out on time dear.
   x
   J

FROM   Patricia Gillot
TO   Holly

For less than the price of a new Merc, I could have her disappear?

FROM   Holly
TO   Patricia Gillot

I haven't got that much.
   What about the price of a second-hand Mini with engine trouble?

FROM   Patricia Gillot
TO   Holly

I'll have one of her nails broken?

FROM Holly
TO Patricia Gillot

Real or false?

FROM Patricia Gillot
TO Holly

*For real, I'll give you a number, he hangs out down The Gun. (Joke —
I know what you meant.)*
    So, you writing back to the cow upstairs?

FROM Holly
TO Patricia Gillot

I think I might send her one back.
    *I really want all this to end — I'm really tired of it and to be
honest I can't carry on much longer.*
    *It makes me so on edge and my heart races and I get worked up
and angry. I don't want to feel like this at work, I don't want her
getting to me, but she's so good at being awful. It's hard keeping up
with her. She's a nasty piece of work.*

FROM Patricia Gillot
TO Holly

What goes around comes around, I just wish it would hurry up.
    PS — Don't you dare leave me!
    xxx
    Go on, write something back she deserves it, I dare you ...

FROM Holly
TO Patricia Gillot

She's even started signing off with J — like he does ... grrrrrrrrrr

Subject: Important

FROM   Holly
TO   Jennie Pithwait

Jennie
  My parents are very proud of me, because I've turned out to be a well-balanced human being, with moral values; not a psychotic tart with delusions of grandeur.
  Love
  H??
  xx

Subject: Aisha

FROM   Holly
TO   Jason GrangerRM

Any news from our miscreant friend yet?
  Her phone's still off.

FROM   Jason GrangerRM
TO   Holly

Zilch.

FROM   Holly
TO   Jason GrangerRM

Are you OK?

FROM   Jason GrangerRM
TO   Holly

Yes, just tired.

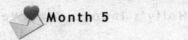

FROM Holly
TO Jason GrangerRM

I was thinking of telling Trisha the truth?

FROM Jason GrangerRM
TO Holly

Good luck sweetie.
* xxxx*

Subject: I'm sorry ...

FROM Holly
TO Patricia Gillot

I'z been lying to you.

FROM Patricia Gillot
TO Holly

About what darlin?

FROM Holly
TO Patricia Gillot

Quite a lot, but it's not my fault.

FROM Patricia Gillot
TO Holly

Don't tell me you're gay?
* If you're about to come out to me darlin, I'm happy for ya and all, but you're not my type. I like girls with more meat.*

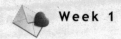

FROM Holly
TO Patricia Gillot

I'm serious Trisha.
Anyway how much meat do you want?

FROM Patricia Gillot
TO Holly

A lot more than you've got. So what's up?

Subject: Little white lies

FROM Holly
TO Patricia Gillot

When I first met you, I didn't know you well enough to tell you the truth. Then I did start knowing you better but by then it was too late to tell you the truth. So I didn't.
You see it's really not my fault Trishy.

FROM Patricia Gillot
TO Holly

You posh people really don't know how to spit things out do you.
Come on you dirty lying whore-bag, tell your Aunty Trisha!!!

FROM Holly
TO Patricia Gillot

I only spent 2 weeks as a receptionist in a hotel.

FROM Patricia Gillot
TO Holly

I could have told you that. I've met some bad receptionists in my time, but you took the biscuit. I guessed you were lying about doing the job for years, either that or you were as thick as f*ck.
So come on, what you been up to?
You weren't working as a Mile End slapper were you??

FROM Holly
TO Patricia Gillot

No Trisha I wasn't. I ran a small events company with my husband.

FROM Patricia Gillot
TO Holly

I know you did. He was a right b*stard from what I heard, used to beat you up and everything. I had a man like that before Les, talking of which that was him on the phone, got to go meet him.
    It's dead anyway, I'll see you tomorrow.
    xxx
    Ha ha, love you,
    you lying cow.

Subject: PS ...

FROM Patricia Gillot
TO Holly

You should have a word with your friends, they haven't half got mouths on them. That Jason for instance, can't keep secrets.
    ha ha

FROM Holly
TO Patricia Gillot

I'll kill him!!! Have a good night.

Subject: Bad bad girls!!!!

FROM Jason GrangerRM
TO Holly

I just called Aish and I'm sure it rang with a foreign ring tone before going dead, I think she's still in Ibiza, or Russia or Egypt. Actually I don't have a clue where she is, but she's not in this country and not in this hotel.
    I'm going to give that young lady a steeeeeern talking to when she resurfaces.

THURSDAY

Subject: Hold the front page!!!

FROM   Jason GrangerRM
TO   Holly

Aisha's coming in!!!!
  Today gets more exciting by the second.

FROM   Holly
TO   Jason GrangerRM

At last!! What else is exciting??

FROM   Jason GrangerRM
TO   Holly

Oh Holly, so many many things, it's a funny old world really isn't it?

FROM   Holly
TO   Jason GrangerRM

What's a funny world? Have I missed out on some celebrity gossip?

FROM   Jason GrangerRM
TO   Holly

No. Promise.

Subject: What a great day it is

FROM   Patricia Gillot
TO   Holly

Morning Holly.

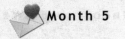

FROM   Holly
TO   Patricia Gillot

Morning. Why are you beaming at me?

FROM   Patricia Gillot
TO   Holly

Didn't know I was beaming.

FROM   Holly
TO   Patricia Gillot

You are and it's scaring me, please stop.
   What's wrong, have you put something sticky on my seat again?

FROM   Patricia Gillot
TO   Holly

No.

FROM   Holly
TO   Patricia Gillot

My skirt wasn't tucked into my knickers was it?

FROM   Patricia Gillot
TO   Holly

I'm just happy. Life is just one big surprise init?

Subject: Ibiza chick

FROM   Holly
TO   Jason GrangerRM

Is she there yet? I still couldn't get hold of her last night either.
Where is the little misfit?

FROM Jason GrangerRM
TO   Holly

She's sitting about four metres away, sniffing, and snuffling and hoping someone notices she's got a cold, trying to look very sorry for herself.

FROM Holly
TO   Jason GrangerRM

Are you buying it?

FROM Jason GrangerRM
TO   Holly

Am I hell.

FROM Holly
TO   Jason GrangerRM

Can I email her or has she been sent to Coventry?
*   And what's the news? Is she or isn't she?*

FROM Jason GrangerRM
TO   Holly

Well that's where the confusion lies, I've no idea.
*   She said it's a long story and she's not well enough to tell it yet. She knows we're both dying to know so she has every intention of dragging it out until I'm nice to her.*
*   She's trying to check people out without opening her mouth to speak to them.*

FROM Holly
TO   Jason GrangerRM

Oh poor love, she might be ill??

FROM Jason GrangerRM
TO Holly

She's not sick, unless the doctor has started prescribing whisky for colds — she smells like an old drunk from the park, she's just hung over. I'm watching her now and she knows I'm watching at her and she's trying to look as feeble as she can.

Oops there she goes, head up, and at last she's seen me.

Subject: To the sick one

FROM Jason GrangerRM
TO Aisha; Holly

To the sick one:

Hello sweetie, not feeling well are we?

A long week in bed recovering from life-threatening illnesses?

Say hello to your friend Holly, she's been worried about you too!

FROM Aisha
TO Holly; Jason GrangerRM

Holly

Hi baby, how are you?

Have you heard how horrid Jason is being to me?

I'm trying to recover from the flu and he's made me do all the checkouts, he doesn't love me any more.

☹

FROM Holly
TO Aisha; Jason GrangerRM

I think he's being very patient young Aisha.

Now I would call you Aisha Peters, but I've no idea if that's your name — is it or not?

FROM Aisha
TO Holly; Jason GrangerRM

I'll always be Aisha Peters to you Holly, although Jason just calls me 'the sick one', poor me.

☹

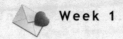

FROM Holly
TO   Aisha; Jason GrangerRM

Stop doing those faces — as Jason always tells me, it's not cute or clever. Now are you married to your boss?

FROM Aisha
TO   Holly; Jason GrangerRM

No.

FROM Jason GrangerRM
TO   Holly; Aisha

Holly
*   I can see that mischievous smile creeping on to her face.*
*   She's trying to hide it under her hand but I can see it there.*

FROM Aisha
TO   Jason GrangerRM; Holly

Oh, you are really on my case Mr Jason, poor Aisha and on her honeymoon too.
*   ☹*

FROM Jason GrangerRM
TO   Aisha; Holly

TELL US!!!!!

FROM Aisha
TO   Holly; Jason GrangerRM

OK, are you sitting comfortably?

FROM Holly
TO   Aisha; Jason GrangerRM

YES!

FROM   Jason GrangerRM
TO   Aisha; Holly

YES!

FROM   Aisha
TO   Jason GrangerRM; Holly

Then I shall begin.
    Firstly Jason, can I have a lickle break? I'm ever so hot and tirsty and my poor lickle head is so hot, I tink I shall surely die.

FROM   Jason GrangerRM
TO   Aisha; Holly

OK OK whatever you want, you can go home after this, just tell us!

FROM   Aisha
TO   Jason GrangerRM; Holly

OK, it was just a fancy dress party.
    Thanks Jasey, love ya, I'll call you tomorrow Holly.
    Jason I'll tell Maria to take over on this desk.
    See you tomorrow.
    Love and kisses
    Aishy

FROM   Jason GrangerRM
TO

I need a drink.

Subject: Story time

FROM   Patricia Gillot
TO   Holly

Tell us about this company then?

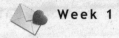

FROM Holly
TO Patricia Gillot

We used to do events, weddings, parties, lots of fun at the beginning.

FROM Patricia Gillot
TO Holly

What happened? Why did it go bust?

FROM Holly
TO Patricia Gillot

Who said it went bust?

FROM Patricia Gillot
TO Holly

Then where is it? What happened to your house?

FROM Holly
TO Patricia Gillot

I'm a little ashamed to admit it, but I was a bit of a mess when he left. He was frightening, he got me to sign over the company and took all the equity out of the house we had.
I messed up really, couldn't pay the bills, and just left it all to rot, just couldn't get everything together to sort things out.
Jason was great, he was such a sweetie, looked out for me, got me back on my feet etc. He's just the best friend anyone could have.

FROM Patricia Gillot
TO Holly

Don't you dare be ashamed. Where's Sebastian now?

FROM Holly
TO Patricia Gillot

Don't know where he lives. I know the company is doing well, it's in Canary Wharf.

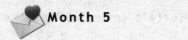

FROM   Patricia Gillot
TO   Holly

How well?

FROM   Holly
TO   Patricia Gillot

Very well.

FROM   Patricia Gillot
TO   Holly

Like?

FROM   Holly
TO   Patricia Gillot

*Like they recently did the music awards, they do all the biggest
shows. Jason's really annoyed, he wants to meet all the celebrities.
Anyway, it's gone, it's over.*
  I'm very happy now.
    ☺

FROM   Patricia Gillot
TO   Holly

I wouldn't be, I feel as sick as a parrot, can't you get it back?

Subject: Aisha

FROM   Jason GrangerRM
TO   Holly

She's lying.
  *I know she's married and I promise I didn't mean to Holly, but I
clicked into her phone line earlier, and she was telling her daughter
about it.*
  Just don't know who to.

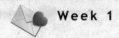

FROM   Holly
TO   Jason GrangerRM

???
> *But why would she lie to us?*

Subject: Toby

FROM   Holly
TO   Mum and Dad

Mum,
> *I've been thinking about Toby more and more recently.*
> *What did you really think of him?*

FROM   Mum and Dad
TO   Holly

Holly
> *Darling it's good to hear from you.*
> *But why are you asking me about Toby?*
> *Love Mum*

FROM   Holly
TO   Mum and Dad

I'm asking you, because you might be able to add something. You met him a few times, I don't know anyone else that knows him.

FROM   Mum and Dad
TO   Holly

He was nice enough, bad manners, I remember he had bad hair, terrible hair Holly.
> *But I don't see why you want to know, you're not thinking about getting back together with him are you darling?*
> *I didn't think you were talking to him?*
> *Mum*

FROM   Holly
TO   Mum and Dad

He has better hair now Mum, you'll be pleased to know. How did he leave when he came around that day? What did he say to you?

FROM   Mum and Dad
TO   Holly

I told him you were very upset and probably that you were both too young to be having such an obviously sexual relationship.
    We argued, he left. Holly, have you been speaking to him again?

FROM   Holly
TO   Mum and Dad

He has blue eyes, I didn't think about them much at the time, but they are blue. James has brown eyes.
    No Mum, I'm not. Don't worry.
    Just thinking.

FRIDAY

Subject: Wedding

FROM   Jason GrangerRM
TO   Aisha; Holly

So where was this fancy dress party then Aish?

FROM   Aisha
TO   Holly; Jason GrangerRM

Dhurrrrr — Ibiza?

FROM   Holly
TO   Aisha; Jason GrangerRM

And it had a wedding theme?

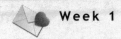

FROM Aisha
TO Holly; Jason GrangerRM

That's what I said, yes.

FROM Jason GrangerRM
TO Aisha; Holly

I presume someone went as a priest or vicar Aisha?

FROM Aisha
TO Jason GrangerRM; Holly

Yes?

FROM Jason GrangerRM
TO Aisha; Holly

Aisha — did this vicar or priest get you to repeat some vows during the evening?

FROM Aisha
TO Holly; Jason GrangerRM

Maybe.

FROM Holly
TO Aisha; Jason GrangerRM

Baby, at some point did you exchange rings?

FROM Aisha
TO Holly; Jason GrangerRM

Maybe.

FROM Jason GrangerRM
TO Holly; Aisha

That wasn't a party. That thing you were attending was what we call a 'wedding' Aisha, and it sounds suspiciously like you were the 'bride'.

Subject: Urgent

FROM   Judy Perkins
TO   Holly; Patricia Gillot

Dear Trisha and Holly
   I've just had a very angry call from Adam Yastovich regarding our new policy of NOT escorting clients up in the lift when we can't get through to the relevant host.
   I was unaware of this new policy — can someone explain to me what all this is about?
   Regards
   Judy

Subject: MY WEDDING

FROM   Aisha
TO   Jason GrangerRM; Holly

OK you two.
   I've had enough of this spotlight, grilling thing.
   I got married to a millionaire, he's handsome and rich and it was a fabulous wedding, I just didn't want you being jealous OK?!

FROM   Holly
TO   Aisha; Jason GrangerRM

Sweetheart, that's wonderful, why would you not want to tell us? I'm really happy for you.
   Tell us about him, where did you meet him, have you got any more photos?

FROM   Aisha
TO   Holly; Jason GrangerRM

No I'm so upset, the camera was stolen.
   It was fantastic though, I didn't invite you because I thought you'd think bad of me. Because we hadn't known each other for long.
   So I wanted to keep it a secret.
   His name is Julian and he's so kind, and sweet and caring.

It was amazing, I was in that dress in the picture I sent you and it was in this huge beautiful old church.

There was this big reception afterwards, I arrived there by horse and carriage. Guests drinking champagne in the sunshine, flowers everywhere, it was so pretty.

FROM Jason GrangerRM
TO Aisha; Holly

Are you OK Aisha?

FROM Aisha
TO Holly; Jason GrangerRM

I'm happy, so happy OK.

FROM Jason GrangerRM
TO Aisha; Holly

Aisha take a break, go on.

FROM Aisha
TO Jason GrangerRM; Holly

I wanted that wedding, I wanted it just like that, I did.
It's just lies, do you want to know why I got married?????

Subject: Jason, what's happening there?

FROM Holly
TO Jason GrangerRM

Is Aisha OK?

FROM Jason GrangerRM
TO Holly

I tried to put my arm around her and she ran off, she's crying her eyes out. I've sent one of the other girls to go after her, she's gone to the toilets.

FROM Holly
TO Jason GrangerRM

What's up with her? I'll see if I can take my lunch early and come over?

FROM Jason GrangerRM
TO Holly

OK, just wait, she's coming back. I'll keep you informed.

FROM Holly
TO Jason GrangerRM

If you get to give her a hug, give her one from me!!!
    xxxx
    and loads of kisses

Subject: Sorry

FROM Aisha
TO Holly; Jason GrangerRM

Sorry, I lied.
    I got married in Spain — to Shona's dad.

FROM Holly
TO Aisha; Jason GrangerRM

What, that man who ran off and left you both?
    Don't tell me you're back with him Aisha????

FROM Aisha
TO Holly; Jason GrangerRM

I'm not back with him. I had to pay him to go OK.

FROM Jason GrangerRM
TO Aisha; Holly

I don't understand?

FROM Aisha
TO Holly; Jason GrangerRM

There was no huge wedding, no carriage, no flowers, he turned up drunk.

I paid for him to have a holiday in Ibiza otherwise he wouldn't do it, that was the condition.

I paid for my fucking husband to marry me OK. There was no lovely church, I signed some bits and pieces, he f*cked off.

I've spent my life dreaming about the perfect wedding, Holly, remember you and me always wanted it just perfect?

it wasn't f*cking perfect

i'm relaly really relayl slukupset OKUPSET

and now Jason, can I go home.

FROM Jason GrangerRM
TO Aisha; Holly

Only if I can give you a hug, why did you marry him Aisha?

FROM Aisha
TO Holly; Jason GrangerRM

For Shona, she's at scholl and I wanted her to say she had a dad, stupid I know, but taht's it.

FROM Jason GrangerRM
TO Aisha; Holly

Go home sweetie.

xxx Holly, I'll give her kisses for you.

FROM Holly
TO Aisha

We all love you Aish.

Don't worry.

Subject: Clients

FROM Patricia Gillot
TO Holly

When you come back on Monday, don't worry about Judy's email, she's just trying to cover her own a*se.
    If they're Jennie's clients, I'll take them up so you don't have to see her nasty face.
    Trish

TRISHA'S INBOX

WEEK 2

MONDAY

Subject: Pssssssssssssssst

FROM   Jason GrangerRM
TO   Les; Trisha

I hear the Russian Ballet is good at this time of year, but why are you wearing a Tutu?

FROM   Les
TO   Jason GrangerRM; Trisha

What?

FROM   Jason GrangerRM
TO   Les; Trisha

I said 'I hear the Russian Ballet is good at this time of year, but why are you wearing a Tutu?'

FROM   Les
TO   Jason GrangerRM; Trisha

Because it's cold and me nuts are freezing. Look Jason, I don't want to be 'The Fish' any more, it's sounds sh*t, I want to be 'The Jackal' or Wolf?

FROM   Trisha
TO   Les; Jason GrangerRM

Les, grow up. So what we doing next?

FROM   Les
TO   Jason GrangerRM; Trisha

Why don't we meet up?

FROM   Jason GrangerRM
TO   Trisha; Les

What's the name of that pub we went to last time?

FROM   Les
TO   Jason GrangerRM; Trisha

The Prince Arthur in Eversholt Street?

FROM   Jason GrangerRM
TO   Trisha; Les

I can be there by 6pm?

FROM   Trisha
TO   Les; Jason GrangerRM

Sounds good, see you both there and let's get a plan together.

FROM   Jason GrangerRM
TO   Trisha; Les

OK, I'm bringing Aisha along, I thought she could be useful.
    From working with her for a while I can vouch for her deviousness and ability to lie.

FROM   Trisha
TO   Jason GrangerRM; Les

That's agreed, and remember Les it's your round.

Subject: Holly

FROM   Toby
TO   Trisha

Hi Trisha,
    has she mentioned me at all?
    Toby

FROM Trisha
TO Toby

Not for a while sweetheart. If I thought I could change her mind I'd say something again. I did try for you a couple of times.

FROM Toby
TO Trisha

I know you did Trisha, thanks.

FROM Trisha
TO Toby

So when you off?

FROM Toby
TO Trisha

Last day here tomorrow, I start work in France on Monday.

FROM Trisha
TO Toby

Good luck darlin.
Trisha

Subject: A letter for me?

FROM Holly
TO Trisha

Here's a letter addressed to Holly Denham, Staples and Paperclips Division.

FROM Trisha
TO Holly

Sorry babes, I told you I was bored, you shouldn't spend so much time up there.

TOBY'S INBOX

WEEK 2

MONDAY

Subject: Holly

FROM Trisha
TO Toby

So when you off?

FROM Toby
TO Trisha

Tomorrow night, I start work in France on Monday.

FROM Trisha
TO Toby

Good luck darlin.
    Trisha

Subject: Coming home

FROM Toby
TO Steve

I'll be expecting a beer waiting for me at 11pm on an outside table, opposite the square in Deauville tomorrow.

FROM Steve
TO Toby

I'll line them up mate, I thought we'd just have a few drinks, have a big night out on Friday. I've got a girl I want you to meet.

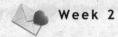
FROM   Toby
TO   Steve

Who, Elise? I've met her?

FROM   Steve
TO   Toby

Not for me for you, she's a friend of Elise's. She's got that independence you wanted from a woman. I'm sure she's just like Holly, no difference.

FROM   Toby
TO   Steve

You haven't met Holly, anyway independence as in — she doesn't want to hang around you two all night?

FROM   Steve
TO   Toby

Yeah yeah, whatever, I try and do you a favour. So this girl I've found you is one of your lot (unless you've had enough of nice girls and want to go back to bad ones????)

FROM   Toby
TO   Steve

I just want to lie on the beach and forget it all.

FROM   Steve
TO   Toby

The beach is a good place to start, once you've seen these French women you'll forget your own name.
*   I said you were wasting your time in London. I did say you were mate.*

FROM   Toby
TO   Steve

Everyone thinks about their first girlfriend, you've mentioned yours before.

FROM   Steve
TO   Toby

But I didn't take a job just to be with her did I?????
    Did you tell her in the end?

FROM   Toby
TO   Steve

What?

FROM   Steve
TO   Toby

That you only joined the company to be with her?

FROM   Toby
TO   Steve

No, she still thinks it was a coincidence, I couldn't see the point.

FROM   Steve
TO   Toby

Good, you would have looked like an even bigger idiot (if you'll pardon the honesty). At least you've kept some of your pride intact, kind of.
    I'd take the piss a bit more but I'm guessing you might be a bit cut-up about it all, so I'll let you off the hook for a couple of days.

FROM   Toby
TO   Steve

I didn't think she'd still be mad at me.

FROM   Steve
TO   Toby

Mad is the right word, just as well you didn't get back with her, you did everything you could to get her back at the time.
    You were in France for God's sake, in a boarding school, you wrote to her, you said you were sorry.

It wasn't your fault anyway, your parents put you there and she never wrote back to you, not once.
How many letters was it?

FROM   Toby
TO   Steve

Don't remember.

FROM   Steve
TO   Toby

A lot, a lot of f*cking letters you wrote her.

FROM   Toby
TO   Steve

A few.

FROM   Steve
TO   Toby

Right, so forget her.

FROM   Toby
TO   Steve

I'll see you tomorrow.
  Toby

HOLLY'S
INBOX

WEEK 2

MONDAY

Subject: A letter for me?

FROM Holly
TO Patricia Gillot

Here's a letter addressed to Holly Denham, Staples and Paperclips Division.

FROM Patricia Gillot
TO Holly

Sorry babes, I told you I was bored, you shouldn't spend so much time up there.

TUESDAY

Subject: Clients

FROM Jennie Pithwait
TO Holly

Receptionist
*   I heard I'll soon be seeing you scurrying past me with my clients.*
*   There's a good girl, behaving at last, it's just a shame it had to come to this ...*
*   I really didn't want to make you feel so small, but I guess you know your place now?*

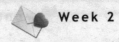

FROM   Holly
TO   Jennie Pithwait

Sadly, you won't see me taking your clients past, because Trisha is very kindly doing yours (on the odd occasion you can't be contacted).
  love
  Holly

FROM   Jennie Pithwait
TO   Holly

By the way, if you hadn't already guessed it ...
  I was shagging James the night before you both went to Spain, he was late to work ... because he wanted to do it again.
  Maybe I gave him something you weren't very good at??
  PS I was there in Spain too, took a flight out after you, he came and met my family before yours in Marbella.
  PPS We're so so in love now and at last he's told me he's ready to settle down, that's right Holly we're thinking of getting married.
  Kiss kiss.
  Have a fab day.

Subject: You OK?

FROM   Patricia Gillot
TO   Holly

You don't look so good, anything I can do?

FROM   Holly
TO   Patricia Gillot

I'm OK.

FROM   Patricia Gillot
TO   Holly

Is it more hate-mail from Jennie?

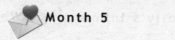

FROM Holly
TO Patricia Gillot

A bit.

FROM Patricia Gillot
TO Holly

Forward it on?

FROM Holly
TO Patricia Gillot

Can't, I feel sick.

FROM Patricia Gillot
TO Holly

Hold on to it darlin.
  xxxx

Subject: Your References

FROM Roger Lipton
TO Holly

Dear Holly
We have been unable to obtain an accurate reference to cover the period of time you said you were working for the LHS Hotels Group.
    Can you explain why this is the case?
    Yours sincerely

FROM Holly
TO Roger Lipton

Dear Roger
    Yes, sorry I was self-employed.
    My husband and I ran an events company during the time I should have been working in the hotel.

I did work at the hotel, but for just two weeks.

I have no explanation other than I really wanted to work here and prove myself. My CV wouldn't have been noticed without having previous reception experience. In the last few months I hope I have managed to show you the dedication, loyalty and vigilance you require from a member of your reception team.

Kindest regards
Holly

Subject: Got rumbled

FROM   Holly
TO   James GrangerRM

Think Shella got me in trouble ... I've been rumbled by HR and they don't sound happy. I told the truth, think it's the best thing to do.

Subject: Your references

FROM   Roger Lipton
TO   Holly

Holly
So you admit you were lying on your CV and you have no previous receptionist experience?

FROM   Holly
TO   Roger Lipton

Yes, apart from the two weeks in the hotel.
Holly

FROM   Roger Lipton
TO   Holly

Holly
Since your employment here we have come to believe you are a dedicated worker and have fitted in well, carrying out your responsibilities to the standard we require from employees.

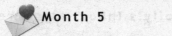

Huerst & Wright is a financial institution and our clients empower us with a huge amount of responsibility in dealing with their financial operations.

Security is therefore at the forefront of all our minds and employees who have fabricated their previous work history, exam credentials, address or any other such details, are dealt with according to company rules. This is an area we take very seriously.

This position as 'Receptionist' had always been offered subject to references and you are still within your six month probationary period, therefore it is with deep regret that I inform you of the termination of your contract with Huerst & Wright as of today.

Please hand your pass back and any other Huerst & Wright property to Judy Perkins at 5pm.

Yours sincerely
Roger Lipton

Subject: Gone

FROM   Holly
TO   Patricia Gillot

That's it, I'm out. They're getting rid of me Trisha.

FROM   Patricia Gillot
TO   Holly

What????

FROM   Holly
TO   Patricia Gillot

Something about security and me lying on my CV.

FROM   Patricia Gillot
TO   Holly

Yeah yeah, very funny.

FROM   Holly
TO   Patricia Gillot

Trish, look at me.

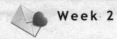

FROM   Patricia Gillot
TO   Holly

They're F*CKING having a f*cking laugh!!!!

FROM   Holly
TO   Patricia Gillot

It's my own silly fault.

FROM   Patricia Gillot
TO   Holly

OH darlin, what you going to do ???

Subject: Missing?

FROM   Shella Hamilton-Jones
TO   Holly

Holly
*   At 12pm you were meant to be waiting for me in meeting room 5, which is where I am?*
*   Have you forgotten???*
*   Are you still on reception or have you been sacked?*

FROM   Holly
TO   Shella Hamilton-Jones

Yes I've been sacked.
*   I imagine someone's had a word with HR about me and they're getting rid of me (well done Shella??).*
*   So no, I can't be bothered coming up for your meeting, because I don't have to take any more crap off you.*
*   Holly*

Subject: What happened???

FROM   Jason GrangerRM
TO   Holly

Have they come back to you yet ??

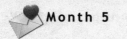

FROM Holly
TO Jason GrangerRM

Yes I'm out the door, gone.

FROM Jason GrangerRM
TO Holly

You're joking?

Subject: Oh dear dear dear ...

FROM Jennie Pithwait
TO Holly

Ex-Receptionist
  It looks like I WIN, after all.
  After finding out you had lied to us all, it only took a couple of calls to set the ball in motion ...
  So it's goodbye from me and goodbye from James.
  Taraaar

Subject: Missing?

FROM Shella Hamilton-Jones
TO Holly

What a ridiculous thing to say, why would I be happy?
  I'll have to find someone else who's good at this now, why on earth are they sacking you?
  Shella

FROM Holly
TO Shella Hamilton-Jones

Jennie told them I lied on my CV. (I've never been a receptionist before.)

FROM   Shella Hamilton-Jones
TO   Holly

So what has Holly been up to?

FROM   Holly
TO   Shella Hamilton-Jones

I managed an events company with my husband.

Subject: Holly Denham

FROM   Shella Hamilton-Jones
TO   Holly; Roger Lipton

Roger
   I must say I find the way you have reformed company policy within the whole of HR rather refreshing.
   Your ability to remove the 'bad eggs' within our company is always achieved with so little fuss and your decisions in this area are always spot on.
   In the case of Holly Denham I cannot believe however, what a total pig's ear you've made of it.
   For what reason are you sacking her?
   Shella
   PS Please keep Holly involved in your reply as I may need to verify some facts with her.

FROM   Roger Lipton
TO   Holly; Shella Hamilton-Jones

Shella
   I am sorry you feel this way, however Holly has lied on her CV and our company policy is clear and unambiguous in this area.

FROM   Shella Hamilton-Jones
TO   Holly; Roger Lipton

What was she doing instead of reception Roger?

FROM   Roger Lipton
TO   Holly; Shella Hamilton-Jones

Shella
I think it would be better if we had a chat in my office tomorrow regarding this matter, however I believe Holly was self-employed.
   Roger

FROM   Shella Hamilton-Jones
TO   Holly; Roger Lipton

She ran an events company with her husband, Roger, and what project are we currently working on together?

FROM   Roger Lipton
TO   Holly; Shella Hamilton-Jones

The annual results.

FROM   Shella Hamilton-Jones
TO   Holly; Roger Lipton

The annual results, very good. It is if you've failed to notice the biggest event of our calendar.
   Holly Denham ran an events company which is exactly the kind of experience I need to help me put together this conference in such a short space of time.
   Will you cancel the termination immediately and let's not hear another word about it.
   I know you meant well Roger, but now I am thoroughly busy with the conference and time is running out.
   Please do not email me again unless it's about a different matter.
   Regards
   Shella
   Ps You may like to look into why Jennie Pithwait sounds like she's taken it upon herself to do her own referencing?

Subject: Working

FROM Shella Hamilton-Jones
TO   Holly

So you will have to take more cr*p off this 'Viper' then won't you?
Oh and if you get any more trouble from that woman — the one who I can see today has come in wearing a skirt which would shame a prostitute, then let me know.
I'm the only one who can be mean to people in this company.
Shella 'Cruella'
PS I really think you should chase after Toby, he's much better-looking.

FROM Holly
TO   Shella Hamilton-Jones

Not sure what to say!!!!
Thank you so so much Shella, you've just made me so happy!
Holly
xxx !!!
(Sorry about the Viper thing.)

Subject: Sad news

FROM Holly
TO Patricia Gillot

Only joking! I'm BACK!!!
YIPEEEEEEEEEEEE ha ah aha aha ha ha
Trisha I love ya 'Darlin'' !!! hee hee hee
!! I want to give you a big kiss, but first, I've got an important message to send someone.

FROM Patricia Gillot
TO   Holly

What???
How?
Tell me now!!!!!!

FROM Holly
TO Patricia Gillot

*She knew!! She read that email I sent about her!!!
    And she is still nice??? ?? What?
    I think the world is turning upside down today.
    Oh, got an email to send, taraaaar.*

FROM Patricia Gillot
TO Holly

???

FROM Holly
TO Patricia Gillot

*Don't be starting with the question marks trishywishy.
    Hee heee
    ☺*

Subject: Wake Up

FROM Holly
TO Aisha; Jason GrangerRM

*Stinky and stinky??
    I've got something to tell you!*

Subject: Going

FROM Holly
TO Jennie Pithwait

OH, I guess I'm off.

FROM Jennie Pithwait
TO Holly

You still here?
　　Would you like to hand ME your pass before you go?
　　If you want I can send you down an empty box of cornflakes to put your pens and pencils into?
　　Boo hoo
　　☹
　　It's the end of an error.

FROM Holly
TO Jennie Pithwait

Don't be dumb; I mean I was just popping over the road to get a coffee ...
　　They haven't sacked me, it was just a terrible error (you were right), got a call from Roger Lipton apologising.
　　Such a shame for poor little vindictive you ... BOOO HOOO
　　HA HA H A HA
　　This feels good der na ner na ner na ner —
　　like I knew it would
　　Love and kisses
　　mwah mwah
　　Holly
　　PS ...... Shella says to watch your back.
　　Ooops naughty naughty Jennie

FROM Jennie Pithwait
TO Holly

Is that so???
　　WELL I'LL SHOW YOU SOMETHING THAT WILL BREAK POOR LITTLE HOLLY'S HEART ANY MOMENT!!

FROM Holly
TO Jennie Pithwait

What is it?
　　OH MY GOD!!!
　　You're not ... about to show me you've had your breast enlarged again???
　　You're right, that would be SO sad.

☹

Or maybe you're about to reveal you're dating Mr Big, that WOULD break my heart.
Oh no, forgot you can't be, you're still dating my cast-offs.
Shame.

Subject: Here

FROM Holly
TO Jason GrangerRM; Aisha

You two just won't believe what's been happening here!!!!!
Are you around????
Holly
x

Subject: Jennie

FROM Holly
TO Patricia Gillot

What d'you think she's up to? She just said she was coming down to quote 'break my heart' — psycho???
Having said that, I've had some great fun emailing her.

FROM Patricia Gillot
TO Holly

I hope it's not what I think she's going to do; she wouldn't.

FROM Holly
TO Patricia Gillot

What????

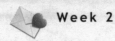

Subject: TELL US!!!

FROM Jason GrangerRM
TO Holly; Aisha; Patricia Gillot

What's happening then Holly??????

FROM Holly
TO Aisha; Jason GrangerRM; Patricia Gillot

Well:
I heard from Jennie that she had been with James all the time I was only holiday with him.
Don't have to say anything, trying to forget that bit.
Then I got sacked (wasn't the best start to a day).
Then reinstated.
Yipppeee (because Shella told them they had to, incidentally she had read that email calling her a Viper) (and she's got a sense of humour, very disturbing?!)
Then I sent a few ha ha emails to Jennie.
Now she's coming down to break my heart (she says).
Oh and here she is now.
With James? Oh I hope they're not going to

FROM Jason GrangerRM
TO Holly; Aisha; Patricia Gillot

WHAT????

Subject: WHAT ARE THEY NOT GOING TO DO?

FROM Jason GrangerRM
TO Holly; Aisha; Patricia Gillot

WHAT is happening??????

FROM Holly
TO Jason GrangerRM; Patricia Gillot; Aisha

She's kissing James in the middle of the reception.

FROM   Patricia Gillot
TO   Holly; Jason GrangerRM; Aisha

Silly girl, she's about to get a huge shock.

FROM   Holly
TO   Aisha; Jason GrangerRM; Patricia Gillot

What?

FROM   Patricia Gillot
TO   Holly; Aisha; Jason GrangerRM

See that client there putting down the newspaper?

Subject: That's …

FROM   Patricia Gillot
TO   Holly; Aisha; Jason GrangerRM

That's his wife.

FROM   Jason GrangerRM
TO   Holly; Jason GrangerRM; Aisha

Sh*t.

FROM   Holly
TO   Patricia Gillot; Jason GrangerRM; Aisha

What? How did you know? What wife????

FROM   Patricia Gillot
TO   Holly; Jason GrangerRM; Aisha

Oh, now that would be telling.
   xxxx

Subject: URGENT

FROM   Judy Perkins
TO   Holly; Patricia Gillot

What is going on down there?
I've just had reports of a security risk and shouting coming from reception? Whoever they are, get security to remove them from the premises, if necessary by force.
NOW!!!

Subject: Do you want to or shall I?

FROM   Patricia Gillot
TO   Holly

Shall I tell them or do you want to?

FROM   Holly
TO   Patricia Gillot

Ooo, I think I can handle this one, might get Ralph to stamp on some feet as he goes.

Subject: Please forgive me

FROM   Mum and Dad
TO   Holly

Holly
I have had a long hard look at myself since our last chat.
As much as this may drive you to hate me, I need to let you know this.
Toby did write to you. He actually wrote to you many times, I didn't let anyone else in the family know, not even your father. I was so angry with him, I tore up most of the letters.
I kept one, this is the final one, which, with the help of your sister, I've scanned and am about to send to you now.
Love Mum

Subject: Happy???

FROM Patricia Gillot
TO Holly

I thought you'd be jumping up and down laughing your head off, what's wrong?

FROM Holly
TO Patricia Gillot

I don't know, I'll tell you in a minute. When did you say Toby was leaving?

FROM Patricia Gillot
TO Holly

Today, he'll be here till 5, why?

FROM Holly
TO Patricia Gillot

I'll tell you in a second.

Subject: Letter

FROM Holly
TO Mum and Dad

Where's the letter??????
    Also how could he have written? I didn't get anything at school, why would he write to you???

FROM   Mum and Dad
TO   Holly

He didn't write to me, I'm sorry, I had the housemaster intercept anything from France.
   Sorry Holly.
   His letter is attached.
   Mum xxxx

Holly Denham
Rosemont School
Guildford
England

22nd Oct 1994

Holly
It's 6am. I'm sitting on my bed in my dormitory.
   I've been lying awake all night again, picturing the same thing, the thing I always picture these days.
   It was different when I first came here. I spent so much of my time thinking of all the funny, crazy things we did together. Even when I was down and you wouldn't leave me alone, you're so damn sexy Holly, even when I wanted to be mad at you, I couldn't be.
   When I wrote to you, I had so much confidence, I had no doubt we'd stay together through this. I knew how I felt about you and I blindly assumed you felt the same way about me. I thought I'd spend a year here and we'd be back together, even if it was two, we'd see each other in the summer when we broke up. I think of how sure I was then and it was only 2 months ago.
   I imagine how you looked at me when you said you loved me, I try to remember that look because, as beautiful as you are, I just need to think of your face, your eyes, how they looked, whether you meant it as much as I did.
   When the post was handed out yesterday, I was there again, hoping there would be one from you. When I see a post mark from England, I realise the writing isn't yours, but then, and how stupid is this, I start hoping they'll mention you in their letter instead. Anything which tells me you miss me as much as I miss you. If I knew you did, I'd run away now, I'd get on a train, I'd walk if I had to. I'd get to you though Holly, if you'd just let me know how you feel.
   I'm not going to write again. I know if you'd have turned out to be pregnant I'd have been the happiest man alive, but that wasn't to be. I know just getting a letter from you saying you're thinking of me would now make me the happiest man alive.

I love you Holly and I just hope one day you'll love me back.

I'm going to go down to the field now at the back of the school. I do this most mornings before everyone else gets up, it's as far away as I can get from people. I listen to the quiet, I enjoy the silence and then I scream as loud as I can, Holly, I shout my head off, I don't know why, I just need to do it.

I love you Holly,
Toby.

FROM Holly
TO Patricia Gillot

Oh my god, I've got to go.

FROM Patricia Gillot
TO Holly

Where? why?

FROM Holly
TO Patricia Gillot

Because I've just realised something.
I'm going upstairs.
xxxx wish me luck.

FROM Patricia Gillot
TO Holly

Go get him now!!!!! go go!!!!

TRISHA'S
INBOX

Subject: So??

FROM Les
TO Trisha

What's happening now?

FROM Trisha
TO Les

Holly's gone upstairs to tell him.

FROM Les
TO Trisha

Tell him what, he knows doesn't he, the whole bank must know now?

FROM Trisha
TO Les

Don't be so dense Les, not James, Toby.

FROM Les
TO Trisha

She's gone to tell Toby what?

FROM Trisha
TO Les

That the photocopier ran out of paper half-way through a print job.

FROM Les
TO Trisha

So?

FROM Trisha
TO Les

And we got Leslie Grantham waiting for him in Reception.

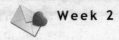

FROM Les
TO Trisha

Leslie who?

FROM Trisha
TO Les

She's gone to tell him she loves him you doughnut!

FROM Les
TO Trisha

How am I supposed to know that then? If you don't tell me, how am I meant to know that's what you're talking about? So, what's he said then?

FROM Trisha
TO Les

I don't know, she hasn't come back yet.

FROM Les
TO Trisha

You got a letter from the doctors here, shall I open it?

FROM Trisha
TO Les

You can if you want, it's probably just giving me the all clear. Hold on, here she comes, this can't be good.

HOLLY'S
INBOX

Subject: He's gone

FROM Holly
TO Patricia Gillot

He's not there, they said he left 10 mins ago, must have gone out the fire escape.

FROM Patricia Gillot
TO Holly

Well, you wouldn't want to walk past us again, would you? Poor lad, so what you doing about it?

FROM Holly
TO Patricia Gillot

I can't do anything can I? I suppose I'll have to get his number or an address for him.

FROM Patricia Gillot
TO Holly

Yeah, just send him a letter, or email, or text or something.

FROM Holly
TO Patricia Gillot

You think?

FROM Patricia Gillot
TO Holly

No, I don't think!!!! I'm not sitting next to you with that wet, soppy love-hurt look on your face, get off your arse and go chase after your man! You love him don't ya??

FROM Holly
TO Patricia Gillot

Yes, a lot.

FROM Patricia Gillot
TO Holly

Then go after him, he's on the Eurostar, it's not exactly hard to find is it? He's going from Waterloo!

FROM Holly
TO Patricia Gillot

Will you be OK here on your own?

FROM Patricia Gillot
TO Holly

Oh, p*ss off! Go before I fling you out!

Subject: That's it

FROM Patricia Gillot
TO Holly

I'm coming over there!

FROM Holly
TO Patricia Gillot

I'm going, I'm going. If he calls, give him my mobile number.
    xxx

FROM Patricia Gillot
TO Holly

He won't call darlin, so run!!!!!!!!!!!!!!!!!!!

TRISHA'S
INBOX

WEDNESDAY

FROM Trisha
TO Jason

Anyone heard anything?

FROM Jason
TO Trisha

No, and I'm worried about her.

FROM Trisha
TO Jason

She can't be sitting up there sulking, we'll have to get her out of her house.

FROM Jason
TO Trisha

If I've heard nothing from her by lunch time, I'm going to her flat.

Subject: Sick

FROM Holly
TO Trisha

Sorry Trisha
I know I can't lie to you, I never could, I was going to say I was sick today, some kind of flu or bug. But I know you wouldn't believe me, the only bug I've got is being in love, so in love it's painful. So I won't be in, until I get over it and I'm really really going to try to get him out of my head Trisha.

Problem is, it's so so difficult when he's lying next to me!!! Heee hee. xxxxx
I caught up with him in the station, I literally saw him by the ticket barrier as I came in. I shouted, he turned around, I didn't know

what I was going to say. I actually said 'Why didn't the HELL didn't you tell me you'd written to me!!!!!'

He didn't answer, he didn't need to.

I ran over and I saw that he was still in love with me, and I'm not sorry to say I threw myself on him. We kissed and kissed and at some stage we were lying on the floor in the middle of Waterloo station kissing, with people passing us by, we actually lay there until we got told to move. Covered in dust, not at all classy, I had a McDonald's wrapper stuck to my bottom when I got up, I now wish I had kept it, as a souvenir.

I'm writing to you right now, from the beach in France. We're lying together, and yes, I'm writing to let you know I'm in love and so I won't be in today. I'm sick. Heee hee hee. No idea what to do next, but got to go, there's a chest which needs my head on it.

Xxxxxxx

Love you Trishy

Holly

PS I'm just about to call Jason (or Dad) to stop him worrying too. Bad Holly.

PPS There's a picture of me and Toby together in the next email I'm sending you. (I think my holiday snaps could be better this year!)

Xxx

Dear Reader,

So that's the end of my story ... for now! I really hope you enjoyed it. Before I go, I wanted to include a few bits and pieces I've collected about my crazy friends and family (and a couple of cringe-making documents of my own) — I hope you like them!

Lots of love,

Holly x x x

PS I'll be back soon!

ONE NIGHT IN JUNE ...

This is a transcript of a conversation overheard between a large man in overalls, a lady in a suit and an extremely well-dressed man, in a pub somewhere in Holborn ...

'I'm the one who found 'er!'

'And you're the one who'll get a slap if you don't shut up, I told you just to sit in the car, not go wandering.'

'I sat in the bleeding car for 6 c***ing hours.'

'Can I have a straw with this?'

' "Don't go wandering," I said, they could have called the police!'

'This isn't a Long Island Iced Tea?'

'No, Jason, it's not a bleeding Long Island Iced Tea. I'm not standing at the bar while he makes you your poncy drink for an hour.'

'Oh he's so tough, can I give him a kiss, Trish?'

'Be my guest.'

'Oi, he's doing it again Trisha, tell him!'

'Oh grow up, Les, so what did you say to them?'

'I told 'em I'd come to read the meter.'

'My favourite line of all time.'

'I said "No one's ever in next door." He said, "So?" I said, "So I've come four bleeding times in the last f***ing week and Mr Lawrence is always out." He said, "Yes but his wife should be around in the day." '

'That dirty c***ing f***ing b***ard.'

'Oh he makes my skin crawl, how's he got away with it?'

'My poor Holls! What shall we do?'

'Tell his wife what he's been up to!'

'I'm not telling her.'

'Don't look at me.'

'What about Aisha?'

'She wouldn't bat an eye lid, she'd be around in a shot.'

'Aisha could tell her in the day, console the poor love, then bring her round the office ... ??'

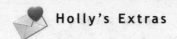

Curriculum Vitae
Holly Denham

Flat 8
121 Springfield Avenue
Maida Vale

Age 28

SKILLS
Self-motivated (*will always try to get on table to sing, however drunk, I need little encouragement*)
People-management skills (*I get other people to watch me while I sing on tables*)
Organizational skills (*able to put my make up on, while sitting on the floor in the toilets mumbling into mobile phone*)
Working in a team or on my own (*I can be equally as ineffective*)

ACHIEVEMENTS
Captain of school hockey team (*got beaten up by captain of hockey team*)
Represented my school in athletics (*got chased by a gang of girls from a rival school somewhere near a lake*)
Duke of Edinburgh Award, Gold (*that's where the lake was, actually got bronze*)
Duke of Edinburgh Award, Silver (*see above*)
Duke of Edinburgh Award, Bronze (*yes, got it, this is totally true — I took this exam*) (*didn't pass it*) (*actually got very drunk during a 2 day map-reading exam by the campfire and me and Toby snuggled up in one sleeping bag together*)(*best holiday/examination I ever went on/failed*)

HOBBIES & INTERESTS
Karate (*Kid — good film then, awful now*) Cooking (*pizza and jellybeans*) Team sports (*lied a bit here*) Literature (*OK!, Hello!, etc*) Long walks (*to the video shop, for popcorn and chocolate essentials*)

WORK HISTORY
LHS Hotels, 5* Hotel, Mayfair   2003 — Present
                                       (2007 till 2007 i.e. two weeks)

Head Receptionist (*trainee*)

Supervising a team of receptionists (*bit of a fib here*)
Meeting and greeting (*definitely, with a big rosy smile*)
Taking guests to rooms (*sometimes their own*)
Using computerised booking system (*Easyjet — for my flight to Spain*)
Switchboard skills (*answered the phone twice, when Jason let me*)
Using Outlook (*to email my CV here*)

Then mainly before this, I was either sitting in my living room, eating chocolate and crying with the curtains closed, occasionally arguing with my mother. Before that worked with Sebastian, ex-husband, in events.

Granny's 20-Step Survival Guide
(to being involuntary re-housed)

1. Insist on travelling with worldly possessions, in van, sitting up-front with driver
2. Read map for driver
3. Direct driver to Ivy Warrington's house, in the north, go for a pee, then scarper
4. If you're forced to go on a plane, insist on travelling with your daughter and get her to pay for first-class ticket
5. Spend the entire flight making friends with other passengers and telling them you're being forced to move against your will by evil daughter. Cry in front of passengers, laugh in front of toilets
6. Begin long term terror campaign against owners of 'The Home'
7. Pretend to be deaf – helps you find out what people really think of you
8. Tell owners of 'The Home' you have a desire to be naked – when they have guests around
9. Go for long walks and forget where you live so you get to talk to lots of lovely young policemen
10. Tell police you were moved against your will, in front of daughter
11. Tell them you were kidnapped
12. Tell them you have no idea who she is (your daughter)
13. Tell them you are the Queen of England
14. When you are bought a hearing aid, wrap it in a hanky and flush it down the toilet
15. Refuse pink toilet paper
16. Insist on pink Gin
17. Use a little whisky to remove the black mark on gin bottle made by daughter
18. Lose walking stick when they attach your address to it (you are not Paddington Bear)
19. Pretend to have a cat, make daughter talk to it and stroke it
20. Pretend to be having affair with owner of the home, so daughter thinks owner of home is a pervert and moves you
21. Watch a lovely film with your family once a week, but always insist on watching the end of the film first; to make sure it's a good one
22. Make '20-step lists' containing more than 20 steps

Who said what?
(for answers see the Competitions page
of www.hollysinbox.com)

1: 'Let me out of here! I'm not a criminal'
James Lawrence
Ferret
Oscar Wilde
Paris Hilton

2: 'Holly's got the horn'
Aisha referring to a game of 'toss the musical instrument'
Jennie referring to Holly's habit of hitting on strangers
Jason referring to the time Holly hung from a wild elephant
Aisha referring to Holly's new-found sexual urges

3: 'I thought I was being mugged'
Trisha referring to children on the estate
Holly referring to Homeless Harry
Charlie referring to the prices charge by suppliers
Jason talking about the lovely Aisha

4: 'Shit or get off the pot'
Holly
Trisha
Les
Jennie

5: 'Getting the sack'
Holly referring to her future employment status
Trisha referring to her future employment status
Jason referring to James' balls
Roger Lipton referring to Holly's future employment status

6: 'Tendency to make your eyes water'

Refers to what?
A lemon
Aisha's perfume
Charlie's club's heating
Holly's jokes

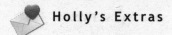
Holly's Crossword
(for answers see the Competitions page
of www.hollysinbox.com)

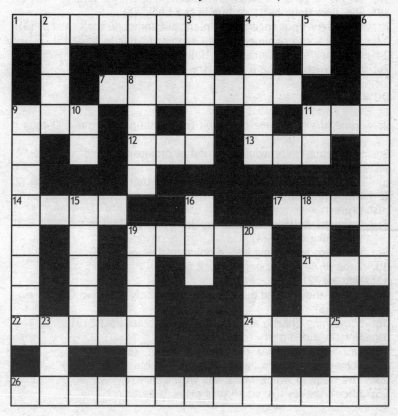

ACROSS

1: Who is Holly referring to when she says 'You're just being silly now aren't you'? (7)

4: Toby had a bad-boy —- (3)

7: What name was invented for an evil PA? (7)

9: Pam will probably have bought a new size of this (3)

11: When Trisha was this, Shella had to cover (3)

12: Jason would never want Aisha to show him one of hers (3)

13: A type of party that Holly and Jason never got to throw for Aisha (3)

14: Jason would not want to wear fluffy ones at Easter (3)

17: This is no good for Holly, she would need two (in a large size) (4)

19: She gave Holly her first hug in the book! (5)

21: The friends put together a 'plan' but someone took the 'p' (3)

22: A good accompaniment with Granny's favourite drink (5)

24: A washer/——- is something Holly would love! (5)

26: Holly, Trisha, Aisha & Jason are all ——————- (13)

DOWN

2: Some of which once belonged to Charlie before the drill took it (4)

3: Something Holly would be good at organising (5)

4: The 'Water boy' (5)

5: Put at the end of an email to indicate there is more to come (2)

6: You may find you're served this at a sophisticated dinner party (9)

8: Essential holiday accessories Holly had packed in suitcase with swimming cozzie (4)

9: Holly enjoyed being kissed down in the ———— (8)

10: Time of day Holly begins work (2)

11: Not out (2)

15: One of these could build roads much straighter than Charlie ever could (5)

16: Something Charlie and Ron are just fabulous at!!! (3)

18: Her favourite party trick is singing (5)

19: Jason can often make a storm in a ——— (6)

20: Someone linked to James was ——— behind a paper (6)

23: The week in which Aisha was with Henry (3)

25: Alice's snakes like to —- rats (3)

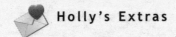

Holly Denham, age 10½
My New Year Resolutions for 1990

1) Take no notice of Charlie – when he's making me angry I'm going to close my eyes and pretend it's the radio. Yesterday we had a fight and I've got scratches all up my arm

2) Don't get angry with Alice when she's bossing me about. She is older and she's only trying to look after me

3) Clean out my rabbit BEFORE Mum starts shouting

4) Practise the piano BEFORE Mum starts shouting

5) Do my homework every night BEFORE Mum starts shouting

6) Don't let Sarah make me cry. I'm going to stand up for myself

7) Get engaged to David Willow. This might not be just for this year, I have to wait until I'm older but that's what I'm going to do

8) Have 10 children called Amber, Crystal, Ruby, Sapphire, Jade, Quartz, Diamond, Emerald, Rock, Stone. This one is for later as well, and the boys names are the not so pretty ones

9) When I get married to David, I want to live in Alison Granger's house in Heathcoat Lane. I think they will move by then

10) Run away and win Horse woman of the year, be in My Pony magazine and marry Horse man of the year, live in Alison Granger's house in Heathcoat Lane

11) Tell David Willow he's no longer engaged to me when I marry Horse man of the year

12) Unless David Willow is Horse man of the year

13) Write to Ice man (in Top Gun) – tell him you prefer him to Maverick

14) Don't cry when you're told off for singing in class again

15) Don't go to the park with Michael, he is childish and stupid grrrrrrrrrrrrrrrrrrrrrr

16) Go to the park with Andy, he has nice hair

THE WAY THEY WERE
Saturday 13th July 1985, 9.55am

At six years old and wearing a pretty cotton summer dress, Holly Denham was sitting on the garden lawn, frowning. She had been told to make a daisy chain by her mother, but it wasn't going well. She put the chain down and sighed, daisy chains were too hard. What she really wanted to do was sit in a big bucket. That would be nice, a bucket full of water, or mud? She got up and wandered over to the garden tap, which was when she heard the explosion ...

Her brother Charlie had been watching her from his bedroom. He was meant to be tidying it, a punishment for convincing Holly that the sun was about to crash into the earth — the only escape being a space rocket he had constructed, a seat on which would cost Holly a bag full of penny sweets. He continued with his job of strapping French bangers to Holly's favourite doll and imagined how sorry they would all be when he grew up and really did own the only space ship off the planet — none of his family would be allowed to come (except Granny of course, but then she knew magic and that could come in useful).

The lady in question was too busy giggling to herself to hear the distant sound of Holly's exploding doll, as she made her way across the field at the back of her house. If anyone had seen her that hot summer's morning in 1985, they may have wondered why this mature, rather striking, beautiful woman, yes beautiful, woman had been hiding apples in the long grass? Not a particularly normal thing to do now was it, Elizabeth? No, but then she did have young Charlie, Alice and Holly over later and in a field with no trees, they always loved the way she knew where the invisible magic apple trees lurked.

As the hour neared 10am, somewhere in Essex in front of two very concerned-looking parents, a boy in spandex tights sang 'Look at me I'm Sandra Dee, if you've got it flaunt it!'

And on the Isle of Dogs a heated conversation was brewing:

'Don't be daft, who's going to come down here?'

'I'm telling you, Les, it's all gonna change, they just said so on the telly!'

'Rubbish.'

'It's not rubbish, Les, it'll be just like the city, big banks, sky scrapers, everything.'

'You're talking bollocks, Trish!'

'Watch your mouth, Les, they said there'll be a rail link from here to the City, it'll be a lot easier to get to that job at Huerst & Wright, if I get it.'

'Shh, it's 10 o'clock, it's starting.'
'Can't we watch this on the big telly?'
'It's not working. Now who's on first?'
'Don't know — Queen, U2, Status Quo or could be Macca.'
'Who's that bloke?'
'Bob Geldof.'
'Fuck me, Trish, he just swore live on TV.'
'He's allowed to, it's for charity init.'

THIS LIST WAS FOUND ON JASON'S WORK COMPUTER ...

My Top 20 Film Scenes
(these aren't necessarily my favourite films, although
some might be)

Bridget Jones's Diary
That fight scene

Bridget Jones's Diary 2
Bridget Jones flopping in the sea saying, 'Beautiful
Bridget'

Love Actually
The scene when Keira discovers Andrew Lincoln has been
filming HER — and not both of them, and he's madly in
love with her. Unrequited love, the poor cherub, I just
want to scoop him up

Notting Hill
When Hugh says being with Julia Roberts was like opening
Pandora's Box and Rhys Ifans says he once knew a girl
called Pandora but didn't get to see her box though

Princess Diaries 1
Julie Andrews giving her Princess lessons

Princess Diaries 2
The sleepover

Grease
In the diner when Oliver Newton John asks a very very
sexy John Travolta if he's jealous of her new man. John
laughs 'oh, ho, a ho ho ho' (as he tries to think of
something cool to say)

Pretty Woman
Dress scene — of course! Julia goes back into the first
shop laden with shopping — my dream experience.

Terms of Endearment
The funeral

Steel Magnolias
The funeral

Big Fish
The funeral once again (sorry it's nothing to do with all
that black believe me, horrible) but when all his dad's
characters turn up, and he realises for the first time
his dad hadn't been lying about his amazing adventures
(my dad was a bit like that)

Maid in Manhattan
When she tries on the lovely dresses and gets her hair
done for the benefit dinner with Ralph Fiennes, I can
just see that happening to me every day in this hotel

Clueless
When she goes shopping (what else??)

What Women Want (and some gay men)
When he realises she's thinking about his package

Sweet Home Alabama
When she goes to find him and it's raining

The Bodyguard
When he gets shot and she's screaming, 'He's my bodyguard!'

Jerry Maguire
When he walks back in the room full of women and does his
speech and you wait to see if that's worked for her and
she says, 'you had me at hello' (you really don't want
to know what I was thinking at that point)

The Breakfast Club
Judd Nelson in every scene

About Last Night
Rob Lowe in every scene

St Elmo's Fire
Rob Lowe in every scene

Actually Rob Lowe in 20 films, the rest, forget!

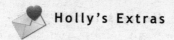
My Dream Wedding
(I'm going to win the lottery)

by Aisha Peters

If I win £15,000,000 ...

Location: France
Venue: Château Le Fantastique (Big Sexy Château)
Wedding theme: Me
Flowers: Flown in from various exotic locations
Dress: Designer – Vera Wang. She will be at the wedding too, adding finishing touches, oh and I want her to call me ma'am as in 'yes Aisha ma'am' and bow when I get stroppy, which I will do
Hair: I like Jennifer Lopez's hair, so I want her to cut it off and give it to me as a wedding present, and I'll have Stella McCartney weave it in for me
Make Up: Lots
Cake: By Jamie Oliver, baking it naked
Live Entertainment: Robbie Williams and Gary Barlow singing a duet, wearing matching T-shirts saying, 'we love Aisha' on them. And they better not argue (Followed by Abba)
Guests: 800 including Will Smith, Jamie Foxx, ~~Martin Luther King~~ (scrub that, Jason tells me he's not likely to turn up), Whitney Houston, as well as the usual faces like Tom Cruise, the Beckham duo and Elton John (once he's changed out of his previous robes as cathedral organist)
Capturing the romantic mood: Film Docu-Crew from OK!, Now, Hello!, Grazia, etc
My mood: Snooty, aloof and stroppy, followed by excitement, tears and joy, finishing in a snooty self-appreciative modest joy

If I win £1,000,000 ...

Location: France
Venue: Château Le Fantastique'ish (Still a Sexy Château)
Wedding theme: Me

Flowers: French
Dress: Vera Wang (she can post me the dress)
Hair: By Nicky Clarke copying Jenny Lopez hair
Make Up: Lots
Cake: By Antony Worrall Thompson (clothed)
Live Entertainment: Lily Allen and Cheryl Cole (and they can argue as much as they like), followed by Chico
Guests: 400 including lots of ex-reality-TV celebs
Capturing the romantic mood: Photographers from OK!, Now, Hello!, Grazia, etc
My mood: Snooty, aloof and stroppy, followed by excitement, tears and joy, finishing in a snooty self-appreciative modest joy

If I win £100 ...

Location: Nth Acton
Venue: Bob's place, because it's got a bigger garden than mine
Wedding theme: Me
Flowers: Already there
Dress: If I have to
Hair: Yeah whatever
Make Up: Myself
Cake: Kwik Save 'No Frills'
Live Entertainment: My Aunt Sally falling into the pond with her skirt over her head like she did last year
Guests: Holly, Les, Trish, Jason and his cats
Capturing the romantic mood: Bob probably on that new camera-phone he always talks about
My mood: Quiet embarrassment followed by drunk as a skunk

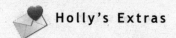

An Interview with Holly Denham

What people annoy you most in London?
Can I give you a list?

Go on then.
People that get on the tube before you've got off.
Teenage girls who sit either side of you on buses or trains and bitch about their friends, across you.
People with enormous backpacks who turn around and knock you out during rush hour.
People who grope your bottom during rush hour.
People who moan about not getting their bottom groped during rush hour (Aisha did this once).
People who eat too much garlic before work.
People who immediately stop after they've gone through the ticket barrier to put their ticket in their purse, so you end up walking into them.
The same people who immediately stop at the top of escalators to fish in their purses for tickets.

What's good about living in London?
The fact I can live here, I mean after all my complaints it really is an awesome place.

What's your earliest embarrassing memory?
I remember when I was about 13 (before Toby) I went on a 'date' with an older boy; he was very confident and popular. We met up in a fast food place (where else) and within minutes a group of his friends had come over to join us, but when they asked who I was, he said just a friend and looked embarrassed to be with me. Later when I got up to empty my tray in the bin I left my purse on it and had to get an assistant to help me, then in front of him and all his friends I had to search through the rubbish for my things. Horrible, just horrible.

Did you see him again?
I saw him, but he wasn't anywhere near me.

What's Trisha's family like?
Lovely, really fun, happy, genuine people; they'd do anything for anyone.

What's your favourite holiday destination?
Spain (I have to say that, Mum might read this).

What's the best thing you heard recently?
I heard a shop owner moaning about the lack of custom to his friend.
He took five minutes to notice me standing there and after I paid he
threw the change down on the counter, turned back to his friend and
said he thought it was probably the bad weather.

What's the best place you've eaten?
Have you ever been to Sketch? They have the most amazing toilets
ever.

I'll remember that. What about your favourite movie?
I watch a lot of films, lots of feel-good tacky stuff, which really
annoys my local video shop in Maida Vale.

Why would it annoy them?
Because they're a cult-film specialist. Another thing I like doing is
pretending not to know famous film stars, just to wind them up. I'll
say, 'What's 'is name, you know, the one with the crooked smile?' And
they'll say, 'Who?? Please don't tell us you're talking about the best
actor of our generation Robert De Niro!' And I'll say, 'that's the one,
Robbie Derro, yes can I have *Meet the Parents* please.'

It's been nice talking to you, good luck with your journey home.
I think my station's closed, thanks. Xxxx

Are you

Take the

1) **You want a promotion... convincing. Do you —**

   a) Write yourself daily re...?
   b) Buy higher heels, a shor... woof' when he passes ...ut
   c) Tell your boss that candid... could escort them off the pr...

2) **You've accidentally 'replied to a... important client has just received ...bit of them a total bitch. Do you —**

   a) Spend the afternoon hiding in the toi...
   b) Send a quick e-mail back saying 'And I'... bitch ... mmmm'
   c) Blame it on the IT idiots who've obviously doctored your email and recommend them for the sack

3) **It's the office party and the gorgeous guy from Sales is there. Do you —**

   a) Stare at him longingly and then offer him a nibble
   b) Crawl under his table and give him a nibble
   c) Grab the nibbles and the champagne and invite everyone back to your fab place, then refuse entry to the competition (if they have the cheek to turn up)

4) **You're taking part in a fire drill at work. Do you —**

   a) Help older colleagues escape from the building first
   b) Sneak out to Starbucks — you're not standing in the cold letting your hair go frizzy for anyone
   c) Run down the stairs, elbowing others from your path whilst reassuring them that it's for the good of the company, you are a more valuable asset and therefore it's much more important you live

hasn't been fixed for a week
k, tell them you're 'weeely tired'
up a chair and sleep with you?
our head on your desk because you
the receptionists on the floor below
gain

726

as organised a day of spiritual enlightenment,
uilding and the development of inner strength
. Do you —

ke the opportunity to cheer up those colleagues who've
been a bit down recently
b) Take the opportunity to remove all your clothes
c) Take the opportunity to build up team morale, especially with
the ones who are lagging behind with the necessary skills,
reminding them it's not their fault, it's simply yours for
employing stupid people

7) **You're about to leave the company and your friends and
colleagues have brought you a goodbye cake. Do you —**

a) Thank everyone, make a short speech, then begin munching
on that lovely cake while singing, 'So long, farewell ...' etc
b) Try to smile while wondering whether it's just worth checking
if they got you a lovely present too? Say, something from Gucci?
c) Grab the stupid cake and throw it back at them, shouting
'Get a life you tossers, I never liked you anyway!'

If you answered mostly As, you are an **Office Dreamer like Holly.**
You are a lovely, lovely person and probably have loads and loads
of adoring friends.

If you answered mostly Bs, you are an **Office Diva like Aisha.** You
are probably the most popular girl in the office, at least with all
the Postroom boys.

If you answered mostly Cs, you are the **Office Schemer like Jennie.**
Oh dear, you must change your wicked ways or risk ending up sad
and lonely and covered in boils and sores (and you might go bald
too).

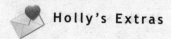

How to be a Fashion Queen (in and out for the office)
by Jason Granger

- Girls, remember it's not what you wear, but how you wear it. A cheap suit can look far better than an expensive one if it fits properly ... by fitting, I don't mean so that it's skin-tight (just wanted to make that clear, Aisha)
- Boys — what are you playing at???? You don't have the complexion to get away with those colours! Look, imagine that all men are not created equal and you'll understand. Digby in Accounts gets away with that because no one expects anything from him. Your friend Kirk gets away with it because he's got a tan, you haven't, so NO!
- Girls, don't wear a suit with frilly padded shoulders, we're not in the circus, we're not in the 80s and frankly it's horrible
- Boys, don't wear a dress to work. My friend Lulu did once, and got some very strange looks. If you do, just remember to shave your chest hair, otherwise you'll scare people
- Girls, don't be tricked into following fashion trends that are put out just to make you throw away your old clothes and buy new stuff, e.g. shoes with heels half-way along (what's that about???); boots like jesters' feet, all pointy (they get trodden on before you've got off the tube); sunglasses upside down (really, they'll try anything to get you to buy new ones)
- Going out ... ! Girls, miss out the grunge/hippy/student/ dressing like a demented schoolboy trend: it's ugly and unflattering. Instead glam it up, wear lots of pink and ribbons and upset everyone around you, it's so much fun (this is actually my friend Lulu's advice — but I included it anyway)

After reading this you are now a registered 'Fashion Queen'. At work, feel free to waltz around the office handing out free fashion tips to those less fortunate who are maybe wearing wrong or unflattering outfits. Invite them to join your fashion seminars after work; I'm sure they'll appreciate it.

PS I've also included my favourite websites to brighten up those dull Friday afternoons (check out my own website first!!!)

www.Jasons101favoritewaystoplayaviolin.com
www.oli.co.uk
www.facebook.com
www.topshop.com
www.clothingattesco.com
www.heatworld.com
www.frontofhousemagazine.co.uk
www.neighbours.com
www.trashionista.com
www.handbag.com

Top 10 Excuses for Being Late for Work
(contributed by Trish, receptionist for 20-odd years, but she still looks really young)

1. I'm not late, I turned up on time, I was just further from my desk than you would have liked (about a mile), however your point is duly noted

2. Sorry I drove to the company I'd prefer to be working for instead

3. I am late AND I think it's incredibly bad manners on your part to mention it, I've never mentioned your halitosis have I?

4. I locked myself in the flat and my dog has eaten my door key, he should poop by tomorrow. Hopefully ...

5. Why Mr Flintstone, I do believe you're wearing your mother's apron, hello Wembley I'm Florence Nightingale so get out of my way! (Scream the last part and you'll find they never mention it again)

6. Go away before I puke on you

7. Up yours stinky

8. I don't have a problem! I think the way you mindlessly agree with GMT is the problem here, have you asked for any proof? No? Exactly!

9. My dog ate my alarm clock. What? He's a hungry dog! When the alarm goes off I might find that report you've been asking for too

10. No speaky de Ingalzy

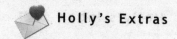

The Soundtrack of My Fabulous Life
by Aisha Peters x

Pussycat Dolls — Don't Cha (*my favourite dance track of all time*)

Pink — Get the Party Started (*for when you're glammin up to go out*)

Madonna — Material Girl (*I used to drive my mum mad with this one*)

Kylie — Spinning Around/Can't Get You Out of My Head (*can't decide, both great*)

Beyoncé featuring Jay-Z — Crazy in Love (*perfect for workin the dance floor*)

Nelly Furtado — Maneater (*Holls and I have a great routine for this one*)

Gwen Stefani and Eve — Let Me Blow Ya Mind (*sexy, and the bit in Friends where Monica strips to it is soooo funny*)

Boys II Men — I'll Make Love to You (*for sentimental reasons — my first snog at the school disco was to this*)

George Michael — Careless Whisper (*forever a classic*)

James Blunt — You're Beautiful (*someone sweet sang this to me once*)

Sugababes — Hole in the Head (*reminds me of my husband — b*****d*)

Justin Timberlake — SexyBack (*I love this man!!!!!!!!!!!!!!!!!*)

Barry White — Just the Way You Are (*cheesy but he is the God of Love*)

Prince — Kiss (*do I need a reason?!!!*)

Calling all City Girls!

Hiya, it's me again. As you know, I've had my fair share of office nightmares: from details of my failed love life being spread round the office (you know who you are), to accidentally sending that e-mail slagging Shella off to ... Shella!, to getting into trouble for those little white lies on my CV ...

To make me feel better (and to give me a laugh!), I'd love to know your most embarrassing office horror story. Maybe you've sent a rude e-mail to someone you shouldn't have, maybe you got caught snogging in the lift (I almost did) or maybe a humiliating photo of you ended up being sent round the whole company ...

If you e-mail your story to me at holly.denham@huerstwright.com, I'll post it on my website and there will be a fab prize for the funniest one — an online shopping spree worth £150, so you can buy yourself a gorgeous new outfit to take you from the office to the dance floor!

So good luck! Can't wait to read your stories!!!

Love

Holly x x x

Competition terms and conditions

1. The prize will consist of £150 to spend online at www.topshop.com
2. In the event of circumstances outside of its control, the promoter reserves the right to provide alternative prizes of equal or greater value.
3. The prize draw is open to residents of the UK, Channel Islands, Isle of Man and Republic of Ireland aged 18 years and over, except employees of Hachette Livre UK and their relatives.
4. Only one entry will be accepted per person.
5. Proof of entering is not proof of receipt of entry.
6. All entries must be submitted via email to holly.denham@huerstwright.com.
7. Print entries will not be eligible for entry.
8. No responsibility can be accepted for lost or misplaced entries and incomplete entries will be disregarded.
9. No purchase necessary.
10. The closing date for entries is midnight on 30th November 2007.
11. The winner will be informed in writing by 14th December 2007.
12. The judge's decision is final and no correspondence will be entered into.
13. The winners' names will be available from 14th November 2007 by writing to The Marketing Dept, Headline Publishing Group, 338 Euston Rd, London, NW1 3BH.
14. By entering this competition you agree to allow your entry to be posted on www.hollysinbox.com at the discretion of the judges.
15. Any entries that involve libellous or criminal activity will be ineligible for entry.

Promoter: Headline Publishing Group